GW00786634

Love and Pain

MARVIN STACEY

Marvin Stacey

M Stacey

authorHOUSE®

AuthorHouse™ UK Ltd.
500 Avebury Boulevard
Central Milton Keynes, MK9 2BE
www.authorhouse.co.uk
Phone: 08001974150

First published by AuthorHouse 3/9/2009

ISBN: 978-1-4389-6123-1 (sc)

Printed in the United States of America
Bloomington, Indiana

This book is printed on acid-free paper.

Chapter One

Such beauty and elegance.

Duncan never failed to notice how beautiful and elegant his wife was, even now as she stood naked in the middle of their marble bathroom. Little beads of water dripping down her back as she dried herself.

The bathroom was like a sauna with the steam bellowing all around. The heat from the shower was all too much, and Duncan was finding it difficult to control himself. He walked over to her unbuttoning his shirt and she was startled as he stroked her back and neck.

He cupped her breasts in his hands from behind and began kissing her neck as she moaned softly. She grabbed his crotch through his trousers that only made him want her more, but the sound of footsteps rapidly approaching bought them both back down to earth with a thump.

'Mom, there's no milk in the fridge.'

It was eight o'clock in the morning and their ten year old son, Mikey wanted his breakfast.

'There's some milk in the fridge in the garage, honey. I'll be right down in a moment.' Grace turned to her husband and smiled. She kissed the tip of his nose.

'I think we should continue this session tonight, don't you?' She growled softly and blew him a kiss, and then she went back to the bedroom and got dressed. She took her long flowing white dress from the wardrobe and laid it out on the bed, and she sat at her dressing table and pulled on her stockings. She smiled to herself in the mirror as she brushed her long auburn hair, and afterwards she slipped into her dress.

At forty-five years old, Grace Philips was always grateful she was able to keep her slim figure. A size twelve. Even after four children, she never had any surgery to retain her slim waist. She examined herself in the mirror now, and she smiled at herself. After a few minutes she went downstairs to the kitchen where Mikey was eating dry Frosties.

'Couldn't you find the milk, darling?' Grace asked as she walked into the kitchen.

'No, but it's OK. I kind of like them like this anyway.'

Grace went to the study and sorted through some papers. She hummed to herself as she was looking forward to when her two eldest daughters would arrive home. Hannah and Danni were travelling Switzerland for two weeks, and would be landing at Heathrow tomorrow evening.

'Bye mom,' Mikey called as he left for school with his friends.

'Bye dad.'

'Bye son. Have a good day at school.' Normally his father would drop him off at school on the way to work, but he chose to walk to school with his friends this morning. The weather outside was glorious. It was only the end of February, and the temperature outside was already sixty-five degrees. Mikey usually wore his blazer and a coat when he walked to school, but this morning he wasn't wearing either. Shortly afterwards, Grace and Duncan left for the office.

At forty-five years old Duncan Philips was a successful lawyer at the family law firm, Philips & Co on Oxford Street, and with Grace as his personal assistant they both had the perfect life together. Hannah and Danni both worked there too and hoped that one day they too would have successful careers just like their parents, but for now they were just happy as they were.

At twenty-five years old Hannah was just two years older than her sister, Danni. They both attended Cambridge where their father studied, and have been working at the office for six months. Duncan has always been proud of his daughters, and even more so that they wanted to work at the family law firm. He hoped that one day their younger daughter, Abbie would join them too, but she was less ambitious than her sisters and more interested in travelling Europe. Abbie was only nineteen years old and wanted to study art and travel the world. She has always talked about being a news correspondent for the BBC. The last letter her family received from her, she was in Rome.

Grace thought of all her children now and how happy they all were as she and Duncan arrived at the office.

'Good morning, Tom,' Grace chirped at the security guard as they pulled in to the secured underground car park.

'Good morning, Mrs. Philips. Mr. Philips,' Tom replied as he pressed the button and raised the barrier.

'Thanks Tom. You have a good day,' Duncan smiled. Duncan pulled into his usual parking space with his name on, and then they both took the elevator to the fifth floor.

Grace went to the kitchen and switched the coffee maker on as Duncan went to his office. Duncan had a conventional office overlooking Oxford Street, with rows of law books on the three bookcases. He was never one for clutter or fancy things. Just a desk and his executive leather high back chair was all that suited him. He switched his computer on as he glanced at the photo on his desk of his wife and children and smiled. He made several calls, and moments later Grace appeared with a steaming pot of coffee.

Duncan had several big meetings today and Grace left to prepare all the files he needed, and when she returned ten minutes later with an armful of files he was on the telephone. She left the files on his desk and walked out shutting the door behind her.

Grace returned to her desk and started typing out some letters to clients and taking notes from the dictator machine. She could see Duncan through the glass partition. He was still on the telephone, his fat cigar resting on the ashtray. Grace didn't mind that he smoked cigars, as long as he never smoked them at home.

Not that Grace disapproved. She just didn't want him polluting their breathing space at home. At nine-fifty Duncan's clients arrived. Grace shown them to the boardroom on the fourth floor and then prepared the pot of coffee Duncan requested, and as Grace returned to the boardroom Duncan was there talking to his clients. Grace knocked the door and entered.

'Thank you my love,' Duncan replied and then Grace left and pulled the door too. She went back to her desk where she had a mountain of papers and letters to go through. It was so unlike Grace to leave things undone at the end of a day, but yesterday afternoon Grace was extremely tired that she didn't seem to have the energy.

The papers were non important at the time. They were just clients' notes that needed to be put into order and filed. She sat at her desk as she felt the last two aspirin she'd just swallowed take effect. Her headache seemed to subside, but she couldn't seem to shake off the nagging pains in her stomach.

She tried to ignore the pains and carried on with her work, but by lunchtime she felt almost sick. She couldn't even stand the sight of food. She decided to take the afternoon off and go and see the doctor.

'You want me to drive you, my love,' Duncan asked when she told him.

'No, I'll be fine. I'll take the bus. The walk might be all I need.' She kissed her husband and left as the phone on his desk rang. He answered it, not taking his eyes off Grace all the time until she got into the elevator.

'Hello, Duncan Philips,' he mumbled incoherently.

Grace took the bus from Oxford Street to the medical centre at St Mary's hospital and sat in the waiting area to see her G.P. She had a rough idea what was wrong with her. All the symptoms were right. Sickness. Nausea. Fatigue. But at her age, she thought.

Seeing the doctor had only confirmed her suspicions, and she couldn't wait to get back to the office to give Duncan the good news. Grace had always wanted a big family ever since she could remember, but had given up on the chance of having more children. Though contented with the children they had, Grace and Duncan had always wanted lots of children.

She was grinning like a Cheshire cat as she skipped through the office when she got back. Duncan was on the telephone again and she went in and sat on his knee. She kissed him while he spoke to his client.

'Yes Mr. Edwards, I will have that letter faxed over to you before five o'clock. Goodbye sir.' He put the telephone down and kissed his wife.

'Well, you certainly look a lot better my love,' he smiled.

'What did the doctor say?' She laughed and kissed him passionately and held up a pair of tiny pink baby booties.

'I think we'll need these in nine months.'

'You serious?' he laughed.

'Yes baby, I'm pregnant.' She kissed him again, and he laughed out loud as the other office staff all looked round curiously and saw Grace sitting on his knee through the glass partition. One of Duncan's partners was standing near the office, and Duncan jumped up and called to him.

'Desmond, I think it's time we opened that special champagne.' Duncan winked at him as Grace stood there grinning and holding her tummy.

'You're not,' he laughed.

'Oh, darling, that's fantastic news,' he said hugging her.

'Well, I think this calls for a celebration.' Desmond went to get the case of champagne and two or three boxes of champagne glasses from the kitchen, and the champagne flowed as Grace had tears in her eyes. She couldn't believe she was pregnant again, and at her age. She sat at her desk and thought of her parents, and she wished they were still alive to see all their grandchildren as she sipped champagne.

It only took a few minutes for the news to spread around the five floors of the office that Grace was pregnant, and the champagne was still flowing well into the afternoon, and by five o'clock Grace felt exhausted and drained. All she wanted to do was go home, put her feet up and go to sleep.

Grace was still smiling all the way home as she and Duncan chatted away about the baby. Grace wanted to wait till the weekend before she told anyone else. At least until Hannah and Danni were home.

Duncan turned into Hyde Park Street where the street was flanked with over grown oak trees and perfectly manicured lawns, and straight ahead beyond the black iron wrought gates was a six bed-roomed house, perfectly situated, on once a patch of wasted land with its electronic gates.

Duncan had acquired the land and was given permission to build the house as a wedding present to his wife in 1978. The house took eighteen months to complete, in which time Grace and Duncan lived with his parents. They moved into the house, which they named "*Graceful*" in 1980 when Hannah was only five months old.

Duncan drove through the iron gates and stopped his BMW convertible in front of their front door, where two stone gargoyles stood either side of the front door guarding the house. Grace got out and let herself in through the huge oak front door, through the magnificent marble floored entrance hall with the winding staircase and went straight to the kitchen and made some iced lemon tea. Mikey was sitting in the lounge watching cartoons on the television.

'Hi mom,' he called. Grace took some aspirin and then went in and greeted him as Duncan came through the front door.

'Hello sunshine. How was your day?' Grace smiled and kissed the top of his head.

Great. I got a gold star in maths.'

'You did. That's fantastic,' she said as he showed his work.

Duncan went straight upstairs and got changed, and afterwards he made a few phone calls.

Grace had gone to the kitchen and started tea. It was Duncan's favourite tonight. Medium T-bone steak with a mushroom sauce, with steamed veg and potatoes. Grace filled a pan with water and put it on the hob while she prepared the veg, and she looked out the window at the angel fountain in the centre of the rear garden.

The kitchen was all white with the double oven and hotplate in the centre, with a marble floor. Grace had designed the kitchen herself. Her masterpiece added to an already magnificent house. When Grace wasn't at work, she was either preparing some fabulous meal in the kitchen or pottering around in the garden.

Grace loved her garden. She could always find something that needed to be done. Something that needed pruning or replanting. Her favourite part of the day was sitting in her garden under the blossom trees reading, or sitting in the hammock in the sunshine.

After tea Grace went to visit her sister in the next street while Duncan was in the study preparing some paperwork for tomorrow. He liked his quiet time as he concentrated on things that needed doing. Though Grace didn't mind, as she could use the time for her needlework or her charities or visiting friends and family, she did miss the quality time she could be having with Duncan.

Though next weekend they would have the whole two days together as they were going to start turning the spare room into a nursery. They were just going to paint it yellow as they didn't know if they were having a boy or a girl, though they both hungered for another boy.

That evening Grace had cuddled up to her husband as they watched a movie on the television. Duncan had got himself a cognac and white wine for Grace. Grace had made some nachos and some other snacks, and Mikey had joined them, though he had fallen asleep on the sofa after a while. Duncan had taken him to bed at nine o'clock, and rejoined Grace on the sofa.

Grace and Duncan have always been a loving couple, at home and everywhere they went. People often commented on them, and saying how well-suited they were. When they were seen as a family, people said they were a nice family. At work, the staff and the clients were always saying nice things about them.

They were married in 1979, when they were both just nineteen. One year later Hannah was born. They were a family. At forty-five years old, Grace and Duncan had been happily married for twenty-six years, and they were both just as much in love with each other as they were the day they were married.

Grace was tall and slender with long auburn hair and sapphire blue eyes, and with long slender legs and a size twelve waist she was the envy of every woman she knew. And with Duncan's rugged good looks and jet-black hair they were the couple everyone wanted to be.

It was two thirty in the morning and Duncan was startled awake to the sounds of Mikey's screams and cries for help, and all at once he was coughing and choking on black acrid smoke.

'Dad,' Mikey cried. 'Mom.' Duncan crawled off the bed and tried to feel for his trousers. He called to his wife and tried to wake her, but she wasn't responding. He knew he had to act quickly. He had to get his family out of the house, and get Grace's dressing gown around her.

'Mikey?' He called desperately to his son, all the time while feeling around him and trying to find the bedroom door. Grace started coughing and calling for her husband. She was panicking as she didn't know where he was. Duncan called to his son and tried in vain to get him to climb out of his bedroom window.

'Duncan,' Grace cried.

'Darling, I'm right here,' he coughed. He went to her and touched her arm so she knew he was near, but it didn't help her to stay calm.

'Darling, everything will be fine. We'll be out of here soon,' he said.

He knew he had no chance of getting them both out down the stairs. This was his family, and he had to get them out. He shut the bedroom door and used something to block the gap under the door to prevent anymore smoke from getting in. All the time he was hoping Mikey would still be able to hear him.

Grace had managed to clamber off the bed and crawl to the window, but she couldn't find the handle through panicking. She was banging her fists against the window trying in vain to break it, but the glass wouldn't budge.

Duncan had had triple glazed windows fitted last year for extra warmth and security.

She could hear Duncan talking to their son, trying to convince him to get out. That much she was thankful for. At least their son would be safe, she thought. And she could hear her husband and he hadn't collapsed in a heap somewhere.

Grace believed they would be safe, Duncan would get them out soon, but the smoke was too much. She lay down close to the floor thinking that she would be safer there, but the smoke was stinging her eyes and searing her throat. She felt herself drifting, all the while she wanted to close her eyes, but she knew she couldn't. She had to stay awake. Stay focused until her husband got to her. Until they were safe.

She called out to her husband, but only a squeak left her lips as she could hardly speak. She was coughing and her eyes were stinging. She collapsed in a heap as Duncan heard the thud.

'Grace. Oh, dear God.' He went to her and tried to wake her, but she wouldn't respond. He went back to the door, all the while praying they'd get out.

'Mikey, can you hear me, son?' he cried.

'Dad, I'm scared. I can't get out.' Tears welled up in Duncan's eyes, and this wasn't from the smoke. It was from the thought of his family not getting out safely.

'Mikey, you must try and keep calm, son. Can you hear me?'

'Yes.' Oh thank God, he thought.

'You must try and get out through your window. I can't get to you. Use the drainpipe and climb down.' Fire and smoke ripped through the hall, stairs and the landing. Tearing up the walls and the wooden staircase. It was impossible for Duncan to get through, and to get to his son. Even if he did, there were no stairs for them to get down.

'Dad, I'm scared. I can't do it.'

'Of cause you can, son. I promise I will be outside shortly too. You can do it.' He wasn't sure how he was going to get out yet. He was hoping he could break the window in his bedroom. He went back to Grace and tried to lift her, but he had to smash the window first. He felt around him. Tried to find something to throw against the window, but all the while he was coughing, his throat was hurting, his eyes were stinging.

The only thing he thought that would be heavy enough to smash the window was the chest of drawers, but they were too heavy. He tried and tried, but he just didn't have the strength to lift them. He crawled back to Grace and collapsed in a heap next to her. He remembered his promise to his son, and tried as he might, but he never had the strength to move. He reached out and touched Grace's face and felt the softness of her skin. He wanted to get up. If only to get his wife and son out, but for the love of God, he never had the strength.

Mikey tried to remember everything his father had taught him in cases of emergencies. Duncan had drummed it into all his children. Mikey felt around him, all the time he was crying. The smoke was stinging his eyes, but he knew he had to get out.

There was no chance of him getting out down the stairs, so he had no choice but to use the window.

Chapter Two

Outside in the street all the neighbours had gathered, waiting in vain and desperate to do something to help. They couldn't see that well up the drive, as three fire engines and two ambulances were parked in the drive. Though some of them had tried getting past to help, but each time the got too close the police kept them back. The firemen had bust through the steal gates, and everyone stood around watching and waiting. Julie Maverick, a close friend of the family was in tears while standing there helplessly. She was so desperate to get inside to help, and every time she edged too close the police and firemen always stopped her.

Around the corner in the next street black smoke could be seen rising from Grace and Duncan's house, and Grace's sister, Lesley was awoken by the sounds of sirens blaring past her house, and she went to the window to see what was happening.

'Oh my God.'

She was hoping no one was hurt. She never gave a second thought that it was her sisters' house, but she grabbed some clothes and went out to see what was happening. The whole area was lit up by the fire and the blue flashing lights. Lesley almost ran as she tried getting her coat and shoes on at the same time, and when she got to the end of her sisters street she stopped dead in her tracks.

For what seemed like a lifetime was only a few seconds as she stood there mesmerised. She felt her legs jolt and she ran at speed.

'Gracie . . . Gracie . . .' some of the neighbours looked round and Julie and Tony ran to stop her.

'Grace.' Lesley crumbled in their arms as they cried and comforted each other, but then someone grabbed their attention as Mikey could be seen at his bedroom window. Mikey had grabbed the chair from by his computer desk and threw it at the window. The sound of smashing glass had got everyone's attention.

'Mikey.' Lesley managed to find her feet and ran at high speed, though Julie and Tony had tried to stop her. She ran screaming his name, until a policeman stopped her.

'Get off me. That's my nephew up there.' Lesley screamed and cried and kicked him to get free, but the police officer kept his grip on her.

One of the firemen gestured to his colleague to bring the fire engine further up the drive, and using the ladder on top he started climbing up to Mikey, but before he even got half way the whole side of the house collapsed, burying Mikey in bricks and rubble.

Everyone in the street gasped and screamed as some backed off. Some even fought past the police and around the fire engines in the drive to help free Mikey from under the rubble, but Lesley just collapsed in Tony's arms. Julie and other people from the street scrambled over the rubble to find Mikey.

'He's over here,' Don Davidson called. They began moving bricks and rubble and found Mikey. An ambulance approached and the firemen freed him as one paramedic came and tended to him. Moments later they lifted him onto a board and carried him to the waiting ambulance.

'I'm going with him,' a voice spoke. Hollie Kilpatrick climbed in the ambulance and held Mikey's hand all the way to the hospital while the paramedic tended to him. When Lesley came round she saw one fireman bringing Grace down on the ladder, closely followed by another with Duncan. Lesley scrambled to her feet.

'Gracie.' She ran to her sisters' side and took her hand in hers while the paramedics checked her.

'We've got a pulse.' The paramedics whisked her away as Lesley went with them. Julie was holding Duncan's hand as a medic gestured to the police officer standing by that he was dead. Julie looked at the medic in disbelief, and then to the officer and Duncan as tears filled her eyes.

'No, please. He can't be dead. No,' she cried.

'I'm so sorry, Miss,' he said covering him with a sheet. Julie sobbed uncontrollably as the medics tried to take him away, but Julie refused to let go of him. Tony went to her and comforted her.

'Miss, we have to take him now,' the medic said.

'Please, just give us a few minutes,' Tony said as he comforted Julie. Duncan was like a father to Julie, after her own father died of cancer two years ago. When Julie let go of Duncan, the paramedics got him into the ambulance and they drove off.

The whole street was numb with shock. Some were sitting and crying and comforting each other. Others were standing and crying. Some were just pacing, looking around in disbelief, all the time they were all thinking: How could this happen? How could this happen to such a wonderful family?

Some of them were thinking of Grace and Duncan's daughters off somewhere in the world, not knowing what had happened, and not knowing what they were coming home to.

At the hospital there were a colossal of people and nurses and doctors all bustling around. There were paramedics bringing in other accident victims, and all the time Julie sat huddled in the corner, being comforted by Tony.

Julie hadn't stopped crying once thinking of Grace and Duncan. She just sat there, not moving. Her shoulder length dark hair was all knotted and twisted, her brown eyes were glazed through crying, and she wiped her eyes now and rested her head on Tony's shoulder. Lesley was crying, occasionally calling Grace's name as Hollie sat comforting her, and moments later the police officer from the scene walked in.

He stood there in the middle of A&E just looking around. Then he saw them as he took his helmet off. He walked sombrely with his head slightly bowed and stood next to Tony.

'Sir, I'm so sorry about your losses. I just came to see if there was anything I could do, and to offer my condolences.' Tony looked up briefly and nodded in thanks and the officer went and sat down.

PC Steve Radcliffe knew the family briefly. That was to say he knew them as part of him community. His beat. His rounds. He walked past Grace and Duncan's house most days on his beat patrol, and spoke often to them, as he did to all the neighbours. He was feeling their loss just as much as the others.

It was a couple of hours before a doctor came to see them. PC Radcliffe had just come back from the drinks machine with coffees for everyone when he saw the doctor talking to them. He placed the drinks on the table and went to hear what the doctor was saying.

'Grace and Mikey are both doing fine at the moment,' he said as Lesley breathed a sigh of relief.

'Though in Grace's condition it's a little more complicated, what with her being pregnant.' Everyone looked stunned. No one more than Lesley. Grace and Duncan hadn't told anyone yet. They were waiting till the weekend so they could tell Hannah and Danni as well.

'Mikey's resting now. He has a few broken bones and some minor bruising, but he's just fine. You can go and see him in a while.' Lesley couldn't stop thanking him through her tears. She couldn't thank him enough. They all sat down now, just thinking and praying for Grace and Mikey. Lesley still couldn't believe Grace was pregnant and couldn't understand why she hadn't told her, but she was just grateful she was alive. Though now her thoughts went to her nieces. Hannah and Danni would be flying home this evening from Switzerland.

'Oh, God, Hannah and Danni,' she said as Tony and Julie turned to her.

'They'll be coming home tonight.' Tony breathed a heavy sigh and buried his head in his hands. PC Radcliffe overheard and went to listen.

'What are we going to do?' Tony asked.

'They're going to expect to see Grace and Duncan at the airport.' Lesley started pacing as she thought.

'One of us is going to have to go and meet them.'

'And what about Abbie. Does anyone know where she is?' Hollie asked.

'Oh Jesus Christ, what am I going to do?' Lesley was starting to feel the burden of it all already. The things that had to be done. Greeting her nieces and telling them the bad news. Finding Abbie and bringing her home. She started crying at the thought of it all as it all hit like a tidal wave. She sat down and buried her head in her hands. She looked to Tony and Julie now, fresh tears streaming down her cheeks.

'What am I going to do? I can't do this on my own.' Hollie went to her and held her hand.

'But you're not alone, Lesley. We're all here to help.'

By now half the street had arrived at the hospital to find out news of Grace and Duncan and Mikey. Hollie's two daughters, Jade and Keeley were there, and Duncan's partners, Raymond and Desmond from the office were there too with Raymond's wife and daughters.

Hollie and Tony had offered to drive out to Heathrow to meet Hannah and Danni, though they weren't looking forward to it. Just the looks on their faces would scare Tony.

At twenty-six years old, Tony Craven was a year older than Hannah, and they were childhood sweethearts. Though now they were just best friends. There was nothing they didn't share together. They even shared some of their intimate secrets and problems. They always knew they could trust each other and never betray each other.

All day people had come and left as they visited. At least Lesley had had company to keep her mind occupied. PC Radcliffe had left and was coming back this evening.

He had promised to drive Hollie and Tony to the airport to meet the Hannah and Danni.

It was only a couple of hours to go before they left for the airport, and Tony's stomach was doing somersaults. All day long he'd been seeing the girls' faces when he told them the news, but at least he knew he wouldn't be alone.

Mikey was doing alright now. He'd woken up a couple of times, though not for long as he kept drifting off to sleep again. The doctor had given them the bad news that Grace had lost the baby, and that Grace was left in a coma. He couldn't see any long term problems, but warned them all that it didn't mean good news.

Grace had suffered internal bleeding and a nasty gash to the side of her head. She had a lot of smoke inhalation and one of her lungs had failed. If she survived it would mean long term care. Lesley would give her life to have her sister back and would put her life on hold to care for her. After losing their parents eight years ago, Grace and Lesley only had each other.

At seven-thirty Hollie and Tony were ready to leave for the airport. Tony looked at the police officer and shook his hand.

Thanks for coming with us, Steve. This means a lot. You too Hollie. I couldn't have done this on my own.'

'It's OK Tony. We're all here to help you,' Hollie smiled. All the way there Tony was in knots thinking of what to say when he saw the girls. Steve noticed after a while that he was all tense.

'Don't worry Tony. I'll be right there with you if you need me.' Steve was in plain clothes today, as he thought the uniform would scare the girls too much. It was a nice easy drive to Heathrow Airport. It was quite chilly that evening, and the heavy clouds ahead looked as though it was going to rain.

Steve pulled into a space on the car park and they headed for the arrivals. They went to the enquiry desk and asked about the flight and then they took a seat and waited. There was only fifteen minutes to wait and Tony was getting really nervous. Every time he spoke to Steve and Hollie he stuttered and his voice was shaking.

Steve tried to calm him a little as he asked about Hannah and Danni. What they were like. Tony told him how he and Hannah were still in love, but decided to just stay friends, and after a while Tony started to calm down, but when he saw the girls come through he started shaking again.

'There they are,' he said. Steve and Hollie looked round and saw two women screaming and running towards them.

'Tony,' Hannah squealed. Tony smiled gloriously, trying to hide what he felt inside. Both girls were wearing flip flops and summer hats. Hannah was wearing light beige shorts, showing off her long slender legs and a white blouse, and Danni was wearing her favourite jeans and T-shirt. Tony kissed the girls now and cuddled them, and he noticed Danni was looking all around. Steve stood close by with Hollie, and the girls started wondering what was happening. Hannah was concerned as she looked at Tony now and saw only pain in his eyes.

'Tony, you're shaking and trembling. You OK?' Tony couldn't stop shaking now, and he only held Hannah in his arms.

'Tony, you're trembling. Baby, what's wrong?' He pulled away from her now, and she kissed him as he tried to smile.

'Girls, I have something to tell you. Let's go and sit down.' Before Tony could take hold of Hannah's hand, she pulled away from him and looked into his eyes again.

'Tony, what's happened?' She looked around then and noticed their parents weren't there. Their parents were always there to pick them up from the airport whenever they returned from a holiday, and seeing Tony's face now only worried them.

'Where're mom and dad?' Danni asked. Tears filled his eyes now, and all he wanted was to wake up from this horrible nightmare. Anything so he didn't have to tell them what had happened. Hannah and Danni looked from Tony to Hollie to Steve, and they just wanted to know what was happening.

'Tony. Hollie, please. You're scaring me now. Where're mom and dad?' Hannah asked. Tony just broke down as Hollie comforted him. He couldn't say it, and the girls just looked at him as they couldn't believe he was crying like this.

'Tony?' By now the girls were near tears themselves. Seeing Tony like this, they knew it wasn't going to be good news, but nothing had prepared them for what he had to say.

'Oh, God. Tony. What's happened?' Hannah cried.

'Miss Philips, I'm PC Radcliffe of Marylebone police station. Could we please go somewhere quiet, we have something to tell you?' Steve held out his arm, gesturing to some seats in the waiting area, and nervously they followed.

'Please, sit down Miss Philips.' Tony took a deep breath as he stopped crying, and he held the girls hands in his while Hollie sat next to Hannah.

'Girls, there was an accident early this morning.' He stopped talking and took a deep breath, and he caught a glimpse of Hannah's face and it almost killed him to carry on.

'Tony, where're mom and dad?' Tears filled her eyes as her bottom lip trembled.

'There was a fire early this morning . . .' Hannah stood up now and clasped her hands over her mouth as she realised what Tony was trying to say. Hollie stood there ready to assist the girls now, as tears welled in her eyes.

'No, please. It's not true. Please.' Silent tears trickled down her cheeks, and Tony went to comfort them as they both cried, but Danni held her hand out to him, as though stopping him from getting too close to her.

'Please Tony, tell me you're lying,' Danni cried.

'I'm so sorry, baby, but your father died this morning,' he cried. Tony and the girls crumbled to the floor holding each other as they cried, and some of the airport staff looked on in concern. After a few minutes Hannah asked about Mikey.

'Mikey's fine. A few bruises and a couple of broken bones, but he's fine. He's at St Mary's with Lesley and Julie, and he was just sleeping when we left.'

'And mom?'

She's doing fine at the moment, though she's in a coma. The doctors can't say when she'll wake up.

'We need to see them. We want to see Mikey.' Steve and Hollie grabbed the girls' luggage as they made their way out of the airport. Tony walked with the girls, comforting them both all the way.

In the car the girls cried all the way back to the hospital, and once there they ran inside and straight to upstairs. Lesley was in bits waiting for them to get back, and once she saw them they just ran to each other.

'Auntie.'

'Oh girls, I'm so sorry.' Lesley cried.

After they all stopped crying they all sat down as the girls wanted to know everything, and after a while they went back to the ward to see Mikey. The girls sobbed as they saw him, all bruised and broken. Danni went to him and took his hand in hers and kissed him.

'Is he going to be alright?'

'The doctors said he'll be alright and he'll make full recovery in a few weeks,' Hollie said. His left arm was in a cast, and both his legs were in casts up to his hips. He was covered in bruises and a few cuts around his face. The girls stayed with Mikey for half an hour, and then they went to see their mother.

Grace was in intensive care, lying in a coma. The girls walked in with their aunt, and the girls cried when they saw their mother. Lesley had told them Grace was pregnant and that she lost the baby, and they just cried holding their mothers hands. The surgeon that operated on Grace came in shortly afterwards, and he stood in the doorway holding his notes as he watched the girls, and Lesley smiled briefly through her tears when she saw him.

'Girls, this is Dr Hanson. He's the one that operated on your mother.'

'How is mom doing?' Hannah asked.

'Your mother is in a coma, and like I said to your auntie, she is doing just fine at the moment, but I don't want to lie to you and say she will always be fine. There're no guarantees that your mother will fully recover. If she wakes up from the coma she may need a lot of care and attention. Maybe even for the rest of her life.' Lesley watched the girls all the time and their expressions.

'What are you saying doctor, "if she wakes up?" I thought you said she was going to be fine,' Danni said.

'No, I said she is fine at the moment. Your mother has suffered greatly. She suffered a nasty gash to her head, which I'm a little concerned about, and she has suffered internal bleeding and a collapsed lung. Right now, she is very lucky to be alive.'

'Oh Jesus Christ.' Hannah brushed her fingers through her long black hair and turned away as tears filled her eyes.

'And how is that "fine?" She looked at her aunt now.

'Why didn't you tell us auntie? She's our mother, how could you keep this from us?' Tears filled Lesley's eyes now as she went to her nieces and comforted them.

'I'm so sorry, darling. I'm sorry.'

'What else is there, doctor?' Danni asked.

'That's it, I promise. Only time will tell if your mother improves. But I must warn you, if she does wake up, she will need a lot of care. Maybe even constant care.' Hannah smiled briefly as she wiped her eyes.

'Thank you, doctor. And I'm sorry for being rude to you.'

That evening Lesley and the girls were sitting with Mikey. It was almost ten o'clock, and everyone had gone home. Steve said he'd pop back in the morning to say hi, and Tony and Julie would be back in the morning too.

Hannah and Danni were sitting holding Mikey's hands when he twitched his fingers. Danni was almost asleep and was startled when she felt Mikey gently squeeze her hand. She sat up quickly and brushed his hair away from his eyes with her hand.

'Mikey?' She saw his eyes fluttering, and everyone gather round now looking at him.

'Sis', he squeezed my hand.' Lesley went to fetch the doctor while Hannah and Danni stayed with Mikey.

'Mikey, can you hear me? Mikey, come on open your eyes. It's Hannah.' Mikey stirred a little and breathed in heavily, and he turned his head towards the sound of Hannah's voice.

'Sis'?' he croaked. Hannah laughed a little through her tears as she kissed him.

'Yes Mikey, I'm here. Danni's here too.'

'Hi ya bro', Danni cried.

'Sis', what happened? Where am I?'

'You're in hospital, Mikey. Remember?' He opened his eyes and looked straight at his sisters, and then to his aunt.

'Hello Mikey. We've all been so worry about you,' Lesley said. A single tear trickled from the corner of his eye as he tried to remember what happened. He looked up at Dr Hanson standing over him as he moved in to check him.

'How you doing champ? Do you know where you are?' he asked as the doctor shone a light in his pupils. Mikey was silent for a moment and then he croaked.

'My mouth is dry?' The doctor smiled a little as Lesley got him some water and a straw.

'Do you hurt anywhere Mikey?' Dr Hanson asked as he continued examining him. He just shook his head.

'That's good.'

'Sis', where're mom and dad? Why am I in hospital?' Everyone just looked at each other now, not knowing what to say. Hannah leaned over him and took his hand in hers.

'Mikey, you're in hospital, remember? And mom and dad are . . .' she turned away so he couldn't see her tears.

'Auntie, I can't . . . I can't tell him.' Lesley went to her and comforted her as she cried. Mikey was getting confused and upset now and he started crying.

'Sis', what's happening?' Lesley went to him and held his hand.

'Mikey darling, there was an accident at home and you were bought here by ambulance.' Images of the incident flashed through his mind now. He was trapped in the house . . . Smoke everywhere . . . He tried to get to his parents . . . Smashing the window . . . It was all coming back to him now.

'Mikey, daddy died last night,' Lesley said softly as tears welled in her eyes. Mikey opened his eyes wide and looked at all of them. Then he burst into tears.

'Sis', I'm sorry,' he cried.

'I'm so sorry.' Hannah and Danni just stared at him now as they saw the fear on his face.

'Mikey?'

'It's all my fault, I should have stayed in the house and got them out,' he sobbed. He was convinced his sisters were going to be angry that he didn't help their parents get out of the house. Hannah and Danni just stared at him in disbelief. Hannah climbed on the bed and just held him in her arms.

'Mikey, it's not your fault. It's nobody's fault,' she said and kissed him. Hannah could physically feel him shaking as she held him, and tears filled her eyes at the thought he'd think they would punish him.

'Mikey, we love you. We wouldn't expect you to risk your life to go looking for them.'

That night Hannah and Danni stayed at the hospital with Mikey. Lesley had gone home to get some rest and she said she'd be back in the morning. Mikey was in a private room. It was something Lesley insisted on so they could spend time with him, and Hannah and Danni were grateful for that.

Lesley had gone to see her sister in ICU before she left, and then she left and called a taxi. Hannah and Danni had fell asleep holding Mikey's hands, but he kept waking up screaming after a nightmare.

Dr Hanson seen to Mikey several times throughout the night and he seemed happy enough with him. He had given Mikey a sedative at one o'clock to help him sleep, and he prescribed him some medication to help with the nightmares.

It had been almost twenty four hours since they have been in the hospital, and Dr Hanson popped in to see to Mikey one last time before he went off duty. He spoke briefly to the girls about Grace and Mikey and how he'd known the family since before the girls were born.

'I assure Miss Philips. As soon as I know anything I will tell you. But please remember, your mother isn't completely out of the woods yet. It'll probably be a few weeks before we see anything positive.'

'Thank you,' Hannah said.

Chapter Three

Over the following weeks Grace had deteriorated rapidly. Dr Hanson had talked to Lesley and her nieces frequently on any changes, and tried in vain to prepare them for the worst, though he wasn't giving upon Grace completely. Not without a fight. He had told the girls that he'd do everything in his powers to keep her alive. Though he was beginning to question himself now.

Grace was slipping through his fingers fast. Her body was rejecting all the medications they gave her, and she'd gone into cardiac arrest twice.

Hannah and Danni were grateful for everything Dr Hanson was doing for their mother, but even they started to realise it was going to take a miracle to keep her alive now.

Mikey and his sisters were sitting with their mother. Lesley was there too with Steve, and Raymond and Lyndsey were there too with their daughters, Caroline and Debbie. Mikey was lying very cautiously on the bed with his mother. There were tubes and wires connected to the cardiograph and Hannah told him to lie still.

Mikey wasn't completely well yet. He still had his legs in plaster, and he has to use a wheelchair to get around. Raymond had lifted him out of the wheelchair and lay him next to his mother, and he was falling asleep as he held her hand.

It was the weekend and some of the office staff had visited to see how Grace was. By now everyone in the office knew of Duncan's death, and they all rallied around to help. Hannah and Danni knew it was their duty now to take over from their father, but that was the last thing on their minds right now. Besides, they knew between all the staff in the office, they'd cope.

Raymond had taken over all of Duncan's appointments and temporarily cancelled any future ones. Desmond had taken charge of booking Duncan's funeral. It was booked for a week on Tuesday. By then they were hoping there was some good news about Grace. Though that looked unlikely at the moment.

At forty-four years old, Desmond Jacobs was a young black student when he came to London from Philadelphia in 1981. He studied law, and achieved all his degrees by the time he was twenty-four, and the following year he was taken on at Philips & Co by Duncan's father. It was Duncan who took Desmond on as a partner in 1990.

At forty-two years old, Raymond Layton has lived in London all his life. He lived with his family in North Islington until he was eighteen. He wanted a better life away from the squalors he was bought up in, so he was determined to get out of there and find a better life for himself and his family. He started working at Philips & Co when he was twenty-one in 1984. He too was taken on as one of Duncan's partners in 1990, and together the three men have had a close personal and business relationship for fifteen years.

Raymond had met and fell in love with his wife, Lyndsey when he was just sixteen, and two years later their daughter, Caroline was born. His light brown hair and brown eyes are what attracted Lyndsey to him. They were married in 1982 when Caroline was just one years old.

It was almost four o'clock in the morning now. Hannah and Danni had fell asleep on a couch they were given from the waiting area, and Mikey was asleep in an armchair. It was all quiet and peaceful across the ward. The night nurses were just wandering around, occasionally checking on the patients, and the ward sister was at her desk going through some paper work.

Dr Hanson was on duty tonight and he'd checked in on Grace a couple of times, and the nurse had been in and fiddled with the machines and the tubes. Hannah had fell asleep reading a book she had bought back from Switzerland, and it fell from her hand now and hit the floor, just as a loud high pitched squeal aroused her. She was instantly alert, and she looked in horror at the cardiograph.

Flatline.

'Heeelp . . . somebody please.' Hannah hit the panic button on the wall above her mothers head, just as Dr Hanson and two nurses burst in through the door. Hannah shouting for help had woke the others. Danni had gone to Mikey and was comforting him, while Lesley comforted Hannah, but two more nurses came in and tried ushering them out of the room.

'Mom . . . Mom.' Mikey cried in Danni's arms as he wanted to get to his mother, and his sisters comforted him as they all cried and watched through the window. Danni had lifted Mikey from the armchair and carried him out after the nurses ushered them out, and she just comforted him now as they sat on the floor crying together. Even Steve had tears in his eyes watching.

Steve was on duty, and he'd dropped by to see how Grace was. He had radioed control and told them he was going off duty for a couple of hours. Dr Hanson tore open Grace's gown with one swift action, baring her chest.

'Stand clear,' a nurse shouted. Dr Hanson pressed the defibrillator to Grace's chest. Her body jolted as the electric shock passed through her, and all the while Mikey and his sisters were watching and crying as Lesley and Steve comforted them.

'Come on Grace, don't you dare do this to me. Not now.' Dr Hanson growled as he hit her one more time with the paddles. A nurse was doing compressions, and all the while trying to call Dr Hanson off.

'Dr Hanson, you must call it.' They'd been going now for almost six minutes, and the nurse knew Grace had gone.

'Dr Hanson, call it. She's gone,' she said as she held two fingers to her neck. He looked up in the heat of the moment. Sweat dripping from his temples, he glanced at the clock on the wall and threw down the paddles.

'Goddamn it.' He walked out in frustration as the nurse covered Grace up, and he saw Mikey and his sisters sobbing and holding each other on the floor.

'Kids, I am so sorry.' Danni stood up and went to him with open arms, and they stood there as tears filled the doctors' eyes.

It was almost eight o'clock in the morning when they left the hospital, and they went home to Lesley's. Hannah and Danni sat on the sofa comforting Mikey while Steve made some drinks, and all the while Lesley was thinking about Abbie.

'Hannah darling. Do you know where Abbie is? I think we should find her and bring her home as soon as possible,' she said as she wiped her eyes. Hannah sat up slightly and thought.

'Well, the last time we had a postcard, she was in Rome, but she could have moved on from there by now.' Steve came in a few moments later with a tray of coffees for everyone and a coco for Mikey. Mikey was still crying quietly, and he nearly spilt his coco as Steve passed it to him.

'There you go Mikey. Be careful, it's hot.' Hannah smiled a little as she watched Steve with Mikey, and she went to him and hugged him.

'Thank you, Steve. You're so kind, and the way you've helped us, especially with Mikey. We'll never forget it.' Mikey had taken well to Steve, and Steve loved helping him. Lesley smiled a little as Hannah hugged him. He pulled away from her and held her hands.

'You're welcome, darling.' Steve sat down on the sofa next to Hannah, and he took a sip of his coffee.

'I have a mate who works at Heathrow. I think he'd be able to put an all port call out to find your sister. How about it?' Wherever Abbie was, Steve was sure they would find her soon.

'Oh, Steve. That'd be fantastic,' Hannah said.

'How soon could we go and see him?'

'Well, how about right now?' Hannah hugged him then and smiled.

'Thank you, Steve.'

After they all finished their drinks they all got into Steve's car and drove to the airport. Steve made a few phone calls before they left and used his connections, but to no avail. Mikey was still using the wheelchair from the hospital, and Lesley folded it up now as Steve put Mikey in the back seat of his Renault Picasso, and they drove to Heathrow.

Steve Radcliffe could have made sergeant ten times over by now if he wanted. At forty-two years old he has been a police constable for twenty four years. He joined the force simply because his father was in the force too, and Steve has always been popular amongst the community. He was always out there talking to the community, and someone always offered him cups of teas and cakes and biscuits.

His thick brown hair and bushy moustache. His trademark braces and flat cap made him the lovable and well-known police officer he is today.

Steve had gone straight to the airport police once they arrived, and Mikey and his sisters waited with their aunt while Steve spoke to the woman sitting behind the desk.

'I'd like to speak to the sergeant please,' he said flashing his I.D.

'Is the sergeant expecting you?' she asked curiously.

'No, but it's . . .'

'It's alright, Sally. I'll take it from here.' Steve looked up and saw a tall thin grey haired man in uniform smiling at him, and a smile spread across Steve's face.

'Frank, you son-of-a-bitch. I thought you retired years ago, mate.'

'Well, you know what they say. You can't keep an old dog down for long.' Both men laughed as they shook hands.

'What happened to Guilford?' Steve was way out of his jurisdiction now, but he had friends, and those friends had the power to make things happen.

'He couldn't handle it. You know, the long shifts and not seeing his family as often as he liked. I think last months riot at the airport finished him off. He quit last month.' Steve introduced everyone, and then they sat down in Frank's office as Danni got Mikey settled in his wheelchair, and a few minutes later Frank's assistant bought in a pot of coffee.

'Thanks Sally, I'll take it from here,' Frank said. Sally left the office as Frank offered everyone a cup of coffee.

'Well, Steve. What up matey?' Steve looked a little sombre now as he put his coffee down on Frank's desk and looked at Mikey and his sisters, and Frank looked concerned for his old friend.

'Frank, it's like this. You read in the paper about a tragic fire in Marylebone a few nights ago?' Frank nodded as he remembered reading it.

'Well it was these kids home and both their parents died.' Danni bowed her head now and silently cried into her hand. Frank leaned back in his chair as he looked at all of them, and Hannah went to her sister and comforted her.

'The problem we have Frank, is their sister Abbie is somewhere in Europe, unaware of what's happened. We need to find her fast and bring her home. Can you put an all port call out in Europe?' Frank sat there as he looked at Mikey and his sisters, and he was overwhelmed.

'Oh, Jesus. Kids I'm so sorry.' He stood up and took some tissues from the box on his desk and passed them to Danni.

'There you go, sweetheart.' Frank paced the room then as he thought, and then he sat down and looked at Mikey and his sisters.

'Well how about this? I can put an all port call out, and every airport in Europe will be notified within an hour. We'll have your sister calling home before the end of the day.' Hannah looked concerned for a moment. She wiped her eyes and looked at her Steve.

'No, she mustn't be told anything. If you can just locate her, and we'll go and bring her home.'

'What would you like us to say to her when we find her?'

'Don't tell her anything, because she will just get scared and frantic and try to phone home. If you can just locate her and we'll go and bring her home.' Frank smiled a little now.

'Consider it done, Miss Philips.' The girls smiled a little through their tears and Hannah stood up and took Frank's hand in hers.'

'Thank you Mr. Andrews.'

'Frank, please, he smiled.

'Don't worry Miss Philips. I'll have your sister home before you know it. I'll contact you as soon as we've located her.' Hannah stood on tip-toe then and kissed his cheek.

'Thank you, Frank.'

Mikey had fallen asleep while they were talking to Frank, and when they got to the car Steve gently picked him up and put him in the car and they drove home.

'Don't worry girls, Frank's the best I know. He used to work for a private investigator. Abbie will be home soon,' Steve said as they drove home.

Steve carried Mikey in the house and took him upstairs to bed while Lesley made some fresh coffee.

Hannah and Danni were sitting together on the sofa when Lesley came in with the coffee, and Hannah was asleep. Her long black hair draped over her face as she rested her head on Danni's shoulder.

Hannah was a spitting image of Grace, except for the black hair. Her sapphire blue eyes and ivory skin was one of the things people loved about her, and with Danni's long auburn hair and blue eyes, there was no mistaking they were sisters.

Tony had come round once he saw Steve's car outside Lesley's house, and shortly afterwards Raymond and Lyndsey had come to visit with their daughters, Caroline and Debbie. Lesley had got some photos of the family out and was telling Steve about the whole family. She told him about Grace and Duncan and about when they met.

'All the boys at school had loved Grace at one time or another, and were totally envious of Duncan,' she said.

'I was always the jealous sister, and sometimes I think Grace used to thrive on it,' she said as Steve smiled.

When Grace was at school she was the beauty queen four times in a row and was the prom queen. Grace had kept all the memorabilia's from her school days. The day trips they went on and all the times she and Duncan had spent together. Though now they were all ruined in the fire.

It was just before five o'clock in the evening when Frank had contacted them about Abbie. Lesley was cooking tea for everyone, though none of them were in the mood for eating. Raymond and Lyndsey were staying for tea with their daughters. Mikey was still asleep upstairs, and the phone made everyone jump when it rang. Danni jumped up and answered it.

'Hi, it's Frank', he said.

'Have you found her? Have you found Abbie?' she almost cried. Lesley had come through from the kitchen and they all stood around anxiously listening, and when Danni started crying they knew Abbie had been found. Danni fell to the floor crying whilst continually thanking Frank, and Steve went to her and took the phone from her.

'Hi matey.' Steve started smiling and he turned to all of them.

'Frank's found Abbie. She's in Paris.' Steve went on talking to Frank for a few minutes and then he put the phone down.

'We're leaving for Paris this evening. We have to leave now to be at Heathrow. Frank's booked us all seats on the seven o'clock flight to Paris.' He went to Danni then as she was still sitting on the floor crying.

'Abbie's coming home, sweetheart.' He helped her up, and Danni stood there holding him as she cried.

Lesley went upstairs and woke Mikey, and she started packing a few things for everyone. Frank had booked the flight and a one night stay at a hotel, and they'd fly back the next morning.

Mikey and his sisters hadn't got anything, except the clothes on their backs, and the luggage the girls bought back from their holiday, but Lesley had got a few spare clothes for them. Maybe they would go shopping in Paris for a few clothes if they felt up to it.

They drove to the airport and they met Frank in the departure lounge. Frank had collected their tickets for them, and Frank's assistant, Sally Evans was there too to see them off.

'Frank, thanks for everything mate. I know Mikey and the girls really appreciate all you've done to help,' Steve said as they arrive. Frank saw them all now, and he walked over to Mikey.

'Don't worry son, your sister will be home soon.' Hannah smiled as she hugged him.

'Thank you Frank. I can't believe you found her so quickly.'

'That's alright, sweetheart. Just seeing you smiling is thanks enough.' Frank took Steve aside then to chat quietly.

'Listen matey. I've booked you all a suite at The Hilton Paris at Charles de Gaulle. It's the same hotel Miss Philips is staying at. I had the feeling the girls wouldn't want to fly back the same day, and booking hotels would be the last thing on their minds.' The two men shook hands and Steve thanked Sally too for all her help, and then they walked over to the departure lounge.

The girls couldn't believe they were seeing Abbie in a couple of hours, though they wished it was under happier circumstances. Abbie was staying at The Hilton Paris, and Frank had made all the necessary arrangements. All they had to do when they arrived at the hotel was book in.

Chapter Four

The flight to Paris only took a couple of hours, but the waiting as they sat on the plane was like a lifetime. It was just after nine o'clock in the evening, and they went straight to the hotel and booked in and afterwards they went to find Abbie.

They left their room and went straight downstairs to reception. Steve made a few enquires, and then the receptionist called Abbie's room. Luckily she was there, and moments later she came down, looking frumpy in her dungarees and her oversized woolly jumper.

She wasn't expecting them, as Hannah told Frank not tell her they were arriving, so naturally Abbie was suspicious, though happy to see them. Abbie squealed with delight when she saw them, but her sisters were less joyful. They were almost crying when they greeted each other.

'Sis', what are you all doing here? And how did you know where I was?' she asked excitedly. Abbie noticed Mikey then and the wheelchair.

'Hannah, why is Mikey in a wheelchair? What's happened to you, Mikey?' she asked as she went to him. Both his legs were still in plaster, and Abbie was naturally concerned. Hannah never answered her sister as she looked to her aunt, and Abbie stood up and glared at her.

'Hannah, answer me. What's happened to Mikey?' Hannah looked round at everyone now, and her eyes stopped on Steve. She held out her hand, and Steve went to her and held her hand.

'Abbie, this is Steve Radcliffe. He's the police officer that helped us find you.' Abbie looked at Steve and instantly grew nervous.

'Sis', why would the police be looking for me? What's happened?' Abbie looked at Mikey again and to Steve and her sisters, and she was getting nervous.

'Abbie, darling. Let's go and find somewhere quiet so we can talk. What about your room?' Lesley asked. Though Abbie was curious and nervous because they were all there, she led them all to her room without question, but once there Abbie started crying.

'Hannah, what's going on? You're really scaring me now.' Abbie saw the tears in her brothers and sisters eyes, and obviously she was concerned. Hannah went to her sister and held her hand as they sat down.

'Ab's, we're all here because we have something to tell you,' Hannah said. Abbie kept looking at Steve as he smiled gently. She wiped her eyes and held Mikey's hand.

'Sis', why are you all here? And why are the police here?' she asked sternly.

'Abbie, something's happened at home. There was a fire, and mom and dad . . .' Tears filled Hannah's eyes as she bowed her head.

'Hannah, what are you saying? Where're mom and dad?' she asked as her bottom lip trembled.

'I'm sorry Ab's. Mom and dad are gone. They're dead.'

'No . . . please.' She held out her arms, as though stopping them from getting too close to her as she sobbed. Mikey was crying as their aunt comforted him, and Hannah and Danni just pulled Abbie close to them as they comforted each other.

'Sis', please tell me they're not dead. Please tell me you're lying.' Though Abbie knew they wouldn't lie to her. Certainly not about something like this. Abbie broke down, and they all sat huddled on the floor crying and comforting each other as Lesley comforted Mikey.

Steve quietly stepped out the room to leave them alone for a while. He went downstairs to the bar and got himself a scotch, and sat down reading his newspaper. It was almost ten o'clock, Paris time, and the bar had started shutting up, but Steve sat quietly as he drank his scotch.

It was a while before Mikey and his sisters had calmed down a little. Lesley had gone to get Mikey and his sisters a drink, and when she returned, Mikey had fell asleep in Abbie's arms as they lay on the bed.

'There you go darling, drink that. It'll make you feel better.'

'Thanks auntie.' Abbie took a sip of her steaming coco and set it down on the bedside table.

'So what happened?' Hannah explained she and Danni knew as much as she did. That they had come back from Switzerland to find out the news.

'Steve told us that dad died before the firemen got him out,' Danni said.

'Mom was still alive when Danni and I got to the hospital, but the doctor at the hospital that was caring for mom told us that she had suffered internal bleeding that led to too many complications. In the end mom wasn't strong enough to fight it. Mom died this morning.'

'Auntie told us the house had collapsed while mom and dad were still in there. The doctors think that that's what caused the internal bleeding,' Danni said. Abbie looked at Mikey as he slept in her arms. She stroked her hand over his face and kissed him.

'And where was Mikey when all this was happening?'

'Mikey was in the house too, darling,' Lesley said.

'Auntie told us that when part of the house collapsed, Mikey was standing at the window, and he was trapped under the rubble,' Danni said as fresh tears welled in Abbie's eyes.

'Dr Hanson at the hospital told us he was very lucky. He only had a few broken bones,' Hannah explained.

'There's a couple of other things I think you should know too, Ab's. Mikey blamed himself for what happened, and I think he still feels guilty that he didn't stay and help dad get mom out quicker. You should have seen his face when he woke up in the hospital. He was so scared, Ab's. He thought we'd punish him for not getting mom and dad out.' Abbie looked horrified as she looked at Mikey, and tears filled her eyes as she kissed him.

'Oh, Mikey, I'm so sorry,' Abbie whispered. She wiped her eyes and took a deep breath.

'What else is there to know?'

'Mom was pregnant. She hadn't told anyone apparently. I only guess is mom and dad wanted to surprise us,' Danni said as Abbie cried.

That night they all slept together in one room. Steve slept on the sofa, as the girls felt there was no need for him to go to a separate room on his own. Mikey and his sisters slept together on the king size bed, and Lesley and Steve slept on the two sofas.

The following morning Abbie was awake early. Though she never slept much. Every time she closed her eyes she could see their parents. Mikey had a few nightmares about being trapped in the house, but he soon got off to sleep again as Abbie sang to him.

At seven o'clock Steve ordered room service. They had breakfast bought to the room, and afterwards Abbie took them all sightseeing around Paris. Though none of them were entirely in the mood, Steve and Lesley thought it would help take their minds off things.

Abbie shown them the Eifel Tower and The River Seine and the Opera Palais Garnier and the Conciergerie, and afterwards they took the early flight back to London. None of them were in the mood for sightseeing. Though Lesley had always wanted to see Paris.

Lesley honeymooned in Paris when she married her ex-husband, and she always dreamed of going back. She planned to take a trip to see Paris and Rome next year, but now she was having second thoughts. Or at least postponing the trip. She knew her main priority now were her nieces and nephew.

A last gift to her sister. To take care of her children.

Chapter Five

It was almost twelve o'clock midday when they arrived back at Heathrow, and Frank and Sally were waiting for them in the arrival lounge. They were all exhausted after the flight home. Mikey had fallen asleep again, and Steve had carried him from the plane while a stewardess got his wheelchair

'Hello matey, good flight?' Frank asked as they shook hands. Frank had offered them all some refreshments before they went home, but they were all too tired and Mikey was falling asleep again in his wheelchair.

'Thank you, Frank. For everything,' Hannah said as he held her hands.

'I'm just happy you're all together and that your sister is home.' Hannah stood on tip toe and gave Frank a cuddle, and then she looked to Abbie and held her hand.

'Frank, Sally. This is our sister Abbie.'

'Hello Abbie. It's nice to meet you,' Frank smiled.

'Thank you for bringing me home, Mr Andrews,' she smiled through her tears. Abbie had cried most of the way home as she thought of her parents.

'You're welcome, sweetheart.'

Steve carried Mikey out to the car park, and they all got in his car and drove back to Lesley's. On the drive back home Mikey and his sisters decided to visit the neighbours in their street, and to see the remains of their house, though Lesley thought it was too soon.

'It's alright auntie. We discussed it last night, and besides we can't avoid the area forever,' Hannah said.

They all stood there in the street mesmerised by what they all saw. Mikey and his sisters sobbed as they examined the remains of their once beautiful home, and Hannah walked over as she saw some of their personal items scattered about. She crouched down and pulled from the rubble what was left of one of her expensive dresses from Milan. She saw her mothers dressing table and what was left of her fathers desk from the study.

Danni stayed with Mikey as Abbie walked over the rubble to her sister. Most of the personal items were irreplaceable. Collectors' items they bought back from the different countries they'd visited. CD's and vinyl's that they would never get again, but most of all it was their home. The only home they had ever had with their family. It was all gone. The cherished memories they would never have again.

Some of the neighbours started coming out once they saw them. Hollie and her daughters and Vera Tibbit, the old lady on the corner.

'Hannah?' Vera stood crying as she leaned on her walking sticks, her shawl draped over her shoulders. Hannah went to the old lady, and they stood there comforting each other.

Vera Tibbit was like the grandmother of the street. At eight-three years old she was the oldest resident on the street. All the children called her grandma, and she was always giving them sweets and biscuits and cakes. Her favourite was gingerbread men. She was always baking fresh biscuits cakes and gingerbread.

She never had any children of her own, and her husband and family had all gone. Sometimes she was seen giving money to the children too. At first the parents would disagreed in her giving her money away, but she had nothing else to spend it on, and with no family left to leave it to she didn't mind.

'Hello granny Vera,' Hannah cried in her arms.

'Oh, my child. I'm so sorry,' Vera cried. Vera saw Mikey and Abbie and Danni now as they all greeted each other. Afterwards they went back to Lesley's. Tony got Vera's wheelchair and she joined them too round at Lesley's. Tony and Julie made everyone some coffee and a coco for Mikey, and Lesley had got biscuits and cakes out and they spent the afternoon remembering and talking about the happy times the family had together.

Lesley had got all the family albums out and videos Grace and Duncan had made over the years. Raymond and Lyndsey had joined them too with Caroline and Debbie, and Desmond was there too.

Abbie had sat with Desmond the entire afternoon, and it wasn't long before she fell asleep in his arms. Desmond cherished Abbie like his own daughter. As his goddaughter, he was always spoiling her. Grace was always giving him disapproving looks every time he spent money on her.

'You're spoiling her again, Desmond,' she would say. The truth was that Desmond never had the chance of his own family, and Abbie was the next best thing. It was Desmond who paid for her driving lessons and bought her first car. A little MG. She drove it everywhere. She even took it on her trip around Europe. She's just waiting now for it to be collected from Paris, as she left it parked in the car park at the hotel.

Tomorrow morning Hannah and her sisters were going to the office to sort through things, and have a meeting with Raymond and Desmond. The girls were happy enough to stand aside and let them carry on for the time being, but the girls knew they would have to do it sooner or later. It's been almost two months since the tragedy that took their parents, and the girls knew it was time to move on.

It was only five days to go before the funerals, and there were still a lot of preparations to do. Desmond had managed to reschedule Duncan's funeral after Grace died so they could be buried together. He knew that their children would want to do something special for them.

Mikey and his sisters had all been shopping for new clothes. Mikey had a new suit for his parents' funerals, and the girls had picked out new dresses. Though it felt strange for Abbie wearing a dress.

Abbie was always seen in dungarees and baggy jumpers. No matter what the weather was like. Grace and Duncan always saw her as a tomboy, and sometimes joked that she was meant to have been a boy.

Before Abbie left for her European trip, she always liked to scrum with the lads as they played rugby, or she'd be kicking a football around with the children in the street. Abbie was a dab-hand with cars. She was sometimes seen with her head under the bonnet of one of the neighbours' cars, covered in oil and grease and wearing a dungarees and a baseball cap on backwards.

Hannah was twenty-five years old and nothing at all like her sister, Abbie. Hannah was always seen in designer clothes, and she always had a different hat to wear and new shoes to wear. Danni liked to wear designer clothes too, though she less obsessed as Hannah. Her long auburn hair and blue eyes and her designer Gucci bags, there was no mistaking they were sisters.

Mikey was only ten. Though he like nice clothes and he was always dressed smartly, he wasn't at all bothered about designer wear. His dark hair just like his father and blue eyes, he was sure to get all the girls falling for him.

The night before the funeral, Mikey and his sisters were all sitting in the lounge. Steve was at work tonight and Tony and Julie were there at Lesley's. All the preparations had been made. The local church had got involved in some of the preparations too. Mikey and his sisters thought it would be nice to have the wake in the street. *Kind of like a street party*, Abbie told her aunt.

They had borrowed tables and chairs from the local community hall, and all the neighbours had prepared some food that they left in fridges.

All the residents always come together on occasions like this. Grace and Duncan had even had their reception in the street. One big street party with all their neighbours and friends, and Mikey and his sisters thought it would be nice to send their parents on their way the same way they started. Beside it was a nice afternoon, and what better way to celebrate your parents lives together with friends and neighbours.

Mikey had slept a bit more soundly that night, though he woke a couple of times with pins and needles in his legs. Dr Hanson told his sisters that he had to keep the casts on his legs for a couple of months so the bones started to heel, and then he'd see about reassessing him. It would probably take a few months before Mikey would be able to walk without crutches again, but he seemed alright for the moment.

Lesley was the first to wake the following morning, and though the funeral wasn't till eleven-thirty, she had plenty to be getting on with.

Raymond and Lyndsey came round just after nine o'clock with Caroline and Debbie, and Desmond was there too. Tony and Julie prepared all the tables and covered them all with paper table clothes, while Caroline and Debbie were helping with all the chairs.

The vicar had come round too that morning before the service to visit and to offer his condolences. At fifty-seven years old Reverend Joe Watson had had the pleasure of seeing most of the children in the street grow up, and he had christened all of them.

Sometimes the residents would go to him for all kinds of advice. Whether it would be of a personal nature or sexual advice or anything else, the reverend always seemed to have an answer.

'Hello reverend, how are you this morning?' Abbie asked when she saw him.

'Hello my child. I'm very good thank you.' Abbie went to him and hugged him then and the reverend blessed her as she smiled briefly.

'May the Lord be with you my child.'

At ten thirty Mikey and his sisters went to get changed. Mikey had his new suit Danni bought him and his new black shoes. Though Mikey wasn't able to stand up for too long unaided, he seemed to manage, though he had trouble doing his tie. He called to Hannah in the next room where his sisters were getting changed.

'Sis', I can't do my tie,' he called from his room.

'Hang on Mikey, I'm coming.' Hannah was sitting there in just her bra and knickers. She was putting her tights when Mikey called to her. Hannah grabbed her silk dressing gown and went to help Mikey. When they were all dressed they went downstairs. Steve had arrived, and Frank and Sally were there too.

'Frank, Sally. You came. Oh it's good to see you again,' Danni said as she and her sisters greeted them. Frank didn't know the family that well, but the sisters invited him and Sally to the funeral.

'We bought these wines and some cakes. Steve said you were having a wake. I hope they're appropriate.'

'Thank you, Frank. They'll be appreciated.' From the moment Frank and Sally arrived they instantly felt the love these people had for each other, and it almost made Sally cry that such tragedy had fallen on this nice family.

Chapter Six

At the service, the church was filled with friends and loved ones, and in the front pew Mikey and his sisters, all dressed in black sat together with their aunt and Steve. Lesley was wearing a simple grey flannel suit and a white hat with a red ribbon around it.

At the end of each pew, down the isle there were carnations and red roses, two of many of Grace and Duncan's favourite flowers, and at the front laid out in front of the coffins more roses spelt out their names in a wreath.

Grace and Duncan's caskets were laid open at the front as the reverend Joe Watson read from the bible. Mikey was crying as he sat there holding Abbie's hand. Hannah was trying to keep herself composed, though there were a few visible tears.

'It's alright to cry, darling. They are your parents after all,' Lesley said.

'I know auntie. I just don't want Mikey getting anymore upset than he is. You know how he gets when I cry.' Danni was the same too, though she was wearing dark shades to hide her eyes from him.

The sisters always put Mikey's feelings first. Ever since he was born they were always looking out for him. It was one thing Grace and Duncan were happy about. At least they would always be there for him and each other. No matter how old they get.

Hannah and her sisters had got up in front of the congregation and read from the bible too. And they told how they are a loving family, and that no matter where their parents were they were always going to be a family together.

That had made some of the congregation cry just listening to the girls. Even Steve had tears in his eyes after the girls' speech.

After the service everyone was invited back to the street. It was a glorious afternoon as the sun shone, and with the cool breeze it was quite a refreshing afternoon. Lesley was fluttering through the street as she spoke to people and offered lemonade, and not too far away, Mikey and his sisters sat quietly by the door of number 23 watching everyone.

Frank and Sally were there too. Sally had cried at the service listening to the girls' speeches, and seeing Mikey and his sisters now sitting on their own it made Sally want to cry again. She saw Lesley going over to them now, and she noticed she looked grieved seeing them on their own, and she went to speak to Lesley. She got four cups of lemonade and walked over to Lesley and smiled.

'Lesley, do you mind if I try talking to them?'

'That's so sweet, Sally. Thank you,' she smiled. Lesley went back to Steve, as Sally smiled and approached Mikey and his sisters.

'Hi ya girls. Hello Mikey. Do you mind if I join you?' Sally smiled and gave them each some lemonade.

'Thanks Sally.' Sally found a chair and sat quietly for a moment.

'You know, I lost my mother when I was only twelve years old.' Mikey and his sisters looked at her now as they listened.

'It's a hard process to grieve sometimes. Especially when you lose a loved one. I know it was for me. I never knew my father, so I ended up staying in an orphanage. I never had no one until I met Frank,' she said.

'Frank's been good to me over the years. He and his wife adopted me when I was fourteen, and they took me in and cared for me, and gave me a home and a job. There are a lot of people here today that love and care for you. I know you're grieving right now, but you're not alone.' Hannah thought about what Sally had just said as tears trickled down her cheeks. She breathed sharply and started crying.

'I just miss them so much. I want them back,' she sobbed as Sally stood holding her in her arms.

'I know you do, sweetie. I know. Shhh.' Lesley saw them now, and she went to run to Hannah, but Steve stopped her.

'Just leave them be for a while, darling. Sally's got it all covered.'

'I know Steve, but I can't stand to see them so upset,' she cried.

'I know, but just leave them be for a while.' Danni and Abbie and Mikey started crying now, and Sally was there comforting them all.

'That's it, you all have a good cry and get it out of you system.' It was the first time in a long time that Mikey hadn't tried to stop his sisters from crying.

At thirty-six years old, Sally Evans lives alone in Ashford, and has been working for Frank for twenty years. She had studied law at Oxford, and completed her degrees last year, and is now considering a course at medical school.

Steve's sergeant, Bill Holts was there too today. Bill stood talking to Steve for a while, and he was watching Mikey and his sisters. Mikey and his sisters were a lot better now, considering. After Sally had spoke to them they started to mingle a little bit and talk to their friends.

'I can't get over how loving these people are, mate. It almost breaks your heart to watch them,' Bill said.

'I know. This street is part of my beat, and I see all of these people everyday, but I've never known a group of people come together like this before.'

'Well, it's surprising what tragedy can do to people, matey.' Steve had been watching Lesley all afternoon, and he saw her now as she was talking to Sally, and he'd started getting those old feelings for her that he never thought he'd have again.

'Whatever you said to Mikey and the girls, Sally, it seems to have worked. Thank you.'

'Oh, you're welcome, Lesley. I just think they haven't allowed themselves to grieve. Grieving is important, I should know.' Lesley sensed then that Sally had suffered a loss too, and as she thought about it she noticed Steve was watching her, and she turned away shyly.

At forty-two years old, Steve Radcliffe had been married once, but the divorce had almost devastated him. He didn't like being single, but he was scared of starting over again. He'd said as much to his sergeant. Bill had known Steve for over thirty years, and he couldn't be more proud of Steve, even if he was his father.

'Believe me matey. Men are not supposed to be on their own. If every man had a loving woman, the world would be a brighter place. You'll know when the times right and when it's the right time, I'm sure things will be right for you.' Steve smiled a little, and he felt a bit bashful talking to his sergeant about his feelings.

Steve was never the sort to open up to someone, least of all to a colleague, but he had known Bill for a long time. Lesley smiled when she looked at Steve again. He was talking to Bill, and she took him some lemonade over as Bill left them too it.

'Listen Steve, I never got the chance to thank you properly for everything you've done for us. Especially helping to bring Abbie home. She'd probably still be in Europe somewhere now if you hadn't helped. We all do really appreciate it.'

'That's alright. Just seeing you all together is thanks enough.'

'The girls want to have some kind of ceremony for their parents and have a private burial ground for them. I wouldn't even know where to begin to enquire about something like that. Could you help in any way?'

'Well I have a few connections. Let me make a few calls and I'll see what I can do.' Mikey and his sisters were not going to have their parents buried just yet. They wanted to see if they could make it a bit special.

Over the next couple of days Steve had made a few phone calls and called in a few favours. He got on to the council and arrange for a section of land at the cemetery to be fenced off. Hannah and her sisters were willing to pay for it, they just wanted somewhere private so they could be alone with their parents.

It took a few weeks to organise, but Steve managed to get the planning permission. In the meantime Hannah and Danni had arranged for their parents burial at the site. Grace and Duncan were being kept at the morgue at St Mary's for now, and the girls were just happy they could finally lay their parents to rest.

The evening after the wake they were all sitting in the lounge at Lesley's. Steve was on duty tonight, and promised to pop in on his rounds to say hello. Julie and Tony were there too with Vera.

At twenty-five years old, Julie Maverick was orphaned two years ago after her father died of cancer. She never really remembered her mother, as she died of tuberculosis when Julie was only three. Her father was her whole life, and when he died it was like a part of her died too.

Though Julie had inherited everything from her father, she moved in with Grace and Duncan after the funeral. They were concerned for her after she tried to commit suicide. Julie only wanted to die and to be with her father in heaven, but every time she tried, Grace and Duncan were there to stop her.

They never gave up on her, even when Julie kicked and screamed when they intervened. 'Please just let me die,' she sobbed in Grace's arms one night. Julie had owed her whole life to Grace and Duncan, and now they were gone too.

The morning of the ceremony, everyone from the street was there. Tony had pushed Vera along in her wheelchair, while Hannah and her sisters walked behind the coffins with Mikey in his wheelchair.

Steve and Frank had joined the pallbearers. They carried the coffins through the street as the neighbours came out to pay their last respects to two dear friends.

Some had joined the congregation as they walked to the cemetery.

As they walked the streets with the coffins, there was an eerie silence over the streets as pedestrians stopped and watched. They felt as though they were in a military march and people stopped and listened.

There was a lot of respect for Grace and Duncan, and the disaster of the fire and their deaths had shocked the community. Grace and Duncan were major fund-raisers, and when Grace wasn't at the office, she was always helping out at local nurseries with the children and different other charities, and they did endless work with the disabled children.

Duncan was always the local Santa, and visited schools and hospitals each year. People of all ages had respect for them. Ten years ago Grace and Duncan had helped a small group of kids quit the drugs and glue sniffing. Duncan had donated twenty thousand pounds to the AIDS charity, and a lot of people that wanted to kick the habit were immensely grateful for his contributions.

When they reached the cemetery, they laid the coffins down as the line of people slowly came through the gates, though there wasn't enough room for all of them. As far as they could see people waited in line to pay they last respects.

'Oh my Lord. Sis', look at all them.' They looked back as far as they could see. There were hundreds of them.

'Where've they all come from,' Danni laughed.

'I know mom and dad were popular, but not this well.' Literally hundreds of people had lined the streets to wait their turn to pay their last respect. The police were called in to help divert the traffic as people blocked the road.

It was several hours before Mikey and his sisters had a moment to themselves with their parents. Lesley had said her goodbyes to Grace and Duncan, and they all left Mikey and his sisters alone for a while.

"Their Garden" as they liked to call it now turned out nice. Steve had arranged with the local council to fence off ten metres square of space. They had a fence built around that gave them a bit of privacy. Though people could still see over the fence, it was their space, and there was a door with the words "The Philips Garden" on it.

Over the next few weeks Mikey and his sisters and their aunt would plant flowers and plants in their garden, though Mikey was going back to school in a couple of weeks and the girls had the office to contend with.

Duncan had left the business and all the families' possessions and money in his will. A total of four and a half million pounds.

It was Monday morning, and Mikey was going back to school today, and his sisters were going into the office on their first day. Though Abbie had never studied law, Hannah and Danni had, and they were going to teach her everything they knew. In the meantime Abbie was going to enrol in college for next September. Hopefully at Cambridge.

Mikey wasn't at all nervous about going back to school, though he had butterflies in his stomach. He enjoyed going to school and being with his friends, and most of all he was looking forward to seeing his friend, Vanessa Harris.

'You all ready to go Mikey,' Hannah asked

'Yeah. Just got to put my shoes on.' Mikey wasn't using the wheelchair now, though he still used the crutches, and his casts had come off his legs now. Danni helped him put his shoes on and tied the laces. His sisters had bought him a complete new uniform to go back to school with. A new bag for his books and a new coat, and just as they were ready to leave the door bell rang.

'Good morning Vanessa,' Danni smiled when she opened the door.

'Come on in for a moment. We're dropping Mikey off at school. Do you want a lift?'

'Yes please.' Vanessa liked riding in Hannah's Bentley. It was really posh and comfortable, she thought.

They all left as Lesley stood and waved them off. Hannah dropped Mikey and Vanessa off at school, and then the girls went to work.

Philips & Co occupied five floors of and Knights Court on Oxford Street. Duncan was hoping by now that they occupied the whole ten floors, but they never got the permission to expand. It was Duncan's grandfather, Isador who started the business in 1924 when Philips & Co was just a small shop.

In 1934 Isador expanded and moved to Oxford Street and took over the first floor office space. It was Duncan's father, William who made Philips & Co the way it is today.

Hannah pulled into the underground car park and waved to the security guard.

'Good morning Tom.' She pulled into Duncan's space and the sisters made their way upstairs.

'Mornin' Dolores,' Danni chirped at one of the receptionists.

'Miss Philips? You're back.' Dolores was extremely surprised to see them and jumped up and greeted them. Though she knew they were back from Switzerland, Dolores wasn't expecting them back in the office for a while.

'Oh it's so good to see you all. I wasn't expecting you back so soon.'

'Thanks Dolores. We thought it was about time we came in. Besides we can't stay away forever,' Hannah said.

'Can you ask Raymond to come to my office when he comes in please?' The girls went to leave then, but Dolores stopped them.

'But Miss Philips. Raymond's already here. He was in his office ten minutes ago.'

'Oh. Thanks Dolores. You have a good day.'

'You too Miss Philips. And by the way, it's good to have you all back.'

Dolores Channing was thirty four and was always a live wire. She always brightened everyone's day with her infectious smile and her bubbly personality. At ten thirty, Dolores put a call through to Hannah.

'Miss Philips, there's a situation downstairs in the meeting room. I think you should get security and come down.'

'Well what is it Dolores? Can't security sort it? I have a stack of papers to go through before five o'clock.'

'Not really Miss Philips.'

'OK, I'll come down.' Hannah left herself a note on her desk to remind her to make a phone call when she got back. She had been so busy that morning that she hadn't noticed nearly everyone had left the office. She looked around suspiciously as she made her way to the stairs. Not even her sisters were there, and it was only ten-thirty. She opened the door to the main boardroom on the fourth floor and stared into the darkness.

'What the hell's going on?' she mumbled. The blinds were closed, and as she stepped inside the lights flashed on.

"HAPPY BIRTHDAY!!!" they all shouted. Hannah screamed and fell over with fright. It took her a moment for her to compose herself, and as the security guard helped up off the floor she started laughing as she saw everyone there. Her sisters, Raymond and Lyndsey and Desmond, and Lesley and even Tony and Julie were there. They were all there.

'Oh you guys. What are you like?' She saw Dolores then, and smiled.

'I thought there was something fishy going on,' she said, and she hugged Dolores as they both laughed. Hannah had totally forgot it was her birthday, what with everything that's happened over the past couple of months. She wiped her eyes now and greeted each of them as Desmond opened the champagne.

'I wondered where you two had disappeared to,' she said as she hugged her sisters.

'And you thought you could let your birthday go by without being noticed?' Desmond laughed.

'Happy birthday, darling.' He kissed her and gave her some champagne.

'I should be working, you know. I have a stack of papers to go through. You and Raymond can help me this afternoon, she laughed.

It was the school summer holidays coming up soon, and Hannah and her sisters were planning a trip to Bude in Cornwall. Though Mikey seemed to be getting better now, he was still having the odd nightmare and he was sometimes depressed, and his legs were sometimes playing him up.

He had had the casts off his leg now, but he still couldn't do gym at school and join in with any sport activities, which he enjoyed doing. Mikey was crazy about football. He was on the school team and hasn't played since before the accident.

He still has to go to therapy once a week, but he didn't mind that. As long as he could start playing football again soon.

His sisters thought it would be a nice treat for him to go to Bude after everything that's happened. They had discussed it with their aunt and they had invited Steve too.

Steve and Lesley had been spending a lot of time together lately and Hannah had noticed which made her happy for her. Hannah asked her aunt if there was something going on between them one evening as they sat watching television, and Lesley smiled.

'I'm absolutely crazy about him, darling. I haven't felt this way for years, and it's kind of scary.'

'Why's it scary,' Danni asked.

'Well I haven't had a relationship since John left me twenty years ago and I don't think I know how to anymore.'

'Don't be silly, auntie. Of cause you do. It's just natural you're scared, and Steve obviously makes you happy, so just go for it.'

'You sure, darling. I mean, I do have you three and Mikey to take care of now. I made a promise to your mother I'd take care of you.'

'Don't be daft, auntie. You're just making excuses now. Besides, we're old enough to take care of ourselves and Mikey's coping a lot better now,' Abbie laughed. Lesley laughed and kissed her.

'Anyway, seeing how happy you are, Steve's obviously good for you.' Lesley giggled then like a lovesick teenager, and they all laughed as Lesley told them about her and Steve. Steve was taking her out for a meal tomorrow night to the Locanda Locatelli, an Italian restaurant in Marble Arch, and Lesley was kind of scared.

She knew Steve would never hurt her in any way, and they both had the same feelings for each other, but it was the first date Lesley had been on in twenty years.

The following morning Lesley was dancing around the kitchen as she prepared breakfast for everyone, and moments later Mikey stood in the doorway staring at her.

'Good morning darling. Do you want some scrambled eggs, my special little diddykins?' Mikey stared at her as though she'd gone mad, and Hannah laughed at her as she came in.

'*Love is in the air,*' Lesley sang. The girls laughed as they saw the expression on Mikey's face.

'Don't worry bro'. Auntie's in love,' Danni laughed.

All day Lesley was on cloud nine as she bounced around and sang. She went through her wardrobe a dozen times thinking she hadn't got anything to wear.

'I must go shopping for new clothes,' she thought, so that afternoon she took the bus down to Oxford Street and bought an entire new wardrobe. She bought half a dozen new dresses and some new suits. Some new shoes and a new handbag. She spent hours trying on different necklaces and chains and earrings. Then she went to Harrods and spent a couple of hours sampling all the perfumes and jewellery there.

By five o'clock she was exhausted and took herself home. She showered, and then tried on a few outfits in front of the mirror. She had got herself a new perm at the hairdressers, and she stood in front of the mirror examining herself as she tried on each outfit.

Lesley was always proud of her figure. A size fourteen. She stood in front of the mirror examining herself.

'Not bad, not bad,' she mumbled. Her long black perm cascaded sensually over her shoulders as she pouted her lips at herself. Her dark brown eyes with a little eye shadow and mascara, she stood back examining herself in the mirror, and she liked what she saw.

'Mmm, maybe I should get a boob job as well,' she thought to herself pushing up her breasts in front of the mirror.

Mikey was in his bedroom reading comics when Lesley got home. Lesley had a huge six bed roomed house on Connaught Street, and Mikey and his sisters had a room each. She had bought the property with her ex-husband when they were married, so there was plenty of room for all of them. It was one of the few things Lesley managed to keep hold of after the divorce.

Lesley was thinking recently about selling the house. 'It's too big for just me,' she had told her sister, Grace once. Though now she was thankful she never sold it. Steve rang the door bell at six thirty and walked in, and he stood in the hallway as he saw Lesley.

'Wow, you look fantastic,' he said. Lesley blushed and giggled, and Hannah laughed as she watched them both. Steve had bought a new suit as well. Beige, with a blue shirt. They left shortly afterwards and Mikey and his sisters watched as they left.

'Behave yourselves,' Danni joked as they walked to the car.

'Of cause we won't,' Lesley said, and they all laughed as Steve opened the door to his Mercedes and drove off.

At forty-seven years old, Lesley Clifford had been married and divorced twice. Her first marriage only last less than a year. Grace had convinced her that he was no good for her after he continually abused her. It was a bitter divorce that he dragged on for years, though she found some comfort in her second marriage. Lesley had a blissful marriage the second time, until she found out about his countless affairs with his younger floozies. They were only married for seven years. Lesley has been single for twenty years now, and she has always been happy until now, that is.

It was only two weeks left before Mikey broke up for the summer holidays, and his sisters had booked the holiday to Bude. They hadn't told Mikey yet, as they wanted to surprise him.

Hannah was in charge of booking the hotel, and Danni was in charge of booking the train tickets. The girls had bought Mikey all new clothes for the holiday, and they had invited Steve and Tony and Julie, and Lesley was going as well, though Tony couldn't get the time off work. At twenty-six, Tony was a high-flying executive in his uncles law firm, and had several big meetings over the next few weeks that he couldn't afford to miss, though Julie was thoroughly excited about going to Bude.

The girls had packed Mikey's case and hid it in Abbie's bedroom. They had bought him all new clothes, a couple of pairs of trainers and some flip flops and swimming shorts.

Mikey and his sisters still visited their parents graves everyday, and spent a couple of hours there. They were truly grateful to Steve for doing "The Garden" for them at the cemetery. At least they could be there as long as they wanted without disturbing anyone.

The memorial garden was nice too. Steve had arranged it with the council to turn the land where their house was into a memorial garden.

Hannah and her sisters were still waiting for the forensics test to come back to say what caused the fire and destroyed their beautiful home. Steve had tried to rush it up now, as it had been almost three months. The council had the go ahead to clear the remains away after the fire brigade had finished taking samples, and now they were just waiting.

Grace and Duncan had had a six bed-roomed house at the end of the street, which was a convenient space for the memorial garden. They had planted a blossom tree, which was Grace's favourite, and some of Grace and Duncan favourite flowers and plants. There were tulips and roses and daffodils and carnations, and in the summer when it would all be in bloom they knew the garden would look fantastic.

Some of the residents in the street often sat in the garden to be close to Grace and Duncan. There were two benches and a rose bush either side of the entrance. And on the gate, a simple message read:

In loving memory to a loving couple and a loving mother and father. Grace Olivia Philip and Duncan Stephen Philips. 1960-2005.

Chapter Seven

On the evening before they departed for their holiday, they were all in bed by nine o'clock. Steve had packed a suitcase and stayed the night at Lesley's in one of the spare rooms, and Julie stayed the night too.

Mikey could barely contain his excitement when his sisters told him they were going to Bude. Grace and Duncan had promised to take him again this year, though they hadn't told him. The family had holidayed in Bude at least two or three times a year. It's where they had all their family holidays, and Mikey was always excited about going back each time.

Steve couldn't believe he was going on holiday with them all. Only a few months ago they were just people to him. Steve had got his house over on Kensington Gore, just the other side of Hyde Park, but he had been thinking of selling recently. It was only a small two bed-room house on the end of a terrace that he shared with his ex-wife, but there were too many memories there for him. Lesley had offered a place to stay a few weeks ago, but he hasn't made his mind up yet. Though he spent most days with Lesley and her nephew and nieces.

Lesley and her family were just someone he stopped to talk to on his beat and maybe have a coffee with them. Now he couldn't imagine his life any other way. Steve and Lesley's relationship was a bit more intense now that everyone knew, and his sergeant couldn't be happier for him. And he was even more thrilled for him when he told him he was going on holiday with them.

They were all awake the following morning at seven o'clock. The train from Paddington was at ten-thirty, and though everything was packed and ready they wanted to make sure they had everything and got to the station on time.

Lesley made the last checks around the house as she ticked off her checklist, while Hannah and Danni cooked breakfast for everyone. Hannah was still in her night clothes, and Abbie was still upstairs in the shower.

'Come on Ab's. Breakfast is ready,' Danni shouted.

It was one thing Lesley insisted on was a good hearty breakfast in the mornings. Though Mikey enjoyed a full English breakfast, and would eat it everyday if he had the chance, his sisters were quite the opposite. Maybe once or twice a week they had a full breakfast. Though they could eat enough food together to feed an entire football team, the sisters were quite petite.

'Where do you put all that food, girls,' their mother asked them once.

After they all finished eating they cleared everything away and washed up, and they started to leave. Steve and Lesley both checked through the house one last time that the windows were closed and they'd got everything, and then they all left.

Tony had come round to see them off before he left for the office. He was really sorry that he wasn't going with them, but he had deadlines at the office. But maybe next time, he thought.

'I really wish you were coming with us, Tony. I'm gonna miss having you around for the whole week.'

'I know babe. I'll miss you too, but this holiday will be good for you all. Hell knows you could all do with the break after everything you've been through. Besides I've got plenty to be getting on with while you're away. Seven

days isn't that long. You'll be home before you know it.'
They held each other for a long time as they kissed.

'Come on you two lovebirds, get a move on. Mikey's
getting restless,' Abbie laughed. Hannah looked round
and laughed and she kissed Tony one last time.

'Love you,' she said.

'Love you too, babe.'

Hannah and Tony's relationship had started to
blossom again over the past couple of months. Though
they both agreed to split up eight years ago, they still
remained friends. And still madly in love. Grace and
Duncan could never understand why they split up.

'Have you two had a fight or something?' Grace
had asked once. There was no logic reason to it, Grace
thought. Neither of them had had a relationship with
anyone since they split up, because they promised each
other they would get back together again one day, and
Danni and Abbie had noticed as much over the past
couple of weeks. Only last week Danni saw them kissing,
and it made her happy to think they had rekindled their
love.

At twenty-three years old, Danni has never had a
serious relationship. 'A good man is as rare to find as
a rare diamond, you don't get many of them,' she said
once. Danni had only had one relationship. A childhood
sweetheart, she liked to call him. They were only eight
years old when they started hanging around together,
and they were deeply in love by the time they left school,
but his family emigrated to Spain soon after, and Danni
never saw him again. She hopes one day their paths
would cross again.

They arrived in Bude and took a taxi to the Falcon Hotel. After they booked in they unpacked and went straight out. They had booked four rooms. One for Mikey and his sisters, one Julie, one for Steve and another for Lesley. They all met in reception and went out to look around.

Mikey and his sisters always loved going to Bude. They especially couldn't wait for the summer holidays when they went as a family. Hannah stood on the sea front and looked out to sea and breathed in the sea air as she smiled, and it was almost like a homecoming.

'Oh, mom,' she said as she looked out over the ocean. The sun glistened and sparkled on the sea like a million diamonds, and Danni smiled and looked round at her sister.

'You alright, sis'?'

'I just wish mom and dad could see this now.' Lesley smiled as she took Hannah's arm.

'I'm sure they can, darling. I'm so proud of you.' Lesley looked at her nieces and nephew now and smiled.

'I'm so proud of all of you. The way you've handled everything since you came home. I was sure you'd get messed up over it.'

'We did, auntie, but we have to move on. We can't wallow in the grief process forever. Mom and dad are gone, and they're never coming back. But they will always be here,' she said as she put her hand to her heart. A single tear trickled from Julie's eye as Lesley held her niece, and Julie could almost feel her fathers love surround her. It was a small slice of heaven. It was the first time Julie had felt that, and she knew from that moment her father would always be with her.

They had arrived in Bude just in time for lunch, and at twelve thirty they went to find somewhere to eat. It a gorgeous sunny day, and it made you want to stay outdoors forever. They ordered lunch and sat down outside on the patio. They thought they would hire a car and drive around the scenic route that afternoon.

The girls had ordered the seafood salad, and Mikey ordered fish and chips. The others were still inside the restaurant looking through the menu.

It had been years since Steve took a holiday anywhere. He rarely even took time off work, unless he had doctors appointment, so to be here, he thought, in Bude was like another world for him. He still couldn't believe that they invited him. He felt a part of their lives now, and couldn't possibly imagine his life any other way.

Julie had decided on the crab salad and Steve and Lesley had pie and chips, and after they finished eating Steve paid the bill, and they went to hire a car for the week. They walked along the sea front and along Summerleaze Crescent to the High Street. The girls stopped occasionally to look through the shop windows and to speak to the locals they knew.

One local that saw the girls walk by was Mrs. Springer. Mrs. Springer was in the butchers buying some meat when she spotted the girls. She paid the butcher and went out.

'Hannah? Danni? Abbie?' The girls looked round and smiled when they saw the woman.

'Oh girls, it's wonderful to see you again.' She saw Mikey and Lesley then and greeted them all.

'You all on your own? Are your parents with you?' Hannah looked round at everyone then as she realised not all their friends had been told of their parents deaths.

'Oh Mrs. Springer, I'm sorry. We forgot about everyone here.' The Philips family had known many people in Bude over the years, and with the commotion of dealing with their parents loss and the funerals, they had totally forgotten about their many friends in Bude. Hannah paused for a moment and looked deeply grieved as she held Mrs. Springer's hand.

'Our parents died a few months ago,' she said. Mrs. Springer looked as though she'd just walked into an invisible wall. Totally stunned.

'Oh, Lord. I'm so sorry. What happened?'

'There was a fire at home and dad died, and mom died a few weeks later in hospital.' It was too much for her to take in. She was deeply shocked. Hannah and Danni supported her as they went to find a café to sit down. Lesley introduced Julie and Steve, and then Julie ordered some drinks and they sat quietly for a while thinking of Grace and Duncan.

'Hannah, you know if there's anything any of us can do. Just give us a holler, won't you?' Abbie was thinking of notifying all their friends in Bude, but hadn't got a clue how to notify a whole town. Though she knew Mrs. Springer would spread the news fast enough now. Letters of condolences would soon come flying through the post.

After a while they found a car rental showroom, and Steve hired a Renault Picasso for the week. They thought it would easier to see the sights, and a lot easier than using the buses. Beside the buses were few and far between in Bude, they thought.

They drove down to Boscastle and Tintagnel to see the historical sites on their first day. Though they came to visit Bude, they thought they'd go further a field as well as they'd got the car for the week. Steve and Lesley had gone for private walks occasionally just to be alone, and the girls whistled and joked as they left.

'Off for a trip down lovers' lane,' they'd say. Bude was a nice place to be, Lesley thought. Lesley had been with Grace and Duncan a few times when they visited Bude, and she always thought it would be a nice place to live. Danni had said just the same as they sat in their hotel that evening.

'I think we should move here, sis'. Mikey looked hopeful as he listened. Though he didn't like the winters there. Especially if it snowed.

'Be serious, girls.'

'Why, what's wrong with it?' Abbie asked.

'Well, for one, the winters here can be terrible. You could get snowed in.' Steve raised his eyebrows hopefully, and Hannah laughed.

'Steve, stop encouraging them,' she said and slapped his leg.

'And secondly . . .' She couldn't think of another reason.

'Come on auntie, you know it's a good idea. You said yourself Bude's a nice place to live,' Danni said.

'Well what about Mikey and school. And what about the office. You still have all that to consider,' Lesley said. Steve was in the middle of things. He thought it was a nice place to live too. He loved Lesley, and if she moved with them he wouldn't be able to see her as often, unless he moved with them. But he had his career to consider too.

'You're just making excuses now. And besides, we can find Mikey another school easily enough,' Abbie said. Mikey went to his aunt now and sat next to her.

'Pleeeease.' Abbie and Hannah joined in too with their pleading eyes and Lesley laughed.

'Oh, alright. I give in. But I still say it's a bad idea.' Mikey whooped with glee then as he punched the air.

That evening Lesley and Steve went for a walk along the coastal path. They discussed moving too, but Lesley was concerned for him and his career in the force.

'Steve, I can't expect you to give up your career after twenty odd years to move to Cornwall, and I don't want to be somewhere without you.' They carried on walking for a while in silence as they thought, and then he turned to her and kissed her.

'My darling. I love you with all my heart, and I want to be with you too. No matter where that would be.'

'But what about? . . .' He put his hand over her mouth to stop her from talking and he kissed her.

'You know I've been married before, and the divorce almost killed me. I don't want to ever feel like that again. And I don't want to lose you. After eighteen years I can honestly say I've found happiness again. I found it with you, and a family to go with it.' He kissed her passionately as tears trickled from her eyes.

'I love you Lesley Clifford.'

'I love you too, Steve.' He held her and kissed her passionately.

They took a slow walk back to the hotel along the sea front, and when they got back Julie had just made a pot of tea. Lesley decided not to tell the others yet that she and Steve were thinking of moving with them. They wanted to be absolutely sure before they did.

That night after they all went to bed, Lesley crept into Steve's room. She slipped off her silk dressing gown and let it fall to the floor, and climbed into bed with him. Steve was almost asleep, but he didn't say anything as he cuddled up to her, feeling the soft satin night shirt against his skin.

He rolled her over and took her in his arms. Kissing her lips, her face, her neck, she moaned softly. He teased her nipples through the soft satin night shirt, then slipping it gently over her head he kissed her naked breasts. She lay in front of him with only her knickers on, feeling very vulnerable. After all it had been over twenty years since another man had seen her naked, and though she felt safe with Steve, she still felt that vulnerability. Steve noticed after a while and wondered if she really wanted this. He kissed her lips and looked deep into her eyes.

'You sure you want to do this?' he asked. She never answered him. She only slipped her knickers off and pulled him close. She kissed him passionately as his hand caressed every inch of her naked flesh. Teasing her nipples with his tongue while his hand disappeared between her legs.

Her back arched against the soft linen sheets, she moaned as he teased her. His fingers roamed and burrowed deep between her legs until she could take no more.

'Oh, Steve. Make love to me.' She gasped sharply as he entered her. Slow at first as they both savoured every moment and the pleasure, then as she felt the tip of an orgasm he started thrusting harder and faster.

'Steve. Slow down. I want to savour every moment.' She moaned and groaned with every thrust he made. The intense pleasure she thought she would never experience again heightened immensely. She held him in her arms as they both clenched. The sheer joy as she felt the orgasm. Every part of her body shook as an explosion of feelings went off like a firework.

'Jesus Christ.'

Thrusting deeper, they both climaxed. Like a single second froze in time, they lay there afterwards exhausted and confused with mixed feeling. Tears of joy sprang from her eyes as she lay there, and he held her close and kissed her passionately.

They lay there afterwards in each others arms. Both of them thinking it wasn't possible to feel the way they did, they fell asleep happy and contented.

Chapter Eight

The following morning they were all dressed and ready by eight o'clock. They went downstairs to the restaurant and had breakfast and they went straight out. It was a glorious morning, so the girls thought it would be nice to hire some bikes and explore the countryside.

They walked along down the High Street, and Hannah smiled devilishly at her aunt and Steve as they smiled and chatted about last night.

'You look as like the "cat that got the cream", auntie,' she said.

'I'm just happy, darling. It's a glorious day and I'm here with my nephew and nieces.' Hannah looked at her curiously and smiled, and then joined her sisters and Julie. It was a glorious morning. Almost eighty degrees, and a gentle breeze as they breathed the sea air.

'You don't suppose they heard us last night, do you?' she asked Steve nervously.

'Nah. They couldn't have,' he said wondering the same thing.

When they got to the High Street, they hired some bikes and cycled off up the street. Lesley hadn't been on a bike in years. She took one look at the saddle and laughed.

'You don't expect me to sit on that thing, do you? It's like sitting on a razorblade.' The girls laughed and rode on ahead.

'Girls, wait for me.'

'Come on, auntie. Race you to the end of the street,' Abbie laughed. The girls had bought their hats and smothered Mikey's back in sun cream before they set off.

Mikey had got such sensitive skin, and his sisters were always cautious whenever the sun came out. He was only wearing shorts and a T-shirt and his baseball cap.

They cycled over a small hump in the road where a stream passed underneath and Lesley stopped to take a sip of water from her water bottle, and a mile down the road they stopped outside an old rundown barn and admired the view. They stopped for a while to rest, and the girls laughed watching their aunt getting off her bike.

'Oh God, my arse is sore,' she said rubbing bottom.

'How do you kids manage to sit on them saddles?' Lesley sat down on the grass and rested for a while with the others and Mikey went to explore the old barn. The barn looked a hundred years old, with it's crumbling structure, but the scenery was magnificent. Wide open fields as far as the eye could see. There was a couple of houses along the lane, and outside the barn was a wreck of an old Volkswagen Beatle.

'Mikey, please be careful,' Hannah called to him as he disappeared into the barn. Mikey was used to his sisters protective ways, but their aunt sometimes gave disapproving looks.

'Sorry auntie,' Hannah said when she noticed.

'Darling, he's a young boy. He's aloud to fall over and scrape a knee occasionally. That what all boys do once in a while,' she said.

'I know, but I just love him to bits. I don't want him getting hurt.'

'I know you don't, darling, but just ease off a little. Just let him be a young lad.' They all got on their bikes after fifteen minutes and cycled off, and Mikey nearly slipped in the road. Lesley just shook her head disapprovingly as Hannah winced and cringed.

That afternoon they were cycling through the country lanes, just outside of Bude when they came across a for sale board outside a house. They stopped as the girls read the board, and they went to peer in through the windows.

'Careful girls. Someone still might be living there,' Lesley said. Though it didn't look possible, she thought. The exterior of the house looked as though it had been deserted for years, but inside was immaculate. No furniture, as the previous occupiers had moved out and took everything with them, but it was clean, and there were some red velvet curtains left in the lounge. It looked as though it had recently been decorated, and the fittings in the kitchen looked brand new.

They tried to look around the back of the house, but the gate was locked. Mikey and his sisters all looked at each other curiously, wondering if the place was still for sale. They continued to look around the property, and after a while they found another gate that led to the back garden.

They all went through cautiously, though expecting someone to be there, and they all stood there in surprise.

'Wow.'

'Oh auntie. This is fantastic,' Danni smiled. Julie peered in through the patio doors into the dining area and smiled.

'Hey, guys, come and check this out.' They all peered in and saw a lavish dining suite and a side unit. Newly decorated and a chandelier on the ceiling.

'I wonder if this place is still for sale, auntie?' Abbie asked hopefully. It was perfect, and just what Mikey and his sisters were looking for. The house stood on one and a half acres of land. There was a huge back garden with a water feature, and a stream that ran past at the bottom of the garden.

The driveway at the front of the house was easily big enough for six or seven cars and decorated with coloured pebbles. There were two blossom trees in the front garden, and the wooden bench for lounging on in the summer looked wonderful.

'Oh, girls. This is beautiful,' Steve said.

'You'd be crazy to let this go, darlings,' Lesley said. They all sat down on the lawn in the back garden as they discussed it. Financially they knew they could afford it. They had their inheritance from their parents and their own savings, and they had enough to buy the house and still have enough to live on.

'So what do you think, sis'? Mikey asked.

'Well I love it. There's no question about it,' Hannah said.

'Well let's get down to the estate agents and see if it's still for sale,' Lesley chirped. They all talked excitedly about the house as they cycled back into town, and about moving. Lesley still wasn't thrilled on the idea of them leaving London, but she was happy for them. The house was nice, she thought, and it would be nice to visit them and stay occasionally. And it would be especially nice in the summer.

They were still talking excitedly about moving when they walked into the estate agents. Mikey and his sisters enquired about the property, and were thrilled it was still for sale. They filled in some forms while they were there and told the woman they wanted to pay cash outright. She tried to convince them to take a mortgage but the sisters were adamant.

'No thank you. We don't want to be tied down with a mortgage for the next twenty five years. We want something that would be ours.'

They paid the necessary fees, and down payments, and then they were taken out to the property so they could view it. Mikey and his sisters loved the place. The only part of the property they hadn't seen before was the upstairs, but once they saw it they took it.

They went back to town and collected the keys. The estate agent checked all their references and the payment was taken from their bank a week later. Then they could move in.

They still had three days left of their holiday, so they used the time to buy furniture and anything else they needed. They took a better tour of the house after they got the keys, and they examined every nook and cranny.

There were five bedrooms upstairs and a guest room downstairs, which would come in handy for visitors. Two bathrooms and two en suite upstairs with showers. The large kitchen would come in useful for when they have visitors and outside parties.

They couldn't wait to get back to London to tell everyone. The girls had already decided to leave Raymond and Desmond in charge, and the girls would commute. They had found a school for Mikey, and managed to enrol him for September, which they were thankful for, and on their last day they used the time to make sure they'd packed everything.

They all sat in Lesley's room at the hotel that evening discussing moving. Though Steve and Lesley had decided to move with them, they hadn't said anything yet, though Steve wasn't looking forward to telling his sergeant. Steve had been with the force for nearly twenty five years, and he knew Bill wouldn't take the news well. Though he knew he would be happy for him.

'I wish you two were moving with us, auntie,' Abbie said as she cuddled up to her on the sofa. Lesley and Steve looked at each other then and smiled briefly.

'I know you do, darling. But I've got my house, and Steve's got his job. We can still visit each other, and you'll be commuting every now and then. And besides, you kids need your own space. You don't need me hanging around forever.'

'I know, but it won't be the same without you.' Lesley was distraught when they told her they wanted to move, and she couldn't understand why they wanted to move anyway, but now she was warming up to the idea. She knew that when the girls wanted something badly enough, they wouldn't give in until they got what they wanted. Danni went and sat with Steve and put her arms around his shoulders.

'Please come with us, Steve.'

'I don't know, darling. Like your aunt said, I do have my job.'

'Please uncle Stevie. We do love you.' She kissed his cheek as they all laughed.

'Uncle Stevie?' he laughed.

'Looks like we've got no choice now, Steve. They'll keep hounding us until we say yes,' Lesley said as Abbie and Danni started kissing him.

'Ok, Ok. I give in. I would love to move to Cornwall with you,' he laughed.

At two o'clock they went down to reception and handed in their room keys, and they took a last cycle out to their new home for one last look before they returned their bikes. Steve returned the rental car, and afterward they headed for the train station.

Mikey and his sisters couldn't wait to return to Bude. Though they wanted to live in Bude, they loved their new home, and they could still travel into Bude whenever they wanted. The girls were going to start looking for part time work to fill in some of their spare time once they move.

They were still going to commute to London, and maybe stay the odd weekend at their aunt's house. They had a lot of friends in and around Bude. The girls thought they would catch up on the gossip, and find out what's new in the area. They knew they had a lot of good times there with their parents, so maybe they'd visit some of the attractions they went to, they thought.

At the station, Steve got all their tickets ready, and they sat waiting as Mikey was playing his gameboy his sisters bought him. Steve and Lesley sat talking about their future plans. Steve wasn't sure if he wanted to sell his house or not after he moved, but Lesley was going to keep hers. Steve and Lesley knew there would be times when they wanted to be alone, and Mikey and his sisters would always have somewhere to stay when they commuted to London.

Mikey had fallen asleep on the journey back to London, and Steve had carried him when they changed trains, but his aunt woke him up when they arrived in London. He was still using the crutches occasionally, but he tried to get used to walking without them now, It was nearly eight o'clock in the evening when they returned home and Tony and Desmond were waiting for them at Paddington.

'Tonyyy,' Hannah squealed as she ran to him. They locked themselves in a passionate embrace and locked lips.

'Oh, God I missed you,' he said and kissed her again.

It had only been seven days, but Hannah missed Tony too, and she was starting to realise now how much they needed each other and how difficult it was going to be to tell him they were moving.

Hannah knew he had his job in London and how difficult it would be for him to leave. He could quit, but he had a lot riding on his career.

'Oh I missed you too,' she laughed.

They walked out to the car park and got into Tony's car, and all the way home they were talking about the holiday. Hannah was dreading telling Tony about the move. She was going to wait till they got home. They were still talking about the holiday when they got back to Lesley's

Julie went to make some coffee while Hannah disappeared upstairs with Tony. They sat on the bed and

Tony kissed her passionately, but then Hannah turned away from him.

'Babe, what's wrong?' By now Hannah was in knots. She started pacing as she thought, and Tony was getting worried. He went to her and held her hand, and looked deep into her eyes. There was nothing Tony and Hannah couldn't hide from each other. They had known each other too long.

'Hannah, what's wrong. You're worrying me now.' She held his hand and kissed him now.

'Tony, I love you. You know that, right?'

'Yes,' he replied nervously.

'There comes a time when people have to move on, and after everything we have all been through since mom and dad died, I just don't feel I belong around here anymore.' Tears welled in her eyes now as Tony listened intently. He kissed her lips and looked at her. She folded her arms across her chest and walked slowly to the window.

'Babe, whatever's bothering you, you know you can tell me.'

'We found this nice house in Cornwall, just outside of Bude. Oh, it's such a wonderful place. It's got five bedrooms and a guest room. It's out in the country, and Mikey and I and Danni and Abbie, we kind of bought it. We're going to live there.' She looked at him now not knowing what he was thinking, and he smiled at her.

'Oh baby, that's fantastic.'

'It is?' she asked nervously.

'Yeah, cause it is. You love Cornwall, and we both know how much you want to live there.' He cupped her face in his hands and kissed her lovingly.

'But what about us? I know how difficult it will be for you if you left your job, and I couldn't stand it if we lived apart,' she told him. He thought about it now as he realised why she was worried so much when she got back.

'Hannah, baby. I love you, and if that means giving up my job and moving from London to be with you, well so be it.'

'But Tony, everything you've worked for and everything you've achieved. You're prepared to give all that up?'

'Yeah, if it means we can be together. Besides everything I've achieved will help me to get a better position in life. There're bound to be jobs available for me in and around Cornwall. And who knows, I might even start my own business.' He kissed her lips now, and she laughed.

'I don't think you realise what you've just done for me,' he laughed. He jumped off the bed and spread his arms wide, as though inviting her into his arms.

'You've given me the greatest opportunity of my life,' he said. He kissed her and ran from the room and whooped with glee. Then he turned and looked at Hannah as she laughed. He went back to her and kissed her passionately.

'Sorry babe, gotta go. Gotta go and tell my boss to shove his job up his arse. Wahey.' Hannah laughed watching him, and he bumped into Abbie on the stairs. He held her face in his hands and kissed her hard on her lips as she was shocked.

'Ab's, I love you. Wahey.' He whooped with glee as he ran down the stairs and out the front door, and Abbie and Hannah looked at each.

'What the hell you done to him, sis'? Abbie asked as they both laughed. Hannah went downstairs and joined the others after a while, and she told everyone that Tony was moving with them.

'He's just gone to hand his notice in to his boss,' she said.

The following morning Steve went into work and spoke to Bill. By now the whole station knew of his relationship with Lesley, and they were happy for him, though some of the officers teased him. Bill was in his office when Steve arrived. He knocked the door and walked in.

'Hi ya matey,' Bill said as Steve sat down and exhaled deeply.

'How was the holiday?' Bill poured them both a scotch as Steve told him all about their holiday, and then Steve looked a little more serious.

'What's up matey, you look troubled.'

'Well Bill, it's like this. You know about my relationship with Lesley, Right?' Bill nodded as Steve continued.

'Mikey and his sisters have bought a property in Cornwall, and Lesley is moving with them. And so am I. I'm going to quit the force and move to Cornwall.' Bill almost choked on his biscuit then as he stared at Steve.

'You're what?'

'I leaving the force and London.' He paused for a moment and saw Bill's face, and Steve was almost sorry to leave.

'I'm going to ask Lesley to marry me this weekend,' he said then. Bill was almost speechless for once as he stared at Steve.

'Well, for the first time in my life, matey. I'm speechless.' He stood up then and congratulated him, and then he went out and spoke to his assistant.

'Rosie, sweetheart. Here's fifty quid. I want you to go and buy a bottle of the best champagne there is,' he said. She went to leave, and then he gave her another fifty.

'There, that should do it,' he said. Rosie smiled curiously looking at Steve and then she left.

At fifty-two years old, sergeant Bill Holts had been in the force, and has served the Marylebone and Paddington area since he was eighteen. There wasn't many people in town he didn't know, and he especially knew all the gangs and the hooligans, and where they hung out. Over the years Bill had made a name for himself, and was well known in most parts of London. "The Raging Bull", people called him, cause he was well known for charging into places to catch the criminals.

Bill sat down at his desk, looking over the top of his half moon spectacles. The light from the overhead fluorescent lamp was shining down on his grey balding head, and he took two cigars from the box on his desk, handing one to Steve.

'Steve, matey. I never thought I'd see the day that you'd leave the force.' Bill had got high hopes for Steve. Though by now he had hoped Steve had made sergeant.

'Well mate, I can't say I'll be glad to see you go. You'll be missed around here.'

'I know, but there comes a time when you ask yourself, are you really happy with your life, and Lesley has given me fresh hope. And this past week has made me realise what I'm missing out on.' Even if Lesley said no to his marriage proposal, he knew he'd still be happy with her, and Lesley felt the same. When Rosie returned with the champagne Bill made his speech.

'Gather round everyone, gather round. I have some rather happy news.' He looked to Steve as he held up the bottle, and he felt a bit embarrassed that Bill was putting him on the spot.

'I never thought this moment would come, but it has.'

'Bill, you're not trying to tell us that you're crazy in love with me, are you?' Zoë laughed.

'No, but that's a nice thought. Thank you, Zoë,' he said as they all jeered.

'Steve has found himself a new life. And he's leaving us. I'm not saying that's the happy news, but he is going to ask Lesley to marry him tonight.' Everyone fell silent then and looked at Steve.

'Steve, buddy, you're not leaving, are you?' Johnus asked.

'But why?' Queenie asked worriedly. Steve laughed and put his arm around her shoulders.

'Well Queenie. I've found myself a new love. I'm sorry sweetheart, but you just don't satisfy my needs anymore.' They all jeered again as Queenie blushed, and Steve kiss her cheek.'

'Because I've found something that I never thought I'd find again. Love and happiness. And a family to go with it,' he said then. There were some visible tears amongst his colleagues now as he looked across the room, and he felt almost sorry he was leaving. Zoë went to him and congratulated him as she wiped her eyes.

'You silly fool. I don't care what you say, you're gonna miss this place.' She kissed him as Bill popped the cork and started pouring the champagne.

'Here's to Steve and Lesley and their new life together,' Bill added.

Zoë has always had a liking for Steve. Not in a sexual way, but she always saw him as an older brother. At thirty-six years old, Zoë Wilson had always respected and admired Steve and looked up to him as a perfect example of how a police officer should be.

Chapter Nine

That afternoon Steve left the station and went home to Lesley. Mikey and his sisters were upstairs packing a few things, and Steve called them downstairs as he waited in the lounge with Lesley. Steve felt quite nervous now as he paced the living room waiting. He wasn't sure how Lesley was going to respond. He hoped she'd say yes, but if she said no, would it ruin what they had already?

Mikey and his sisters sat on the sofa waiting curiously for what Steve was going to say, though Abbie had her suspicions. Abbie had been watching her aunt closely over the past few weeks, and noticed they were getting extremely close. Steve stood in the middle of the lounge now as he looked at Lesley.

'Lesley, I know we haven't known each other that long, and these past few months I've spent with you has only proved our love for each other.' Lesley was getting embarrassed now as Hannah realised what Steve was doing. She laughed a little as she put her hands over her mouth. Steve took the ring from his pocket and knelt in front of Lesley.

'Oh, Jesus.' Steve never said another word as Lesley realised. Tears filled her eyes as she kissed him. They had both felt so strongly about each other that there was no doubt in either of their minds that they were doing the right thing.

'Will you marry me?' he asked, poised to putting the ring on her finger.

'Yes. Yes,' she cried. Hannah was crying and Abbie and Danni were near tears too. Steve pushed the ring completely on her finger now and they locked themselves in an embrace as they all cheered.

'I suppose I can officially call you Uncle now,' Danni laughed. She hugged and kissed him them.

'Congratulations auntie,' Abbie said hugging her.

At lunchtime Steve took Lesley for a celebration meal at the Auroru at Piccadilly Circus and afterwards they spent the afternoon shopping on Oxford Street and Covent Gardens and Harrods, and at five thirty they saw a show at the Phoenix on Charing Cross Road.

Mikey and his sisters carried on packing once Steve and Lesley left. They had got a lot more belongings now since they moved in to their aunts. Danni had started building up her CD collection again and Hannah had got all her designer clothes and hats and her many pairs shoes. The girls were talking constantly amongst themselves about moving, and Mikey was singing along to a Westlife CD, which he only did when he was thoroughly excitedly about something.

Hannah smiled as she could hear him in the next room. It was the weekend now, and the girls were hoping to be moved in to their new home by next weekend. The girls had many things to sort through at the office. They had several meetings this week, and they wanted a meeting with Raymond and Desmond too.

Raymond and Desmond were partners and practically ran the business anyway. Even when Duncan was there, Raymond and Desmond were second in charge. The girls were happy enough to step aside and let them run things, as long as they occasionally showed their faces. The girls would have plenty of time for themselves. They could contend themselves with shopping and lazing on the beech in the summer.

That evening when Steve and Lesley returned home Hannah was in the kitchen cooking tea. Beef Stroganoff, one of the families favourite. And always their fathers favourite. Hannah smiled to herself thinking back when she cooked it for the first time for her fathers birthday. It was raining that day and Duncan arrived home from the office drenched just from walking from the car to the front door, and he was welcomed by the smell. He had thought it was Grace cooking at first, as Hannah was only eleven years old, but was surprised to see his daughter cooking.

Hannah was wearing the apron she'd made at school, and a makeshift chefs hat. Her face was covered with flour, as she had being making pastry as well, of course Grace was aiding her, but Hannah had done everything herself except using the oven. Hannah remembered it all now, and how proud her father was of her as her sisters walked in the kitchen.

'Ooh, Beef Stroganoff,' Danni said as she smiled gloriously, sniffing the air. They all sat round the table as they told stories of old times. Julie and Tony had gone home earlier, so it was only Mikey and his sisters, and Steve and Lesley. Steve smiled as he heard all the family stories.

'Do you remember, sis', when mom and dad bought us those new bikes for Christmas and grandpa came to visit and spoilt the surprise?,' Danni said.

'And the time mom came home late one night after a show with auntie, and she set the house alarm off and dad thought it was a burglar,' Hannah said. The sisters laughed and cried as they told and heard the old stories, and Steve listened as he felt their bond strengthen.

The weekend before they moved they used the time to ensure they had packed everything. Tony had handed his notice in, though his boss had tried relentlessly to change his mind. Hannah and Danni had dealt with the meetings with Raymond and Desmond while Abbie helped Mikey pack the last of his belongings.

Abbie had notified Mikey's school, and they were sad he was leaving, but most of all his friend, Vanessa was really upset he was leaving. Hannah and Mikey had gone to visit Vanessa at home on the Saturday afternoon before they left. Vanessa's mother answered the door, and she smiled warmly as she invited them in.

'Hello Hannah. Hello Mikey, Vanessa's in the lounge, feeling very upset. You carry on through.' Vanessa was sitting cuddling her teddy and watching television with her father when Hannah and Mikey walked in.

'Hello Vanessa,' Hannah said as she walked in.

'I've bought someone to see you,' she smiled. Vanessa was really upset Mikey was moving, and looked as though she'd been crying. Hannah stood over her now and held out her arms.

'Come here, Vanessa, darling. Come and sit with auntie Hannah.' Hannah used to baby-sit Vanessa, and still does occasionally when her parents go out somewhere, and Mikey joins them sometimes. Hannah sat on the sofa while Vanessa cried in her arms. Hannah thought the world of Vanessa, and Vanessa secretly saw Hannah as mother figure. Though she hadn't told anyone. Mikey sat next to Hannah for a while as he listened.

'You know, Vanessa. Just because we're moving away, it doesn't mean you'll never see us again. We'll come and visit, and you're more than welcome to come and stay with us whenever you like.' Vanessa stopped crying now and Hannah wiped her eyes and kissed her.

'How would you like that? You'll have the beach to play on and the house is a nice place to be. And when we get settled we were thinking of getting some horses. You'd like to go horse riding, wouldn't you?' Vanessa looked hopeful then as she wiped her eyes.

'Would you teach me horse riding?' Hannah laughed a little then and kissed her.

'Of cause I will, darling. I'll teach you anything you want,' Hannah said as she cuddled her.' Vanessa felt a little better now and disappeared somewhere with Mikey, as Hannah spoke to her parents.

'Hannah, I can't thank you enough. Vanessa's been so upset since you announced you were leaving. I didn't think anything would cheer her up.'

'You're welcome Mr. Harris. And I meant what I said. We have a guest room that Vanessa can use any time she wants to stays, and we'll leave you our phone number if she wants to call us. We'll come and pick her up and drop her home again.'

'I tell you what. Why don't we arrange it for a week on Monday so Vanessa can spend some time with us before she goes back to school? She can stay the week and we'll drop her back home again. What do you say? It'll be a surprise for her and Mikey.' Mr. and Mrs. Harris looked at each other and smiled.

'It's alright with me,' Mr. Harris said.

'I think that'll be a nice idea, Hannah. Thank you. As long as you're sure she won't be in the way,' Mrs. Harris said.

'Of cause she won't. It'll be lovely to have her, Mrs. Harris,' Hannah said.

'Teresa, please. We've known each other long enough,' she said.

'You're so kind, Hannah. It's hard to believe sometimes that such tragedy has befallen you and your family. Teresa and I knew your mother and father from school, and they were always such nice people. I always knew they'd do well for themselves.' Hannah smiled as she listened, and it made her cry a little talking about her parents.

Hannah left after she finished her coffee. She had left Mikey with Vanessa upstairs in her bedroom, and would be back later to pick him up. The girls were almost packed. They had their night clothes and wash stuff they would pack in the morning after they had showered. Mikey was all packed and ready, and at eight o'clock the girls sat down and watched a movie with their aunt and Steve. Tony and Julie were there, and Hannah and Tony were cuddled upon the sofa.

Tony was all packed and ready, he only needed to bring his bags over in the morning. They were hoping to be leaving before nine o'clock, so they got most of the day to unpack when they arrived.

Julie was sad they were moving too, though she had plenty to occupy herself with. Her fathers business, Maverick's & Partners was flourishing now. Though Julie owned it all now after her father died, she wasn't always there. Though next week was going to be extremely busy, as she had several clients to deal with. Two of them being a criminal law.

Her father was set on defending clients that had wrongly been accused of a crime. And he never once lost a case. "Let a new kind of justice be unravelled" was her fathers motto, and it was something Julie stuck by too. Only last week she free a man wrongly accused of rape. Only because she proved her client was in the wrong place at the wrong time.

That evening they all were hoping to be in bed by ten o'clock. They wanted an early start in the morning. At eight-thirty they were all sitting in the lounge watching a film when Bill knocked the door, and Abbie smiled and greeted him.

'Hello, Bill. This is a surprise. What brings you here?' Bill was in uniform and looked a little sombre as he greeted everyone.

'Hello matey,' Steve said as the two men shook hands.

'Er, Steve. I'm here because I have the forensics results on the fire.' Everyone fell silent as they listened, and Mikey went to Hannah as she sat on the sofa.

'It's not good, is it Bill,' Hannah asked.

'No, sweetheart, it's not. The forensics seem to think the fire started in garage. And it looks as though it was arson.' Abbie took a deep breath as tears filled her eyes.

'You mean it was deliberate. Who would want to do that?' she cried as her aunt comforted her.

'Bill, everyone knew mom and dad one way or another. I mean there's no one around here that would do such a thing,' Hannah said.

'Well it doesn't mean it was a local. It could have been anyone from anywhere. Maybe someone who had a grudge against your parents, for what they did and stood for. Or maybe someone that your father helped put in prison. It could have been anyone.' He paused for a moment, thinking.

'There was an excess amount of accelerant found at the scene. Do you know if your father ever kept any flammable liquids in his garage?'

'No, none. Only the diesel in mom and dad's cars,' Danni said quickly. Bill gave the report to Steve so he could look through it himself. All the evidence was there. He looked at Mikey and his sisters.

'I'm sorry kids, but it's conclusive,' he said passing the report to Hannah. Steve walked to the front door with Bill and chatted for a while, and then Bill left. They had all grieved for their parents for so long now, that this extra news was none important. Though they were still shook up at the thought that someone would want to deliberately hurt the family.

The following morning they were all awake at eight o'clock. Mikey went for a shower while the girls prepared breakfast. Julie had come over at eight fifteen to see them off before she left for the office.

The usual fry-up was on the menu this morning, though Hannah only had a bowl of cereals, and once everything was cleared away they started leaving. They loaded the cars last night, and once they were ready Lesley locked up and they all left. Half the street was out this morning to say goodbye to them all. Hollie and her daughters were there and Vera Tibbit.

Mikey and his sisters were starting to feel guilty they were leaving now, as they saw the old lady. At eighty-three years old, Vera was more than just the grandmother of the street. She was more than just the old lady on the corner that gave sweets and cakes to the children. Vera had moved to the street in 1951 with her husband, when they were just twenty-nine years old, and she is the oldest living tenant, and the only living tenant to remain there from 1951.

Grace and Duncan moved there thirty years later, and instantly became friends with the residents. Duncan had become firm friends with Vera's husband, Jeff, until he passed on in the winter of 1989. Hannah greeted Vera now as everyone said their goodbyes.

'I love you granny Vera,' she said as she cuddled the old lady. Vera had tears in her eyes, and Hannah smiled and wiped her eyes.

'We'll be back next week to visit,' she said. After Vera said goodbye to all of them, she stood on the pavement holding her walking stick as she waved.

'Goodbye my darlings,' she muttered.

Chapter Ten

They pulled up in front of their new home, and Hannah got out and breathed in the fresh air and smiled.

'Home at last.' Lesley went up to her and took her arm.

'Come on darling. Let's go and look at our new home.' Lesley kissed her niece and they all went inside, as Tony jokingly carried Hannah over the threshold. They all went in, and Mikey ran upstairs and chose a bedroom. They had ordered the beds, and they were hopefully been delivered today, along with the three piece suite. All the other bedroom furniture was already there.

New carpets were going to be fitted next week, and the girls had bought new curtains for all the windows. After a while they went outside and started unloading the cars. Hannah started unpacking the kitchen utensils and loading them all in the drawers. There was a space in the middle of the kitchen for a double oven, and a space under the work surfaces for a washing machine or a dish washer. Though there was a utility room off the kitchen they could use for the laundry. Their new cooker was going to be delivered tomorrow morning along with the fridge freezer.

The first thing Steve saw too was the heating. The house hadn't been lived in for almost ten years, and Steve was concerned the heating was all seized up. There was a coal fire in the lounge, and they used the coal they bought with them to get some heat in the property.

There was a coal shed in the back garden they would keep stocked up, especially for the winter. Steve was in the cellar checking the boiler when Danni bought him a coffee.

'Any luck, Steve.'

'Not yet, darling. I usually know what I'm doing around a boiler. I'll have this thing running soon,' he said.

That afternoon they were almost settled. Some of the furniture had been delivered, and the fridge freezer had been deliver at eleven o'clock, and that afternoon Lesley and Danni had gone into town to buy food and stock up the cupboards, and when they got home Hannah laughed when she saw how much they bought.

'Have you bought the whole store, auntie?'

'There's no harm in being prepared, darling. Don't forget we could get snowed in out here in the winter, and we won't be able to go shopping, so a little bit extra of everything each week will be alright.'

They had a large walk-in pantry they could stock up on tinned food, and the girls thought it would be a good idea to buy a chest freezer so they could store plenty of meat. Abbie had suggested baking their own bread as well, which would come in useful too.

When they finished unpacking the shopping they all sat in the garden by the water fountain and took a break. Danni had made ice-tea for everyone and they sat talking about their new home, their plans and their future, when they heard a vehicle approaching. Danni went out to look who it was, and she was happy to see more furniture had arrived.

'Sorry I'm late, Miss. Took a hell of a job finding this place.'

Everyone joined in to unload the wagon. There were beds and two three-piece suites, and some garden furniture. Wardrobes, Chests of drawers, and dressing tables for the girls.

At five-thirty they all sat down to their first meal, sitting around all the lavish dining suite.

'Can you believe this dining suite, sis'? I mean ten years this place has stood empty and no one's tried to break in and nick it,' Danni said. It was a completely isolated area, and no one would see strangers hanging around. Their closest neighbours were two and a half miles away up the road.

Steve had got the heating working now, though officially it was still summer, but it wouldn't be long before they would need it. Over the next few days Mikey and his sisters shown Steve and Tony around Bude and started to familiarize themselves with Bude and the locals. Every time they went out they were stopped by someone that knew them.

It wasn't long before winter would start to settle in, so they started stocking up on coal and logs for the fire. Tony and Steve had spent a couple of days chopping wood, and some of the locals advised them where to get wood from.

The weekend after they moved, Hannah had drove to London and brought Vanessa back to spend the week with them. It was still the summer holidays, so Mikey and Vanessa weren't due back to school till the first week of September.

Mikey had so much fun telling Vanessa about their new home, and the nights they used to sit up talking when his sisters thought they were asleep. Vanessa thought it was wonderful being there, and couldn't wait till they got some horses. Hannah and her sisters thought it would be nice to get some cattle as well, but not till next year though.

Hannah and her sisters took Mikey and Vanessa on a shopping trip on the Wednesday around Bude, and at lunch time they stopped in at the Carriers Inn for something to eat. They sat down at the table by the window. Hannah ordered a bottle of Chardonnay for her and her sisters and some pepsi for the Vanessa and Mikey.

'Can we have the menus as well please?'

Danni glanced over the menu and smiled shyly when she noticed a young dark haired gentleman staring at her. He was wearing a chefs jacket and hat, and she assumed he was the chef from the Carriers Inn. But then her eyes fixed on him as he started advancing towards her. Only then did she realise there was something very familiar about him. His face. She could never forget a face.

Then she noticed his eyes. She had seen those eyes somewhere before, but where? she thought.

'Good afternoon, Miss, and welcome to the Carriers Inn. And my restaurant.' He took her hand as he greeted her. There was something about the way he spoke to her. Hannah and Abbie watched as the chef spoke to their sister, and they were amused just watching him.

'I am delighted to tell you madam, this afternoon we . . .'

'Don't I know you from somewhere?' Danni asked.

'I don't think so, madam.' And then as if she had a sudden brainwave, her hands flew to her mouth.

'Jason Thomas.' The chef stood back as though shocked.

'Sis', it's Jason. Jason Thomas,' she squealed.

'Sorry Miss, but how do you know my name?'

'Don't tell me you've forgotten about me? We were at school together. Childhood sweethearts. I'm Danni Philips.'

'Oh my golly gosh,' he said as he put his hands to his mouth.

'Little Danni Philips.' He laughed out loud and made everyone in the restaurant stare at them, and they flew into each others arms as they laughed. Hannah and Abbie smiled watching them. They were happy for their sister. They remembered how distraught she was when Jason moved away. Danni and Jason pulled away from each other now and laughed.

'What are you doing here, Jason? I thought you emigrated to Spain with your family.'

'I did. But I came back two years ago and opened my own pub and restaurant. What about you, you on holiday?' Danni tried to compose herself now as tears trickled from her eyes. She was so overjoyed that she was standing in front of a man that she thought she'd never see again.

'No, I live here now.' Danni introduced everyone then as she held Jason's hand.

'We moved here 1st August. We bought a house just outside Bude.'

'What about your parents. Are they still in London?' Grace and Duncan were always fond of Jason, and always treated him like their own son. Danni sat down now and held Jason's hand.

'Jason. Mom and dad died six months ago.' Jason took a deep breath and slowly sat down.

'Oh, Danni, I'm so sorry. What happened?'

'There was a fire at home. Me and Hannah were in Switzerland and Abbie was travelling Europe. Dad died, and then mom died a few weeks later in hospital. We lived with our aunt for a while, and then we came out here.' Danni explained how she and her family used to take holidays in Bude quite often, and they liked the place. Jason held her in his arms now, and Danni felt so happy that she had found her only true love.

'Oh baby. I'm so sorry,' Jason said.

After they finished eating Danni and Jason went for a walk, leaving the others to themselves. It was like a dream for Danni to see Jason again. She had dreamt of this moment ever since he left, but never thought they would actually see each other again.

They walked along the beach holding hands and talking as though they'd always been lovers. They walked out to the lighthouse and sat on the rocks, and as though they had always been lovers, they kissed. Their lips met. A single moment of passion, and so many feelings came pouring out that it almost made Danni cry. She pulled away from him, and Jason looked concerned, as he saw her damp eyes.

'Baby, you OK?' She turned away from him as tears filled her eyes, and holding her chin he made her look at him.

'Danni, baby, what's wrong?'

'Jason, you have no idea how many times I've dreamt of this moment. That we'd meet somewhere, fall in love all over again, and carry on from where we left off. But it's not that simple.' Jason smiled at the idea, and took her in his arms, but she pulled away from him.

'Is there someone else? I mean if there . . . '

'No, there's nobody else,' she cried.

'It's just my life is so complicated now. I mean, mom and dad have only been gone for six months, and it's still too fresh for me. And we have Mikey, my little brother to care for now.' She turned and looked at him as tears streamed her face, and she touched his face.

'Jason, I love you. I've loved you all my life, and I'll carry on loving you, no matter what. But my main priority now is Mikey. He's only ten, and though he seems happy enough now, we just need to get him through the next few years until he leaves school.'

'But what about you? What about love? I seem to recall someone telling me not to give up on it. That we'd find a way to be together. I never gave up. Though I tried looking for you many times, but it's as though you'd just disappeared.'

'And we have. We found each other. I'm not saying I don't love you anymore. I do. If anything I love you more now,' she cried.

'I'm just asking for a little time to see how things pan out. We've only been in Bude for a few days,' she said.

'I love you Jason, and yes I want to be with you, and no, my feelings haven't change towards you. I just need some time to get my head sorted out and to get settled here.' Jason smiled and kissed her. He took a tissue from his pocket and wiped her eyes and cuddled her.

'OK baby. That'll do for now. As long as you know I'll always be here for you, and I'll always love you.'

'Thank you,' she said. They stood holding each other for a long time then, and she smiled to herself as she thought the only man she'd ever loved was there. There right in her arms.

That evening Jason had taken the evening off and spent some time with Danni and her family. They were all sitting in the lounge telling stories, as Danni sat with Jason on the floor as she cuddled up to him.

It was another couple of weeks before Mikey started at his new school. He was excited about going to a new school, but nervous as he wouldn't know anyone there. He never had any trouble making friends, and knew it wouldn't be long before he was running around enjoying himself.

He had a complete new uniform and new shoes, and his sisters had bought him a new school bag and gym bag, and a gym kit. He was starting back to on the 2nd September, and the school bus would collect him from home and drop him off afterwards. Though his sisters would take him the first few days.

Over the next few days more and more furniture started to arrive. The carpets had been fitted throughout and new curtains. All the bedroom furniture had arrived and they had bought a chest freezer and filled it with joints of lamb and beef and pork. Vanessa had joined in to help too, though Hannah insisted she and Mikey played together and enjoy themselves, and by Friday evening Vanessa was sad she was going home in the morning.

Like Hannah promised her parents, she would drive her back to London. Abbie and Danni had ensured Vanessa had packed everything, and like promised Hannah gave

Vanessa their phone number. The phone was going to be installed next week, but they already knew their number, and at ten o'clock Hannah tucked Vanessa up in bed and kissed her goodnight.

'Goodnight Vanessa, darling. Sleep tight.'

'Goodnight Hannah.' Hannah left the room then and switched the light out and went upstairs to say goodnight to Mikey, and afterwards she went back downstairs and cuddled up to Tony on the sofa with a steaming hot cup of coco as the watched an old movie.

Chapter Eleven

Back in London, Hannah and her sisters contended themselves with various meetings. Mikey had joined them in London too. He had spent all day Monday with Vanessa and her family while his sisters were at the office. Mikey was due to start his new school in the first week of September, and he was thoroughly looking forward to it.

Hannah and her sisters met with Raymond and Desmond before they headed for the boardroom on the fourth floor. There was only half an hour before their clients arrived, and they sat going through the paper work.

'Girls, we've a problem. Me and Desmond have been going through these papers for a few days now, and we haven't been able to get a single witness to come forward. This case is going to court next month, and out of all the material witnesses, none of them are willing to testify. Unless we get someone, or we get some seriously convincing evidence, we don't have a case.'

'There must be someone who's willing to come forward,' Danni said.

'I mean Mr. Clarke is a highly respected member of the community and he's looking at fifteen years to life because some lowlife creep has embezzled millions from the companies funds and laid the blame on our client.'

'I know, darling. But unless we can get the proof and the witnesses, we don't have a case,' Desmond said. Hannah sighed heavily and dropped into a chair.

'Isn't there anything we can do?' As they sat talking, Mr. Clarke and his partners were shown into the boardroom on the fourth floor.

'Hannah,' Desmond's secretary said.'

'You're clients are in the boardroom now.'

'Thanks Jen,' Raymond said. Desmond gathered all the paperwork, and they all headed for the fourth floor. Hannah flipped her long black hair over her shoulder as she pushed the door open and stepped into the boardroom, and she smiled warmly when she saw the clients.

'Mr. Clarke. Mr. Adams, I'm Hannah Philips,' she said extending her arm to greet the gentlemen.

'These are my sisters, and we will be conducting this meeting today, and if you don't have any objections my partners, Mr. Layton and Mr. Jacobs, will be observing this meeting,' she said.

'I'm sorry Miss Philips, but I was told Duncan Philips would be conducting this meeting today.'

'I'm sorry, Mr. Clarke if you've been misinformed, but Mr. Philips hasn't been with us now for seven months. We are his daughters, and we're quite capable of conducting this meeting.'

'I'm sure you are, but unless we see Mr. Philips, we'll take our business elsewhere.' Desmond stood up then and tried to take charge, but Hannah stopped him.

'Sit down Desmond. I'll handle this.'

'Mr. Clarke. Mr. Philips is our father,' she said gesturing to Danni and Abbie as well.

'And he died seven months ago. We are his daughters and are now in charge.' The clients fell silent now as they sat down.

'If you have a problem because we're not our father, that's fine. If you don't want us to help you, you can take your business elsewhere, but don't presume to think that we don't know what we're capable of.' Raymond and Desmond were stunned to hear Hannah's little speech, and almost told her to keep calm, when they saw Mr. Clarke smiling.

'Miss Philips, you have a sharp tongue. I like that. There's no question that you're Mr. Philips daughter,' he said as his partner agreed. He stood up and extended his arm.

'I'm sorry Miss Philips for my rudeness. I'm sorry about your loss.' He sat down again and opened his briefcase and withdrew some files.

'Shall we carry on?', he asked.

They had spent the afternoon going through all the paperwork with a fine tooth comb, and it was almost four-thirty before they emerged from the boardroom, and Mr. Clarke smiled apologetically as he and Hannah shook hands.

'Thank you Miss Philips for all your help and advise,' he said looking at the three sisters

'And please except my apologies for my rudeness, and of course my condolences. I've heard many great things about your father. He was quite an fine gentleman.' The gentlemen left and Hannah and her sisters all looked at each other and laughed.

'Whoa, sis', I see you haven't lost your touch,' Abbie laughed. Hannah started pacing then as she ran her fingers through her long black hair.

'Oh, man. I did not mean to say that. I did not mean to say that,' she said. Desmond laughed and put his arm around her.

'Darling, you were incredible.' Hannah walked out of the boardroom, all the while she was tense.

'I did not mean to say that. I did not mean to say that.' She went for a walk to calm down and to clear her head while Raymond and Desmond cleared the boardroom.

Though Abbie was officially working at the office now, she was still training. Raymond and Desmond would always discuss different cases with her and she sat in on meetings to see how to conduct a meeting. She was still going to Cambridge next year, just as her father and sisters did, but for now she was enjoying being with her sisters, and being close to her godfather, Desmond.

That afternoon Mikey and his sisters spent some time in the memorial garden and visited their parents graves. Lesley and Steve had stayed in Bude, so it was only Mikey and his sisters, and at five thirty they went back to their aunts house and had something to eat. The girls had another big meeting in the morning, and they were going to leave Mikey with Vanessa's parents again.

Mikey and Vanessa were talking about going down to Oxford Street to look through the shops with Vanessa's mother. Mikey wanted to get something for Danni's birthday next week. His aunt had given him some money before they left Bude, as he wanted to look for something special.

That night Mikey had stayed with Vanessa at her parents. Vanessa's mother, Teresa had made the spare bed up in Vanessa's room, and they were in bed by nine o'clock. The two kids had stayed awake talking for a while until Vanessa fell asleep, and then Mikey did the same, and when he woke up the following morning just before eight o'clock, Vanessa was downstairs in the kitchen eating her cereals.

'Morning honey,' want some breakfast?' Teresa was cooking a bacon sandwich for herself and did one for Mikey too, and afterwards Mikey went upstairs and showered. Vanessa was all ready to leave for Oxford Street as her mother tidied up the breakfast dishes, and fifteen minutes later Mikey came down showered and dressed.

'So what you kids want to do this morning? You still want to go to Oxford Street?' Vanessa's father stood in the kitchen putting his jacket on. He worked for the council and was off on his morning rounds. He was late this morning though. He grabbed a piece of his wife's brown toast, kissed her on the cheek and dashed out the door.

Goodbye, my love. Have a good day kids,' he shouted as he waltzed away, and moments later Teresa and the kids left and got in the car. Teresa made a pit stop at the cash point machine and then to buy some petrol, and then she headed for Oxford Street.

It was only nine-thirty, and already Oxford Street was bustling with the crowds. Teresa parked up, and they started down the street as Mikey stopped occasionally to look through shop windows. Teresa had given her daughter some money to spend as well, as Mikey had got some from his aunt. Though Mikey was only shopping for his sisters birthday.

He stopped to look through the window at the jewellery store and saw a pendant for best sister. Lesley had given him fifty pounds, so he knew he'd got enough.

'You found anything you like, honey?' Teresa asked.

'I like that one there,' he said pointing to the sister pendant. They went inside to look at the pendants, and the assistant took the one he wanted from the window to show Mikey.

'Yeah, I like that one,' he said. He paid for it and the assistant put it in a box and gift wrapped for him, and afterwards he wanted to look for a birthday card. They walked out of the shop and stood by the kerb to cross the road. Teresa held her daughters hand to cross the road.

'Mikey, honey, come and hold my hand to cross the road,' Teresa said, but Mikey never heard her over the noise of the traffic. They were standing at the kerb ready to cross the road as Mikey was examining the chain he'd just bought for his sister. He went to step out onto the road as Teresa was checking for traffic. There was a sudden screech of brakes, car horns blaring and Teresa looked round. Her face white with sheer terror.

'Mikey.' There was a split second decision as Teresa screamed and released her daughters hand, hurling herself forward between Mikey and the oncoming van, but it was too late. Mikey's legs went from under him as the van struck him, the gold sister chain fell from his hand to the ground as he was hurled through the air, over the van and onto the hard tarmac street.

Angry drivers blared their horns as the traffic came to a standstill, and in the distance looking out through the window on the fourth floor of the office block towering over Oxford Street, Hannah pressed herself against the window. Hannah and her sisters were in another meeting with Raymond and Desmond, and she froze mid-sentence as she saw the commotion outside on the street. Her legs buckled, and fear gripped her from within.

'Mikey,' she screamed and crumbled to the floor. Raymond and Desmond rose from their seats in a split second movement and raced to Hannah, and looking out onto Oxford Street they saw a figure lying in the street in a coat that looked almost like Mikey's.

'Jesus wept,' Desmond said, his face rocked with fear. Desmond and Raymond bolted from the office, leaving their clients somewhat confused.

'Jenny. I need an ambulance, police now. 999,' Raymond said as he and Desmond headed for the stairs. Jenny was startled, as though out of a trance, and she fumbled with the phone as she dialled 999. She hadn't got a clue what had just happening, but she pressed the buttons on the phone anyhow, and moments later Raymond and Desmond emerged outside on the street. Teresa was kneeling over Mikey, sobbing as she attempted to call an ambulance, while Vanessa stood on the pavement crying, and Desmond took Mikey's hand.

'Teresa, what happened?' Teresa was crying as she tried to tell Desmond what had happened and talk to the operator at the same time, and minutes later an ambulance came screaming up the street, followed shortly by a police car. The two officers immediately started to disperse the crowd as the paramedics tended to Mikey. Desmond managed to get Teresa away from Mikey and tried to get her to tell him what happened, but she was too hysterical to talk.

Raymond took Vanessa upstairs to the office as she was crying, and one of the secretaries took care of her while Raymond went to Hannah and her sisters. The girls were sitting on the floor crying as their clients tried to comfort them, and Raymond grabbed Danni and tried to stand her up.

'Come on, girls. They're taking Mikey to the hospital now.' He told their clients to speak to his secretary to reschedule the meeting as he helped the girls outside to his car. They were just getting Mikey in the ambulance when they got outside, and seeing him only made the girls cry even more.

Raymond got them in the car and he followed the ambulance to St Mary's. Teresa tried to compose herself as one of the officers helped her up, and then she went upstairs to the office to collect her daughter. Teresa had noticed the gold chain in the road that Mikey had bought Danni when she came back down, and she knelt down and picked it up, and then she and Vanessa went back to the car and drove to the hospital.

When Teresa and Vanessa arrived at the hospital Raymond and Desmond were pacing backwards and forwards as the girls sat crying and comforting each other. Teresa stood in the middle of A&E as she cried and watched the girls.

'Hannah, I'm so sorry.' Hannah never saw or heard Teresa as she was crying too much. And Desmond went to Teresa and sat her down while they waited.

'Has the doctors said anything yet?' she asked. Desmond just shook his head and went to speak to Raymond. Raymond had phoned his wife at work, and she come straight over.

'I'm going to call Steve and Lesley. They should be here,' Desmond said.

It was a couple of hours before the doctor came to speak to them. By then the girls had almost cried themselves to sleep, but they jumped up now as they saw the doctor. It was the same doctor that treated their mother after the fire, and Dr Hanson was somewhat beside himself with grief.

'How's Mikey. Is he alright?' Danni cried.

'Mikey is resting now, but he has suffered an enormous head trauma.' Raymond and Desmond got the girls to sit down. Somehow they sensed it wasn't going to be good news. Dr Hanson couldn't believe he was treating Mikey again in such short space of time. Though this time it was a little more serious for Mikey.

'Girls, I want to be honest with you, and I'm sorry to be after losing your parents, but Mikey's injuries are extremely critical. He's suffered a massive head trauma, and there was some bleeding in his brain. We've done all we can for now, and only the next twenty-four hours will tell. In the meantime Mikey will be kept under close observation.' He paused for a moment as his words were absorbed.

'I'm sorry,' he said.

'Dr Hanson. Is Mikey going to die?' Hannah asked. Her words echoed in her mind, and though standing outside her own body she could hear herself speak the words as though it was someone else in the room. Dr Hanson never answered for a few seconds, and though he finally said he didn't know his face told another story.

'I don't know, Hannah. I really don't know.' Dr Hanson left them then, and the girls sank on the sofa in the waiting area and cried. Teresa was beside herself with grief, and as she stood over the girls now, she was not sure she deserved their forgiveness.

'Hannah?' Hannah looked up through blurry eyes at a distraught Teresa. Teresa had explained to Desmond exactly what happened, and though they all knew Mikey was usually sensible when it came to the roads Hannah stood up and went to comfort Teresa, but she pulled away from her.

'Hannah, please. I don't deserve your forgiveness. I should have been watching him. I should have took more care of him.' But her words fell on deaf ears as Danni and Hannah pulled Teresa close to them and comforted her.

'Oh, girls. I'm so sorry.'

'Teresa, it's not your fault. Desmond told us what you told him, and we believe you. We know you never intentionally meant for this to happen,' Danni said wiping her own eyes. The girls sat down comforting each other after a while and Teresa comforted her daughter, and moments later Dr Hanson came back out.

'You can go and see him now. He's sleeping now, but please be warned. What you're going to see in there is not a pretty sight.' The girls followed the doctor to the recovery room with Raymond and Desmond, and when the doctor pulled the curtain back the girls sobbed as they saw Mikey lying there. Hannah went to him, as though floating to him, and she took his hands in hers and kissed him.

'Oh, Mikey. What's happened to you?' Hannah couldn't believe that it's only been seven months since they were last at the hospital fearing for their brothers life, and now it was happening all over again.

'He will survive doctor, won't he?' Danni cried.

'We will do everything we can, Danni.'

'He can't die . . . I won't let him . . . I won't let you die, Mikey. You hear me?,' Abbie said as though giving him a stern warning.

Steve had answered the phone when Raymond called him about Mikey, and they left straight away. It was not even lunchtime, but Lesley was preparing a stew for her and Steve and Tony for tonight's tea, but they left straight away once Steve told Lesley. It was a four and a half hour drive from Bude to London, and it was plenty of time for Lesley to fear the worst.

All the way there Lesley prayed as she held her cross of Jesus. Hannah and her sisters were sitting with Mikey in ICU when Lesley and Steve and Tony burst through the doors into A&E. Steve went to enquire about Mikey, but then Lesley saw Dr Hanson and she ran to him.

'Dr Hanson, where's my nephew?' she cried. Steve tried to keep Lesley calm as the doctor took them to Mikey and his sisters, and Lesley stood in the doorway as she saw her nieces sleeping as Danni held Mikey's hand. Lesley cried and touched Abbie's face.

'Darling, wake up. It's auntie.' Abbie opened her eyes slowly, and for a second she forgot where she was, but then she saw Mikey and started crying as her aunt comforted her. Steve had picked Jason up on the way, and he comforted Danni as Tony comforted Hannah.

'What happened, darling?' Lesley asked and kissed her niece. Danni tried to compose herself as Jason wiped her eyes. Teresa was still there, and she stood up as she took the gold chain from her handbag Mikey had bought.

'Mikey wanted to go shopping on Oxford Street for Danni's birthday next week.' They all looked at Teresa now as she explained.

'He bought this chain with sister on it, and he wanted to go and look for a birthday card. We stopped to cross the road, and I called to Mikey to hold my hand before we crossed, but he couldn't have heard me as he was looking at the chain. I was checking to see if it was safe to cross, when I looked round and Mikey had already started crossing.' Teresa held the chain up now as Danni cried.

'Oh, Mikey. You silly boy,' she cried holding the chain. Danni went to Teresa and comforted her as the doctor left them, and Lesley went to her nephew and sat in the chair opposite the bed and took his hand in hers.

Chapter Twelve

Mikey had suffered a severe head trauma and a broken leg, and was left comatose. The doctor had tried to give them all some hope, but they all knew how it was. Mikey was lying broken and bruised, and they knew it would take a miracle to save him.

The bleeding to his brain had been stemmed, but he was still critical. The next twenty-four hours was the longest the girls had endured.

Mikey had been transferred to ICU, and was closely monitored. The girls wanted to stay by his side until he woke up, but the doctor insisted that Mikey should get complete rest. They all went back to Lesley's, and Tony and Jason went with them. Teresa and Vanessa went home when the others left. Vanessa was too distraught and her mother wanted to get her home. Steve had called Julie to let her know what had happened, and moments later she was knocking Lesley's door in tears after running all the way.

Steve answered the door, and Julie cried in his arms at the door. After a while she went in and saw Hannah and her sisters.

'What happened?' Julie asked as she sat next to Danni. Danni explained what Teresa had told them, and then Danni introduced Jason as Steve came in with coffees for everyone. Hannah and her sisters were getting restless not knowing what was happening at the hospital, and within the hour they were wanting to get back to Mikey.

'But Dr Hanson said he will call you girls, if there's any change.'

'I know what he said, auntie, but we can't sit around here doing nothing. What if something goes wrong and we're not there? What if he wakes up and we're not there?,' Hannah asked.

'Nothing is going to go wrong, darling. Mikey's in the best care.'

'Oh wake up, auntie,' she snapped.

'Mikey has suffered a massive head trauma. Bleeding in his brain,' Hannah cried as Steve tried to calm her. It was the first time in her life that Hannah had shouted at her aunt, and it had scared Lesley.

'That's critical. You wasn't there when we saw the look on the doctors face when I asked if Mikey was going to die.' Lesley went to her niece now and tried comforting her, and Hannah broke down in her arms.

'I can't take this anymore. I'm losing my family . . . I'm losing my family,' she sobbed. Tears welled in Lesley's eyes now as she held her niece and felt her whole body shaking.

'Oh Jesus wept.'

'I'm losing my family,' Hannah cried.

It took a couple of hours to calm Hannah down, as Abbie and Danni cried too, and afterwards Lesley decided to take the girls back to the hospital. Steve had given them a lift, and when they arrived the girls waited while Lesley went to find Dr Hanson.

All the while Hannah was sitting crying quietly and slightly rocking herself in the chair. Steve watched her closely and was already concerned for her, and when Lesley came back with Dr Hanson, Hannah never even acknowledged them until she heard Abbie speaking to the doctor. She immediately jumped up and walked over to him.

'Doctor, I know what you said before, but we need to be close to Mikey at all times,' she said interrupting her sister.

'Please. Please just let us be with him,' she said as tears welled in her eyes. Dr Hanson smiled briefly and noticed that Hannah was anxious to see her brother.

'OK.' Dr Hanson took them to ICU, and they all sat around the bed as Danni held her brothers hand and gently kissed him.

'Hi ya bro'. We're back,' she said and kissed his hand. They sat quietly, and occasionally whispered when they spoke to each other.

That evening Hannah was sitting holding Mikey's hand as she sang quietly to him. Steve and Lesley had gone for a walk around the hospital grounds for a while. Just to get some fresh air, she told her nieces.

There was nothing else the doctors could do now except wait. They wanted to see how the next twenty-four hours go, and the swelling around his brain. His head was all bandaged up, and occasionally his sisters would kiss him gently through the bandages.

Though Mikey was in a coma, his sisters believed, as they had believed with their mother, that somehow Mikey would be able to hear their voice, so occasionally they would speak softly to him to urge him to open his eyes, but he never did. He just lay there motionless as they just continued to talk to him.

As the sisters took it in turn to sit next to Mikey, Steve started noticing a dramatic change in Hannah's behaviour. As every hour passed by and after each time she opened her eyes after having a nap, she seemed to change. Steve was getting worried and spoke to Dr Hanson about it one evening. Steve didn't want to concern Lesley about it yet, unless he needed to.

'It's probably a mixture of various things,' Dr Hanson said.

'Tiredness, anxiety, stress. It could even be borderline depression. I wouldn't be surprised considering everything she's been through in the past seven months.' The doctor had suggested that Hannah may be carrying all the weight of everything. Being the eldest, she may feel responsible for her sisters and Mikey.

Though Abbie and Danni look as though they're dealing with it, they weren't. Quite often they would be seen crying somewhere away from Hannah. Hiding in some corner to be alone. Steve and Lesley found Abbie crying outside the hospital one afternoon when they went for a walk.

It's been two days since Mikey's accident, and though he hasn't got any worse, he hasn't been showing any improvement either. He was still critical, and as each hour and day passed, Hannah was slipping further away. And Steve had noticed. He had found her wandering the corridor at two o'clock in the morning, mumbling incoherently to herself. When he approached her, she seemed startled as though he had just woke her up.

Steve didn't want to concern Lesley with it, but he saw no other choice now. She was her aunt, and in effect her guardian. Steve took Hannah back to the ward, and asked Lesley to join him out in the corridor. Lesley smiled and kissed her niece and walked out of the ward with Steve.

'What's up?' she asked. Steve seemed flustered, as though not sure how to tell her, but he knew he had to. He sat her down in a chair outside ICU and held her hand.

'I'm concerned for Hannah. I was talking to Dr Hanson yesterday about her. I think she is showing all the signs for depression. I mean, she's not eating properly. She's not sleeping properly. She's always tense and stressed.'

'Well, we all are Steve. We're all under a lot of strain' she snapped.

'Darling, I've just found Hannah wandering the corridor, mumbling to herself. I think she was sleepwalking.' Lesley looked surprised, but laughed it off.

'Hannah doesn't sleepwalk.'

'I just think we have to keep a close eye on her, that's all,' Steve said.

They went back to ICU then and sat quietly. Lesley kept her eye on Hannah, and she was thinking about what Steve had just told her. She was beginning to think the same the past few hours, but she didn't want to believe it.

The following morning had only confirmed what Steve had told her. Danni was sitting with Mikey, while Hannah was sitting in the chair by the window, and she seemed disorientated and hugging her knees. Lesley went to her and took her hand in hers.

'Darling, why don't you and I go for a walk? It'll do you good to get out of here for a while.'

'No, I want to stay with Mikey.' She shrugged her off, and Lesley only had tears in her eyes as she looked at

Steve. Danni and Abbie noticed then what was going on, and they were concerned and led Steve and their aunt out of the ward.

'What's going on?' Abbie asked.

'I don't know, darling, but it seems it's hit Hannah hard and fast,' Steve said.

'What's hit her?' Danni asked raising her voice slightly. Steve got the girls to sit down and he sighed heavily.

'Girls, I didn't want to say anything unless . . .'

'Steve, just tell us what's wrong,' Abbie said as she was getting annoyed.

'It looks like Hannah is suffering from deep depression. I found her early this morning wandering the corridor mumbling to herself. She was sleepwalking.'

'Oh Jesus,' Danni cried. She stood up and started pacing.

'Auntie, is Hannah alright. Is what Steve saying true?' Abbie asked.

'Yes, darling,' she said taking Danni's hand in hers.

'It looks as though Hannah is taking it the worst.'

Over the next forty eight hours Mikey only got worse. The operation to release the pressure on his brain had failed, and the surgeon hesitated on doing a second operation. Dr Hanson had already told Lesley and her nieces that it was a dangerous operation at best, without doing a second one. Lesley talked to her nieces and tried to tell them what was happening, and it only made them cry.

'Mikey's going to die, isn't he?,' Abbie cried. Lesley never answered, and her silence only confirmed what they were all fearing.

They all sat quietly around Mikey as they prayed for his recovery. The constant beeping of the machines that surrounded him were only delaying the inevitable, and moments later Dr Hanson came in with a nurse and stood at the foot of the bed. Lesley stood up when she noticed them and she wiped her eyes. Dr Hanson stood silent for a moment as he gathered his thoughts.

'Miss Philips.' Danni and Abbie looked up straight away, but Hannah was sitting staring out the window, and she looked round slowly through blurry eyes as the doctor spoke. Tears streaming her face, and Danni went to her and held her arm. This was the moment Dr Hanson always dreaded. When everything had failed, and not even a drop of hope existed. He had failed yet another patient. First Grace, and now Mikey. Two patients in too shorter time.

'Come on sis'. Mikey's waiting for us,' she said gently as tears streamed her face. Mikey was as good as dead. There hasn't been any brain activity for almost forty eight hours, and the machines were only delaying the inevitable as he lay there amidst the wires and tubes. Everyone was there now. Hannah and her sisters, Steve and Lesley, and Tony, Julie and Jason, and Raymond and Lyndsey and their daughters and Desmond. Lesley stood comforting her nieces as they all cried, and Steve stood behind Hannah as he supported her. Tears streamed his face too as Hannah and her sisters went to their brother now, and Hannah climbed on the bed and held him in her arms.

'We love you, Mikey. Hannah loves you,' she sobbed. The girls all cuddled and kissed their brother, and Lesley signalled to Dr Hanson.

'I love you, Mikey,' Danni cried.

'I love you, Mikey,' Abbie cried.

Dr Hanson flicked the switch, and the beeping slowed down as Lesley held her nephews hand.

'Goodbye my darling. Mommy and daddy are waiting for you,' she cried and kissed his cheek. Hannah lay so still holding her brother in her arms as she sobbed uncontrollably.

'Mikey, I'm so sorry . . . I'm sorry . . . I'm sorry.' Tony wanted to go to her as he cried, and he just wanted to hold her. He wanted to hold her and tell her that everything will be OK. He wanted to protect her forever, but she seemed so fragile lying there next to her brother, that he didn't dare touch her, as he feared she would break.

He just stood by her side and touched her, just to let her know he was there for her. Her whole body was shaking through sheer grief and torment, and she was mumbling incoherently to herself. Dr Hanson had left the room to leave them alone for a while. He went back to his office, and he buried his head in his hands and cried like a baby.

Dr Clive Hanson had known the family for over thirty years, and after losing Grace nearly eight months before, losing Mikey now was too much for him to bare. He knew Mikey was critical, and it would have took a miracle to save him, even from the moment he was bought into A&E, but he always believed in hope.

Hannah had been holding onto Mikey for almost an hour now, and she was nearly asleep as she lay there. Danni and Abbie were sitting holding Mikey's hands as they cried, and Tony gently lifted Hannah off the bed, so not to disturb the tubes around Mikey, and they all left quietly. Tony carried Hannah outside to the car as she slept in his arms, and Steve went to find Dr Hanson to tell him they were leaving now.

They drove back home in silence as Tony comforted Hannah. She was mumbling to herself, though she was asleep, and when they arrived home they were all like robots as they walked from the car into the house. Tony carried Hannah upstairs and lay her on her bed, and moments later Hollie and her daughters knocked the front door and walked in. They stood in the doorway to the lounge and looked at each of them, and Hollie knew instantly that Mikey had died, and her hands flew to her mouth as she started crying.

Jason had gone back to Lesley's too, and he sat with Danni in the armchair comforting her as she cried. He had decided to take some time off work and spend it with Danni. He wanted be there for her and help her through her grief.

By three o'clock in the afternoon Hannah was still asleep upstairs. Tony had checked on her a few times, and he sat there by the bed. He held her hand and stroke her face. She looked so peaceful as she lay there. As though she hadn't got a care in the world.

'Baby, I love you so much. Please come back to me.' He kissed her gently on her lips, and then her eye.

'I love you' he whispered. She mumbled something in her sleep then and he sat there just watching her sleeping.

Chapter Thirteen

Over the next few days, Hannah's health seemed to worsen. She had fallen into deep depression with episodes of uncontrollable crying. Often she would be found crying in her bedroom, and her sisters would just sit and comfort her. Sometimes she'd be sitting watching television with her aunt and sisters, and she would suddenly start crying.

Abbie and Danni were obviously feeling their brother's loss too, but they were too concerned for their sister now to worry about their grieving. The sisters had become Hannah's carers as they cared for her around the clock. Sometimes someone else would take over while Abbie and Danni got some sleep.

It had only been three days since Mikey died, but Lesley and Steve went to the funeral directors and booked his funeral. Lesley had cried while doing it, and she turned to Steve who comforted her.

'Steve, he's only ten years old.'

Lesley and Steve took a break afterwards and took a walk through the park. Lesley was so grief-stricken having just booked her eleven year old nephews funeral, that Steve had to settle her down before going home to the girls. Hollie and her daughters offered to sit in the house and watch the girls while they were away.

Jade and Keeley had taken time off to spend some time with their mother while they cared for Hannah. At twenty-three years old Jade Kilpatrick owned her own beauty salon on Edgeware Road. Her long blonde hair down to her bottom and ocean blue eyes were quite distinctive. Her twenty year old sister, Keeley, with shoulder length blonde hair and blue eye was studying law at Kings College. Though Keeley needed to get back to college soon before she missed too much, she stayed by her sister as they cared for Hannah.

All the neighbours in the street had rallied around to help the family since they heard about Mikey's death, and Lesley was extremely grateful. Hollie and her daughters were an enormous help as they sat with Hannah when the Danni and Abbie were tired. Desmond was always a big help too, and of cause Raymond and Lyndsey and their two daughters, Caroline and Debbie were a big help too, as Caroline and Debbie sat with the girls to keep them company.

At twenty-four Caroline Layton was just two years older than her sister. Her short cropped blond hair and brown eyes, and her little button nose was what she like best about herself.

Caroline was her fathers personal secretary. She loved being near her father, and enjoyed organising his work schedules. Caroline was always a daddies little girl, and Raymond loved having her around him. Her sister, Debbie was studying catering and homecare at Queens College in Marylebone. She wanted to open her own restaurant in Covent Garden.

It was almost three o'clock in the morning, and Abbie and Danni had fell asleep in their own beds as Jade sat up in Hannah's room. Everyone had volunteered and took their turn to care for Hannah through the night, and they each took extra care to keep an eye on her. Though it wasn't always easy.

Jade was reading a book to see if it would help keep her awake, but her eyes kept dropping. It wasn't necessary to stay awake all night, Lesley had told her. 'Just be there for her if she wakes up,' she said. Jade closed her eyes for a moment, and what seemed only moments later she jolted awake. The bedroom light was off, but the light from the small table lamp was enough for her to see that Hannah's bed was empty.

She jumped up and dropped her book, and instantly became aware. She called out for her, thinking she had woke up and gone to the toilet, but after checking the toilet and bathroom, fear gripped her.

'Hannah?' There was no response. No sound, except that of Jade's heavy breathing. Jade went to go downstairs to see if she was there, but she stopped dead in her tracks at the top of the stairs as she stared at an open front door.

'Oh dear God.' She ran down the stairs and out the front door and looked around, but Hannah was no where to be seen. She ran back up the stairs and woke everyone up.

'Lesley, wake up.' Lesley was instantly awake and she saw the panic in Jade's face.

'What? What's happened? Is Hannah alright?'

'Hannah's gone, and the front doors wide open.' Everyone jumped out of bed and ran outside in the pouring rain. Still in their nightwear, they all ran in different directions calling out for Hannah. The commotion had woke some of the neighbours, and they had come out to look for her too. Hollie and Keeley came out looking too after Jade ran home to tell them what happened.

'Oh Hannah, where are you?' Danni cried.

'Hannah.' She ran to the end of Connaught Street and looked up Hyde Park Street.

'Hannah.' She looked straight ahead up Hyde Park Street, and there lying in the memorial garden was a white figure. She called out to Steve and Lyndsey, who were searching along the street, and Danni ran into the garden and knelt at her sisters side and held her hand. Hannah was soaked and freezing, and Abbie and Danni sobbed as they held their sisters hands.

Limp and lifeless, Steve carried Hannah back to the house. Abbie and Danni had got her changed and dried and into clean pyjamas, and Steve put her back into bed. Abbie cried as she got into bed with her sister and cuddled up to her. Everyone had gone back home and changed after Lesley thanked everyone, and now she stood watching Hannah sleeping as tears filled her eyes.

Danni was crying as she paced the bedroom. She was still grieving for her parents, and now Mikey. And now her sister. How could life be so unfair?, she thought. She cried now as she pulled at her hair.

'I can't do this anymore. Why is this happening to us, auntie?' Lesley looked round and saw Danni's distraught face, and she went to her and comforted her.

'Danni, Danni. Don't you go losing it now, darling. Hannah needs us all now more than ever,' she said comforting her.

'I know you're grieving, darling. We all are, but Hannah needs us all to stay positive.' She stood comforting Danni for a while, and then the sisters all got into bed together and comforted each other, and Lesley stood watching her nieces sleeping together in the bed.

It had bought so many memories flooding back for her as she remembers when the girls were children. Tears filled her eyes just watching. She wandered where the years had gone, and how tragedy has torn the family apart. She went downstairs and saw Steve thanking Raymond and Lyndsey for their help, and after they left Lesley cuddled up to Steve on the sofa.

The following morning everyone was awake by seven o'clock, except Hannah. Hannah was still sleeping, as her long black hair was fanned out on the pillow. Danni lay there in bed just watching her sister sleeping, and occasionally touching her face and kissing her.

'I love you sis'. Please come back to us.' She kissed her again and gently got out of bed without disturbing her, and she went downstairs to find the others all in the kitchen. Raymond and Lyndsey were there too. They had come over early that morning with Caroline and Debbie to see how Hannah was.

'Morning, darling. Do you want some coffee?' Lesley asked. Danni mumbled something and sat at the table and buried her head in her hands.

'Oh man, my head is banging.' Both Danni and Abbie looked terrible this morning, and they both look as though they had been crying half the night.

'Is Hannah still asleep, darling?'

'Yes.' Raymond looked at Abbie and Danni now as they nursed their sore heads.

'Listen, girls. I just want you to know that everything is in hand at the office. Me and Dessy's will manage. You just take as much time as you need,' Raymond said.

'Thanks Raymond. It's nice to know that something in my life is going alright.' Lesley and Raymond looked at each other then, and then Raymond kissed his wife and daughters and left for work.

'Bye daddy. I'll in the office by ten o'clock,' Caroline said.

At eight-thirty, Hollie and Keeley came round to see how Hannah was. They hadn't had much sleep either after last nights commotion.

'We stayed up mostly this morning after we got home, as Jade felt guilty for what happened,' Hollie said as Steve poured her some coffee.

'Oh no. I must speak with her and reassure her,' Lesley said.

'She's alright. She'll be round soon. She was in the shower when we left.' No one was in the mood for breakfast that morning, but Steve and Lesley had got some bacon and eggs on the go, and asked if Lyndsey her daughters wanted to stay for some. Caroline was off to work soon, but Lyndsey and Debbie stayed for some. Hollie was off to work soon too, but Jade and Keeley stopped for some breakfast as well.

At forty-one, Lyndsey Layton was the head chef at the Cigala Spanish restaurant, where she's worked for the past twenty years. Her manager, Carlos Benning had personally recruited her straight from college. He had trained her up himself in the different styles of cooking, and now twenty years on she runs the kitchen single handed. Though now, Carlos has got his nephew to stand in while Lyndsey is off.

Moments later Jade walked in feeling refreshed after her shower. Her blonde hair tied up in a bobble as she wore jeans and T-shirt. She sat down at the table as Lesley put a plate of bacon and eggs in front of her.

Lesley was always cooking something. Before the fire claimed her sisters life, she always had someone to lunch. Always someone there for breakfast as she dished up bacon and eggs. In the thirty years Lesley had live on Connaught Street, there hasn't been a week gone by that she hasn't had someone to lunch, or someone to breakfast.

Lesley had a large kitchen with a breakfast bar and a huge dining table. There was always a delicious smell wafting in the air after she'd cooked something. At forty-seven, Lesley hasn't worked since she was twenty-nine, after she won a huge payout in an out of court settlement after she sued the council for personal injuries.

Lesley was walking home from work one evening, and she slipped and broke her leg falling down a manhole that wasn't properly signed and covered. She won the court battle, with Duncan's father by her side, but she has been waiting for fifteen years for a new hip replacement.

'Jade, darling. It wasn't your fault what happened this morning with Hannah. It could have happened to any one of us.' She touched her face and smiled.

'You shouldn't feel guilty, darling.' Jade shot her mother a look, as much to say: *you didn't have to tell her.*

That morning Lesley decided to take Hannah to see Dr Hanson again. It wasn't something that was usually done, unless it was an emergency. Hannah would normally have to be referred, but Dr Hanson did say to go back to him if there was any problems. And he did know the history of the family.

Steve had drove them to the hospital, and he and Lesley supported Hannah as they walked slowly across the car park and into the hospital. They sat Hannah down and went to the enquiry desk and asked to see Dr Hanson.

'Have you got an appointment?' the nurse asked.

'No, but we saw Dr Hanson a couple of weeks ago after my nephew was bought in, and he told me to come back if we needed to.' The nurse asked Lesley to take a seat while she paged the doctor, and all the while Hannah was mumbling to herself.

'Dr Hanson . . . Dr Hanson to outpatients please. Dr Hanson to outpatient,' a voice said over the intercom system.

It was by chance they were hoping to see Dr Hanson that morning. Normally he worked on appointments only, unless he was on call or working in A&E or the theatres. He walked through to the waiting area in the outpatients department looking quite refreshed, and he smiled as he saw Hannah. At forty-eight years old, Dr Clive Hanson was tall and muscular with slightly receding grey hair, and he was the only doctor qualified in most areas around the hospital. By the age of thirty he was already a qualified surgeon and G.P. He went back to medical school at thirty-five and studied a course in paediatrics, and afterwards he studied a course in obstetrics and gynaecology. He smiled warmly now as he greeted Steve and Lesley, and he squatted to talk to Hannah.

'Hello Hannah. Do you remember who I am?' Hannah just stared blankly at him. Then she pointed her finger at him.

'Man.' The doctor smiled and held her hand as he helped her up.

'That's right, Hannah. I am.' Hannah had worsened since the doctor last saw her, and he was concerned as he and Steve helped her to an examining room. Hannah sat in the chair opposite the doctors chair, and Lesley went to her, and spoke to her as though she was talking to a child.

'Hannah, darling.' Lesley held her chin and made her look at her.

'Hannah, this nice doctor is going to take care of you now.'

'Man?' Hannah pointed to the doctor again, and Lesley sat there while Dr Hanson examined her.

Hannah seemed in a better mood this morning. Though she had a bout of crying during the night as her sisters comforted her. Hannah giggled occasionally as Dr Hanson examined her, and afterwards he listened to her chest and checked her weight as he and Lesley helped her onto the scales.

'I see she's lost a bit of weight. Is she eating properly?'

'Yes. I mean we have to spoon feed her, but yes, she eats regularly,' Steve said. Hannah started crying as Dr Hanson got his stethoscope and listened to her chest. Lesley took some tissues from her bag and wiped her eyes.

'Darling, it's alright.' Hannah looked at her aunt, and for a moment she seemed almost terrified of her. Like a small animal wanting to bolt from the room. She flinched as Lesley went to wipe her nose, and went to get up out of the chair, and Lesley touched her arm.

'Darling, it's OK. It's me, auntie,' she said as she smiled.

'Auntie?' Hannah seemed confused as she tried to remember. She calmed down a little then and Lesley held her hand as she listened to the doctor.

'Well physically Hannah seems to be alright. I think it's just a simple case where she's just been through a few months of terrible loss and grief, and she hasn't adequately dealt with it,' he said.

'Hannah probably never dealt with the loss of her parents properly, as she may of felt she was responsible for her brother and sisters welfare. It's not uncommon for the eldest child to take on the burden and the responsibility of their younger siblings. I think Hannah just didn't have that grieving period after her parents died, and losing Mikey after such short space of time was too much for her.' Everything the doctor told them was almost true.

Hannah did feel guilty that she wasn't the one that took Mikey shopping for Danni's birthday, instead of being in the meeting. She did feel responsible for him because their parents had gone.

Lesley thought about it all the way home, and after they got Hannah settled and Steve had made some coffee, they all sat down and discussed Hannah's welfare.

'So what did Dr Hanson say?' Julie asked.

'He just said that he thinks Hannah hasn't adequately dealt her loss properly, and she may have felt guilty that she didn't live up to her responsibilities of caring for you two and Mikey because you are her siblings.' Danni had tears in her eyes as she thought of Hannah. Danni knew all too well what her sister was like, and she went to her and cuddled her now.

'I love you, sis'.

That afternoon they were all sitting in the lounge. Julie and Tony were there as well, when Frank and Sally arrived, and Danni seemed stressed as she answered the door.

'Oh hi Frank. Come on in,' she said matter-of-factly, and walked straight back in the lounge. Frank and Sally looked at each other and wondered if they were disturbing them. They stepped into the hall and Frank shut the front door behind him, and then they walked into the lounge. They stood in the doorway and looked around the room. Danni was feeding Hannah some cottage pie, as everyone seemed glum.

'What's happened?' Sally asked nervously. Hannah smiled when she saw them, and she jumped up to greet them.

'Hello, you're a nice man. Nice lady,' she said looking at Sally. Lesley stood up and went to Hannah and held her arm.

'Hannah, darling. Come and sit down and finish eating.'

'What's going on in here? What's the matter with Hannah?,' Frank asked worriedly. Steve put his mug of coffee down on the table and led Frank and Sally to the kitchen. He stood there against the cooker and rubbed his hands over his face as he thought for a moment.

'Frank, Mikey died last week, and now Hannah's blaming herself.'

'Oh, Jesus wept.' Frank sank slowly in the chair at the kitchen table as Sally cried.

'What happened matey?'

'He got run over on Oxford Street. The doctors had said he'd suffered a massive head trauma. Hannah saw it happen as she was in the office, and now she suffering deep depression and a nervous breakdown.' Steve carried on telling them about Hannah and her mood swings, and about not recognising people. Sometimes not even her family, and afterwards they went back into the lounge and sat down.

Danni had finished feeding Hannah, and Sally sat there holding Hannah's hand as tears filled her eyes.

'Are you my friend?,' Hannah asked Sally excitedly, and Sally smiled and cuddled her.

'Yes sweetie, I'm your friend.' Hannah seemed restless and agitated then as she sat there, and suddenly she started crying as she rocked back and forwards.

'Hannah, sweetie. What's the matter?' Hannah stood up and paced the room as she cried, and Abbie went to her to calm her down, but Hannah pulled away from her and went to walk out the front door. Tony jumped up, and he and Abbie tried to bring her back, but she was trying to get away from him too.

'Go away, leave me alone. You're not my friend.' Frank sat there watching the commotion. He was stunned to see Hannah the way she was, and he couldn't believe how much she had changed. She was like a whole different person.

'Hannah, baby, it's me, Tony. Remember?' He tried to get her to look at him, but she was trying to get away from him, almost as though he was a stranger trying to hurt her. Everyone sat there watching, as Sally started crying. She couldn't bare to watch her like that, and she stood up and left the room crying as Steve followed her. Lesley went to help Tony, and they got Hannah back to the sofa.

She was still agitated as she rocked back and forwards. She was still crying, as Tony comforted her.

'What can we do to help?' Frank asked now.

'I'm afraid there's not much anyone can do. We just have to be there for her, and keep reassuring her when she gets confused. Dr Hanson at the hospital has prescribed some medication, and we have to go back once a week to see Dr Manns for psychotherapy,' Danni said.

'We have to care for her twenty four-seven. There's always someone that has to watch her. She's started sleepwalking now, and she managed to get out the other night, and we found her in the memorial garden,' Steve said.

'If there's anything you want us to do, you just call us, and we'll be right over,' Frank said. Danni smiled and thanked them, and she went to Frank and hugged him.

'Thank you Frank.'

Frank and Sally had stayed with them for a few hours, and then they went to leave, but as Sally stood up Hannah seemed scared and ran to her and threw her arms around her.

'Please don't leave me . . . please,' she cried. Sally comforted her now as tears welled in her eyes, and she sat down on the sofa with her.

'OK sweetie. We won't leave you.' They sat on the sofa together, and Sally kissed her and brushed her hair away from her eyes as everyone watched them, while Frank and Steve disappeared into the kitchen to talk. Steve made some fresh coffee and they sat down at the table and talked.

'What else did the doctor say, mate? Did they indicate how long she could be like this?'

'No, not really. It could be a matter of weeks, or maybe months or years. We just have to be there for her, and hope she snaps out of it soon. In the meantime she's got her depression tablets, and we take her to psychotherapy sessions once a week.' Frank seemed shaken as he sat there, he looked at his friend now with sincere feelings.

'I mean what I said matey. You call me anytime night or day if you need any help. If you need me to sit with her when you go out, just give us a bell, OK' The two men shook hands, and when they returned to the living room Hannah had fell asleep in Sally's arms. Tony gently lifted her up and took her upstairs to bed, and Frank and Sally left. Steve shown them out, and then he went back inside.

Chapter Fourteen

It's the second week in October, and Danni remembered that Mikey was suppose to have started at his new school in Bude last month. She was sitting in the lounge with Hannah, and she told her aunt. The school has bound to have tried to contact them, and Danni check her phone. Twenty seven missed calls.

'I'm going to have to phone the school and notify them. Or go down there,' she said. Steve had decided it was best to go to Bude and notify the head teacher in person rather than over the phone. Danni contacted the school and apologised for missing all their calls, and informed them that Mikey was no longer going to the school, and that her aunt was going to visit the school and explain why. Danni had left it at that as she didn't want to explain it all over the phone.

Danni wasn't feeling up to going back to Bude yet anyhow. She said that it would just remind her of the house they bought, and that it's likely they won't be living in it anymore. At least for a while, anyhow. Jason had gone back home to Bude now, as he had the restaurant, and Danni had asked him to go by the house everyday to check things are alright.

It was Mikey's funeral tomorrow, and as they all sat in the lounge that evening there was deep sense of gloom in the air. No one spoke to each other as they all gathered their thoughts.

Frank and Sally had travelled up from Ashford the day before the funeral, and Bill Holts was there too. Raymond and Lyndsey were there too with their daughters, and

Desmond was there too as he sat comforting Abbie. Tony sat comforting Hannah, as she mumbled to herself.

Outside in the street neighbours and friends from far and wide had gathered and laid flowers and wreaths outside Lesley's house. There were cards and letters of condolences from all of Mikey's friends, and the following morning sitting outside on the pavement was Mikey's only best friend, Vanessa Harris.

She sat there on the pavement holding a teddy bear someone had left, and Lesley saw her and went out to her. She stood on the doorstep as she watched Vanessa, and she slowly walked out to her as Vanessa looked up with tears streaming down her little cheeks. Lesley stood with her arms outstretched, and Vanessa cried and ran to her.

'I so sorry, darling.' Vanessa's mother stood in the street watching, as Lesley took Vanessa in the house. Teresa went home then to her husband. She knew Vanessa would be alright with Lesley.

At eight-thirty that evening everyone started going to bed. Bill went home, and Lesley made the spare rooms up for Frank and Sally. Bill had dropped Vanessa home when he left, and the following morning Lesley was awake at six-thirty. She had hardly slept all night thinking about the next day. Abbie and Danni stood outside in the street at seven o'clock looking at all the cards and letters people had left.

Hannah seemed to be more aware this morning of what was happening. She hadn't stopped crying from the moment she woke up. Jade and Keeley had come over at nine o'clock with their mother, and Jade was upstairs helping Hannah get dressed. Jade had washed her in the shower, and Hannah stood so still, as Jade dried her off.

All morning Hannah had cried as she kept calling for Mikey, and Jade sang softly to her as she got her dressed, which seemed to calm her a little, and moments later they came downstairs and Jade smiled supporting Hannah.

'There we go. Hannah's all clean now,' she said as she helped Hannah to the armchair. Lesley smiled and went to Jade.

'Thank you Jade. You're so sweet for helping Hannah.' Lesley went to Hannah now and kissed her.

Hannah was wearing the same black dress she wore for her parents funeral. Jade had tied Hannah's hair into bobble, and tied it with two black ribbons

It was a gorgeous morning outside with a gentle breeze in the air as the sun shone, and outside in the street neighbours had gathered as a horse drawn carriage came up the street carrying Mikey's coffin. The funeral was booked for eleven-thirty, and the reverend Joe Watson arrived moments later in a black limousine. The reverend stepped out of the back seat slowly and greeted some of the neighbours, and Danni and Abbie opened the front door and smiled bleakly as they greeted him.

'Good morning, reverend,' Abbie said.

'Hello, my children.' Everyone stopped and watched as Mikey's coffin was lifted out from the carriage and into the house. Hannah was sitting on the sofa with Jade as they walked in, and Hannah started crying when she saw the coffin. A simple white coffin with white carnations.

The coffin was laid in front of Hannah, half opened. Mikey was dressed in the new suit that his aunt bought him, and he lay there with hands across his chest as

Hannah advanced towards him. Tears ran down her cheeks as she cried in to her hands, and she touched his face and kissed him.

'Hello Mikey. Hannah still loves you.' Lesley wasn't sure it was a good idea bringing the coffin in the house, but Steve thought it might be good for her to see him one last time before the funeral. Hannah stood there with her sisters as they talked to Mikey, and moments later Bill walked through the door with Rosie.

Bill looked very smart this morning with his grey hair combed back and the grey suit. At thirty-seven years old Rosie Adams has been Bill's secretary for twenty-one years. With her blond curls and blue eyes, she was always the flirt at the station. She had flirted with Steve often enough, and teasing him with her short skirts. Bill and Rosie stood in the doorway to the lounge watching the sisters now, and then Bill saw Steve and went to speak to him.

'Listen matey. I've arranged for the roads to be blocked off between here and the cemetery, and there will be four men on bikes leading the cortège. They wasn't going to have the service at the church. It was a glorious morning, and the girls thought it would be nice to have the service at the graveside. In the presence of their parents.

The sisters stood outside with their aunt and Steve as Mikey's coffin was bought from the house and put back in the carriage, and the neighbours started falling in behind as the four police officers on bikes slowly led the possession up the street. An eerie silence fell across the streets as people stopped and watched.

Vanessa sobbed the entire time as she walked with her parents, and not far behind was Mrs Hope, the head teacher from Mikey's school in London, and some of their pupils. Mrs Stone, the head teacher from school in Bude had travelled to London for Mikey's funeral too, and Danni and Abbie had thanked her for coming.

Danni and Abbie had supported their sister the entire way, as they cried and walked behind the carriage. In the window of the carriage, flowers spelt out Mikey's name, and engraved on a brass plaque on the coffin was the message:

Our dear beloved brother. Michael William Philips. 1995 - 2005.

At the cemetery Mikey's coffin was laid on the ground as the reverend read from the bible, and mourners gathered round as they paid their last respects. A plot had been dug out between Grace and Duncan. Frank stood comforting Sally all the while as she cried. She was thinking how so much tragedy had befallen on the family in such short space of time. How cruel life could be sometimes, she thought.

Sally had thought the world of Mikey, and it only seemed like yesterday when Mikey was crying in her arms after his parents deaths.

Mikey's coffin was lowered into the ground as some of the congregation prayed, and Vanessa walked over and dropped a single white rose and her favourite teddy in on top of the coffin. She stood there crying as she held a piece of paper, and read out loud a poem she had wrote.

'To my best friend in the whole wide world. You are gone from my life, but not from my heart. You live with God and the angels up in heaven now. I hope you visit me at night in my dreams, where we

can always be friends. Where I will always love you. Love from your best friend. Vanessa.'

She looked up with tears streaming down her cheeks, and she kissed the note and dropped it into the grave.

'Goodbye Mikey.'

After the service, most of the congregation had gone back to Lesley's. Some of the neighbours had gone home, but Lesley and Steve had a gathering in the garden for their friends.

Lesley had prepared a small buffet for the wake. Just for family and close friends, and they all gathered now as Danni and Abbie stood to speak to them all.

'We would like to thank you all for all your kind thoughts and wishes over the past few weeks. And most of all we would like to thank you for all your help and support. Not just since our dear brother, Mikey fell ill, but since our parents died too,' Danni said as everyone gathered and listened intently.

'As you all know so well, our dear sister, Hannah is in dire need of our prayers and thoughts,' Abbie said as she held Hannah's hand. Lesley and Steve helped Hannah to stand up and face everyone, and Vanessa went to Hannah and put her arm around her waist.

'Please give generously your thoughts and prayers and help our dear sister, Hannah to a speedy recovery,' Abbie continued.

After their speech, Danni and Abbie had gone round greeting everyone and talking to them as they walked round slowly with Hannah.

Hannah had got another session of psychotherapy tomorrow with Dr Manns, and Lesley was going to give her some more medication after the wake. The two head teachers Mrs Stone and Mrs Hope stood talking to the sisters now as they offered their condolences again.

Hannah's ability to walk unaided was getting slightly worse. She used the walls for support sometimes at home, though there was always someone there to assist her. Dr Manns had said it wasn't uncommon for someone to lose their sense of co-ordination. Hannah had fell asleep that afternoon on the sofa after the wake, and Frank and Sally sat in the lounge with her.

At forty-nine, Frank and his wife Patricia have been happily married for thirty years, and had one daughter. Frank and Sally have always had a close relationship. Sally owes her whole life to Frank and his wife. If it was not for them, she would probably died years ago.

Hannah sat at the table now with her sisters and Lesley and Steve as they ate dinner. It was almost six o'clock in the evening, and after they finished eating Danni had give Hannah a bath and they sat in the lounge with their aunt and Steve as they watched a film that Steve had rented from the library. Jason was still there, and so was Julie and Tony, but everyone else had gone home.

Danni cuddled up to Jason on the floor as Tony sat with Hannah. Julie had made coffee for everyone, and after a few minutes Hannah had fell asleep as Tony cuddled her. He kissed the top of his head and smiled.

'I love you babe.'

Chapter Fifteen

The morning after Mikey's funeral, Hannah and her sisters sat by their parents and Mikey's graves in "The Garden" at the cemetery rearranging the plants and flowers. Hannah sat there staring blankly, occasionally pulling up a plant or flower that her sisters would have to replant.

Danni and Abbie thought it would be good for Hannah to visit the graves, just to be close to their parents and brother. Hannah seemed in a good mood this morning, though she cried a little when Danni got her dressed.

It was almost ten thirty in the morning, and Lesley was preparing the meat for tonight's tea. Not that anyone was in the mood for eating, but she waltzed around the kitchen as she prepared the veg and the potatoes, and she washed the meat before she diced it up, and mixed the gravy. She was just filling a saucepan with water when someone rang the doorbell.

Steve answered the door, as Lesley waited to see who it was, and moments later she heard voices. They sounded foreign, and Lesley frowned and washed her hands, and when she got to the lounge she saw two strangers with backpacks on.

'Yes, can I help you?'

'We are looking for Miss Abigail. We went to the address that she gave us, but we could not find it. A lady said that Miss Abigail lived here with her auntie,' the man said.

'Yes, that's right. I'm her auntie. Who are you?' Steve stood next to the two people as he listened.

'Oh, I'm so sorry. I'm Philippe DuPree, and this is my wife Marie-Claire. We met Miss Abigail in Paris, and we arranged to visit today.' Lesley realised then who they were, and she sat down. She had heard Grace mention their names before, and she had read some postcards that Abigail had sent home from Paris.

'Abigail has gone out at the moment with her sisters, but she should be home soon.' She offered them some drinks while they waited, and ten minutes later while Lesley was in the kitchen Abigail walked in supporting Hannah. Philippe and Marie-Claire stood up, and Abigail squealed with delight when she saw them.

'Philippe. Marie.' Abigail went to her friends and greeted them as Danni sat Hannah down.

'Oh, guys. It's wonderful to see you. When did you get here?'

'About fifteen minutes ago,' Marie-Claire said.' Their English was quite good, as Abigail had taught them different phrases. Abigail composed herself now as Lesley came through from the kitchen.

'Auntie. This is Philippe and Marie-Claire. We met in Paris.' Abigail introduced the others then, and all the while Philippe was watching Hannah as she sat in the armchair staring blankly at the floor. Abigail looked at Hannah now and kissed her.

'Philippe, Marie. This is Hannah. My sister.' Philippe and Marie-Claire had remembered Hannah from when Abigail spoke of her in Paris, but they never remembered her like this. Philippe and Marie-Claire sat down as Lesley bought some coffees in.

'Philippe, Marie. My sister is suffering from severe depression and a nervous breakdown, because our brother,

Mikey died almost a month ago. It was his funeral only
yesterday.'

'Oh, Miss Abigail. I'm so sorry.'

'We also lost our parents almost nine months ago.'
Marie-Claire was almost crying now as she stood up and
hugged Abigail.

'Oh, Miss Abigail. Why didn't you contact us. We'd
have come to see you?,' Marie-Claire cried as she hugged
her friend. Abigail explained that their house burnt down.
She explained that it happened in February when she was
in Paris, and that her sisters were in Switzerland. Abigail
had been in Paris for the third time when Frank had
found her after the fire. Abigail has always loved Paris.
So romantic, she thought. It was the second time she was
there when she met Philippe and Marie-Claire.

After they finished their drinks, Abigail took her
friends to see her parents graves and the memorial garden.
Abigail spoke fluent French, and she explained to them
that the memorial garden was where their house was.

Philippe and Marie-Claire was stopping in London
for the week. They had booked into a hotel when they
arrived, but Lesley offered them one of the spare rooms.

'No, no, it's OK. We have hotel room,' Philippe
said.

'Please. I'd like you to stay. You are friends of Abigail's,
and it would be nice to have the company.' Marie-Claire
smiled and thanked Lesley, and then Abbie shown her
friends upstairs. It was a lovely room with pink velvet
curtains and a beige carpet. There was a double bed with
a cotton sheets and a satin bedspread. Abigail had got
some fresh sheets out and changed the sheets on the bed
for them.

She got some fresh towels for them, and afterwards she left them to unpack. Lesley had had all the bedrooms redecorated two years ago, and all new carpets throughout. Though at the time she never had plans to use the rooms, it always looked nice and clean and fresh if she ever had visitors stay over.

Lesley had got some more meat out of the freezer to prepare, as Philippe and Marie-Claire were eating with them that evening. Though they felt a bit awkward and didn't want to impose.

'Please, I insist. It'll be lovely to have you here. You're friends of Abbie's. Besides it'll cost a fortune to eat out everyday in London,' Lesley said.

'Fortune?' Philippe didn't quite understand, so Abbie translated it for them. Philippe smiled then and thanked Lesley for her hospitality.

Abigail took her friends out for a few hours around London. They visited some of the museums and galleries, and Trafalgar Square, and at lunchtime they found a café and had sandwiches and coffee.

Abbie wanted to show them different parts of London while they were there. That afternoon after they finished lunch they went to see a play at the Phoenix on Charing Cross Road.

That evening everyone was in bed by ten o'clock as Abigail stayed awake for a while talking to her friends. She still couldn't believe her friends were there, although she remembered they were coming. They had stayed awake till nearly two o'clock talking, and then they went to bed.

Abigail was awake the following morning by eight o'clock. She wrapped her dressing gown around her and checked if Hannah was awake yet, and then she went downstairs to find her friends eating breakfast. Lesley had cooked them a full breakfast, and Abbie smiled and kissed her friends.

'Morning guys. Did you sleep well?'

'Like a . . .' Philippe was thinking of the English phrase.

'What is it the English say. Like a loog?' Abbie smiled as she understood, and she corrected them.

'That bed is really comfortable, Lesley, thank you,' Marie-Claire said then.

Abbie was going to show her friends the office, and introduce them to Raymond and Desmond this morning.

That morning Steve and Lesley took Hannah out for the day. They had borrowed a wheelchair from the hospital, and they took Hannah on a trip around London to see the sights. It was better than being cooped up in the house, Steve thought, and it gave everyone a break.

They visited Trafalgar Square and Westminster Abbey and Buckingham Palace, and after they had lunch along the River Thames they took a trip to see the Horse Guards Parade and the Household Cavalry, where Hannah had her photo taken with the guards outside Buckingham Palace.

Danni and Abbie had more or less cared for their sister since Mikey died, and it was starting to tell on them. Though they were concerned all the while, and couldn't wait to get back to their sister, they enjoyed the day to themselves as they visited Covent Gardens and had lunch, and they had a girlie afternoon in Harrods as they tried on clothes and jewellery, and afterwards they went to see a show at the Piccadilly.

The sisters had had fun all afternoon, and laughed and giggled as they tried on different clothes, but they couldn't help feeling guilty, as their sister was so depressed. Abbie had shown her friends around London too that day, and by four o'clock they made their way home with their bags of shopping. They caught the train to Paddington and walked the rest of the way, and as they walked through the front door they were exhausted.

They dropped onto the sofa and kicked off their shoes, and moments later Lesley came through the door with Hannah. Danni and Abbie jumped up excitedly and greeted their sister, but Hannah looked as though she'd been crying. Danni kissed her and went to help her out of the wheelchair, but Hannah started crying again and tried to push her away. Abbie's friends sat on the sofa watching, and Marie-Claire had tears in her eyes watching them.

'Hey, hey, sis'. It's me, Danni.' Danni held her hands and tried to get Hannah to look at her. She held her chin and looked at her.

'Sis', it's only me.'

'Friend?' Hannah asked confusingly, and Danni smiled and touched her face.

'Yes, I'm your friend.' Danni held her hands and helped her out of the wheelchair, and walked her to the sofa, where she comforted her sister. Hannah started crying again, as Abbie sat with them, and Abbie only smiled and wiped her sisters eyes.

'Sis', I love you,' Abbie said and kissed her.

'I can't remember you,' Hannah cried. Her sisters only comforted her, and Abbie pulled away and looked at her sister.

'You will soon. One day you'll be all better,' she said gently. Lesley got some photos out after a while, and she thought it would be a good idea to sit with her nieces and show Hannah the family photos. Maybe it will help her to remember if she saw them all together in the photos, Lesley thought.

Steve had made some fresh coffee, and moments later Julie and Tony knocked the door and walked in. They spent a few hours together as they discussed each photo. Hannah smiled occasionally when she seemed to recognise someone, and Lesley smiled and kissed her niece when she pointed to a photo of her mother when she was younger and said "Mama".

That evening Hannah was upstairs asleep. It was almost eight o'clock, and she started moaning in her sleep. Julie and Tony were downstairs, and Bill had popped by to visit with Rosie. Abbie's friends had left, and they were staying at a hotel for the night before flying back to Paris in the morning. Abbie was sorry they were leaving, but she understood, as Marie-Claire was getting upset seeing Hannah the way she was.

Danni and Abbie were in the kitchen talking, when Hannah started screaming loudly. It had made Bill jump, and he almost spilt his coffee. Danni and Abbie bolted up the stairs, closely followed by Steve and Tony, and Lesley and Bill and Rosie. Hannah was asleep, but she seemed almost hysterical.

Danni and Abbie jumped on the bed and sat Hannah up trying to wake her, but all the while Hannah kept screaming and flapping her arms. It was almost as though someone was trying to attack her in her dream. Her arms flapped all around as though she was trying to fight someone off.

Danni was gently slapping her face to bring her round, but nothing seemed to work. Her sisters started crying as they were scared and confused, and Lesley grabbed her niece and slapped her hard across her face. Abbie and Danni stopped crying as everyone jumped. Everyone was shocked, but no one more than Lesley as her hands flew to her mouth. Hannah stopped screaming and sobbed.

'What did you do that for?,' she cried holding her face. Lesley took her niece and held her in her arms now as they both cried.

'I'm so sorry, darling, but you were hysterical.' Lesley had never in her life raised her hand to her nieces, and she shocked herself to think she was even capable of it. Lesley sat on the bed now comforting her niece as everyone went back downstairs, and moments later Hannah had fell asleep again in her arms. Lesley lay her down gently and sat there watching her sleeping as tears filled her eyes.

'Come back to us, darling. We all love you so much.' She kissed her cheek where a red hand print was after her aunt slapped her, and she smiled down at her.

'I love you so much, darling. Please come back to us.' Hannah slept soundly that night, and never woke up once till almost nine o'clock the following morning. She lay there in bed just quietly talking to herself, until finally she called out.

'Sissy. Sissy.' She almost sounded like a little girl calling for her mother, and moments later Abbie smiled as she saw Hannah awake. Hannah touched herself and started crying. She had urinated in the night, and Abbie smiled at her and helped her out of bed as Tony came upstairs.

'Tony, I'm sorry, but she's wet the bed. Can you change the sheets for me please?' Abbie took Hannah to the bathroom and got her undressed. She ran the shower, and afterwards she got her dressed and helped her down the stairs as Hollie came through the front door.

'Well, don't we look all smart this morning.' She went to Hannah and kissed her, and Hollie held her arm and led her to the front room.

At forty-six, Hollie Kilpatrick work as a receptionist at a branch of solicitors in Mayfair, where she's worked for the last fifteen years. She never really wanted to work at the beginning, but after her husband walked out on her for a younger woman she had no choice. She had the mortgage to pay and two daughters to support.

Hollie had always been Grace's best friend ever since they were at school together. They did everything together and went everywhere together, and when Grace met and fell in love with Duncan, Hollie was so jealous. She had always been the school flirt, and hoped to catch Duncan's eye, and Duncan often teased her at school.

Her long blonde mane that she's had ever since she was fourteen, and her ocean blue eyes, was what attracted her ex-husband, though now Hollie wore her hair short. Easier to manage, she told Grace once. Hollie was always one for designer labels and expensive jewellery. She always looked simply desirable every time she went out, though just lately she was all for jeans and T-shirts. Clothes that she wouldn't have been seen dead in twenty years.

Chapter Sixteen

It was only three weeks to Christmas Day, and all along Hyde Park Street and Connaught Street coloured lights decorated every tree and every house. Everyone in the street had got together and decorated the street, and the memorial garden. It was something they did each year, and thought it as extra special this year because of Hannah.

Vera Tibbit had done her usual cooking of different cakes and cookies and gingerbread men, and Raymond and Lyndsey had stringed lights around the lampposts in the street and flashing signs of "Merry Christmas".

At night everyone gathered in the street as the children sang Christmas carols. On the Saturday night they held a barbecue in the street, and they roasted chestnuts on the open fire. Raymond was going to dress up as Father Christmas this year and have some of the children dress up as elves.

It was seven o'clock in the evening, and as Steve and Lesley cuddled on the sofa they could hear the children singing Christmas carols outside. Julie and Tony were there, and Vera was there too. Hannah had had another session with Dr Manns that afternoon, and the doctor seemed happy with her progress.

Hannah was starting to recognise people more often now, though sometimes she forgot their names. Lesley had told him about the episode she had the other night, and that she got hysterical. He told Lesley she was probably just dreaming of her parents and brother.

Dr Manns did regular exercises with Hannah to stimulate her mind, and to keep her active. Quite often

Hannah would just sit motionless at home when she was awake. Sometimes her sisters would read to her, and Dr Manns suggested trying to involve her in daily tasks, even if it was just tidying things up or allowing her to try and get herself dressed in the morning.

'Get her used to doing some everyday tasks,' he told her aunt.

Danni had let Hannah try and feed herself last night, though she had got most of the food on her face instead of in her mouth, but it was a start, the doctor had said.

Over the following few days everyone in the street had prepared something for Christmas, and on the afternoon of Christmas Eve everyone gathered in the local community hall and sang hymns. Hannah stood with her aunt and Steve as they kept her steady. Hannah was dressed in her white dress and red sweater that her mother knitted her. Her long black hair hung loose with a red bow in her hair.

Danni and Abbie were dressed in their matching red and white dresses with the little red cherries sewn into the collars. Abbie was getting used to wearing dresses now, though it wasn't very often she wore one. Even at the office she sometimes wore her jeans and T-shirt. Though if there was a meeting scheduled for that day she wore a skirt.

Danni stood so still now as she stopped singing. Her heart was racing, as she swore she felt Mikey's presence. She breathed sharply as she thought she heard him speak. She looked all around, and then at Abbie. She thought she'd only imagined it, but for a single solitary moment she looked at Abbie again, and then at Hannah, and it was almost as though they had all just experienced the same thing.

Danni and Abbie walked out of the community hall together as their aunt watched them and wondered where they were going, and they stood outside in the snow talking.

'Did you just feel that, sis'?' It sounded almost impossible, and it sounded even more impossible as they heard themselves talking about it, but they went back inside to join the others, and Hannah was crying and smiling at the same time. Danni and Abbie looked at each other, and wondered if what they felt really did happened. Danni and Abbie had discussed it with their aunt after the service in the community hall. She told them it was just their imagination, but all three of them experiencing the same thing at the same time. It was either impossible, or a miracle.

'Things like that just don't happen, darling,' Lesley said back at the house.

'It's nice to think that they do, and it'll be nice to think that your parents and Mikey are still here in that way, but it just doesn't happen, darling.' The more the girls thought about it the more what happened seemed real. They couldn't be sure if Hannah had felt the same too, or whether she just happened to be crying and smiling at the same time, but they knew what they felt was almost real.

The girls had discussed it with Tony and Julie as well, and Julie had told them of the moment she felt her fathers presence that first day when they arrived in Bude. Danni and Abbie convinced themselves it was not their imagination, and from that moment they hoped it would happen again.

Steve had gone to the kitchen to make some fresh coffee when they got back. Julie and Tony were there too, and Hollie and her daughters. Danni and Abbie sat on the sofa cuddling Hannah, and Lesley went in the kitchen to help Steve with the coffees. She told Steve what the girls had said, and he smiled as he poured the coffees.

'You know, when my grandfather passed away I was only nine years old, and I grieved for months. I had no friends to turn to, and my only comfort was my teddy bear.' Lesley smiled as Steve shared some of his past with her.

'I used to talk to that teddy all the time. I convinced myself that he could hear me, so I told him all my secrets and fears, and one day I just stopped grieving. From that moment on I was sure that when my grandfather died, his spirit lived on in that teddy bear. I kept it for years. I'd kept it till well into my twenties, until I told myself that my grandfather wasn't really in my teddy bear,' he said. Lesley smiled as he told her his story, and part of her really wanted to believe that Mikey was still there somehow.

'But it didn't mean that I stopped believing that he was still with me,' Steve continued.

'If the girls believe they heard Mikey, then I believe it really did happen,' he said then. Lesley kissed him and smiled.

'Have I ever told you that I love you?' Steve thought about it, and smiled.

'No,' he said jokingly as they both laughed. They went back into the lounge with a tray of coffees, and

Lesley smiled as she watched her nieces on the sofa. She was actually hoping that it was true now, that they did feel Mikey's presence. She was hoping that she too would feel it. And of cause her sisters and Duncan's.

Lesley lay awake for a while that night still thinking about it. It was almost one o'clock in the morning on Christmas Day, and she could hear Hannah mumbling to herself in her sleep. Danni and Abbie were fast asleep in the other room, and Tony and Julie were asleep in the spare rooms. Jade and Keeley had stopped the night too as they sat up in Hannah room. Keeley was dozing, and Jade was reading a book.

The curtains were slightly apart in Hannah's room, and the street light outside the window was shining through. Jade looked up now as she thought she heard a noise, almost like a whooshing noise. She got up and looked through the curtains to the street outside, and Keeley was startled awake. Jade and Keeley both looked at each other, both of them wondering if the other felt what they did, and moments later a flickering light appeared in the corner of the room.

They both stared in amazement. Wondering if they should be scared and run from the room, but something about the light kept their gaze on it, that was now getting brighter. It was as though the light was shining through a hole in the wall, forcing the hole bigger, and for a moment the girls shielded their eyes against the light.

'Do you see that, Jade?' her sister asked. Jade never answered, keeping her gaze on the light all the time. Quiet distorted voices vibrated around the room, almost echoing, and Danni was startled awake. She sat up and breathed sharply, wondering if she had just dreamt what just woke her, and she went to investigate.

'Hannah . . . Hannah . . .'

The voice sounded as though it was coming from the light, and moments later Danni stood in the doorway, as images of Mikey appeared and flickered out like a candle. She stood mesmerised watching the image. She saw her mother, and then her father, and they too flickered out like candles. She ran and woke the others, all the while hoping what she saw was still there when they got back.

'Auntie, Steve. Wake up,' she said shaking them awake. Steve and Lesley both sat up, and wondered what was happening.

'Is it Hannah, is she alright?' Steve asked.

'No, Hannah's fine, but you must come and see this.' Danni sounded almost delirious and excited. She ran back to the light, and everyone followed. Lesley stood there as her jaw dropped, and Steve was almost speechless as images on Grace and Duncan and Mikey appeared and disappeared in front of them. Danni felt for the bed and shook Hannah awake, all the while not taking her eyes off the light.

'Sis', wake up.' She shook her again and again until Hannah woke up, and then, as though someone had just flicked a switch, Grace and Duncan and Mikey all appeared in front of them. All smiling, and all as clear as day. The light was still there, flickering like the ever-changing images of a kaleidoscope, as Grace and Duncan and Mikey stood in the light. Hannah opened her eyes and looked dreamy at her sister, and Danni smiled helping her to sit up.

'Sis', there's someone here to say hello.' Danni held her chin, and turned her head towards Mikey and their parents, and all at once Hannah cried.

'Mikey?'

'Hello sis'. It's good to see you again,' Mikey said. Hannah cried wondering if she was dreaming.

'Mama? Daddy?' The image of Grace seemed to float towards her daughter as Hannah got up onto her knees.

'Hannah, sweetheart. I love you so much, and it's no good for you to punish yourself for what happened.' Hannah only cried more as Danni and Abbie sat on the bed with their sister and aunt.

'But, mama, I should have been watching him. Mikey died because of me,' she sobbed. Jade and Keeley, and now Hollie stood watching in amazement at what they were seeing. Jade had ran home to fetch her mother, and they ran back, all the while Hollie was wondering what was happening. Julie was crying tears of happiness as Tony stood mesmerised. Duncan and Mikey floated over to the bed now, and Duncan reached out to Hannah.

'Sweetheart, please stop this silliness and be happy. We all love you so much, and we want you to be happy.' Mikey reached out and touched his sister now.

'Please don't cry, sis'. You know I don't like it when you cry.' Hannah tried to laugh a little then.

'I love you so much, Mikey, and I'm so sorry I wasn't there for you,' Hannah cried.

'Sis', it's nobody's fault what happened.' Mikey leaned forward now, almost as though he was going to kiss his sister, and Hannah closed her eyes and felt her lips tingling.

'I love you, sis'. Please hurry up and get better.' Mikey reached out and touched her knee then, and turned to see the others. Grace floated now, and turned to Abbie and Danni. Danni and Abbie were crying, and they smiled now as their mother reached out to them.

'Mama,' Danni smiled.

'Hello my precious daughters. I love you both so much, and I'm so proud of you. The way you've put your lives on hold and cared for Hannah, and of everything you've achieved since you were babies. Be happy my angels.' Grace's voice was almost angelic and dreamy as she reached out to them. Her long flowing hair and blue eyes were unmistakable. Danni and Abbie only smiled through their tears and closed their eyes as they imagined their mothers touch, and then Grace turned to her sister, and Lesley smiled.

'Gracie.'

'Lesley, my dear sister. I love you now more than I ever have. The way you've cared for our children is wonderful. You make me so proud to be your sister, and someone that I always looked up to.' Hannah sat on the bed watching all the time. All the time wanting to reach out to her brother and parents. Grace and Duncan spoke to Julie and Tony, and then to Hollie and her daughters, and then as though heading back to the light, Grace and Duncan and Mikey all turned and looked at everyone.

'Be happy my darlings. Be all that you can be. To all of you, just keep smiling, and we'll always be there to guide you along your way,' Grace said. Just then Raymond and Lyndsey and their daughters and Desmond came through the door in their pyjamas after Tony had gone and woke them, just in time to see Grace and Duncan and Mikey smile before they disappeared.

'Holy Mary Mother.' It was barely a whisper, as Desmond stood wide-eyed and watched them disappear like a wisp of cloud.

'Mama, don't go . . . daddy,' Hannah cried getting off the bed to go and stop them.

'Be happy, my precious angels. Be happy,' Grace's voice echoed and vibrated around the room. Everyone stood there mesmerised, and wondered if what happened really happened, and Hannah sobbed as her sisters and Tony and Julie comforted her.

Grace and Duncan had spoke to Steve, and gave him many thanks for taking care of their family. They'd spoke to Julie, and told her that they'd always be with her, and to Tony, for his endless love and care he has given Hannah over the years.

Everyone had stayed awake for most of what was left of the morning. Desmond, still in his pyjamas went to make some fresh coffee, and they all gathered in the lounge, and sat quietly as they gathered their thoughts of what just happened.

At seven-thirty that morning Steve and Lesley sat at the table together in the kitchen in silence as they drank coffee, when Danni and Abbie walked in. Everyone was still there that had gathered to see Grace and Duncan and Mikey, and they all started to filter into the kitchen now.

'Morning darling,' Lesley said as Danni sat at the table. Steve poured her some coffee, and she sat there thinking.

'How do you feel this morning?' Steve asked. Danni only gave a little laugh as she leaned back in her chair.

'I don't know. I don't know how I feel.' It took them all most of the morning to gather their thoughts of last night, and at ten forty-five when Hannah walked into the kitchen looking a bit worse-for-wear, they all stopped and stared at her. Her long black hair was all tangled and knotted, and her face looked as though she's been crying half the night. She never even realised that she was only wearing a T-shirt and her knickers.

Raymond and Lyndsey were still there with their daughters, and Desmond was still there too.

'You alright, darling?' Lesley asked as Hannah sat down. It was Christmas Day, and no one even give it a second thought to what day it was as they sat in the kitchen. Hannah stood up and went to pour herself some coffee, and everyone just stared at her.

'Sis', you OK this morning?' Abbie asked.

'Yeah. I've got a banging headache, but I'm fine. Auntie, have you got any Aspirin?' Hannah was talking as though nothing had ever happened. As though the events of the past three months hadn't happened. As if Mikey hadn't died, but as she looked round at all of them now she realised what her sister meant, as she noticed they were all staring at her. She was walking unaided and without leaning on anything. Tears filled her eyes as she looked around. The memories of last night came flooding back to her now, and she was almost ecstatic.

'Auntie, look.' She pranced around the kitchen, almost as though she'd just discovered her feet for the first time in her life, and her sisters laughed watching her.

'I guess last night really did happen,' Jade laughed watching Hannah. Hannah cried as she put her hand on her heart.

'Oh Mikey. I love you so much.'

Chapter Seventeen

Over the next few days, Hannah started getting used to things again. Her speech was still a bit poor, and she was still taking the antidepressant tablets that Dr Manns prescribed. She was due to see him again after Christmas, and her aunt couldn't wait to see what he said.

They all gathered in the lounge after lunch and unwrapped Christmas presents. Everyone had gone home and bought all their presents over to Lesley's, and they all sat around together.

Desmond had made some punch, and gave everyone some, and Hannah was smiling and laughing as she unwrapped gifts that everyone bought her, and that afternoon when Frank and Sally, and Bill and Rosie visited with a sack full of presents for everyone, they were amazed to see Hannah laughing with the others. Frank had bought his wife and daughter with him as well. Hannah stood up and greeted Frank, and he was happy for her.

'Hello, sweetheart. It's good to see you happy.' Frank introduced his wife and daughter, and they all sat as they unwrapped the presents Frank had bought. Sally sat with Hannah, and she watched her face as she unwrapped her presents. Frank and Steve disappeared into the kitchen to talk, and Steve made some fresh coffee.

'So what happened, mate?' Steve laughed a little as he didn't know where to begin. He was still having trouble believing it himself. Steve had always believed in the afterlife, and that your soul goes somewhere, but he was having trouble believing what he saw last night.

'Do you believe in the afterlife, and that you can come back in some form or another?' Frank looked at his friend not fully understanding, and as Steve explained last nights event, Frank looked shocked.

'So you're saying that somehow Mikey and their parents are still with us?' Frank looked non-believing for a moment, but he knew Steve wouldn't make up such a story, and seeing Hannah the way she is now, he knew whatever it was, it was powerful stuff. Moments later Hannah walked into the kitchen, and smiled as she went to Frank. He put his arm around her waist, and she sat on his knee and hugged him.

Thank you Frank. Auntie has just told me about everything you did to help me.' She kissed his cheek, and they went back to the lounge. Frank had many times sat with Hannah and fed her and read to her when she was ill. Sally sometime read to her too, but mostly she just sat with her and comforted her when she cried.

That afternoon Tony and Hannah disappeared upstairs and talked in her bedroom. Tony had told her about everything since Mikey died, and how bad Hannah was. He told her of the night she got out of the house and went to the garden. They sat cross-legged on the bed facing each other, and Tony kissed her as he thought for a moment.

'Hannah, you know how I feel about you, and you know just how much I love you.' Hannah smiled as she listened, and she kissed him.

'These past few weeks since Mikey died, and you being so ill, it's kind of got me thinking about us, and well, I was kind of hoping we could carry on from where we left off eight years ago.' Hannah smiled and kissed him again.

'You know, It's kind of scary that we know each other so well, Tony, because I think you must be able to read my mind.' Tony smiled and kissed her again.

'Yeah, well, I'm thinking that you want to kiss me right now.'

'Is that so?' she laughed. They leaned into each other, and their lips met for that long awaited and overdue kiss. They'd locked themselves in an embrace and held each other as he gently lowered her onto the bed. Their bodies entwined as she ran her fingers through his short blond hair, both of them breathing heavily as they explored each other.

It was the moment that they had both waited for, but both being scared of what to expect. Both of them had saved themselves for each other, only promised to each other. They slowly undressed each other as their hands explored each other. He gently squeezed her breasts and teased her nipples as she undone his jeans. Kissing every square inch of her soft naked flesh, his hands wondered freely over her soft skin.

She moaned softly as he teased her nipples, and then kissing her nipples his hand drifted slowly to her crotch. Her back arched against the satin bedspread, feeling his fingers exploring between her legs. It only made her want him more, and as she could take no more, she screamed and shuddered.

'Oh, Jesus. Make love to me.' He never responded as he continued to arouse her with his tongue. She grabbed his arm and pulled him on top of her, and she gasped sharply as he entered her, and moaned with every move he made. Slowly, as they both savoured every moment. He grabbed her soft milky white breasts and teased her nipples and kissed her passionately, and she let out a loud scream as she felt the edge of an orgasm.

He covered her mouth to muffle her screams as the intense pleasure heightened, and thrusting deeper she screamed louder as her whole body shuddered. They both clenched, feeling the intense pleasure of the orgasm. He continued thrusting, pushing deep inside her until they both climaxed. They both lay there afterwards, naked on top of the sheets and in each others arms, both of them spent and exhausted, and he kissed her lovingly on the lips.

Downstairs in the lounge Lesley was handing out the mince pies. Frank and Sally were still there with Frank's wife and daughter, and moments later Hannah and Tony came down. Danni and Abbie smiled wickedly at their sister and Tony as they walked into the lounge. They had only guessed what they'd been up to, and moments later after Hannah spoke with Frank and his wife she and Tony disappeared out the front door.

Hannah felt as though she had so much to catch up on, so many weeks that she'd been depressed. She wasn't going to waist a second more on grieving. They took a walk to the cemetery and visited Mikey's and her parents graves. She knelt down and looked at the headstone over her brothers grave and smiled.

'Thank you Mikey. I love you so much.' She kissed her fingers and touched the headstone, and afterwards she and Tony took a walk through Hyde Park. It's been a long time since they had just walked together and talked and enjoyed each others company. They walked through the snow holding hand as they chatted about their future.

Though Hannah and Tony had moved into the house in Bude with her sisters and Steve and Lesley, Hannah thought about buying a little retreat somewhere just for her and Tony. Somewhere where they could escape to, to be alone. Tony had always loved Devon. Maybe they would buy a cottage there sometime. Though it's only been a couple of days since they saw Mikey and their parents, Hannah was considering moving back to Bude soon.

Though she was still on her medication, and still had to visit the hospital once a week to see Dr. Manns, she thought about discussing it with everyone. Maybe they'd move back there in the Spring, she thought. Hannah didn't want to waste another moment. She had believed her brother and parents had somehow cured her. There was no other possible reason for her getting well so quick, and after Lesley explained what happened to Dr Manns, he had to agree.

'How would you like to buy a small cottage in Devon. You know, just you and me?' Hannah asked now as they walked along. Tony raised his eyebrow at the thought and smiled, but at the moment he was more concerned for Hannah and her health.

'But, baby. What about the house in Bude? And what about you?' They stopped walking and he took her hand in his and looked at her.

'Baby, you've only just got over losing Mikey. You were poorly for a long time. Are you really over Mikey now?' His concerns for her only made her happy. She knew he would always be there for her and care for her, no matter what.

'No, I don't think I'll ever get over losing Mikey. His death has scared me for life. Even more so than mom and dads. It's just that I've grieved for so long now, that I'm beginning to wonder if anything else matters.' Her bottom lip trembled as she spoke, and a single tear trickled from her eye.

'Tony, I've loved you for as long as I care to remember. I don't want to lose another minute grieving and being depressed. Mikey has gone now, and so have mom and dad. I'll love them all forever, but I have to carry on, and I want to carry on with you. All I want to do now is spend time with you.' Tony smiled and wiped her eyes, and he kissed her now. They both discussed it further as they walked along.

It was dark now, and the stars glimmered in the sky like diamonds. It was still Christmas Day, and they were enjoying the evening together. They walked out of the park now through Cumberland Gate and along Bayswater Road as they held hands. Anyone that saw them together knew they were in love. They always looked so happy together, and as they walked home they stopped on the corner of Connaught Street. He took her in his arms as kissed her passionately.

'Baby, I love you so much, and I just want to be with you. No matter where that is.' She smiled and took his hand in her as they walked home.

That night Hannah and Tony made love again. His big muscular arms engulfed her and protected her. He lowered her gently onto the bed, resting her head on the soft feather pillow, and he allowed himself a moment to let his fingers roam and explore her softy creamy ⌣ teasing her nipples as she lay naked in front of him.

She closed her eyes and savoured the moment. He kissed her tummy, and then her breasts. He teased her clitoris that only heightened her pleasure. He kissed her lips as she kept her eyes closed, and he ran his fingers lightly over her bare skin, sending a cold shudder through her body.

He took a piece of satin cloth and blindfolded her, as she moaned with pleasure. Then he took another and bound her wrists to the bed frame.

'Mmm, Tony. I didn't know you could be so kinky.' She almost whispered, and her voice was sexy. He ran his fingers the length of her body, from top to bottom. He reached over to the bedside table and took the bottle of massage oil, and let it trickle like maple syrup on to her soft pure skin. She flinched and giggled as the oil first touched her skin, and moaned with pleasure as he rubbed it softly into her soft skin.

The aroma from the scented candles was only heightening her pleasure. As every moment passed she wanted him more and more, but he was waiting for the right moment. She felt his hand touch and caress every part of her body, and after a while he untied her binds and turned her over. He bound her wrists again, and dribbled the scented oil on her back. She was startled as the lukewarm liquid touched her skin, and she groaned intensely as he massaged her back and neck, and feeling his hard erection against her soft skin only made her want him more.

'Oh, God, Tony. Make love to me. Make love to me.' He only ignored her pleas as he continued massaging her neck. He was waiting for the right moment, until she could take no more.

'Oh, baby, please. I want you so much.' He slowly untied her wrists, and the moment she was free she grabbed his crotch.

'Oh, baby, give it to me.' She took her blindfold off now and pushed him down onto the bed and straddled him.

Pushing herself down onto him she groaned as she felt him deep inside her. He grabbed her breasts as she felt the edge of an orgasm. She almost screamed, but managed to control herself as he reached a climaxed. Her face contorted as she felt every drop, and moments later she felt the warm slippery goo leave her body as she too reached a climax.

They lay spent and exhausted next to each other, both of them naked with only a thin satin sheet covering her middle.

'Oh, Tony, that was fantastic.' She reached over and grabbed his face and kissed him passionately. It was almost midnight when they finally switched the light out and fell asleep, contended in each others arms.

The following morning Hannah and Tony were still asleep at nine thirty. Lesley had cooked a full breakfast that morning, and she and Steve were eating the last of the bacon in a sandwich when Hannah and Tony finally surfaced. They both walked into the kitchen and plonked themselves at the breakfast table.

'Do you want some coffee darlings? I've just made a fresh pot,' Lesley asked. Tony had been giving Hannah's suggestion of moving to Devon a lot of thought since she mentioned it, and the more he thought about it, the more it appealed to him. He had always loved Devon after holidaying there with a group of old school pals seven years ago. Now that he's quit his job at his uncles law firm, maybe he'd start his own business in Devon.

He'd given it a lot of thought all that day and mentioned it to Hannah at lunchtime. Hannah was of cause thrilled, but the idea of mentioning it to her aunt and sisters didn't exactly sit well with her. Though they wouldn't be living there permanently. They would just escape there once in a while, and it would be perfect for them if they ever got married.

At five-thirty Lesley started preparing tea. Steve prepared the potatoes while Lesley contented herself with the joint. There was only Steve and Lesley, and Tony and the sisters and Julie for tea. Everyone else had gone home, and after lunch was prepared and cooking Hannah and Tony gathered everyone in the lounge to discuss their idea.

Hannah was smiling. In fact almost ecstatic at the idea of having somewhere private just for her and Tony, and she couldn't wait to start looking. They all sat curiously in the lounge now as they waited, and Hannah stood up holding Tony's hand.

'Tony and I have been doing a lot of thinking over the past couple of days, and with everything that's happened since Mikey died, we've decided to go for it.' Everyone looked curious now, and Abbie smiled.

'Well, what is it?'

'We want to start looking for another property. Somewhere for me and Hannah to escape to sometimes,' Tony said.

'I know we've got the house in Bude, but sometimes me and Tony just want to be alone.' Hannah caught a glimpse of her sisters faces now and she realised that they must have heard them making love last night, and Hannah blushed a little.

'What are you saying, darling,' Lesley asked as she went to her niece.

'We're obviously keeping the house in Bude, as it's where we all live, and I hope we go back there soon, but Tony and I just want somewhere private together. So we're going to start looking for somewhere in Devon. It's not that far from Bude,' Hannah said then. Lesley was a little confused and unsure of their ideas, but they were all happy for them. Steve went and shook Tony's hand and hugged Hannah as her sisters eyed her curiously.

'There's another reason why we are all gathered here,' Tony said now, and even Hannah looked curious as her sisters noticed.

I've also been doing a lot of thinking about something else, and after nearly nine years I'm finally going to do it,' he said as Hannah smiled curiously. He turned to Hannah now and took her hand in his, as Abbie and Danni nearly laughed.

'Hannah, baby. We've loved each other for as long as I can remember, and I think it's time we sealed that bond.' Tears welled in Hannah's eyes now as she realised, and Lesley got the tissues ready. Tony pulled the ring from his pocket, and held it for Hannah to see.

'Hannah, will you make me the happiest man on earth, and be my wife?' Lesley passed Hannah a tissue now as she cried.

'Yes. Yes,' she cried. Tony stood up and whooped with glee, and picked Hannah up and spun her around. Tony placed the ring on her finger as she laughed, and she turned to her sisters who hugged her now.

'Congratulations, sis', Danni said. Steve went to Tony and shook his hand and congratulated him, and Lesley laughed as she went to her niece and hugged her.

'Congratulations, darling.' With all the commotion going on Lesley had forgot all about the potatoes, that were now burning.

'What that smell?' Abbie asked.

'Oh darn, the potatoes.' Lesley ran into the kitchen as the smoke alarm started beeping. Steve opened the back door and the kitchen window as Lesley dropped the saucepan in the sink.

'Oh, bugger.' They all looked at each other now and started laughing, and after a while Lesley prepared some more potatoes.

Chapter Eighteen

It was only a couple of days to the new year, and everyone around London was preparing for the biggest party celebration they'd ever seen, but in the quiet street of Hyde Park Street and Connaught Street the celebrations were not quite so extravagant.

Lights hung from every street light and in every window along the street, and over at the community hall food and drinks were being prepared for the streets party. The reverend Joe Watson was going to lead the community in a mass prayer on New Years Eve.

Hannah and Tony were going to Covent Garden today on a shopping trip, and then on to Harrods and Leicester Square and Piccadilly Circus. There was a sharp chill in the air, and Hannah shuddered and wrapped her scarf tighter around her. They held hands as they walked along, whispering sweet nothings to each other and talking about the engagement. Hannah still wasn't a hundred percent better after her breakdown. Though she was a lot happier now, she still had the odd nightmare about Mikey and her parents, and sometimes she was seen crying when she thought no one was looking.

It was only Tony that seemed to fuss over her now, and just last night he comforted her when she woke up crying. She was still taking antidepressants, and her mood swings had stopped. Steve had said just last night how much happier she was.

At one-thirty Hannah and Tony went for some lunch at the Cigala Spanish restaurant on Lamb's Conduit Street to celebration their engagement. The grand piano played softly in the background, while all around secret lovers dined and talked romantically under the soft lights.

Lyndsey was at work today at the restaurant, and Hannah couldn't wait to tell her the happy news. Hannah was wearing her long flowing red and white dress, buttoned down the front, with a simple scarf rolled and tied at the waist. Her long black hair, shiny and loose. She smiled warmly as they were greeted and shown to a table, where the waitress lit a candle on the table, and moments later she bought them two menus as Lyndsey came through from the kitchen with a selection of cakes and pastries she had delicately made for the counter display. She smiled warmly when she saw them, and went to greet them. Hannah casually held her hand out, and gently tapped her fingers on the table, and Lyndsey smiled gloriously as she saw the gleaming diamond.

'Oh, Hannah, that's fantastic.' She kissed her and looked to Tony.

'And it's about time too,' she said hugging Tony. Tony wore his light beige suit, with his shirt collar loose, and he smiled shyly as Lyndsey congratulated them both. Tony was never short on the romance when it came to Hannah. He always liked to wine and dine her, and show her off and let everyone know they were together. Even when they split up nine years ago, they were still often seen out at some lavish restaurant together.

Lyndsey had all her hair tied up under a hairnet and wearing her tall chefs hat. Not very flattering, she always thought, but even when she greeted and talked to the customers, she always looked professional in her whites.

A waitress came over, and Tony ordered the bottle of Chardonnay. He ordered the Buey a la brasa, and Hannah ordered the Paella de pollo y pilotes.

Tony was always so romantic. Ever since he and Hannah left school, he was forever wanting to wine and dine her in expensive restaurants.

Hannah was positively radiant as she sat there. She kept looking at the ring on her finger, and wanting to pinch herself to see if she was dreaming. Ever since Hannah could remember, she always wanted to be Tony's wife. She always wanted to be Mrs Hannah Craven.

Everyone at school was always jealous of them. The girls were always eyeing Tony and chatting him up, and the boys were always following her around. Tony was "The Stud". He was the one that won Hannah's heart. He was the one trailing around with her and holding her hand. He was the one always caught behind the bike sheds with Hannah in his arms.

Though Hannah always seemed timid and shy at school, she did had a wild side. It wasn't very often she shown it, and it wasn't very often she needed to, unless she saw some tart trying to get off with Tony at school.

Hannah beamed now as she sat across the table holding Tony's hand. Everyone who noticed them walk into the restaurant could tell they were in love, and more than once someone went over and commented, and congratulated them when Hannah shown her ring. Lyndsey's manager saw them now, and he smiled and greeted them.

'Miss Philips and Mr Craven. Always such a delight to see you both,' he said and kissed Hannah's hand.

'Mr Benning. I see Lyndsey has delighted herself in telling you our happy news,' Hannah said as he took her hand and kissed her fingers. Hannah stood up and greeted him as she smiled. Her long black hair cascading sensually over her shoulders.

'Carlos, please. We're almost family, you know,' he said.

'OK, then I insist you call me Hannah,' she smiled. Carlos snapped his fingers and a waitress went over to their table.

'Hannah, Tony,' he said as Hannah smiled.

'This is Louisa, and she will be your waitress this afternoon. Please take a moment to look through our menus, and please accept your choices on the me.'

'Oh, Carlos, no. We can't do that.' Hannah felt awkward and guilty now.

'Yes you can. I insist. Just a small token of best wishes to the both of you.'

'Thank you Carlos. That's wonderful,' She stood up and kissed his cheek and smiled.

'Louisa, these are two of my finest customers. Please give them anything they want from the menu,' he said as Louisa smiled.

Hannah and Tony carried on talking as they waited for their food, and moments later Hannah looked round and saw a little Spanish girl, with the brownest eyes and the cutest smile standing next to her. Her hair tied in braids with little red bows on the ends. She smiled, showing all her teeth, and she gave Hannah a flower.

'*Es una señora muy bonita.*' Hannah smiled, and looked puzzled.

'Sorry.' The little girl skipped away smiling, and Hannah smiled as she watched her disappear around the corner.

'She said, you are a very pretty lady. And I have to agree with her.' Hannah looked up and saw a tall dark haired gentleman standing there with the little girl in his arms.

'Benito?'

'Hello gorgeous. I see you haven't changed. You're still looking as beautiful as ever.' Hannah smiled embarrassingly as Benito put the child down and Hannah hugged him as they both laughed. Benito was the same age as Hannah, and they hadn't seen each other for nearly ten years. Hannah pulled away from him now and smiled. Benito saw Tony then, and the two men shook hands and greeted each other.

'So Benito, what brings you around here? The last I heard you had your own restaurant in Spain.'

'Yes I have. I just flew into England yesterday to visit my uncle.' Benito looked at the little girl now as she sat on his knee.

'Hannah, Tony. Say hello to my eight year old daughter, Maria.' Hannah went to speak to the child, but Benito stopped her.

'Sorry, she only understands Spanish.'

'*Eres una niña muy bonita.*' The little girl smiled as Benito raised his eyes brows curiously.

'I'm impressed. I didn't know you could speak Spanish.'

'Mmm. There's a lot you don't know about me Benito,' she smiled.

Moments later the waitress bought Hannah's and Tony's order, and Hannah turned her attention to Tony and her meal, as Benito disappeared with his daughter.

Lesley and Steve went out for the evening that night. Steve had booked tickets for a show at the Phoenix. It was New Years Eve, and as they walked down the street holding hands new year celebrations were all in full swing all across London.

In the distant fireworks exploded and music was playing, but Steve and Lesley were more interested in each other than the goings on around them. They were looking forward to their wedding in May, and after Hannah and Tony announced their engagement, they booked their wedding for the same time.

'Why not a joint wedding, auntie?,' Hannah had suggested. Lesley and Steve thought it was a wonderful idea. Hannah had always wanted to see Las Vegas, and was looking forward to when they went there for their honeymoon. Steve and Lesley wanted something a bit more romantic, so Steve was going to surprise her with a trip to Venice. Lesley didn't know yet, though she knew they were going on a honeymoon, but Steve wanted to surprise her.

It was almost nine o'clock in the evening, and Steve and Lesley were looking forward to seeing their first New Year in together. Steve had bought some champagne, and they were all going to see the New Year in together.

Bill and Rosie were coming round, and so were Frank and Sally. Frank was bringing his wife and daughter, and Sally was bringing some of her friends as well. Steve thought about doing a barbeque, and there were cases of beer and champagne and wine, and Lesley had got some pepsi and lemonade for the children too.

Everyone in the street were involved, and they were going to have one big street party together with friends and family.

Steve and Lesley walked together holding hands along Bayswater Road and Park Lane. Lesley always felt unnerving walking alone in the dark, especially alongside the park, but with Steve she felt safe. In fact she felt more than safe. She felt secure and protected.

It had been so long since Lesley had felt safe walking anywhere at night. Usually she got Duncan to take her somewhere, or she got a taxi. It was very rare she used public transport, unless she was with someone she knew.

Steve and Lesley were talking about the wedding, and Lesley was already talking about the honeymoon. Lesley didn't know that Steve had already planned and booked the trip to Venice. He wanted to wait till the last minute to tell her.

All along Hyde Park Street and Connaught Street, all the neighbours and friends stood together as the minutes counted down to midnight, but somewhere along the Thames Steve and Lesley held hands as they counted down.

Five . . . Four . . . Three . . . Two . . . One . . .

In the distance, the neighbours could hear the chimes of Big Ben, and streets full of cheers and screams, as Steve and Lesley had their first kiss of the New Year. For Lesley it was the most thrilling moment of her life. To be kissing the man she loved as they saw in the New Year, and as Steve held her face he felt tears on her cheeks. He pulled away, and smiled. Then he pulled her close and their lips met again, and it seemed forever until they finally pulled away from each other again.

They took a slow walk back to the street. They walked along Whitehall and onto Pall Mall and onto St James Street and Piccadilly. It was almost one o'clock in the morning when they arrived back to the street, and the party was still in full swing.

There were burgers and hotdogs on the barbeque, and all around the neighbours sang and danced in the street. No one cared how much they drank. Not even Steve and Bill. Bill wasn't on duty again until the fourth of January, so he had plenty of time to sleep it off.

Steve and Lesley spotted Hannah and Tony, and Hannah smiled wickedly as she could only guess what her aunt had been up to.

Steve got himself and Lesley some champagne and they disappeared again somewhere. Probably to his car outside Lesley's. Not so discreet, he thought, but as everyone was enjoying themselves in their own way, they wouldn't be noticed, and moments later Danni disappeared with Jason.

Jason had come down from Bude the day before yesterday to spend time with Danni. His restaurant was closed till after the new year, so he had plenty of time to spend with Danni and catch up on old times.

Though Jason was still cautious around Danni, especially since Mikey died, they both seemed to be hitting it off together now. Now Hannah was a lot better, and happy again with Tony, Danni and Abbie could concentrate more on their own grieving, and Danni chose to let Jason help her through her troubled times.

Danni walked off up the street as she held onto Jason's arm, and as they turned the corner at the end of Connaught Street, Danni leaned into Jason and stole a kiss. Hannah smiled watching them as they disappeared around the corner, and she was happy for her sister.

Danni and Jason had a lot of catching up to do, seven years to be precise. It was almost three o'clock in the morning, and Danni wasn't the slightest bit tired. She smiled as she cuddled up to Jason on a bench along Edgware Road. Their lips met, and their arms entangled around each other, but Jason pulled away from her. Danni looked confused as he looked lovingly at her.

'Are you sure you're ready for this?' Danni only smiled and pulled him close and kissed him.

'Jason, my mind all so messed up at the moment. I'm sorry I seemed distant when we first saw each other in Bude, but I can't grieve for Mikey anymore. Helping Hannah through her depression has sort of helped me to grieve. Mikey's gone, and I'll always love him, but I need to carry on living, and I want to do it with you.' Jason smiled and kissed her.

'I'll always be here for you, Danni. No matter what. I thought I lost you once, and I had got used to the fact that I would never see you again, but that day you came into my restaurant I couldn't believe my luck. I had the chance of love again.' He pulled further away from her now and looked deep into her blue eyes.

'I love you Danni Philips. I don't think I've ever stopped loving you. I don't ever want to be away from you again.' Danni smiled and kissed him now as Jason brushed his fingers through her long blond hair.

'Danni, I don't know if it's too soon, but I'm prepared to wait either way, but I hope in time you get used to me being around, because I don't ever want to be away from you again.' She leaned into him, and their lips met again. Running his fingers through her hair, he felt his heart pounding. For Jason, Danni had been his only sweetheart, and now he knew he had found his only true love.

It seemed hours before they pulled away from each other as they sat on the bench on Edgware Road, and he looked at her now and laughed.

'Jesus, Danni. What're you doing to me?' Jason seemed all hot and flustered as he stood up and paced. He couldn't ever remember feeling like this before, even when he and Danni were at school.

'I don't know what you're doing to me, Danni, but I like it.' Danni laughed now as she took his hands in hers.

'Jason, baby. I think it's amazing that we found each other again, and I think we should take it as a sign.' She looked deep into his green eyes now and ran her fingers through his short brown curls, and she seemed to be floating on love, and it wasn't long before they'd locked themselves into another embrace.

Hannah and Tony walked along holding hands as they looked across the Thames to see the first of the sunlight creep across the land. A cold frost had settled, and Hannah felt chilled in only her thin blouse and cardigan. She stood in Tony's embrace, and their lips met again before they headed home.

Traces of last nights party was still strewn across Hyde Park Street and Connaught Street. The barbeque was still standing at the end of the street by the entrance of the memorial garden, and the street looked like a ghost town. Everyone was under the covers of their homes now, as some were just going to bed, but Hannah and Tony weren't the slightest bit tired. They crept quietly into the house and up the stairs, and switching the light off they both climbed into bed.

Hannah snuggled up to Tony and wrapped her arms around him. Tony could feel her nice warm body against his, her long black hair tickled his face, and he leaned into her and they kissed.

It was electric as their lips sparked. His hands were all over her, caressing her soft skin. His hands cupped her soft white breasts, and seemed to wander all over her naked flesh, feeling every curve of her voluptuous body. Her fingers running through his short bond hair, both of them ravaging, both of them hungry for each other. Kissing every square inch of her silky smooth skin, his hand disappeared between her legs.

Her back arched against the soft silk sheets as he teased her clitoris. He kissed her crotch, and then her hips, working his way back up her body until their lips met again, and she let out a scream as he pushed his way in.

'Oh, Jesus.'

She held him tight in her arms feeling every move he made, their bodies entwined, like twigs growing around each other. Thrusting deeper, she only screamed louder as he covered her mouth. His hands cupped her breasts, and then they both clenched as she reached a climax.

Like a single moment froze in time, he paused, feeling her body shaking, then thrusting deep he only continued to pleasure her, until they both lay spent in each others arms.

Chapter Nineteen

It was ten-thirty in the morning on New Years Day, and as Abbie sat at the breakfast table nursing a sore head, everyone else was still in the warmth of their beds. Abbie had found the paracetamol, and swallowed two with a mouthful of coffee. Coffee that was now almost cold. She poured the rest down the sink and poured herself a fresh cup, as Jason walked into the kitchen.

'Morning Jason. There's a fresh pot of coffee there if you want some.' Abbie was only in her nightshirt, and had gone upstairs now for a shower, leaving Jason in the kitchen.

Abbie stripped off and turned the shower on and let the water run hot before stepping in. She went to the mirror and stared horribly at herself with disgust.

'Oh, man. Did I get wasted last night?,' she mumbled to herself. Abbie always got drunk too quick when she drank alcohol, especially when she was on the vodka. Though she was rarely sick. She just regretted the next morning. She wasn't usually a heavy drinker. She only drank on special occasions or at parties.

She peeled off her knickers and let them drop to the floor and she stepped into the shower. She stood there for a moment and just let the hot steaming water caress every part of naked body.

At twenty years old, Abbie had always prided herself on her ample figure. Though she has always come across as a tomboy over the years, Abbie had turned into a fine lady over the past few months. Her size twelve waist, her long auburn hair, and her ample bosom made her look every bit a lady.

Ste stood naked in the middle of the bathroom drying herself, and her aunt knocked the door.

'Abbie, darling. Is that you in the bathroom?'

'Yes, auntie. I'll be out in a sec.'

'Would you like some bacon a eggs?'

'Yes please.'

Abbie went to the bedroom and got dressed. She was feeling a bit better now, though she was still feeling the effects of last night. She walked into the kitchen with a towel wrapped around her head, and plonked herself at the table as Lesley put a full breakfast in front of her, and moments later Steve walked in tying his dressing gown around him, having just got out of bed.

'Morning, darling,' he said and kissed Lesley. He picked up a two week old newspaper and sat at the table.

'How you feeling this morning, Abbie?'

'Like I've just been dragged from the bottom of the scrap heap,' she said and smiled.

'I think I had just a little too much to drink last night,' she said then.

'Well, it is the New Year. You're allowed to go wild occasionally. Just as long as you don't go round swinging your knickers in the air every time,' Steve said and winked at Lesley. Abbie looked horrified for a moment and looked to her aunt.

'Auntie, I didn't, did I?' Steve laughed then, and Lesley hit him on his arm.

'Don't pay any attention to him darling. He's just teasing you.'

'Oh, Steve, you rat.' She threw a newspaper at him then, but he ducked out the way as she laughed. Abbie had been known to go a little crazy when she's been on the booze, especially if she was drinking with the lads from the rugby team, but she was thankful that that wasn't very often. And she never got that drunk she forgot what she'd done the night before.

By eleven o'clock it looked as though Lesley was cooking breakfast for the entire street. Julie had stayed the night last night in one of the spare rooms, and Hollie and her daughters were there with Raymond and Lyndsey and their daughters, and Desmond had come round just after ten o'clock looking a bit worse-for-wear.

Lesley has always liked a good crowd around the table, whether it be for breakfast or lunch, and she was always happy to dish up her favourite bacon and eggs for friends.

Hannah was improving all the time now, as her memory was slowly coming back. She wasn't taking her medication anymore either. She didn't see the point in taking them anymore, as she was improving.

She had felt a bit embarrassed when her aunt and sisters told her how she wanted to strip off in front of everyone one afternoon, and how she'd gone to the memorial garden in the night and fell asleep, and how they had to feed her and wash and dress her, and she was so apologetic when they told her that she forgot peoples names and crying fits all the time.

Hannah was forever grateful to everyone for all their help, and she can't stop thanking her sisters for everything they'd done for her since Mikey died.

Hannah and her sisters were going back into work tomorrow morning. They wanted to try and get back to normal now that Christmas and the New Year was over. Hannah still had the occasional nightmare about Mikey, and sometimes she seemed depressed, but getting back to normal might help her to carry on, she thought.

Hannah and Tony had gone out together on their own on the afternoon of New Years day. They went for a stroll in Hyde Park. They talked about their future plans and buying a cottage in Torquay. Hannah was going to get onto the travel agents in a few day and book the hotel, in the meantime Tony was seriously considering starting his own business in Bude. Maybe he would start his own hotel and restaurant, he thought, or maybe he would start up his own catering firm. He hadn't decided yet, though.

He had enough savings to tide him over until he decided. For now he was just happy being with Hannah.

Over the next few days, Hannah and her sisters contented themselves with the office. There were several meeting booked for the following weeks, and they had plenty to catch up on in the meantime.

It was the first week in January, and Hannah had her appointment with Dr Manns at St Mary's. She was looking forward for him to give her the all clear, but she was a bit worried that he might say she needs more time to get over her loss, but as she walked into his office on the second floor at St Mary's, she couldn't have looked more radiant.

'Well, Hannah. You certainly look a whole lot better since the last time we saw each other.'

'Well, I feel fantastic, doctor. Though I still get the occasional nightmare, I'd like to think I'm cured.' Dr Manns was looking at her strangely now, and it made Hannah feel awkward as she shuffled in her seat.

'I don't expect you to believe what happened the morning of Christmas Day. I still have trouble believing it myself, but there were fourteen other people who witnessed what happened.'

'I'm not saying I don't believe you, Hannah. To someone who doesn't believe in the afterlife, it would be a very tall story. I believe your parents and Mikey visited you, in some form or another, because frankly, there's no other logic reason for you to get well so quickly,' he chuckled. Hannah smiled now. She was worried that he wouldn't believe her story.

'I see no reason that you can't stop taking your antidepressants, but if you feel you need to take more, then don't hesitate, and don't hesitate in calling me if you feel you need to talk. I had a lot of respect for your parents. Their passing had shocked a lot of people in this hospital.' Hannah smiled and thanked the doctor, and shortly after she left feeling on top of the world.

The following morning Hannah was delighted to be returning to the office, though she wasn't looking forward to see the scene of Oxford Street from her window after Mikey died. She was thinking of moving offices, but she wasn't sure yet.

She smiled to herself as she sat at her dressing table pulling her tights on, and she went to the wardrobe and picked out a dress. It had been so long she wore a dress to work. Normally she only wore a trouser suit.

She stood in front of the mirror examining herself, and she smiled at what she saw. A simple black and white dress with her grandmother broach. Her long shiny black hair hung loose down her back with a string of small pearls around her neck, and her expensive designer gold Gucci watch.

'Perfect.' She grabbed her high heels from the wardrobe and swung her mink jacket over one shoulder and made her way downstairs, and when she walked into the kitchen at just after eight o'clock everyone stopped and stared.

'Wow, sis.' Her sisters thought she looked like a model just stepped out of Cosmopolitan, as Danni went to examine her, and Lesley beamed at her.

'Darling, you look stunning. I haven't seen you wearing a dress for years.'

'What, this old thing,' she joked. She did a twirl, and smiled.

'It does look fantastic, doesn't it?,' she laughed. Tony walked through from the lounge a few minutes later, and stopped dead in his tracks.

'Wow. Who is this sexy model? And what have you done with my frumpy girlfriend?,' he said as he went to kiss her. Danni and Abbie gasped sharply and Tony just laughed as Hannah swung her handbag at him.

Hannah only had beans on toast for breakfast that morning, and just before nine o'clock she and her sisters left for the office. They took Hannah's Bentley, and ten minutes later Hannah pulled into the underground car park at Philips & Co.

'Good morning, Tom.'

'Good morning, Miss Philips. It's good to see you're better again.'

'Thanks Tom.'

At fifty-four Tom Jordan had been the security guard at Philips & Co for almost thirty-six years. He started there in 1970. He has always enjoyed working for the Philips family, and has plenty of happy memories there.

Tom raised the barrier and Hannah pulled into her usual space and the girls made their way upstairs. Abbie went to the kitchen and switch the coffee maker on, and Hannah went straight to her office, and moments later when Raymond came in he stopped and stared at Hannah as she stood at the window talking on the phone.

Tony had spent the morning booking the coach tickets for his and Hannah's trip to Torquay. They were going to travel by National Express. More comfortable than the train, but take a little longer to get there, he thought, and afterwards he went home and surfed the internet to find a suitable hotel. They wanted a hotel near the coast, though they were looking for property out in the country, hopefully somewhere near the town. Tony and Hannah just wanted somewhere private so they could be alone together from time to time.

They could drive out there once or twice a month, have a quiet weekend together and drive back afterwards for Monday morning. Tony has already started looking into starting his own business. He has decided to take up freelance photography, and maybe in the summer he would start a surf club for the Torquay area as well.

That afternoon Hannah and Raymond walked into the boardroom on the fourth floor and greeted their clients, and moments later Danni walked in as their secretary bought in a pot of coffee. Abbie was staying out of the meetings for a while as she wanted to study and read through files.

She had enrolled into Cambridge for September for a three year course in law, and she couldn't wait to start. Though she had said to her sisters that it was just like going back to school. Abbie had always hated school. She wasn't very popular amongst the girls, as she always liked hanging out with the lads. The girls sometimes teased her for being a tomboy and wanting to scrum with the lads when they played football.

Hannah was always the popular one at school, and more than once she had to step in to defend Abbie when the other girls picked on her. Hannah always came across as petite and quiet, and sometimes shy and demure, but she had a temper on her that most of the school saw occasionally. She had more than once put some lad on his back after he'd bullied Abbie, and only once she was sent home after breaking someone's arm for picking on Danni.

Abbie and Danni have always looked up to their sister with pride, though sometimes they were jealous of her for being so popular. Abbie was always contented on the way she was, but sometimes Danni cried because she wanted to be like her older sister.

'You are who you are, sis'. And one day soon people will appreciate you for that,' Hannah had said comforting her one day.

That evening Danni and Jason had gone out for the evening. He surprised her with a candlelit dinner at the Le Gavroche French restaurant in the heart of Mayfair. A swanky restaurant with the personal touch. Jason always tried to provide just the service in his restaurant, but he thought the Le Gavroche was more stylish.

Danni was wearing her new Ralph Lauren black knee-length dress with sequins down the front, with a simple ankle chain. Her new diamond necklace and earrings that Jason bought her for Christmas, and her new Lacoste watch her aunt bought her.

She felt a warm glow as she held Jason's arm and walked into the Le Gavroche, and she leaned into him and kissed him as a young woman came to greet them.

'Hello, and welcome to the Le Gavroche,' she smiled. The woman took some menus from the counter and led them to a table underneath a painting by Picasso, and Danni smiled at the extravagance of the place. She glanced around at the watercolours and the paintings on the walls, and then her eyes met Jason's. She held his hand across the table.

'I love you,' she mouthed.

'I love you too, he mouthed back.

Moments later a waitress came over and took their orders. Jason ordered the *Escalopé de Foie Gras Chand et Pastilla à la Cannelle* for himself, and for Danni she ordered the *Fricassée de St. Pierre Façon Bouillabaisse.*

Soft French music played in the background as the waitresses busied themselves, and Danni smiled as to herself feeling the calm and relaxed atmosphere. She glanced all around at the other patrons in the restaurant as they engaged themselves in conversation, and she turned to Jason and smiled.

At twenty-three, Jason was thinking of expanding his restaurant in Bude and open another one in London.

Now that he had found Danni again, he wasn't prepared to be away from her again. He had spent long enough time in London over the past few months, and he kind of liked the Marylebone area. Maybe he would take a while to look around. First he would need to get back to Bude and speak to the head chef at the Carriers Inn, so he could leave someone in charge while he was away.

Danni held onto Jason's arm as they took a slow walk. It was almost nine o'clock when they left the restaurant, and they walked along Park Lane and Bayswater Road, and as they reached the end of Albion Street Danni turned and faced him. Their lips met and her arms snaked around his waist. He held her tight in his arms, not wanting to let her go, and she whispered sensually into his ear.

'I love you Jason Thomas.' They walked along Connaught Street, and when they reach the front door she turned to him and they stole another kiss, and then they held hands as they walked into the house.

Chapter Twenty

It was the weekend, and as Danni stood on the doorstep waving Jason off, she felt a sudden loss and a void in her life already. She ran to his car and poked her head through the open window and stole a last kiss before he pulled off.

Jason was going back to Bude for a few weeks to sort out the restaurant. He was hopefully only going to be a month at the most, but for Danni it was a lifetime.

'I love you Danni.'

'I love you too, baby.'

'See you in four weeks,' he said. They kissed again, and she stood back and watched him drive off. She walked slowly back to the house, and she saw Hannah in the kitchen. Danni wiped her eyes as she sat at the table, and Hannah smiled and went to her.

'You really do love him, don't you?'

'Yeah, I do. I can't live without him now I've got him back.' Hannah sat down and comforted her now, and Hannah smiled.

'I told you you'd find happiness again one day, sis'. Danni looked confused now and looked at her sister.

'What do you mean?'

'Don't you remember when we were at school, and how popular I was, and you said you always wanted to be like me? And I said, you are who you are. Well, you're happy now, aren't you?' Danni thought about it now, and she smiled remembering that day.

'Jeez, sis'. You remembered that?'

'I remember a lot of things from when we were at school. I remember how you were always jealous of me and Tony. You wished you could have had that kind of relationship with Jason. I remember how you were sometimes sad because you were picked on.' Danni smiled now listening, and a single tear trickled from her eye as the memories came back.

'I remember how you always come to my defence whenever I was picked on,' Danni said now.

'I was always secretly proud of you sis'. You were always a sister I could look up to, and be proud of,' she said then. Hannah stood up and hugged her sister now, and tears filled Danni's eyes.

'I love you sis', Danni said.

'I love you too, Danni. And I hope you and Jason will be as happy as me and Tony are. You deserve a bit of happiness. You just make sure he takes care of you, or I'll find the nearest lamppost and hang him from it.' They both laughed then as Hannah wiped her sisters eyes.

'Yeah. And I can really imagine you doing that as well,' Danni laughed as they both remembered how tough Hannah could be. Sweet, but deadly, Tony used to call her.

It was Saturday afternoon, and Lesley was cooking a beef curry for tea. The smell in the kitchen was delicious as she mixed in her own secret spices, and moments later when Steve walked in the kitchen he seemed carried away with the aroma.

Steve had had a lot of time on his hands now since he gave up work, and he wasn't used to it. Though he and Lesley were engaged now, and they always had something to do together, he was always used to working. Even when he was married before, the force was his life.

Though his ex-wife always moaned that he was married to his job more than her, He had said as much to Lesley one evening, and she had to agree.

'Why don't you ask Bill if you can go back to work now that were back in London?,' she told him. Steve had considered it many times. Even when the girls decide to go back to Bude, and they will one day, Lesley thought, she and Steve could still stay in London and just visit them whenever Steve had time off.

Steve was going to discuss it with Bill on Monday. After all, he was only forty-three, and he could still have a good career in the force.

That evening Steve and Lesley discussed it further as they walked together in Regents Park, and when they returned home they discussed it with her nieces. Lesley was happy with her life with Steve now, and couldn't imagine being without him, but she wasn't thrill on not seeing him while he was at work. Lesley was thinking of doing some part time work too, just to fill in her time. If her nieces decided to go back to Bude she would have a lot of free time on her hands, and if Steve went back to work, she would want something to do during the day.

'Whatever makes you happy Steve,' Danni said as they discussed it.

'We know that you liked your job in the force, and we kind of felt guilty that we asked you to give it up and move with us before,' Abbie said as she went and sat with him. Abbie cuddled up to Steve, and he put his arm around her.

'We love you, and if you return to work it doesn't mean that we won't see each other.' Steve cuddled her now, and she rested her head on his shoulder.

Steve was always so easy-going. It was one of his best qualities that Lesley loved about him. Whenever he walked into a room there was an instant calmness about him that people always noticed.

Lesley cuddled up to him on the sofa that evening as they watched television. Hannah and Tony had gone out, and so had Danni and Jason.

Over the following few day Hannah and Tony prepared for their holiday to Torquay. Danni and Abbie weren't thrilled at the idea of being away from their sister for two weeks, but they realised that they just wanted to alone together occasionally. Though Danni was more upset and lonely as Jason had gone back to Bude for four weeks.

It was Monday morning, and Hannah and Tony were leaving on Friday for two weeks. Hannah was excited about the holiday. Two whole weeks alone with Tony. Tony had booked the tickets, and they were going to travel on the Friday afternoon.

Hannah thought about it now as she stood at the window in her office staring out onto Oxford Street, and she seemed in a world of her own as her secretary knocked the door.

'Miss Philips?' Hannah never answered as she continued to stare out of the window.

'Miss Philips?' She touched Hannah on her arm, and Hannah was startled and looked round.

'Are you alright?'

'Yes thanks, Karen,' she smiled warmly. Hannah seemed flustered as she went back to her desk, and Karen seemed concerned. Hannah gathered up some files and left for the fourth floor. Karen watched her leave, and then went back to her desk.

'Good morning gentlemen. Sorry to have kept you waiting,' Hannah smiled as she walked into the boardroom.

Danni had taken herself down to Oxford Street that morning. She couldn't concentrate at work thinking of Jason. She spent the morning, and most of the afternoon looking around the shops. She took the bus to Piccadilly and Covent Gardens, and when she returned to the office she didn't seem any better.

She sat at her desk trying to shake off the blues, but by four o'clock she took herself home. Lesley was in the kitchen preparing tea, and Steve was in the lounge reading the newspaper. Lesley seemed startled when Danni came through the front door. She wasn't expecting her home till nearly six o'clock, and when she saw Danni's face she was immediately concerned.

'Darling, what's wrong?'

'I couldn't concentrate at work, so I thought I'd come home.' She never said another word as she went upstairs to her room to lie down. She switched her stereo on and put some music on and quietly cried to herself, and when Lesley went to check on her half an hour later she was fast asleep, though Lesley could clearly see that she'd been crying.

Lesley went downstairs to finish tea, and at six forty-five when Hannah and Abbie came through the door loaded with bags, Lesley was beside herself with worry over Danni.

'Darling, what's the matter with Danni? She came home and went straight to bed.'

'I think she's just missing Jason, auntie.' Hannah dumped her bags in the lounge and went to pour herself a coffee. Tea was almost ready, and she went upstairs to speak to Danni, but she was still asleep. She sat on the bed and stroked her face.

'Danni, wake up.' Danni slowly opened her eyes and squinted against the brightness.

'You OK sis'? Auntie said you looked as though you'd been crying.' Danni sat up and rubbed her eyes as she thought.

'I just miss Jason so much. I never thought I could miss someone this much, and it's only been a couple of days.' Hannah smiled and cuddled her.

'Come on, sis'. tea is nearly ready. Go and wash your face and I'll see you downstairs.' Danni looked in the mirror in her room and saw streaks down her face where she'd been crying.

'Oh, man. I look a mess.' She splashed water on her face and brushed her hair, and minutes later she sat down at the table, just as Steve was dishing up the pasta bake.

You alright, darling?'

'Yes thanks, auntie. I was just tired. I'm sorry I was a bit distant when I came in.' Lesley smiled as she poured Danni some juice and she sat down.

Danni stayed silent all through tea as she thought of Jason. Jason had been her only love. Even when he moved to Spain with his family she always thought about him, and now she'd got him back, he was all she thought about.

After they finished eating Hannah and Tony cleared the table and loaded the dishwasher while Lesley prepared dessert. Julie and Abbie started tidying the kitchen as Danni went upstairs to call Jason.

Danni had never been so depressed. She could barely eat her tea as she thought of Jason. All she wanted to do was take him in her arms and never let him go. She lay on the bed talking to him, and she smiled just hearing his voice.

'I miss you so much, Jason. When can you get back here?' She knew he'd got the restaurant to manage, and she was hoping he could get back sooner, but his answer didn't make her happy.

'*I have to stay here for at least two weeks. I've managed to find someone to stand in for me while I'm in London,*' he said.

Danni was now thinking of going to Bude just to be with him, but she didn't want to sound too clingy. If she went, would it scare him too much, she thought, or would it please him too to be near her.

She told him how she felt, and her idea of going there to be near him, and she smiled gloriously. Ten minutes later she hung up the phone and ran down the stairs.

'Well, you certainly look a lot happier, darling,' her aunt said as she sat at the kitchen table.

'I've just been speaking to Jason.'

'That figures,' Hannah joked as she laughed.

'Jason wants me to go to Bude to be with him. I think he's missing me too,' she said.

'Ahh, isn't that sweet. Young love,' Steve joked. Danni skipped off upstairs then to decide what to pack. She was ecstatic that she was going to be alone with him for two or three weeks, and she couldn't wait to see him when she got there.

Chapter Twenty One

It was almost eight-forty-five in the evening, and Caroline was just leaving the London Palladium after seeing a show with her friends. They stood outside on the pavement talking for a while.

'You sure you don't want a lift, Cass'?' her friend asked.

'No, I'll be fine. It's only a fifteen minute walk down the road.' Caroline hugged and kissed her friends and then they went their separate ways. Caroline was listening to some music on her IPod as she walked home. It was dark as she walked along Oxford Street, and though she usually don't walk through the streets at night, she felt safe enough. Besides, she'd got her panic alarm, and she only lived down the road, she thought.

She got her IPod out and changed the music as she reached Marble Arch on the corner of Hyde Park, and up ahead she noticed someone walking towards her in dark clothes. She glanced briefly and crossed the road to avoid him, but moments later she felt the presence of someone near. She took her earphones off and half turned round, but it was too late.

He grabbed her around the throat, and with his free hand he pulled her to the ground by her hair. Kicking and screaming, she cried as she fought to get free. He dragged her into the park and threw her to the ground, and kneeling on her back she sobbed.

'Please let me go . . . Please don't hurt me . . .'

'Just shut the fuck up bitch and do as I say,' he said through gritted teeth. He pulled at her handbag and ransacked it, and seconds later she felt his hand around the waist of her jeans.

'Oh god, don't . . . please,' she cried. She tried to reach out and scratch at him, but he grabbed her by her hair and pulled her head back.

'I said shut the fuck up bitch.' He slammed her face into the dirt and she felt the hard blow of his fist against her face, and she felt almost dazed as she lay there. He turned her onto her back and bound her hands above her head, and she lay there struggling to free her hands as he pulled and tore at her jeans, and she sobbed as he pushed his hand into her knickers.

'Please just leave me alone,' she sobbed. She wanted to call out, but feared another blow to the head. She could see in the distance the passing pedestrians and traffic, but she was too scared to call out.

She felt the weight of him now on top of her, and she sobbed uncontrollably as she felt him inside her.

'Oh God, please help me.'

'God ain't gonna help you now bitch. He's on my side.' His face was inches from hers, but was too disfigured through her tears and the darkness.

He left her lying there afterwards, her clothes dirty and torn. She crawled under the nearest bush and curled herself up underneath it as she sobbed.

At home her parents were going frantic. Raymond had called Caroline's mobile phone several times, but just got her voicemail. It was almost ten-thirty, and Caroline said she would be home no later than nine o'clock.

He called her phone again, and then decided to call the police. Bill was on duty tonight and he called round to Raymond's straight away. Debbie was crying and Lyndsey was near tears when Bill knocked the door and walked in.

'Raymond, it's Bill.' Raymond went out to the hall and saw him standing there.

'Bill, something's happened to Caroline. It's not . . .'

'Raymond, calm down. Just sit down and tell me what's happened.' Bill got them all to sit down in the lounge and he asked where Caroline had been to and who with.

'Bill, Caroline left the concert at eight-thirty when it finished. She text me to say she was leaving, and the Palladium is only up the other end of Oxford Street. It doesn't take this long to walk home.' Bill was taking notes as Raymond talked to him.

'She's not answering her phone, and she should have been home no later than nine o'clock.' Bill knew Caroline just as well as her own father. He knew it wasn't like her not to call home if she was going to be late.

'Raymond, listen to me. I'm not going to waste time asking you all the usual questions, because I know Caroline. So all I can say now is just wait here by the phone and we'll go looking for her.'

'I'm coming with you.'

'Raymond, listen. It's no good you running around half cocked and fired up. Just sit . . .'

'Don't tell me what to do Bill,' he snapped.

'My daughter is out there somewhere in God only knows what state. I'm coming with you.' He never said another word as he grabbed his jacket. He kissed Lyndsey and Debbie, and he held Debbie's face and looked at her as she cried.

'Don't worry baby. We'll find Caroline and bring her home.' He kissed her on her head and then left as Bill was getting in the police car. Bill radioed control and got all available officers searching for Caroline. Lyndsey had contacted one of Caroline's friends, and they told her she was going to walk along Oxford Street. She relayed the message to Raymond, and they started searching along the park, and ten minutes later all the officers gathered around Bill at the entrance to Hyde Park.

'Listen up people. I don't need to tell you the urgency on this. So let's just start looking for Caroline. I want you to split up, and search every square inch of the park and surrounding areas.'

Bill walked away with Raymond hot on his heels. Everyone was calling out for Caroline, and moments later Steve pulled up outside the park with Desmond. They ran into the park calling out.

'Caroline. Caroline.' There was no sound apart from the different voices calling out for her, and the quiet sound of the night. Lights in and around the park gave them just enough light to see where they were going, and Bill had given everyone a torch.

'Caroline. Caroline.' Nothing. No response. Raymond and Bill knew in their gut that Caroline was somewhere in the park. A fathers intuition. Raymond called out in all directions, running in all directions.

'Come on baby, just one little sound. Tell me where you are. Caroline.' Winters was searching under the bushes and the undergrowth, and moments later he stood still as he thought he heard whimpering, but from everyone calling out for Caroline it was difficult to tell where it was coming from. He tried following the sound with his torch, shining the light in all directions.

'Come on Caroline. Give me a clue,' he said. He swung his torch in all directions, and moments later the light fell on a figure under a bush. He stepped closer keeping the light fixed on the bush.

'Caroline?'

Caroline covered her eyes from the beam of the torch, and scurried back and cowered like a frightened animal.

'Caroline, it's me, Winters.' Caroline new every officer from Marylebone by sight and name, but she just huddled there against the cold. Too scared to move. Winters took a closer look then and saw she was almost naked.

'Jesus. Hey guys, I've found Caroline.' He got on the radio then and called Bill who was searching the other side of the park with Raymond.

'Bill, Bill, it's Winters. I'm by the Princess of Wales Memorial Fountain. I've found Caroline,' he said frantically. Everyone ran now and gathered around Caroline as Raymond fought his way through.

'Get out of my way. Let me through.' He stood there and saw his daughter. Cold and weeping. Her clothes torn as she cried.

'Jesus wept,' he cried. Her clothes were torn and almost gone. Her blouse was missing, her jeans were torn down the front. She was dirty and cold and badly bruised around her face and neck. Caroline saw her father now and sobbed.

'Daddy.' She went to jump up and go to her father, but her legs give way. He caught her, and she sobbed uncontrollably in his arms.

'Oh, baby, it's alright now. Daddies got you.' He could physically feel her shaking as she clung to him, and moments later Zoë Wilson appeared with a blanket from her car. She wrapped it around Caroline as her father carried her back to Bill's car.

Bill drove Raymond and Caroline to St Mary's, and he radioed control to let them know she'd been found. Bill asked control to contact Lyndsey to let her know, and she and Debbie left straight away.

Bill pulled up outside A&E with the siren blaring, and Raymond carried his daughter inside. It was almost midnight, and the A&E was ghostly quiet.

'I need a doctor for my daughter,' he demanded. The nurse looked up from behind the reception and gestured for Raymond to take her through. He lay her gently on the gurney, but Caroline cried and clung to him.

'Daddy, please don't leave me,' she cried.

'Baby, it's alright. I'm not going to leave you. This nice doctor is going to take care of you.' He held her hand the entire time as the doctor spoke to Raymond.

'Has your daughter got any allergies?,' he asked.

'No.' The doctor touched Caroline's arm, and she flinched and tried to get away from him.

'Baby, it's alright. Daddies here.' He tried to soothe her so the doctor could talk to her, but she seemed almost petrified of the doctor.

'Caroline, do you feel up to telling me what happened tonight?,' the doctor asked gently. Caroline just lay there holding onto her father, and she shook her head as she started crying, and moments later Lyndsey ran through the doors with Debbie.

'Caroline.' Caroline sobbed when she saw her mother, but Lyndsey saw the bruises and the blood and cuts around her daughters face.

'Oh my god.' Lyndsey covered her mouth and cried into her hands, and she went to her daughter and held her in her arms.

'Baby, what happened?' Caroline only sobbed as her parents and sister comforted her. The doctor stood there as he waited, and Caroline eyed him nervously as she tried to cover herself. She tried to tell her parents what happed, but she kept crying too much. Raymond kissed his daughter, and smiled a little as he tried to get her to look at him.

'Caroline, honey. Will you let this doctor examine you?' Caroline only shook her head as she pulled the blanket further over her.

'Well, what if a female doctor examines you. Will you do that for me?' Caroline thought about it for a few seconds and nodded her head.

'OK baby. You just get some rest now, and the doctor will come and see you.' Raymond kissed his daughter and he and Lyndsey and Debbie left the cubicle with the doctor.

'So what can you tell us doc. Your initial thoughts. What do you think?,' Raymond asked. The doctor sighed heavily and rubbed his eyes as he thought.

'Well, my initial thoughts to what happened is. I think your daughter was sexually attacked. It would explain why she doesn't want a male doctor examining her.'

'Oh, Jesus.' Lyndsey cried now as she paced.

'That's the worst case scenario,' the doctor said.

'At the most, your daughter could have just been attacked.' Though it was unlikely, the doctor thought, seeing as how her jeans were torn.

Raymond and Lyndsey paced now as they waited for the female doctor, while Debbie sat holding her sisters hand. It was almost one o'clock in the morning, and Caroline was curled up on the bed falling asleep when Hannah and her sisters arrived with their aunt and Steve.

'Raymond what happened? Where's Caroline?', Abbie asked.

'She's in the cubicle over there. Were waiting for a female doctor to come and examine her.'

'Did Caroline say anything about what happened?,' Hannah asked.

'No. She just seems scared around the male doctors, and it's worrying me now.' Everyone seemed puzzled listening to Raymond, but Steve understood. Tears filled Raymond's eyes now, and Lyndsey just comforted him.

'The doctor seems to think that Caroline has been sexually assaulted,' Raymond said then.

'Oh my God,' Abbie said as tears welled in her eyes, and moments later Dr Alison Dawson walked through the curtains and smiled warmly. She greeted everyone, and then she went to see Caroline. Raymond and Lyndsey went to their daughter now and woke her.

'Caroline, honey.' Lyndsey touched her face and she opened her eyes slowly. She saw the doctor as she smiled at Caroline.

'Hello Caroline, I'm Dr Dawson. Do you feel up to letting me examine you?' She nodded slowly as her father helped her to sit up. Dr Dawson suggested that

Raymond and Lyndsey waited outside the cubicle while she examined Caroline, but Caroline wanted them to stayed.

'OK Caroline. Can you tell me what happened this evening?' The doctor started cleaning some of the wounds on Caroline's face as she listened, and she pulled the blanket back to clean and stitch her wounds on her arms and body.

There was a big gash on her leg where her attacker tried to stab her. Her jeans were torn, and Lyndsey winced and looked away. There was dried blood around the wound, and her jeans were stuck to her leg. Dr Dawson give Caroline a local anaesthetic before attempting to stitch the wound.

The doctor took some scissors from the tray and cut the leg of Caroline's jeans away. She gently pulled the jeans away from the wound, but it was still too painful as Caroline cried and flinched. She sobbed as she clung to her mother.

'OK, Caroline. I'm sorry, I'm sorry.' The doctor tried to wet the last bit to free it from her leg.

Caroline was only wearing her jeans and bra when she was bought into A&E. What was left of her jeans, anyhow. She had still got the blanket around her that Zoë gave her from her car when they found her.

'I was walking along Oxford Street after I left the Palladium. My friends asked if I wanted a lift, but I said no, as it was only a fifteen minute walk home.' Caroline wiped her eyes now as her father touched her arm to comfort her.

I was listening to my music, and I remember this man walking towards me, so I crossed the road to avoid him, and before I knew what happened someone grabbed me from behind and dragged me into the park.' She sobbed now as her mother comforted her, and moments later she looked up through blurry eyes.

'He raped me, daddy. He raped me.'

'Oh, Jesus Christ.' Raymond held his daughter now as she sobbed uncontrollably in his arms.

The doctor had examined Caroline further and found recent activity of intercourse, and now Caroline was resting. Dr Dawson went to speak to Raymond and Lyndsey out in the waiting area. Bill was still there, and he was livid after Raymond told him what had happened.

'You better hope you find that bastard before I do, Bill,' he snapped pointing his finger.

'Raymond, listen. Don't start thinking you can take the law into your own hands. We'll find whoever did this, and he'll get what's coming to him. In the meantime, I suggest you take Caroline home and give her some TLC.

'Don't tell me what to do, Bill. That bastard is going to suffer for what he's done, and when I find him I'll hang him by his own innards.'

Bill never said anything else as he watched Raymond wrap a blanket around his daughter and carry her out to the car. Bill understood the fathers grief, as he had lost his son twenty years ago to gun crime. He just prayed that he found Caroline's attacker before Raymond did.

Lyndsey got Caroline in the bath when they got her home, though it made Caroline cry more. The warm water was stinging the wounds, and Lyndsey only soothed and comforted her.

'I know it hurts, honey, but I have to try and get the dirt and blood off you.' Caroline held onto her mother as she tried getting in the water. It was nearly fifteen minutes before Caroline sat comfortably in the warm water.

Her mother cleaned all the dirt off her and the dried blood, and afterwards she gently dried her and wrapped her dressing gown around her.

Raymond kissed his daughter as he tucked her up in her bed. He stood there for a while watching her as Lyndsey watched her from the bedroom door.

'I love you sweetheart,' her father whispered. He went to switch the light out when Caroline spoke.

'Daddy?'

'Yes sweetheart. I'm here.' Raymond sat on the bed and held her hand as he wiped fresh tears from her eyes.

'I'm sorry I never got a lift home. I know it was silly of me to walk home.'

'Shhh. It's alright sweetheart. It's not your fault.'

'Daddy. I think I know who it was.' She looked away from her father as he crouched on the floor and held her hand.

'What do you mean, darling?'

'I mean, I think I know who attacked me. It was dark, and I couldn't see his face that well, but there was just something about him. Something about his voice when he spoke.' Raymond touched her cheek and made her look at him now.

'Baby, who did this to you?' Caroline started crying now, and she turned away from her father.

'I just feel so ashamed and so dirty.' Lyndsey walked over to the bed now, and she knelt on the floor by Caroline and touched her arm.

'Caroline, what are you saying?'

'Caroline thinks she knows who attacked her,' Raymond said. Lyndsey looked at her daughter and brushed her hair away from her eyes with her hand.

'Caroline, honey. If you think you know who did this, you must tell us.'

'I can't be completely sure, but I think it was Carson.' Raymond thought about the name for a moment, as though it should mean something to him.

'Carson Davies? Your old boyfriend?' Caroline only nodded as tears welled in her eyes, and Raymond jumped up and dashed from the room.

'Daddy,' Caroline called after him.

'Raymond, don't go doing anything stupid. *Raymond*,' she shouted after him. Raymond completely ignored his wife and ran down the stairs and out the front door as Debbie came through from her bedroom.

'What's going on? Is Cass' alright?'

'Caroline's fine honey. It's your father that I'm worried about now,' she said dialling Bill's number. Bill answered the phone, and he seemed distracted.

'Bill, it's Lyndsey. Caroline knows her attacker, and now Raymond's gone looking for him.'

'Who is it?'

'It's Carson Davies. Caroline's old boyfriend.' Bill seemed shaken now as he heard the name, and moments later he hung up the phone. He dashed from his office grabbing his car keys.

'Winters, Clover, Daniels, Butch, come with me,' he shouted running out the station. Winters was just drinking the coffee he had just made and nearly spilt it when Bill's voice bellowed, and they dashed out confused as they followed Bill. Clover had barely got in the car as Bill skidded off down the road blaring the siren.

'Raymond's gone hunting for Carson Davies. Caroline thinks he's the one who attacked her.' Every police officer in London knew the name Carson Davies and his family. Every time a violent robbery took place, Carson was always at the top of their lists, though the police were not always right. He was one nasty piece of work in Bill's books.

Carson was always in and out of the courts. Though till now the police could never get anything concrete on him. His pathetic excuse for a mother always pleaded insanity for her son, and she was always there to bail him out.

Wilson and Clover hung on for dear life as Bill skidded and took each corner. It was almost four-thirty in the morning as Bill drove the streets of Marylebone, and moments later he turned into Rossmore Road and saw Raymond up ahead outside Carson's house. Bill skidded to a stop and jumped out.

'Raymond.'

'You stay out of this Bill. This is between me and Carson.' Carson came to the door and opened it with the chain on, and he went to shut it quickly as Raymond kicked it open, sending Carson flying. Raymond barged in and kicked Carson in the ribs.

'You fucking mess with my daughter again and I'll fucking kill you,' he raged. His face turning purple, Raymond grabbed him and shoved him up against the wall, as Carson's mother came screaming down the stairs with a baseball bat, and moments later Bill, Clover,

Winters and Daniels barged in and all grabbed Raymond, as Butch restrained Carson's mother.

'Raymond, stop it. Get off him,' Bill shouted. They held Raymond up, but he pulled away from them and managed to get in another kick to Carson's ribs before Winters and Clover decked him. All the commotion had woke some of the neighbours, and they came out to see what was going on. They saw Bill and Daniels holding Carson up, and Butch restraining his mother, and they all cheered.

'Get that scum off our streets.'

'Yeah, get that murdering family off our street,' another one called. Carson's mother just mouthed off at the neighbours, as she lay face down on the grass in handcuffs, and Carson looked at Raymond as Daniels and Butch had him restrained, and he laughed sinisterly.

'That bitch was begging for a good shag. I just gave her what she wanted.'

'You fucking wanker. I'll fucking kill you,' Raymond bellowed as he broke free from Winters and Clover again and lunged towards him. Pent up rage only fuelled his anger as he grabbed Carson by the throat, lifting him off the floor he punched him hard in the stomach and kneed him in the groin. He dropped Carson to the floor and stamped on his groin. Bill, Clover, Winters and Daniels all grabbed Raymond again and decked him, as other officers piled into the house.

'Get that piece of shit out of here,' Bill shouted looking at Carson. They pulled Carson up and handcuffed him, and Carson only laughed at Raymond.

'You just wait. I'll find Caroline again, and next time I'll finish her off. And that slut sister of hers.' Raymond lunged for him with fury, but Clover and Winters tightened their grip on him.

'Get that scum out of here,' Bill bellowed. Bill turned to Raymond then as Winters and Clover loosened their grip on him.

'You're very lucky I don't lock you up Raymond. I told you not to take the law into your own hands. I told you I'd deal with it.' Raymond only ignored him as he made his way outside. He watched as the police van pulled off with Carson and his mother in the back, and he walked slowly back to his car and drove home. Home to his family.

Chapter Twenty Two

Caroline had slept for most of the day after her father got her home. It was almost six o'clock in the evening when she came downstairs. Dr Dawson had stitched her wounds on her arms and legs and treated the bruises, and now it was only her pride that was hurting as she walked into the lounge.

Her face was still badly bruised, and she covered her face now with her hands and bowed her head in shame when she saw her sister. Caroline started crying as her sister held her hands and pulled them away from her face.

'Cass', you've nothing to be ashamed of. And you're still beautiful.' Caroline cried in her sisters arms now as their parents watched.

'I love you Cass'.'

'I love you too Deb's.' Caroline pulled away from her sister and composed herself.

'How you feeling now, hon?,' her mother asked.

'I'm OK. I'm just so tired. Every time I close my eyes I can see him. I feel him touching me, and I feel so dirty all the time.' Raymond took a deep breath as he stopped himself from crying, and he only comforted his daughter.

Caroline pulled her cardigan tighter around her as she sat on the sofa now, and moments later Lyndsey came in from the kitchen with a steaming cup of coco for her.

'There you go hon'.'

'Thanks mom.'

That evening Bill and Winters dropped by to see how Caroline was. Hannah and her sisters were there with their aunt and Steve, and Raymond stood up now as he saw Bill.

'Mate, I'm sorry for the way I acted. I realise now it was dumb. I wasn't thinking straight.' The two men shook hands as Bill smiled.

'Trust me mate. If it was my child, I'd have done the same thing.' They went through to the lounge and sat down on the sofa now. Caroline was upstairs in bed, and Debbie bought a cup of coffee in for Bill and Winters.

'Thanks sweetheart.'

'So what happens now, Bill?,' Debbie asked.

'Well it's more or less an open and shut case. Carson has admitted to it, and the tests from the hospital proves he did it, so he'll go to court and get sentenced. How's Caroline?

'She seems fine. I think it's just her pride that been damaged more than anything,' Lyndsey said.

'I just hope they lock him up and throw away the key,' Debbie said then.

'I wish it was a simple as that sweetheart.'

It was Tuesday afternoon and Danni arrived in Bude at four-thirty. She drove along Lansdowne Road, and moments later she pulled into the car park at the Carriers Inn. She smiled to herself as she stepped out of her VW Beatle and sniffed the sea air, then she went inside to find Jason.

It was busy in the restaurant today and she wondered whether to disturb him or not. She spoke to one of the waitresses, and then she ordered a chardonnay and took a seat in the restaurant while she waited, and moments later Jason popped his head through the door and saw her.

He crept up to her and put his hands over her eyes. She was startled, but smiled joyfully when she saw him.

'Hello gorgeous.' She kissed him, and threw her arms around him.

'I can't talk right now babe. It's really busy in the kitchen. You OK to wait for an hour or so?' She smiled and kissed him.

'OK.' She kissed him again and he went back in the kitchen. She sat there browsing through the menu, and moments later a waitress came over to her.

'Are you Danni?'

'Yes.'

'The chef asked me to bring you this.' The waitress put a plate in front of her, and Danni laughed. The words "I love you" was squirted with whipped cream on the plate, and she scooped some up with her finger.

At six-thirty Jason got changed and went out to meet Danni in the restaurant. She was sitting gazing out the window, and Jason went up to her and kissed the top of her head.

'You ready, babe?' She grabbed her jacket and they held hands walking out the restaurant.

'Goodnight girls,' Jason called to the waitresses. It wasn't closing time yet, but Jason always finished around seven o'clock in the evening, unless it was busy. There was always someone available to lock up at ten-thirty. If not Jason, would go back.

Danni and Jason walked along the beach holding hands as Danni looked out to sea. There were a lot of good and bad memories in Bude for Danni, though now she was learning to deal with the bad ones.

Jason was there for her now, and Danni knew he would always be there for her. Jason stopped walking now and turned to Danni. It was a pleasant evening as the last of the days sun was going down, and Jason held her in his arms and kissed her.

'Danni, these past few days I've been away from you has made me realise how lucky I am that you walked into my life again. I'm not expecting an answer from you now, but I hope you find it in yourself to say yes.'

'I love you Danni Philips, and I want to marry you.' Danni was speechless now as she stared at Jason, but from the look on her face there was no doubt in her mind that she wanted the same thing. She thought about it now as they carried on walking, and as they walked along Summerleaze Crescent Danni turned to him and kissed him.

'Yes.'

'Excuse me?'

'Yes, I'll marry you.' They both laughed and fell into each others arms. Their lips met and they kissed for a long time, and then Jason took a ring from his pocket that he'd been carrying around with him for two weeks. He'd bought the ring in London, and was biding his time. Danni eyed the ring curiously now.

'And where did you get that from?'

'Oh, the fairies must have dropped it in my pocket,' he said jokingly. It was almost eight-thirty in the evening, and a few people were still strolling the street. Jason dropped on one knee, and although Danni had already said yes, he asked her again.

'Danni, will you marry me?' A couple of people stopped and watched as they smiled, and Danni felt embarrassed.

'Get up silly. I've already said yes.' Jason giggled as he knew he was embarrassing her.

'I'm not getting up until you say yes.'

'Jason, you're embarrassing me,' she laughed.

'I know.'

'OK, OK. Alright. Yes. Yes,' she shouted excitedly. He placed the ring on her finger, and a few people clapped and cheered as they watched them. They leaned into each other and kissed as a young couple came over to congratulate them.

Danni and Jason walked back to the Carriers Inn after a while, as Danni had left her car parked on the car park and they drove back to Jason's.

Jason opened the front door to his house, and Danni stepped into the lounge. She smiled as she looked around at the china plates on the wall, and the photos of him and his family on the shelves. There were paintings by Monet and da Vinci and Kandinsky. She stepped cautiously as she looked around, and Jason followed. He stood in the doorway to the kitchen watching her.

'Hey, come here beautiful.' Danni smiled embarrassingly, and he held her in his arms and kissed her lovingly.

'So, what's your bedroom like?' she asked playfully. He eyed her curiously, and took her hand and led her upstairs. She slipped his T-shirt off walking up the stairs, and they leaned into each other and kissed.

He took her hand and led her to his bedroom, where a huge king size four-poster bed stood centre of the room.

More paintings by Monet and Van Gogh and Rembrandt decorated the walls, and Jason went to the stereo and put on some soft music.

Danni stood there looking so vulnerable and so sweet and innocent. Her long blond hair sensually draped across her shoulders. He pushed her hair back, and held her face as he leaned in to kiss her, and lifting her up into his arms he carried her to the bathroom. He turned the shower on as they looked hopeful at each other, and they stood there undressing each other.

Her hands caressing his body as their lips met. He peeled her knickers off and let them drop to the floor, and they both stepped into the shower.

The steam bellowed all around, as their hands wandered and explored each other. He cupped her milky soft white breasts with one hand as the other disappeared between her legs. Her back arched against the wall, she moaned softly as she took hold of his penis.

The hot steaming water caressed every part of their bodies as their arms twisted and entangled around each other. He kissed and teased her pert nipples, and lifting her up, he slowly entered her. She screamed joyfully as she felt him deep inside her. For Danni it was the most exciting pleasure she'd ever experienced. It had been so long since she made love to someone, that she almost forgot what it was like.

She was only twenty-four years old, but Jason had been her only truelove. Though she had had a few relationships over the past couple of years, but nothing ever lasted. Danni always hoped she would meet Jason again one day.

Jason carried Danni to the bedroom, and he lay her on his bed. He dimmed the lights and lit some candles, and she smiled as he turned to her.

'Come here handsome.' She peeled the towel away from him, and he stood completely naked in front of her, his body still damp from the shower.

'Now, where were we?,' she asked sensually. She took him around the waist and pulled him on top of her. Their lips met as she took hold of his erect penis.

'Make love to me,' she whispered in his ear.

She gasped sharply as he entered her, and feeling him deep inside her she held onto him as she savoured every moment.

Danni hadn't made love to someone in almost three years, and now she had Jason twice in one day. She never thought lovemaking could be so pleasurable.

The following morning Jason had gone into work at eight o'clock, and Danni went with him and helped in the kitchen preparing some of the starters and desserts. Danni was happy just being near Jason, but she was enjoying working there with him too. So much so, that that afternoon Jason had the idea of them becoming partners at the restaurant. He had give it a lot of thought since she's been back in his life, and as they sat eating lunch in the restaurant at two-thirty he asked her.

'Danni, how would you like to join me here at the Carriers Inn? We can become partners?' She stared at him as though he'd lost his mind, but deep down she liked the idea.

'Jason, I don't know the first thing about running a restaurant.'

'I know, but I can teach you, and the staff like you. Gina told me just this morning that she loved having you here. We can become partners. Fifty-fifty. Everything split equally, and you'll have shares in the business too.'

'But what about London, and the office. I do have responsibilities there too.'

'I know, but you don't need to be there all the time, and you won't need to be here all the time. You can commute, and I'll commute with you as well when I can.' Danni smiled at the idea now. She loved Jason and being with him. She could share his life, and he could share hers.

At seven o'clock Jason called a meeting with the staff. He'd closed the restaurant early, and all the staff sat around in the restaurant discussing Jason's idea of Danni becoming a partner.

Jason always considered his staff, and involved them in most of the decisions. After all, most of the staff had been there since it opened in 2003, and he valued their ideas too.

'So all hands up if you would like Danni, my gorgeous girlfriend, to be a partner.' Everyone laughed as Danni smiled embarrassingly, and it was clear they all favoured Jason's idea. Jason turned to Danni now and held her hand.

'Welcome to the Carriers Inn.' Danni had tears in her eyes as the staff welcomed her.

'Welcome to our family, Danni. You're gonna really love it here, Claire Woods said as she hugged her.

Danni couldn't believe her luck now as she thought about it. She had only been back in Bude for less than two days, and she got engaged, and has equal shares in

Jason's business. She couldn't wait to get home to London to tell everyone.

It was still over a week before Jason could go back to London with Danni, but she was so excited about telling her sisters that Jason had decided to pack up for a couple of weeks and go to London with her.

Besides, most of what Jason needed to do was done. He knew the business was in good hands, so the following morning Danni and Jason packed their things and left for London. Danni couldn't stop smiling at the thought of being with Jason. She just hoped her sisters would understand.

Chapter Twenty Three

Danni and Jason arrived back in London much earlier than planned. She was going for two weeks to be with Jason, but it had only been two days. Danni had said her goodbyes to Hannah and Tony, as they were going to be leaving for Torquay on Friday. Though Hannah and Tony were going to be back before Danni, and as she walked through the front door at three thirty on the Thursday afternoon they were all surprised.

Hello, I'm back.' Lesley was startled as she was preparing tea, and Steve was in the lounge reading the newspaper when he heard Danni. Hannah was just making coffees, and she smiled joyfully when she saw her sister.

'Danni?' Hannah saw her sister smiling gloriously, and she hugged her and then saw Jason. Abbie come running down the stairs as she heard Danni, and she ran to her sister as Hannah greeted Jason.

'Sis', what are you doing back so soon? We wasn't expecting you.'

'I know, but I wanted to get back to give you the most fan*tastic* news.' They all looked at Danni curiously now, as Danni smiled gloriously.

'Well?,' Hannah asked curiously as she smiled. Danni held her hand out excitedly.

'Jason's asked me to marry him.'

'Oh, Danni, that's fantastic,' Hannah said hugging her. She saw Jason and hugged him too.

Congratulations, sis', Abbie said hugging her sister. They all congratulated them now, and Danni stood there holding Jason's hand.

'There's more,' she said.

'Jason has asked me to join him at the restaurant. He wants us to be partners.' Everyone looked stunned now as Hannah sat down.

'Danni, that's fantastic. But what about the office?' Danni and Jason sat at the table now as they held hands.

'I know I have commitments at the office, but I don't need to be there all the time, and I won't need to be at the restaurant all the time. I can commute, and Jason will commute too.' Hannah was obviously happy for her sister, but she wasn't entirely sure she'd thought it through properly.

'Sis', I know how you must be feeling. I'm committed to the business. I'm giving it my all, and we all don't need to be there all the time. It's just that I love Jason, and I'm trying to be happy. And I am happy.'

'Danni, I am really happy for you. I really am, but are you sure you've thought this through properly?'

'Yes. It's what I want,' she smiled. Hannah held her sisters hands now and smiled.

'Then I'm happy for you, and I wish you both the best of luck.' Everyone was standing around listening, and Steve smiled and congratulated them both. Hannah hugged her sister now and smiled.

'You've really done it sis'. You've found happiness.' Hannah wiped her eyes now and looked to Jason. She held her hand out to him, and she hugged him.

'Just you make sure you look after her.' Danni laughed as Hannah kissed him.

They all sat in the lounge after Lesley made coffees, and Danni and Jason talked about their plans. They spoke about the restaurant and how friendly the staff are, and

Danni told them it was going to be an equal partnership, and it was clear that Hannah was happy for them both.

That afternoon Danni and Jason went to visit Caroline, and to see how she was. It's been three days since Caroline was attacked in Hyde Park, and within twenty-four hours her parents had noticed she had become withdrawn and depressed.

Caroline was upstairs in the shower, the fifth time since she woke up at ten-thirty. Her parents thought she was in her bedroom, so Danni went upstairs now to speak to her. Jason stayed in the living room talking to Raymond and Lyndsey, and as Danni went to knock Caroline's bedroom door she could hear her crying in the bathroom. She stood outside the bathroom door and spoke to her.

'Caroline, it's Danni. Can I come in?' Caroline never answered, so Danni tried the door. It wasn't locked, and she walked in.

'Caroline, it's Danni.' She stepped into the bathroom and saw Caroline in the shower through the steamed glass. She slowly walked over to the shower and slid the glass door open, and saw Caroline sitting down sobbing in the shower scrubbing herself.

'I just can't get myself clean.' Caroline was using a scrubbing brush, and her skin was red raw. Danni crouched down to her and went to get the brush from her now.

'Cass', give me the brush.' Caroline gripped it tight as Danni tried to get it from her.

'Cass', give me the brush. Give me the brush.' She pulled it from her hand and winced as she saw her skin.

She turned the shower off and held her arms out to her as tears welled in her eyes.

'Come on, come here Cass'.' Caroline sobbed in her arms.

'I just feel so dirty and so ashamed.'

'Caroline, there's nothing to feel ashamed of. It wasn't your fault.' Danni could physically feel her shaking in her arms. She helped her out of the shower and wrapped a towel around her.

'Come on, let's go and get you dressed before you freeze.' Caroline cried as Danni dried her. She tried to dress her, but her skin was too sore, and moments later Debbie knocked the bedroom door.

'Cass', it's Deb's.' Debbie walked in and saw Danni comforting her sister, and Caroline looked up through blurry eyes. Caroline's skin was red raw, and bleeding, and Danni went to the bathroom and got some wet towels.

'Deb's, can you go and fetch your mom's first aid box please?,' Raymond and Lyndsey thought Caroline was sleeping, and when Debbie asked for the first aid kit they were concerned.

'What do you need that for?,' he father asked.

'Caroline's been in the shower and scrubbed herself too hard and now her arms and legs are bleeding.' Raymond and Lyndsey ran up the stairs and saw Caroline, and her arms and legs.

'Oh my god. Caroline, what have you done?' Caroline sobbed as she started scratching.

'I just can't get myself clean.' Lyndsey went to comfort her daughter now.

'Oh, Caroline. It's alright.' Her legs were all red and sore and bleeding, and her body was red sore. Lyndsey put some ointment on the cuts, and bandaged her legs.

'Raymond, she going to need to get to the hospital. I haven't got the right stuff here to treat the cuts.' Caroline sobbed now as she saw her legs.

'Mom, I'm sorry, I'm so sorry,' she cried. Lyndsey comforted her daughter.

'Honey, it's alright. It's not your fault.' Lyndsey tried to get her daughter dressed as Raymond went to get the car out of the garage. Danni had tears in her eyes as she watched, and she went downstairs to Jason. Moments later Raymond carried his daughter down the stairs. Lyndsey gave Danni her house keys.

'Danni, can you lock up for me please? I'll get the keys back later.' Lyndsey ran out and shut the front door. Danni went back to Jason, and he held her in his arms and comforted her.

Raymond pulled up outside A&E and carried his daughter inside. Lyndsey went to the reception and asked if they could see Dr Dawson.

'Dr Dawson's not working this afternoon, but there's another doctor available.'

'It has to be a female doctor though,' Lyndsey said.

'Well, Dr Meadows is free. He can see to your daughter.'

No, it has to be a female.' Lyndsey paused and sighed as she ran her fingers through her hair, and then she explained her reasons, and the receptionist smiled understandingly.

'OK. Take your daughter through, and I'll send in a doctor.'

'Thank you.' Raymond lay Caroline on the bed as she cried a little, and moments later a female doctor walked through the curtains. She smiled warmly as she greeted them. Lyndsey explained she had tried to dress the wounds, but hadn't got any antiseptic cream.

'OK Caroline, shall we have a look?' Caroline was only wearing baggy leggings and a loose T-shirt, and as Dr Stone tried taking them off, Caroline cried in pain.

'I'm sorry honey. I know it hurts, but it won't be for long.' Caroline lay there in just her bra and knickers as Raymond waited outside the cubicle. Lyndsey held her daughters hand as the doctor treated her. It looked as though Caroline had used a wire brush to scrub herself, and she winced and cried as the doctor treated her.

'Sorry, honey, I know it hurts. It'll all be over soon.' Dr Stone had bandage the wounds so Caroline couldn't scratch, and afterwards Lyndsey got Caroline dressed.

At home, Raymond carried his daughter upstairs to bed. He pulled the quilt over her as she was nearly asleep. He leaned over her and kissed her cheek.

'Sleep well, my angel.'

'Daddy?'

'Yes, sweetheart?' Raymond sat on the floor by her bed and held her hand. Tears trickled from her eyes, and he gently wiped them away.

'I lost that gold diamond necklace. You know, the one you and mama bought me.' Raymond chuckled a little and kissed her.

'It's alright, darling. I'll buy you another one.' He kissed her and she closed her eyes.

'I love you daddy.'

'I love you too, sweetheart,' he smiled.

Chapter Twenty Four

It was Friday morning and Hannah and Tony were leaving today for their two weeks in Torquay. Though excited about the holiday, Hannah was concerned for Caroline. She didn't feel right about going, and Tony felt the same.

They were packed and ready, and they were leaving about nine o'clock, so they had enough time to visit Caroline before they left.

Lyndsey greeted them warmly as they stepped inside through the front door.

'How's Caroline?,' Hannah asked.

'She's fine at the moments. She's going demented because she can't scratch.' Hannah smiled a bit and she and Tony went upstairs to say hello. Caroline was nearly asleep on the bed as Debbie was sitting on the large beanbag by the window reading a book, but Caroline was wide awake as she heard Hannah's voice.

'Hi, how we doing this morning?' Caroline tried to smile as she sat up, but then she saw Tony and she seemed nervous.

'Hi Caroline. You OK with me being here?'

'Yeah, I'm fine. I'm just a weary around men, but you're OK,' she smiled. She held out her arms to him, and he cuddled her.

'I'm so sorry Cass'.' Caroline sat on her bed and crossed her legs as Tony sat in the armchair by the window

Caroline's face was still badly bruised, but the swelling around her eyes had healed. She was wearing baggy clothes, and she tied her hair up under a hat. Hannah smiled gently now and looked at her.

'I just can't seem to get the ordeal out of my mind, Hannah. I'm so tired all the time because I can't sleep. I don't know whether I'm coming or going.' Tears filled her eyes now, and Hannah went and sat on the bed with her and comforted her.

'Cass', listen to me. I know I will never be able to understand what you're going through right now, but when we lost Mikey, and I went through my depression, I thought about nothing except wanting to hurt myself. I thought that if I couldn't have Mikey back, then I didn't want to live either.' Caroline wiped her eyes as she listened.

I know what you're feeling right now isn't nice, but you will find a way to cope with it. I know it's only been a few days, but I know you're a strong person. We all love you Cass', and we're all here to help you.' Hannah held her now as she cried in her arms. Hannah kissed the top of her head, and she pulled away from her and dried her eyes.

'Come on, Cass'. Let's go downstairs.' Raymond and Lyndsey had just sat down in the lounge when Hannah and Caroline walked in. Lyndsey had made some coffee and sat in her favourite armchair by the fireplace.

The magnificent portrait of the family hung pride of place on the wall over the grand piano. Lyndsey often played the piano, and now sometimes gives lessons to various children. Laminated flooring all around the house, with a simple rugs scattered around, and a glass coffee table in the centre of the lounge. Lyndsey stood up and smiled when she saw her daughter.

'Hello sweetheart.' Hannah told them how she and Caroline had just had a chat upstairs.

'Mom, I think I want to go for a walk with Hannah and Tony.' Raymond and Lyndsey looked impressed as they looked at Hannah.

'OK.'

'We're just going to take a walk up the street and back,' Tony said.

'OK.' Lyndsey looked at Raymond now, and it was clear that they were impressed with Hannah and Tony's effort to get their daughter out of the house for a while. Caroline got her big coat, and she wore big shades to hide her eyes. Hannah opened the front door, and Caroline looked out into the street. At first she seemed nervous, but Hannah stepped out and took Caroline's hand.

'Come on Cass'.' Caroline reached out and held Hannah's hand and stepped out. It was a cloudy morning, and it looked like it was going to rain. Vera Tibbit was looking through her window, and she smiled gently as she opened her front door. Caroline eyed her nervously and froze, but Hannah gently persuaded her.

'Cass'. It's alright. It's only granny Vera.'

'Oh my poor child.' Everyone in the street knew of Caroline's attack, and they all hoped she made a speedy recovery.

'Hello granny.'

'Caroline, my child.' She cuddled her, and then gently held her face and kissed her cheek.

'Granny, we're just going for a walk. Do you want to join us?'

'I think that'll be lovely. Thank you.' Tony went inside Vera's house and got her wheelchair, and they walked off together down Connaught Street.

Vera was watching a repeat of Coronation Street when she saw them walk past, but she'd seen it before. They walked slowly along Connaught Street and along Hyde Park Street. Caroline held Tony's arm as Hannah pushed Vera in her wheelchair, but each time Caroline spotted a strange man she froze and turned away.

They walked over to Grace and Duncan's Memorial Garden, and as they approached they saw a man walking his dog.

'Hannah.' Caroline cried as she stood behind Tony. Vera looked round and saw tears on Caroline's cheeks as Hannah comforted her.

'Caroline, sweetie.' Vera held her hand and smiled gently. Hannah went to her and held her face.

'Hey Cass'. It's alright. He's gone. OK?' Caroline tried to look as she cried, and Tony wiped the tears from her cheeks.

'Hey, Caroline. I won't let anything happen to you,' he said gently. He held her chin and she looked at him. For Caroline, this short walk was helping her to overcome her biggest fears. To face the outside world again, and as they sat in the Memorial Garden Caroline sat staring at Grace and Duncan's plaques.

They sat quietly for a few minutes, and Caroline looked at Tony as he held her hand.

'Why can't all men be as nice and as kind as you?' Tony laughed a little as he kissed the back of her hand.

'Hey, they can't all be as nice as me,' Tony said.

'Or Hannah will be chasing after them all.' Hannah smiled hopefully then.

'Now there's an idea,' she laughed.

'Come here you. Let me give you a kiss,' Caroline said to Tony.

'You're still beautiful, you know. And don't let anyone tell you different, OK?,' Tony said. They took a slow walk back then, and Tony helped Vera into Lyndsey's. Lyndsey was just making a pot of tea when she heard Caroline talking, and she smiled when she came into the lounge, and when she saw her daughter smiling, she was happy.

'Well, someone looks happy.' She kissed her daughter, and then she saw Vera.

'Hello granny.' Nearly everyone in the street called her granny, and Vera liked it. She liked the idea of being everyone's granny. Lyndsey kissed Vera, and she went back to the kitchen to pour the tea as Hannah followed her.

'Thank you Hannah. I don't know what you've done, but I never thought I see Caroline smile for a long time.'

'Well, she was a bit nervous at first, but Tony soon cheered her up,' she smiled.

'What more can I say? Tony's just a big softie. He'll make anyone smile.' Lyndsey smiled then as she put the milk back in the fridge.

'You've got a good catch there Hannah. I know you'll have a happy life together.'

Everyone knew that Hannah and Tony were leaving for Torquay that evening for two weeks, and after that afternoon, Caroline was sorry to see them go.

Hannah and Tony left Lyndsey's at eight forty-five and went home to finish packing for holiday. They were hoping to be on the motorway by nine-thirty. Lesley was a bit upset they were going, but she told herself it was only two weeks.

Danni and Jason were staying in London for a couple of weeks, and They were going to go sight-seeing around London together. Danni didn't have to be at the office all the time. And neither did her sisters. The truth was, they rarely had to go in anymore, now they'd left Raymond and Desmond in charge. Hannah knew that, even when Danni announced she was joining Jason in Bude. It was just an excuse to try and get Danni to stay close. Though now Hannah and her sisters were thinking of returning to Bude themselves.

Hannah was discussing it with her aunt just the other day, and though their aunt was staying in London this time Hannah was looking forward to it

It was just after nine o'clock, and Hannah and Tony were ready to leave. They'd loaded the car, and now they all gathered in the lounge saying their goodbyes.

'I love you sis'. Take care,' Danni said.

'Have fun, darling. Send us a postcard,' Lesley said. Hannah hugged and kissed her sisters and Steve, and they went out to the car. Hannah looked across the street and saw Caroline through the window, and she waved and blew her a kiss, and moments later Hannah pulled off.

Scented candles lay all around the marble bathroom, as Danni slipped out of the thick fluffy hotel bathrobe and threw it over the chair, and standing naked over Jason as he lay in the Jacuzzi he smiled up at her.

'Come here, beautiful.' He held her hand as she stepped down into the tub, and sliding in beside him their lips met. He poured her some champagne, and passing her the glass she moaned pleasurably.

'Mmm, I think we should do this more often.' Jason smiled at the idea, and he leaned into her and kissed her lips.

Jason had decided to give Danni a weeks pampering in one of London's plush hotels. They had booked into the Grange-Holborn Hotel in Bloomsbury yesterday morning, for some exquisite indulgence. Seven days of pampering and luxurious service.

At eight-thirty that morning Jason had called down for room service and ordered breakfast, and afterwards they enjoyed a Jacuzzi before hit the town.

Danni lay there in the Jacuzzi as Jason looked lovingly at her, and pulling her closer he held her in his arms as their lips met. His hand wandered over her naked flesh, and down between her legs. He teased her clitoris, and taking his erect penis in her hand she eased it inside her.

She pushed him onto his back, and she moaned softly as she felt him deep inside her. He reached up and grabbed her milky white breasts. The jets of water from the Jacuzzi only heightened her pleasure as she felt the edge of an orgasm. She screamed, and her whole body shook as she held onto him as she reached a climax, and moments later he climaxed as she smiled dreamily and savoured every drop.

They lay holding each other for a long time, and she kissed him passionately.

'We definitely should do this more often, she then as they both laughed. He kissed her then and reached for the champagne bottle.

'We need some more champagne,' He went to get out now of the tub now, and she giggled a little.

'If I drink anymore of that champagne, you'll carrying me home.' Jason only smiled then.

'I'd better go and get some more then.' She laughed a little as he walk naked over to the bedroom. His body tall and muscular, and lightly tanned from the sands of Cornwall.

Jason always liked to keep in shape. Twice a week he worked out at the gym, and he always liked to top up his tan on the beech whenever he had time.

Danni stepped out of the Jacuzzi and wrapped her bathrobe around her. It was almost midday, and half an hour later Jason emerged from the bedroom looking fresh after he'd showered and shaved and got dressed.

Danni was sitting at the dressing table drying her hair after her shower, and afterwards she got dressed. By one o'clock they had left their hotel room to catch a train from Kings Cross.

Chapter Twenty Five

Hannah and Tony pulled up outside the Osborne Hotel in Torquay at around one o'clock in the afternoon, and Hannah stepped out her Bentley and stretched her legs and sniffed the sea air. She smiled gloriously and squinted against the afternoon sun, and she kissed Tony and held his arm as they walked towards the entrance.

It was still late-January, and they were lucky to get any sun, though this holiday was not just for the sun and lounging on the beach. They were hoping to have found a nice property for themselves before they went home.

'Oh, baby. This is grand,' she said walking to the entrance. There was still a chill in the air, and it was no weather for bikinis, but it was just right.

'Good afternoon, madam. Sir. Welcome to the Osborne Hotel,' the doorman said as he opened the door. They walked in through the magnificent entrance and into the foyer, and Hannah stopped dead in her tracks as she viewed the spectacular surroundings on the hotel

'Oh wow.' She looked all around at the magnificent art and portraits on the walls, the huge chandeliers, and the red velvet curtains, and looking up the long winding staircase and to the spectacular dome skylight, and she was in awe.

They checked in at the reservations, and afterwards they took the elevator to the third floor and they were shown to their room. Hannah went to the window and saw the view of the sea, and she turned to Tony. The porter had left their luggage by the bed and left the room, and Hannah went to Tony.

'Oh, baby. This is fantastic.'

Hannah sat on the king size four poster bed and lay back, and held the drapes around her face as she giggled. There were silk sheets on the bed with a simple throw, and lace drapes hanging at the four corners. Hannah looked lovingly at Tony as she lay on the bed and teased him.

Pouting her lips he went to her, and kneeling on the bed she held him in her arms. She kissed him passionately, and he pushed her long black hair back behind her ears and looked at her.

'Are you happy?' She smiled beautifully and kissed him.

'I am happy. I have the only man I've ever loved.'

'Me?,' he asked jokingly.

'Yes, you. And I'm here in these beautiful surroundings, with that man I love, and I can think of nothing else right now, than staying in this beautiful hotel room all weekend making love to that beautiful man.' Tony raised his eyebrows hopefully and smiled.

'With me?,' he joked.

'Yes, you.'

'Wonderful. When do we start?,' They both laughed as she pulled him on top of her. She kissed him lovingly and smiled.

'How about right now?'

It was almost four-thirty in the afternoon, and though they had gone to Torquay for house hunting, there wasn't much they could do until Monday when the estate agents opened. They were going to look around the town over the weekend, but for now they stayed in their hotel.

Hannah ran her fingers through his short blond hair as their lips met. He unbuttoned her jacket and pushed it over her shoulders, and slipping her sweater over her head she dropped it to the floor. He cupped her breasts in his hands as she unbuttoned his jeans. They dropped to the floor and she stood up and pushed him onto the bed.

'Ooh, I love it when you're so masterful,' he said softly. She smiled and pulled his jeans off, and then his boxers.

He lay there hard and erect, and completely naked. She turned and went to her bag on the floor and took a pair of pink fluffy handcuffs, and smiled devilishly at him. She cuffed him to the bed frame and whispered into his ear.

'Now you're completely mine.' Hannah had packed a few extra essentials that Tony didn't know about, and now she was going to show him just how kinky she could be.

She went to the mirror on the wall a slipped out of her knickers and bra and standing naked before him she took a leather blindfold from her bag and snapped it taut. Leaning over him, she tied it around his eyes as he tried to tease her nipples with his tongue.

'Ah ah ah. Naughty boy.'

'Ooh, is the mistress going to punish me?,' he teased hopefully. Hannah never answered. She only smiled wickedly and licked her lips. She draped a satin nightgown over her shoulders, and standing over him she took hold of his erect penis as he groaned.

She leaned over and took a bottle of massage oil from her bag, and dripping it slowly over his naked body he flinched.

She ran her fingers over his hairy chest, feeling the scented oil between her fingers. The lights were dimmed as soft music played in the background, and Tony was feeling really relaxed, but Hannah leaned over him and took hold of his penis again and wrapped her luscious lips around it, and holding it firmly she squatted and lowered herself onto him. He moaned pleasurably, as she leaned over and freed his hands. He held her now and rolled her over.

He took his blindfold off, and letting his eyes adjust to the dimmed light he took her in his arms. Her long black hair fanned out on the satin pillows. He cupped her breasts in his hands, gently squeezing them and teasing her nipples.

She moaned softly feeling him deep inside her as he grasped her slender neck. He leaned down and kissed her open mouth.

'Oh, Jesus.' Her whole body clenched as she felt the edge of an orgasm. He held her tight in his long muscular arms as she climaxed. They lay there afterwards as he held her in his arms. He brushed her hair away from her eyes and kissed her cheek, and he saw a single tear trickle down her nose.

'Baby, what's wrong?' She smiled and looked up at him now.

'Oh, nothing, I'm fine. I just get like this sometimes. I am happy, baby.' She touched his face now and kissed him as she saw his concerns.

The truth was that Tony always pleased her between the sheets, but it was the first time he had seen her cry after making love. He was worried at first that he'd done something wrong, but she reassured him.

That evening Hannah and Tony went out for a meal at the Al Beb on Torwood Street. Oozing with an oriental atmosphere, with drapes, lamps and low couches. Delicious cuisines from Morocco and the Mediterranean.

They ordered drinks, and a waitress came over and took their order. They sat their quietly, soaking up the atmosphere.

It had been almost fifteen years since Tony was last in Torquay. He used to go their often with his family, though over the years it had changed dramatically.

It was a relaxed atmosphere as they ate and talked about there future plans. They were looking forward to buying their first property together. They were looking for somewhere near the coast. Not too far from the coast, but somewhere secluded and cosy.

They talked all through their meal and as they walked back to the hotel, and that night they snuggled up to each other as Hannah smiled dreamily to herself, and when Tony woke the following morning just after six-thirty, he heard Hannah being sick in the bathroom. He jumped out of bed and ran into the bathroom and saw her leaning over the toilet.

'Baby, what's wrong?' Hannah was sweating profusely, and she leaned back in Tony's arms as he took the towel from the rail.

'Oh God, Tony. I feel so awful.' He carried her back to the bedroom and lay her on the bed, and then he called downstairs to the front desk. The concierge was on duty, and he sent for an ambulance straight away.

Tony went back to Hannah, but she jumped up and ran to the toilet as she was sick again, and he followed her with the towel. Hannah sat there with her head over the toilet while he tried to soothe her. She leaned back in his arms again, and tears rolled down her cheeks. Tony wiped her mouth and her eyes, and he gently kissed her cheek.

'It's OK baby. The ambulance on it's way.' He brushed her hair away from her eyes with his hand and kissed her again.

'Tony, what's wrong with me?,' she asked with her arms crossed over her stomach.

'I don't know, baby.' He sat there leaning against the bathtub with her in his arms, and moments later the concierge knocked the door and let himself in with the paramedics.

'Mr Craven. The paramedics are here.'

'We're in the bathroom.' Tony never moved as he held Hannah in his arms, and the paramedic walked in and smiled gently.

'OK, what do we have here?'

'I woke up earlier, and she was being sick,' Tony said. Tony sat her up and moved aside so the paramedic could see to her. Hannah was ghostly pale, and she seemed dazed.

'OK, honey. Let's have a look at you.' Hannah sat leaning against the bathtub as Tony stepped aside. All the while he was frantic as the concierge tried to keep him calm.

The paramedic asked her if she felt nauseous and checked her pupils and her blood pressure, and moments later they strapped her to a portable chair and carried her outside to the ambulance. Tony grabbed a few clothes for Hannah and quickly got dressed himself, and he followed the paramedics and got into the ambulance and held Hannah's hand.

Hannah was only wearing her nightshirt, and Tony thought they might have find their own way back from the hospital afterwards.

The ambulance pulled up outside the A&E at Torbay Hospital, and they wheeled Hannah inside. Tony stood around and paced as he waited impatiently. They had only been there five minute, but he'd looked at his watch at least ten times.

Tony thought about calling Lesley, but he left it for a while just to wait and see what was wrong with Hannah. Besides, he didn't want to worry her unnecessarily. It would only make her want to go all the way to Torquay.

By the time the doctor emerged an hour later, Tony was going out of his mind. There was no one there to comfort him. There was no one there to reassure him. He was on his own this time. He stood up quickly once he saw the doctor, and Tony didn't know what to think.

'Doc, what's happening?' The doctor smiled gently as he greeted Tony.

'Your wife is doing just fine now, Mr Craven. We've given her something to settle her stomach, and she's just resting now.' The doctor naturally assumed Hannah was his wife, but Tony never corrected him, as he liked the idea of being Hannah's husband.

'So what was making her being so sick?,' Tony asked.

'Well, at first we thought it was food poisoning, but we did further tests, and found my initial tests to be wrong.' The doctor smiled now, and Tony was confused.

'Your wife is pregnant, Mr Craven.' Tony was stunned now, and he sat down slowly not knowing what to think.

'She's what?'

'She's pregnant. I'd say about four or five weeks.' Tony smiled now, and he whooped with glee as he grabbed the doctor and hugged him. He pulled away and looked at him.

'You're sure? I'm gonna be a father?' The doctor laughed as he steadied himself now.

'Yes, sir. You can go and see her now. I'll take you to her.' Tony was so excited, and he couldn't wait to see Hannah, and he smiled gloriously as he walked through the curtain and saw her sitting there looking so pretty.

'Hello gorgeous.' He held her hands as helped her to stand up, and he hugged her. Hannah wasn't sure what was happening. The doctor hadn't told her yet, as he wanted to tell them together. Tony looked at Hannah now and smiled.

'Baby, this is fantastic news.' Hannah seemed more confused as she looked at Tony. Her hair was still a mess, and there were streaks on her face where she had been crying.

'Tony, what's happening? What's wrong with me?' Tony looked at Hannah now, and back at the doctor.

'You haven't told her yet?'

'No sir. I thought it would be nice for your wife to hear the good news from you.' Tony looked at Hannah now and kissed her lips.

'Baby, you're pregnant. We're going to have a baby.' Hannah stared at him, and laughed a little.

'I am? I mean, we are?' Hannah's smile spread further across her face as tears filled her eyes. Tony looked at her now, and he was confused.

'Baby, what's the matter?' Hannah only smiled through her tears and hugged him.

'We're going to have a baby.' She laughed and held him tight now and wiped her eyes.

'I love you, Tony.'

'I love you too.'

.

Chapter Twenty Six

Hannah and Tony were excited all day after they left the hospital. At eight-thirty they stopped in at the café on Victoria Parade, overlooking the Old Harbour and had breakfast. It was a lovely morning, with a gentle breeze, and Hannah smiled happily as she and Tony talked about the baby.

They couldn't wait to get home to London to give everyone their happy news.

After they finished breakfast they took a stroll along Meadfoot Beach. Hannah wore her blue jeans and a loose T-shirt with her denim jacket, and she was wondering how much longer she had before she wouldn't be able to fit into them. She smiled and held her tummy thinking of the baby.

They walked along Meadfoot Sea Road, and up to Kents Cavern, and onto Anstey's Cove. They sat on the beach for a while talking, and after a while Hannah started getting cold. Tony wrapped his jacket over her shoulders and they started walking back to their hotel.

Hannah was thinking of leaving the house hunting for a while now, and was going to discuss it with Tony later. The weather was still too cold to be wandering around by the coast. Though it was a lovely area, and they couldn't wait till they bought their own house together.

When they arrived back at the hotel, the hotel receptionist smiled warmly and congratulated them on their happy news, and the hotel manager had given them a complimentary bottle of champagne.

Hannah lay on the bed rubbing her tummy and smiled. She was only a couple weeks gone, and she wasn't showing yet, but she was happy. Tony leaned over her and kissed her lips, and then lifted her T-shirt and kissed her belly as Hannah smiled.

'How you feeling now?'

'Tired. I didn't sleep that well last night, and after this morning, I think it's just took it out of me.' Tony kissed her lips, and she chuckled to herself.

'Why did that doctor at the hospital call me your wife?'

'I don't know, babe. But it sounds nice, though, doesn't it?' They both laughed then thinking about it. Tony kissed Hannah passionately on the lips, and then he went to the bathroom, and when he returned five minutes later Hannah was asleep. He leaned over her and kissed her cheek.

'I love you, babe.' He left the room quietly and went down to the reception. He left a note on the bed for Hannah, so she didn't worry, and he left a message with the concierge, and afterwards he went for a stroll along the beach.

He left Hannah sleeping on the bed, and he went for a walk to clear his head and think about what he really wanted. He was having second thoughts now about Torquay. Someday he would like to return there and buy a property, but for now he was happy as he was.

That night Tony spoke to Hannah about his ideas of returning to London without looking for a property, and though Hannah was thinking the same, she seemed surprised.

'But I thought you wanted to look for a house?'

'I know babe, but it's not really that important right now, and besides I've still got my house in London, and we've got the house in Bude too. We can always stay at mine when we want to be alone.' Tony had given it a lot of thought while he was out walking, and Hannah had thought about it too.

'So, do you want to go home?,' Hannah asked.

'Not yet. We can still enjoy the rest of the holiday together.'

Steve had discussed with Bill last week about returning to work. Bill was delighted to have him back, but Steve still wasn't sure. He'd been away for almost six months, and he felt quite nervous. It was Saturday afternoon, and Steve popped into the station to see Bill. Bill was in his office talking on the phone, but he waved to Steve to go in.

Steve sat there in the armchair in Bill's office while he waited. He poured himself a scotch and sat back thinking of what to say, and moments later Bill smiled as put the phone down, and he stood up and greeted Steve.

'Well, Steve old buddy. How can I help you?'

Bill, I want to return to work. Can you get me back in the force?' Bill was surprised, but clearly happy. He leaned back in his chair as he thought for a moment.

'Is it really what you want though mate?' I mean, you've been away for almost six months, and you're due to get married. Lesley's a fine lady, and you seem happy enough.'

Steve and Lesley were getting married in four months, and they were both excited. Preparations had already started, and they were having a joint wedding a St Paul's Cathedral with Hannah and Tony

Steve stood up and walked to the window thinking about his future wedding. He looked out to the kids playing football over the road, and he leaned on the windowsill and turned to Bill.

'Bill, I thought that I would be happy if I just found myself a good woman. Settle down and have a family. It's too late for me to be thinking about that now.' Bill narrowed his eyebrows listening to his old friend.

'I've got Lesley now, and the girls. They're my family now, and I couldn't love them anymore, even if they were my children. But I can't help feeling I'm missing out on something. The force was my whole life, just as it was my fathers. I've got another fifteen to twenty years before I consider retirement, and I'd be lost without working.' Bill smiled and poured Steve another scotch.

'Steve, mate. I won't lie when I say that it was a great tragedy when you announced you were leaving. Not just for me, but the whole station. I think it would be an honour to have you back.' Bill extended his arm and shook Steve's hand.

'Welcome back, mate.' Steve laughed out loud, and PC Clover looked round wondering what was happening. Everyone at the station was busying themselves with something. Clover was on the phone to a Mrs "Fusspot" Terrance, that was complaining about the neighbours cat ruining her cabbages again, and Wilson was flirting with one of the male officers, and Winters was just coming through from the kitchen after making everyone a coffee, and WPC Queenie Ward was on the phone to the head teacher at the local school after a bunch of their kids had vandalised the phone box across the street.

None of them had noticed that Steve was in Bill's office, though Wilson tried flirting with him again as he walked in. WPC Zoë Wilson was the stations flirt, and though she was only teasing, she had asked every male officer, including Bill for a date. Though happily married with two beautiful children, Zoë was a terrible flirt.

Steve had asked Bill to keep his return to work a secret until the day he started back. Steve wanted to surprise them all when he walked back into the station in full uniform.

Steve left the station feeling very happy and pleased with himself. He had got the rest of the weekend to be with Lesley, and on Monday morning at six o'clock in the morning he was returning to work for his first shift. He was excited about going back to work again, but nervous at the same time.

It was almost eight-thirty, and there was only Steve and Lesley and Abbie at home that evening. Danni was still enjoying her time with Jason around London. They had moved on from the Grange-Holborn Hotel, and they were staying at the Grange-City now on Coopers Row. A nicely decorated suite with beige carpets and light brown curtain over-looking the Tower of London and the River Thames.

Hannah and Tony were still enjoying their break in Torquay, though they were thinking of cutting their holiday short and going home.

They had only been in Torquay for two days, and though they were staying for two weeks, they had decided to go home after one week.

Lesley was preparing the joint for tomorrows lunch. She was going to leave it in the oven over night and start cooking it slowly in the morning. Abbie was having a soak in the bath, and Steve was falling asleep in the lounge reading the daily telegraph.

Abbie had washed her hair under the shower before stepping into the bath. She lay there with her hair tied up under a shower cap. She closed her eyes listening to the elegant sounds of Celine Dion on her portable cassette player. The bathroom suite, though not as elegant as her sister, Grace's once was, was decorated with white ceramic floor tiles and pink and green pastel shades on the walls.

Though Lesley did like her home comforts and luxury items, she wasn't as fussy as her sister once was.

'As long as it's clean and fresh, it suits my needs,' she told Grace once. Abbie lay there feeling relaxed with the scented bubble bath and the music playing. The bathroom was all steamed up, and moments later she opened her eyes and saw a man staring in at her through the open window.

She screamed loudly, and jumping up she grabbed the towel and covered herself, and seconds later Lesley and Steve were banging on the bathroom door.

'Abbie, it's Steve. Are you alright?'

'Steve, get in here, she screamed. Abbie was standing up in bath covering herself with a large bath towel as her aunt and Steve walked in. Steve saw the frightened look on her face, and then the open window.

'Abbie, what's wrong?,' Steve asked.

'There was a man at the window staring in at me,' she cried. Steve went to the window as Lesley comforted her niece. Steve saw a man running away across the gardens, but he was too far to shout after him. He turned to Abbie as her aunt wrapped a dressing gown around Abbie.

'You alright, darling?,' he asked.

'Yeah, I'm OK. Just a little shaken that all.' Lesley took her back to her bedroom as Steve closed the bathroom window. Abbie got dressed and went back downstairs.

Steve was on the phone taking to Bill about the peeping tom when Abbie walked into the lounge.

'Yeah, she fine, mate. Just a little shaken up. Can you just keep your ears to the ground for anyone prowling around?' Abbie sat in the armchair by the window and curled up as she shuddered thinking of that peeping tom, and moments later Lesley bought her a coffee in.

'There you go, darling.'

'Thanks auntie.'

The huge portrait of the family hung proudly above the fireplace in Lesley's lounge. Her sister smiling down on them all as she held Duncan's arm.

Lesley sat on the sofa now looking at the portrait, and she smiled to herself remembering the day her sister had it done for her. The portrait was almost ten years old, and Mikey was only fourteen months old in his mothers arms. Lesley cuddled up to Steve as he read the paper.

Another episode of Coronation Street was on, as Lesley and Abbie sat glued to it. Steve tried to blank the television, as he did every time the soaps were on. He just sat there, as Lesley liked to call it, looking intelligent with his reading glasses half way down his nose.

Steve was never one for watching television. He never had the time when he was working before, and even now he always insisted that there was nothing interesting on, unless it was something to do with science fiction.

He never sat down in front of the television watching the football or the racing or the cricket. Quality time with Lesley and her nieces was what he liked to do best.

Steve was always the romantic. Taking Lesley out for meals. Candlelit dinners in some expensive and romantic restaurant. He always liked to show her off to everyone, telling them she was his fiancée. Wining and dining, and roses and expensive jewellery. Just last week Steve had surprised her with a three hundred pound diamond ring.

'You spoil me too much, Steven.' she had said. She only ever called him Steven if she disapproved about something he did. It was usually spending his money on her, or spending too much money on her, but she always liked the attention though.

Chapter Twenty Seven

It was Monday morning, and Steve reached out and switch the alarm off. It was four-thirty in the morning, and he stretched and yawned as Lesley rolled over and threw her arm across his chest.

'What time is it?,' she grumbled.

'It's four-thirty, darling.' He kissed her and swung his legs out of bed.

'Go back to sleep, darling.' Lesley mumbled something incoherently as Steve slipped into his slippers and grabbed his dressing gown and went for a shower. He put his clothes in the bathroom last night, so he didn't have to disturb Lesley going in an out of the bedroom.

He showered and had a shave, and he got dressed in the bathroom, and afterwards he went downstairs and cooked himself some breakfast. He sat at the table reading yesterdays newspaper, and moments later Lesley stumbled into the kitchen.

Lesley often got up early in the mornings. She was never one for sleeping past six or seven o'clock in the mornings. She always liked to be up bright and early to start her day, and even more so as she wanted to see Steve off to work each morning.

Steve was going to start off doing the early shifts, and then he would think about doing shifts again. Lesley didn't mind, especially when he started at six o'clock in the mornings. It meant he would be home just after two o'clock, and they would have the rest of the day together.

Lesley was thinking of doing some part-time work. Just to fill in the hours while Steve was at work. Though she wasn't sure yet what to do. She always liked working with children. Perhaps she would get a job working in a nursery or a pre-school day centre. Lesley hasn't worked for almost eighteen years now, since she sued the council for damages.

Lesley was working as a typist for a group of solicitors in 1987, and she quit after she won nearly three quarters of a million pounds for personal injuries, and then in 1996 she won seven hundred thousand pounds after she was wrongly accused for theft from a jewellery store in Islington.

Duncan had offered her a job within the family law firm five years ago. She had plenty of skills as a typist, and Grace and Duncan were willing to train her in other fields. Maybe she could ask Hannah for a job at the office, she thought, but she wasn't entirely sure yet.

At five thirty Steve kissed Lesley goodbye as they stood on the doorstep, and she smiled and waved as he got into his car. Lesley went back into the kitchen and started loading the dishwasher, and afterwards she did herself three slices of toast and a coffee.

Lesley always started her day with the same three slices of toast and her coffee. Ocassionally she had a full breakfast if she was cooking it for Steve or her nieces.

At six o'clock Lesley went for a shower. She sorted her clothes out for the day, and afterwards she saw to tidying the kitchen.

Steve pulled into the car park at the station at five-forty, and throwing his bag over his shoulder he made his way into the station. He was smiling and whistling as he swiped his card over the electronic key pad, and shutting the door behind him the officer behind the desk looked up in surprise.

'Steve. You're back.'

'Morning Dave.' Steve smiled and just walked past. He made his way to the canteen where Bill was waiting for him. Wilson and Clover and Winters were in there eating breakfast, and Steve burst in, and standing in the doorway like a cowboy from the wild west, he just glared.

'OK, who's the jerk that's parked in my parking space?' Bill hadn't told any of them that Steve was coming back, and he laughed now as Zoë stared in amazement. Steve stood there in full uniform, and Zoë cheered, and running to him she wrapped her arms around him.

'Hello gorgeous, you missed me?'

'Hello mate,' Clovers said greeting him.

'You come back then? You missed this place that much?' Bill greeted him, and the two men shook hands.

'Welcome back mate. I never told anyone you were coming back.' Bill called to the chef in the canteen.

'Hey, Lydia. Full breakfast over here please.'

'Right you are, Bill.' Steve sat down as Zoë fetched him a coffee. Everyone was happy Steve was back, and five minutes later Queenie Ward walked in, and she stopped in her tracks in the doorway. They were all chatting and laughing as Queenie stood there.

'Steve?' Steve looked up and smiled.

'Hello Queenie.' She went to him and he kissed her cheek.

'You couldn't stay away from us then, I see?' Queenie laughed. She looked to Bill then and smiled.

'You could have told us he was coming back, Bill.'

'What, and ruin the surprise,' Bill laughed.

'The looks on yours and Zoë's face was priceless,' he said then. At six-thirty Steve put his jacket on, and he turned to everyone.

'Well, ladies and gents. This has been pleasant, but one must go and do some work,' he said with a posh accent. He twirled his hand and curtsied, as everyone jeered, and he went to leave as Queenie called to him.

'Hey, Steve. It's great to have you back mate.' Steve blew her a kiss and walked out of the canteen.

'OK people, parties over. Let's get some work done.' Bill called. They all groaned as they walked out of the canteen, and they went to look at their daily rotas for today. Bill caught up with Steve before he left.

'Steve, mate. It's good to have you back.' The two men shook hands, and Steve left with a smile on his face.

Caroline sat at her dressing table staring at herself in the mirror. Her face was still slightly bruised, but the swelling had gone now. A single tear trickled from the corner of her eye as her sister walked into the bedroom. Caroline got a tissue and wiped he eyes, and she smiled.

'Morning Deb's' Debbie stood behind her sister looking at her in the mirror, and she smiled gently.

'The bruising is going down well now.' Debbie touched her face and kissed her.

'I love you Cass'. Caroline smiled as her sister cuddled her.

'I love you too Deb's.'

'Mom's just doing some bacon rolls for breakfast. Do you want some?'

'Yes please.' Caroline smiled as she watched her sister leave, and afterwards she finished getting dressed. She had tied her hair back into a short ponytail, and went downstairs. She could smell the bacon and sausages cooking, and she smiled as she sat down.

'Thanks mom.' Lyndsey put a plate of bacon and sausage rolls in front of her. She reached for the tomato ketchup as her father came through the door.

'Morning, daddy.'

'Morning, darling. How you feeling this morning?' He kissed the top of her head and sat down as Lyndsey put a full breakfast in front of him.

'Thank you, darling.' He kissed his wife and Lyndsey prepared her own breakfast.

'I'm OK. Daddy, I was thinking of returning to work soon. Is that alright?' Raymond looked to his daughter, and then to Lyndsey.

'Yes, that's fine with me, sweetheart. But do you really feel up to coming back yet? I mean, it's only been a week.'

'I know, but I'm going demented sitting around doing nothing all day, and the more time I have, the more time I've got to sit and think about what happened.' Lyndsey sat down at the table listening. She was concerned for her daughters welfare, and she wasn't entirely sure she had recovered properly.

'Honey. It's only been a week, are you sure you're ready? You're still quite badly bruised, and I don't just mean physically, but mentally too.' Caroline thought for a second as she pushed her empty plate away from her.

'Mom. Do these bruises make me look ugly?'

'No darling,' she said quickly.

'Am I embarrassing to you when I go out?' Raymond and Lyndsey realised what she was saying now, and Raymond sighed heavily.

'Sweetheart, that's not what your mother said.' Caroline bowed her head as tears filled in her eyes.

'Mom, I'm sorry. Please forgive me.' Lyndsey smiled and went to her daughter.

'It alright, darling.' Lyndsey comforted her daughter and kissed her cheek.

'Sorry daddy. I'm just being paranoid.' Raymond went to his daughter and held her hands.

'Caroline, you know we love you, and we would do anything if it meant you would be happy,' he said.

'We're just thinking of you. If you want to return to work, then I'll be happy to have you back, but are you sure you're ready?'

'Yes, I think I am.' Raymond smiled and kissed her hand.

'Then I'll be happy to have you back.' Lyndsey wasn't entirely sure though. Though she was happy that her daughter wanted to go back to work, she also knew that some people can be nasty and stare at her.

Lyndsey didn't concern herself with that too much though. She smiled and tried to be happy for her daughter. Caroline smiled now and kissed her father.

'Thank you, daddy.' Caroline smiled mischievously now, and looked at her father.

'Daddy. You said you'd do anything to make me happy?'

'Yes,' he said cautiously.

'Then give me a cuddle.' Raymond laughed and held his arms out to her, and Lyndsey and Debbie laughed too as they watched.

'I love you, daddy.'

'I love you too, sweetheart.' He kissed his daughter, and Debbie went and joined them as she put her arm around her sister and father.

Chapter Twenty Eight

It was Friday morning, and Hannah and Tony were just going downstairs for their last breakfast before they left the hotel. They had loaded the car, and made sure they'd packed everything, and at eight-thirty they sat in the restaurant as they ate their breakfast.

Hannah had full breakfast, with double sausages and bacon. They were hoping to see the concierge before they left and thank him for his help, though they thought he might be working the night shift.

Hannah was looking forward to returning home. They had contacted their aunt and told her that they would be home sooner. Lesley worried a bit, but Hannah just said they had good news. Lesley was thinking they had found a cottage, but in a week, it was a bit quick, she thought.

Danni and Jason were coming home tomorrow too, and Hannah couldn't wait to see her sisters.

Hannah and Tony went to their room just before nine-thirty and had a last look round. They picked up their hand luggage and made their way downstairs. Collette, the day manager was at the reception when they got downstairs, and she smiled warmly as she saw Hannah and Tony.

'Hello Mr. and Mrs Craven. I see you're leaving us today.'

'Yes. I can't wait to get home and give everyone the happy news.' The receptionist smiled as they thanked her for their stay.

'You're welcome Mrs Craven.' Hannah smiled proudly, as though she was already Mrs Craven, and she held Tony's hand.

'It's Miss Philips actually. But it will be Mrs Craven in four months.'

'Oh, well congratulations then, and we hope to see you again soon,' she chirped. Hannah and Tony walked out holding hands. They said goodbye to the doorman, and then they walked out to the car. It was a glorious morning. There was a slight chill in the air, but the sun shone high in the sky, and Hannah smiled holding her tummy as she got in the passenger seat.

'We're going home now, Junior.' Tony smiled at the name as he pulled off out of the car park.

'Junior, huh?' Hannah smiled gloriously.

'Yeah. Sounds good, don't it?'

'Well, what if it's a girl?' Hannah just carried on smiling as they cruised down the street. Tony sometimes drove Hannah's car. Mainly if they were together and when Hannah was tired. Hannah had dozed off on the journey home, and when Tony pulled into the car park at the roadside café on the A38 for a rest he woke Hannah. She slowly opened her eyes and squinted a little.

'We home already?'

'No. I'm just taking a break. I'm a little tired. Do you want a drink from the café?'

'Yes please. Just a coffee, thanks.' Hannah went to the bathroom, and afterwards she joined Tony at the counter while they were waiting, and all at once she hungered for a bacon and sausage and egg sandwich. Tony looked at her in surprise.

'Bacon sausage *and* egg?'

'Yeah, well. I have got two of us to feed now,' she said cheekily holding her tummy. Tony only smiled as he took her in his arms.

'And what else would Junior like?' Hannah thought for a few seconds as she pouted her lips.

'A really thick milkshake.' The waitress behind the counter smiled as she listened.

'Would you like some mushrooms and tomatoes on that sandwich, honey?' Tony looked round as Hannah smiled.

'Hey you, don't encourage her.' Hannah laughed and kissed Tony, and she turned to the waitress.

'Yeah, I will have mushrooms and tomatoes thanks. And put some extra bacon on as well.

'See? See what you done?,' Tony laughed at the waitress. They sat down at a table as they waited, and moments later Hannah's sandwich was bought over.

'There ya go love. Get your mouth around that.' The chef had put extra bacon and sausages on it for her as well, and the waitress winked at Hannah and then left them alone. Tony sat there watching Hannah tackle that sandwich.

'Mmm, I think Junior likes this. I think he wants another one.'

'Oh, he does, does he?'

Tony was just sitting there drinking his coffee while watching her eat the sandwich. Tony only had two bacon sandwiches, and he was smiling watching Hannah. It was clear that Hannah was enjoying it, and she looked lovingly at the second one the waitress now bought over.

It was almost two o'clock in the afternoon as Hannah turned into Park Lane. They were only minutes away from home, and Hannah was bursting with excitement at the thought of telling everyone that she was pregnant, and when she pulled up on the drive Steve was just driving up the street after finishing work. Hannah and Tony jumped out the car as they grabbed their bags, and Hannah greeted Steve.

'Hi ya Steve.'

'Hello darling. Have a good holiday?' He kissed Hannah and they went inside. Lesley was just preparing lunch, and Abbie was upstairs reading a book in her room, but she came running down the stairs once she heard Hannah.

'Sis', you're back.' Abbie ran to her sister and greeted her, and she hugged Tony, as Lesley came through from the kitchen.

'Hello darling,' Lesley said hugging her niece.

'So, come on, sis'. What's this terribly exciting news you had to come rushing home for?' Hannah and Tony had barely sat down in the lounge as they saw Abbie's excitement. Hannah held Tony's hand as they sat down on the sofa.

'Well, in the early hours after our first night, I woke up being violently sick. I felt awful, and I was rushed to hospital.' Hannah was beaming, but everyone else seemed confused.

'That's you're exciting news?,' her aunt asked going to her and holding her hand.

'Darling, what was wrong? Tony, why didn't you call me?' Lesley was getting worried now, but Tony was smiling as Hannah continued.

'Auntie, it was morning sickness. I'm pregnant.' Hannah screamed with excitement now as everyone smiled and laughed.

'Oh, darling. That's fantastic news,' Lesley said and kissed her and Tony.

'Congratulations, sis', Abbie said.

They sat in the lounge and about the baby and their holiday, and at two o'clock Frank and Sally came to visit. Hannah was just telling them about the hotel when they walked into the lounge

'Hello everyone,' Frank said. Hannah greeted them both and ginned like a Cheshire cat.

'Hello sweetheart. You certainly look happy,' he said as Lesley bought some coffees in. Hannah stood up by the fireplace as she held her tummy.

'Frank, Sally. I'm having a baby.' Frank laughed. He jumped up and hugged her.

'Well, congratulations, darling.'

'That's fantastic,' Sally said as she hugged her.

'How far gone are you?'

'About three or four weeks.' Everyone sat around talking as Steve went to the off licence and bought some champagne. Frank and Sally were excited as they thought of everything that Hannah had been through over he past year. It was about time she had some good news.

Hannah and Tony had gone for a walk that afternoon in Hyde Park. They talked for hours about the baby and their future plans. In four months Hannah and Tony were getting married, and Hannah was thrilled that everything was finally coming together.

She slept soundly that night, and had the best nights sleep she had had for a while, and when she woke the following morning at nine-thirty she sat at the breakfast table and ate a full breakfast with extra bacon and sausages.

Danni and Jason were due home that afternoon. They were only staying at the Grange Langham Court Hotel on the other side of Hyde Park, and it was only a fifteen minute walk home. They had checked out of the hotel at twelve o'clock and decided to go shopping on Oxford Street before they went home, and when they walked through the front door just after three o'clock loaded with bags they were both exhausted.

'Hello, we're home,' Danni called. Hannah and Abbie jumped and greeted them.

'Ahhh, sis', you're home,' Abbie screamed going to her. Abbie kissed Jason and they went through to the lounge. Danni greeted her aunt and Steve, and they all sat down. Danni and Jason were bursting with excitement as they told them all about the hotels they stayed at, and moments later Danni took something from one of her bags and stood up.

'Auntie, Steve, and of cause my dear sisters. Jason and I have got some fan*tastic* news to tell you.' She held up a pair of blue woolly booties and smiled gloriously.

'I think we'll be needing these in about eight months.' They were all ecstatic as they congratulated them both. Lesley and Steve couldn't believe it. Both of them in two days, Hannah stood up and took the booties from her sister now and smiled.

'Danni, I think I'll be needing these too in eight months.' Hannah and Danni both looked at each other now and squealed with delight.

'No way. You too?,' Danni asked.

'What are the odds of this happening?,' Steve laughed. He kissed Hannah and Danni and shook Jason's hand.

'I think we're going to have our hands full in eight months, auntie,' Abbie laughed.

Over the following few weeks Hannah and her sisters spent their time on loads of shopping sprees. They visited Oxford Street and Piccadilly and Harrods and Covent Gardens.

Hannah and Danni were excited about being pregnant together. Even Abbie was, though by the end of February she was exhausted. She felt a bit glum, as her sisters were having babies and she wasn't. But those things never excited her that much. Baby sick and smelly nappies, and waking up in the night and breastfeeding were the last thing on Abbie's mind.

Even now, after everything that's happened over the last twelve months, deep down Abbie was still the tomboy she's always been. Though a lot of people had said she was more a lady now than she used to be.

It was the beginning of April, and Tony and Jason had started preparing the nursery. They had taken one of the spare rooms at Lesley's and redecorated it together. They bought the cots and rocking chairs. They had painted it yellow and white, with Winnie The Pooh curtains.

The girls had bought all the baby clothes and loads of nappies ready, and on the morning of the third of April Hannah and Danni went for their antenatal check-up. They both went in to the examination room together. Tony and Hannah were on one side of the room, while Danni and Jason were on the other, and when the girls were given their scans they all watched in awe at the figures on the screen.

'There's my baby,' Danni cried.

'Sis', I can see my baby.' Jason held her had the entire time as he had tears in his eyes watching the monitor.

'Whoa, wait a minute, wait a minute,' the doctor smiled.

'I think you mean bab*ies*, Miss Philips.' Danni looked at the monitor as the doctor shown her, and she looked at Jason, and then to the doctor.

'Twins? I'm having twins?'

'We're having twins,' she cried looking at Jason. She kissed him lovingly, and looked over at her sister.

'Sis, I've having two babies.'

That morning they walked home from the hospital, and they talked all the way home about the babies and the births.

'Just think, Danni. You're going to have to give birth twice.' Danni rolled her eyes and groaned.

'Don't remind me,' she laughed.

It was only three weeks to go before Hannah and Tony, and Steve and Lesley get married. Hannah and Lesley had bought their dresses. Danni and Abbie, and Caroline and Debbie, and Jade and Keeley were going to be bridesmaids.

The service was at ten thirty on the twelve of May at St Paul's Cathedral, and already the brides had got the jitters. It was seven-thirty in the evening, and Steve and Tony and Jason had gone out drinking. Frank had joined them, and Bill and the lads from the station had joined them too while the girls had a girls night in.

Julie and Sally were there with Lyndsey and her daughters, and they bought a few bottles of wine. Hannah had asked Sally to be her maid of honour,

Hannah and Tony had decided to moved into his house after they were married, and maybe one day return to the house in Bude. It's been almost eight months since they were last in Bude. It's been almost eight months since Mikey died, and the sisters were concerned now about leaving the place unattended.

Though Steve and Tony go down there to check on things, and they asked the local police to keep an eye out for prowlers and burglars.

The sisters hadn't decided yet whether they wanted to live there anymore. Now that Mikey's gone, and they bought it together, they didn't feel right about it.

Steve and Lesley were thinking of spending some quality time together in his house after their honeymoon. Steve had been thinking of selling his house recently, though now he thought he'd keep it.

That night Hannah lay in Tony's arms after making love, and she smiled to herself and kissed his arm.

'I love you Tony Craven.'

'And I love you Hannah "soon to be" Craven.' Hannah giggled and leaned over and kissed him lovingly on the lips.

Chapter Twenty Nine

The night before the wedding, Tony and Steve had gone out on their stag night, while Hannah and Lesley and the girls had their Hen Party at the local community hall.

Male strippers and the Chippendales were ordered to give the girls a wild night. Some of Lesley's closest friends from school and college were there, and it was as much a reunion as much as it was a Hen Night.

Some of the girls she hadn't seen since they left school. It was her nieces idea to get in touch with their aunt's long lost friends, and Lesley had cried welcoming them.

All of Lesley's friends had known each other since they were in primary school. Some had shared their most intimate secrets, and they were all shocked to hear of Grace and Duncan's deaths.

One friend of Lesley's had tried contacting her soon after she read in the papers about Grace and Duncan's death, but it was as though Lesley had disappeared off the face of the earth.

Duncan was always the high-flying lawyer. He had handled many divorce cases, and child custody cases. At school he was the captain of the football and rugby team four years in a row. He was a member of the cricket club, and was the coach for the basketball team, and the most decent respectable person that had ever walked and passed through the doors of High School between 1972 and 1976.

Even after he left school, his friends had idolised him. Most of the lads were jealous of him, as he had won Grace's heart, and the girls adored him. On many occasions the girls had tried to get dates with Duncan. More than once they had cornered him in the changing rooms and tried to tear his clothes off him after they had watched him playing football. Lesley and the girls had spent hours that night talking of old times, and reminiscence the past.

Hannah and her sisters cried and laughed listening to stories about their parents, until one of the male strippers grabbed Lesley and Hannah and dragged them on to the dance floor.

All the women jeered and watched as the strippers got them to dance and perform to music my Rod Stewart and Hot Chocolate.

Hannah had never seen her aunt blush and get so embarrassed before. Normally Lesley was so calm and in control in every situation. Danni and Abbie were enjoying the show, especially when the Chippendales got up on stage, and they enjoyed watching their sister and aunt, but after a while they got up and joined in.

By eleven o'clock that evening, Lesley was getting into the swing, as she was the one teasing and toying with the strippers.

'Go auntie, go,' Abbie screamed as Lesley was caressing and touching the male strippers and pulling at their thongs.

Hannah was joining in too, but she was taking things a bit lightly, as she was pregnant, and Danni was just enjoying herself sitting watching, and at twelve midnight everyone jeered and screamed as more strippers arrived dressed as firemen. One of them had scooped Lesley us over his shoulder as he took her up onto the stage.

The party had gone on till the very early hours of the morning, and by seven-thirty everyone was tired and exhausted. Hannah stood in he bedroom as Lyndsey and Hollie were adjusting Hannah's dress, and moments later Lesley walked in and beamed at her niece.

'Darling, you look fabulous.' She went to her and gently kissed her cheek, so not to smudge Hannah's make-up. Lesley stood back and looked at Hannah proudly.

'If your mother and father could see you now, they'd be so proud of you, darling.' A single tear trickled from Hannah's eye, and she gently wiped it away.

'Don't you start crying now, sweetheart. You'll smudge your make-up,' Hollie said.

It was almost eight-thirty, and Danni and Abbie were in the next bedroom with Jade and Keeley getting into their bridesmaids dresses, and across the street Caroline and Debbie were also getting into their bridesmaids dresses.

Jade owned her own beauty salon on Edgeware Road, so she and her colleague were in charge of hair and make-up, and across the other side of Hyde Park, Steve and Tony and the lads had gathered at Steve's house as they got changed.

Outside in the street the neighbours gathered as two limousines waited, and moments later Hannah and Lesley emerged looking spectacular in their white gowns. All the neighbours cheered and waved as Hannah got into one car and Lesley got into the other.

Hannah was wearing her grandmothers pearls as something old, and she waved gloriously as they pulled off. One of the neighbours had got Vera into his car and folded her wheelchair up, and the congregation of cars followed the two limousines to the church. Raymond and Desmond had closed up the offices for the day, and everyone was there for the big day. Hannah felt like royalty as she sat in the back seat of the limousine.

It was a glorious morning as the sun shone high in the sky. Birds sang in the distant, and the sound of a car backfiring vibrated through the air like gun fire, and as the cars pulled up outside St Paul's Cathedral a little boy rode past on his bike and looked in awe at Hannah stepping out of the car.

The sounds of the church organ rose up to the clear blue sky as Hannah and Lesley walked up the path to the church doors. Hannah pulled the vale over her face as she held Raymond's arm, and stepping inside the foyer Hannah giggled like a small child. She had butterflies in her tummy.

She looked into the church as all the pews were full. She saw all the guests that were standing up around the sides of the church. There were more than two hundred guests, and that was without family members.

Steve's brothers were there with their families, and Tony's parents and sisters were there too. Tony's family had flown over from Greece to be there for his big day. Though Tony has never got on with his family, and he was glad to see the back of them when he left home at seventeen, he was happy they were there.

He has always hated his sisters, especially since his older sister, Stacey had called Hannah a slut to her face after Hannah and Tony were caught kissing behind the bike sheds. Stacey had daggers for eyes once she saw Hannah now.

The church organ started playing as the doors to the church opened. Hannah held Raymond's arm as they entered the church, and all faces were on them now as Hannah beamed. Lesley was holding Bill's arm as they walked behind Raymond and Hannah, following closely behind were the six bridesmaids.

Steve and Tony stood at the alter, proud and smiling in grey top hats and tails. The music stopped and the minister greeted the congregation. Everyone took their seats and Raymond went and sat with his wife. He smiled gloriously and proud as he saw his daughters both dressed as bridesmaids. Caroline's bruises were barely visible now, and being there at the wedding was great healing power for her self-esteem and a great confidence booster too

All the bridesmaids wore matching pastel blue gowns with flowery bonnets. They each held a bunch of flowers, and they too took their seats now as Hannah held Tony's arm, and Lesley, standing beside her niece held Steve's arm. Tony beamed and looked at Hannah and mouthed the words "I love you".

'We are gathered here today, in front of friends and family and the presence of Jesus Christ our Lord,' the minister began. Steve stood tall and proud as Lesley held his arm. For Steve, today was the day he thought would never happen for him. He never thought in his wildest dreams that he would be getting married again.

He had always been proud and happy with the way his life was. He has had a good career in the police force for nearly twenty-five years, and his colleagues and the community were his family. Now he had another family. An extra special family, and a beautiful woman as his wife. A single tear trickled down his cheek now thinking of the events over the past twelve months that led him to be standing there right now.

They each exchanged their own personal vows, and Steve smiled proudly now as he held the ring in his hand and placed it on Lesley's finger.

'With this ring, I thee wed.' He kissed Lesley, and the minister turned to Hannah and Tony. Tony took the ring and placed it on Hannah's finger.

'With this ring, I thee wed.' He kissed Hannah lovingly, and they all turned to face the minister. The minister held out his arms, as though gathering them to him.

'By the powers invested in me, I now pronounce you, Steven and Lesley, and Tony and Hannah, husbands and wives. You may kiss your bride,' he said as he looked to Tony and then to Steve. Tony held Hannah in a loving embrace and kissed her sweet lips. After a few seconds, Steve and Lesley smiled watching her niece and Tony as they continued kissing, and the congregation laughed quietly.

'Ahem,' Hannah looked up and blushed as the minister smiled.

'Sorry.'

The church organ played, and the brides and grooms walked slowly back up the isle as some of the congregation stood and congratulated them.

They stood outside in the morning sunshine, as confetti rained down like snowflakes. Tony had noticed as he walked back up the isle, that his family had disappeared, and he felt his eyes sting as the hatred for his family only worsened. Hannah noticed and realised, and she only comforted him.

'I'm sorry, baby.' He kissed her and tried to compose himself as he saw the photographer.

Tony pushed the thoughts of his family further to the back of his mind. As far as he was concerned now, they didn't exist anymore. His family were right there with him. Hannah and her sisters and Lesley and Steve. Steve and Lesley have been more family to him over he past twelve months than his own family have been his entire life.

Hannah and Tony smiled beautifully now for their photos. The brides and grooms stood together at the entrance to the Cathedral for a couple of photos. Then the bridesmaids. Caroline smiled beautifully as she cuddled her sister, and there was one where Caroline was kissing her fathers cheek.

That afternoon, they all gathered back at the community hall on Wigmore Street for their reception. Hannah and Tony were leaving in the morning for their honeymoon. Two whole weeks together in Las Vegas. Steve and Lesley were leaving in the morning too for their honeymoon to Venice.

Steve had told Lesley last week where they were going, and she was so excited. Steve had wanted to leave it till the last minute to surprise her, but knowing Lesley she would want to plan for such a holiday. Though it was all booked and paid for, and the flight were arranged, Lesley would want plenty of time to pack and to make sure they had everything.

When they arrived back at the community hall, Hannah and Tony, and Steve and Lesley were greeted with a crowd of cheers and welcome from their neighbours and friends and loved ones. The moment Tony arrived he looked around hoping his parents were there.

Part of him still wanted to believe they cared, and that they went on ahead to the reception to surprise him, but they were no where to be seen. Probably on their way back to Greece by now, he thought. Hannah held his hand and kissed him lovingly.

'Come on, baby,' she said gently. Hannah knew, despite what Tony said, that deep down he was hurting that his family wasn't there. He could fool a lot of people, but he couldn't fool Hannah, and that night as they sat upstairs in their bedroom he cried in Hannah's arms.

Hannah and Tony made love that night, and afterwards she fell asleep in his arms, but Tony lay awake for most of the night thinking about his lost family. Wishing they had thought better of him, but he knew it was only a fools hope for him to wish for that.

He knew that he would never see them again, and if they ever did show their faces again he would just turn his back on them, just as they turned their back on him.

Hannah was awake by seven o'clock, and she left Tony sleeping. She kissed his cheek and she went downstairs for breakfast. The usual full breakfast was on the menu, but Abbie and Danni were cooking this morning, as their aunt and Steve were still in bed.

Raymond and Lyndsey were there with Caroline and Debbie, and Desmond and Hollie and her daughters. It's been almost three and half months since Caroline's attack in Hyde Park, and she had been back at work for three months, and she hasn't looked more happier.

The colour had started coming back to her cheeks, and the bruises were barely noticeable. She felt a bit conscious on her first day back to work, but the other office staff soon welcomed her and cheered her up.

Hannah walked in the kitchen and sniffed the air and smiled gloriously.

'Well, good morning, Mrs Craven,' Desmond chirped, and Hannah smiled gloriously at the sound of her new name. Desmond stood up and gave her a cuddle and kissed her cheek.

'Sis', what you doing up? I was going to bring you two breakfast in bed,' Danni said.

Hannah and Tony and Steve and Lesley were leaving for their honeymoon's that afternoon. They had already packed, and Raymond was going to give them a lift to Heathrow at twelve-thirty.

'Well, Tony's still asleep, and I needed to get up to go to the loo anyway. So I thought I'd come down for some breakfast. I'll leave Tony for another hour and I'll go and wake him.'

Hannah and Danni were almost fourteen weeks pregnant, with only a couple of days apart from each other. Tony and Jason had finished the nursery now, and when the girls saw it they almost cried. There were Winnie The Pooh curtains and lamp shades, with laminated flooring. The three cots side by side so the cousins could see each other, with three rocking chairs by the cots. Jason had bought the musical mobiles to hang over the cots, and Tony had bought the baby monitors. It was all ready and finished. All they were waiting for were the new arrivals. Hannah climbed on the bed and kissed Tony's lips. He began to stir, and she kissed his neck, and then his ear.

'Good morning my sexy husband.' Tony smiled and kissed her lips.

'Well, good morning, Mrs Craven.' Their lips met, and she lay down and held him in her arms.

'Do you want some breakfast, my love?'

'Yes please. Though I'd rather have you,' he teased reaching out for her.

'No more sex until after the baby has come, Mr Craven,' she teased walking out of the bedroom. Hannah was only wearing her red silk nightie from Ann Summers, that barely covered her bottom, and her short silk dressing gown. Lying down on the bed, he could just see her red silk knickers under her nightie, and she knew it would tease him, and she laughed standing in the doorway to the bedroom.

'What?' You love torturing me, don't you?,' he laughed. He chased after her, and she screamed going carefully down the stairs.

'Tony, this isn't fair. I can't run,' she laughed holding her tummy. He gently grabbed hold of her in the hallway and gently tickled her and pinched her bottom.

'Tony, stop it. Stop it,' she laughed.

'Tony, I'm gonna wet myself if you don't stop,' she laughed as Danni and Abbie came through from the kitchen to see what was happening.

'What's going on out here?,' Danni asked.

'Tell me you love me,' he said pinching her bottom.

'I love you.'

'I didn't hear you.'

'I love you.' He took her in his arms and kissed her lovingly now, and then they went through to the kitchen where Hannah sat at the table as Tony dished up breakfast for them both.

At eleven-thirty Raymond knocked the front door a walked in. He called out and walked through to the lounge where Hannah and Tony were sitting cuddling. They were all packed and ready to leave. Hannah's and Tony's flight wasn't leaving till one forty-five, and Steve and Lesley's was leaving at ten past two.

They had plenty of time to get to the airport, so Steve loaded all the luggage into Raymond's people carrier while Lesley made a pot of coffee. They all sat in the kitchen around the table talking for a while, and just before twelve o'clock they all started to leave.

'Goodbye auntie. Have a good holiday,' Danni said. She kissed her aunt, and then she hugged and kissed Steve.

'Bye Steve.' Lesley hugged Jason and smiled.

'You take care darling, and look after my nieces.' She kissed his cheek and Danni smiled as she held his hand.

Hannah kissed and hugged her sisters, and after they all said their goodbyes Hannah and Tony, and Steve and Lesley went outside and got into Raymond's car. Julie had come round to say goodbye that morning, and she stood on the doorstep now with Danni and Jason and Abbie as they all waved.

Danni wiped her eyes and waved as she watched them drive to the end of Connaught Street and disappeared around the corner, and Julie put her arm around her waist, as Abbie held Jason arm, and they went back inside the house.

Chapter Thirty

Caroline sat at her desk typing out the dictations she took earlier that morning before her father left for a meeting in Richmond. It was almost eleven o'clock, and Caroline was feeling tired.

Though she had a good nights sleep, she couldn't shake off the tiredness. Her head was throbbing, and the two paracetamol she had taken earlier wasn't doing anything for her. She carried on working, trying to ignore the pain in her head, but just before twelve o'clock she went to go to the kitchen to fetch a glass of water.

She used her desk for leverage and tried to stand up, but she felt as though she had no energy. She stood up feeling dizzy and nauseous. She scrunched her eyes shut and opened them, and everything was blurry, and she called out to Desmond's secretary who was sitting opposite her.

'Jen.' She was getting scared as she could barely see her hands in front of her. She flopped back down in her chair as Jenny looked up from her computer, and she saw Caroline sweating and pale.

'Caroline?' Jenny jumped up and went to her as Caroline tried to stand up again, and she collapsed as Jenny caught her.

'Oh my God, Caroline.' She pressed the intercom on her desk as the other office staff gathered around to see what was happening.

'Desmond, get out here quick.' Desmond looked up as he was on the phone, with his cigar resting on the ashtray.

'Jesus, Caroline.' He put the phone down without saying another word to his client and ran out.

'Jenny, what happened?'

'I don't know. She called out to me, and then she collapsed.' One of the secretaries was already calling for the ambulance as Desmond tried to arouse Caroline.

'Jen, get me an ambulance. And get Lyndsey on the phone and tell her to meet us at the hospital.'

Lyndsey was at work today at the restaurant. It was busy, and an order for a party of forty-five guests had just come in. Carlos answered the phone, and he was as white as a sheet as he told Lyndsey.

'Caroline, sweetheart. Come on Caroline, open your eyes,' Desmond said gently tapping her face.

'What's the matter with her Desmond?,' Heather Wilkes asked.

'I don't know. She's sweating. She's trembling and she's hyperventilating.' Caroline lay unconscious in Desmond's arms, and he felt her whole body trembling now.

'It looks like she's gone into shock from something,' he said. But from what, he didn't know. He was gently tapping her face to bring her round, but she never responded. He put his hand on her chest to check she was breathing, and it was only then he noticed her breathing was short and raspy.

'Oh my God.' It was almost as though she was fighting to breathe.

It was nearly ten minutes later when two paramedics came running through the office. Jenny explained what had happened as Desmond moved aside, and moments later they put an oxygen mask over Caroline's nose and mouth and strapped her to a portable chair, and they carried her downstairs and out to the ambulance.

'What hospital you going to?,' Jenny asked the paramedics.

'St Mary's.'

'Desmond, I'll get onto Lyndsey and tell her where you're going.'

'Call Raymond on his mobile and tell him to get to the hospital. He's in a meeting in Richmond.' Desmond climbed into the ambulance and held Caroline's hand as the ambulance screamed out of the car park and along Oxford Street.

The ambulance screeched to a halt as they pulled up outside the A&E, and the paramedics ran inside with her. Desmond ran behind, and five minutes later Lyndsey came running in. Crying and looking a bit worse-for-wear with her whites still on.

'Desmond.' Lyndsey cried in his arms, and moments later she pulled away from him and wiped her eyes.

'What happened?'

'I don't know. I never saw it, but Jenny said that Caroline stood up at her desk, and just collapsed. When I saw her she was sweating and hyperventilating and trembling.' Lyndsey covered her mouth with her hands as she cried, and all the while Desmond comforted her as they waited.

It was twelve-thirty in the afternoon, and all around them there were a bustle of doctors and nurses rushing around, and when Raymond come through the doors looking pale and shaken Lyndsey sobbed in his arms.

'Darling, what happened? Where Caroline?' Lyndsey composed herself and wiped her eyes as she explained she knew as much as he did.

'Apparently she collapsed and Jenny called the ambulance, and Desmond came with her in the ambulance.'

'Mate, Caroline was sweating and hyperventilating and she collapsed. One minute she seemed fine, and the next time I saw her she was unconscious on the floor.' Raymond extended his arm, and the two men shook hands.

'Mate. I can't thank you enough.' Raymond hugged him, and moments later Danni and Abbie came running in after Lyndsey notified them. The girls were out shopping at Harrods, having a girly day out together.

It's been a few weeks now since the girls had spent any time at the office, and they were wondering what to do with themselves. The truth was, that Abbie wasn't officially working there yet. She was still enrolled for Cambridge in September, but she was having second thoughts now. Abbie would always have her share in the business regardless, but ever since she could remember she has never shown any interest in law.

'Raymond, what happened?,' Abbie asked hugging him.

'I don't know, darling. Desmond said she just collapsed in the office.' They all sat around waiting, and pacing as they all worried over Caroline. Although it had been almost four months since Caroline's attack, Raymond was thinking now that it wasn't such a good idea Caroline going back to work so soon. After all it was only a couple of weeks before she went back.

Raymond was pacing, and Lyndsey was near tears when Dr Hanson emerged just after two o'clock. Lyndsey was staring out the window, and Raymond was just pacing as neither of them noticed him.

'Raymond. Lyndsey.' Dr Hanson smiled warmly as they faced him, and Lyndsey cried going to him.

'Dr Hanson, please tell me my baby is alright.' He touched her arm and they sat down in the waiting room. Dr Hanson had heard about Caroline's attack, and it grieved him that someone was prepared to hurt someone so badly. He smiled gently now as he crossed his legs.

'Caroline is fine now. It was just a panic attack. Probably bought on by many factors.'

'How do you mean?,' Raymond asked. Dr Hanson looked at Caroline's notes for a few seconds.

'Well, given what Caroline's been through with her attack, and coping with it since, I wouldn't be surprised if that's what bought it on.' Raymond rolled his eyes as he knew it was a bad idea allowing her to go back to work so soon.

'Stress is a hard thing to deal with. Unfortunately for Caroline, some people deal with it better than others.' Dr Hanson stood up now and paced, and then he turned and faced them. Desmond was still there, and he was listening carefully, because he wasn't sure if Raymond and Lyndsey were right now.

'What Caroline needs now is complete rest. Housebound her if you have to, but it's essential that Caroline gives herself enough healing time.' He thought carefully now as he knew he was treading on a delicate subject.

'I don't mean to sound impertinent, but did Caroline ever go to counselling after her attack?'

'No. We thought about it, but we thought her returning to work would have been a great healer,' Lyndsey said. The doctor smiled and sat down as he placed his hands together and thought.

'Well, it might just be what Caroline needs. Counselling might seem like a bunch of old farce to some people, but it does do wonders, especially for rape victims.' Raymond and Lyndsey thought about what he said now, and moments later Dr Hanson took them through to see their daughter. Caroline was sitting in a cubicle on the bed when her parents walked in. She looked round and felt ashamed as tears filled her eyes.

'Caroline.' Lyndsey cried going to her daughter.

'Mom. Daddy.' They all held each other as Desmond and Danni and Abbie stood watching them.

'Daddy, I'm sorry.'

'Darling, you've got nothing to be sorry for,' her father said as tears stung his eyes. Caroline pulled away from her parents now as she saw Dr Hanson in the doorway smiling at her.

'Hello Caroline. Do you mind if I come in and talk to you?,' he asked gently. Caroline wiped her eyes and shook her head as her father held her hand and sat in the chair next to her. Caroline smiled a little as Dr Hanson pulled up chair.

'How you feeling now, Caroline?'

'I'm OK. Just a bad headache.'

'That's good,' he smiled.

'Can you tell me what you think happened this morning when you were at work? How did you feel before your panic attack?' Caroline stayed quiet as she thought for a moment, and she frowned.

'I don't really remember. All I remember is that I had a headache, and I stood up at some point, and I felt dizzy and I couldn't breath properly.' The doctor nodded as he listened.

'Well, all you had was a panic attack. And in my opinion it was bought on by stress. Can you tell me if you've been feeling stressed lately? Have you got anything playing on your mind?' Caroline thought for a few seconds and looked to her parents as she wiped her eyes.

'I've been having bad dreams the past few weeks about the night I was raped, and I haven't been sleeping that well. I didn't want to worry anyone about it, so I went to my G.P, and she prescribed me some sleeping tablets and something to help with the nightmares, but they never helped.' Raymond sighed heavily as he ran his fingers through his hair, and he stood up and went to the window. He turned to his daughter now as she sat there near tears.

'Caroline, what were you thinking? Why didn't you tell us?' Caroline cried now as she sat on the bed.

'Daddy, I'm sorry. Please don't hate me.' The look of love was only on his face now as he went to his daughter, and he held her in his arms.

'Hate you? Caroline, don't you realise how much we love you?' He pulled away from her and held her face in his hands.

'Caroline, I love you so much. I could never hate you.'

'Oh, daddy, I'm sorry.'

Chapter Thirty One

Raymond and Lyndsey got their daughter home and tucked her up in her bed. It was only four-thirty in the afternoon, and Caroline wasn't the slightest bit tired, but her father insisted she tried getting some rest.

'But daddy, I'm not tired,' she said as tears welled in her eyes.'

'I know darling, but you do need to try and get some rest.' He sat on her bed and leaned down to her and kissed her cheek. She thought for a moment as she wiped her eyes.

'Daddy, are you disappointed with me?'

'No, darling. Why do you say that?' Caroline never answered as she curled herself up under her quilt. Raymond leaned down and kissed her cheek as she smiled a little.

'I love you, Caroline.'

'I love you too.' Raymond went to leave the room as Lyndsey went to her daughter.

'Daddy, when can I come back to work?' He stood looking at her for a few seconds, and he went to her and held her hand.

'Darling, you know I love having you at the office, and I'd have you right back there tomorrow, but you need to give yourself time to recuperate. I know you think you feel alright, but you went through a very traumatic experience, and what happened today only proves you're not ready,' he said gently.

'I want you back at the office, but I need you to be a hundred percent better before you do.' Caroline started crying now as her parents comforted her.

'But I just get so bored. If I could just come back part-time, it would be better than sitting around all day being bored.

'Honey, you know your father's right. It's no good you going to work if you keep having these episodes.'

'But I feel fine, and it's only happened once.' Caroline knew she wasn't going to win this argument this time, but she did try. She cried herself to sleep that afternoon, and it broke her parents hearts to hear her cry, but they knew they were doing the right thing, and when her sister, Debbie came through the front door just before six o'clock she knew something had happened.

'Mom, dad. What's happened? Is Cass' alright?' Debbie hadn't even took her coat off, as she saw her parents, and the look on their faces told Debbie something had happened.

'Deb's, Caroline's upstairs asleep.' Debbie sat down as she listened, and her mother sat next to her and held her hand.

'Caroline's poorly, honey. She collapsed at work this morning, and was rushed to hospital.' Tears stung Debbie's eyes as she listened and her mother kissed her cheek.

'What's wrong with her? It's nothing serious, is it?'

'No, honey. She just had a panic attack, and the doctor thinks she didn't give herself enough time to get over her ordeal before she went back to work.'

After a few minutes Debbie went upstairs to her sister. Caroline was asleep, and Debbie stood in the doorway watching her. She walked over to the bed and looked down at her. Tears welled in her eyes and she gently got into bed with her and cuddled up to her.

'I love you Cass'. Debbie closed her eyes, and it wasn't long before she fell asleep, and when their mother stood in the doorway half an hour later she smiled watching them.

Over the next few days Caroline seemed withdrawn. She stopped taking care of her appearance and was always wearing baggy sweaters and tracky bottoms, instead of her usual jeans and T-shirts. It had been a week since she collapsed at work, and already she wasn't getting dressed in the mornings. It would be almost midday some days, and she would still be in her pyjamas and dressing gown.

Lyndsey had gone back to work, and Raymond had meetings all week. Abbie and Danni had been spending time with Caroline. Just to keep her company during the day, and to keep an eye on her when she was asleep. Caroline was sleeping more and more during the days, and by the end of the second week her parents were getting worried. The were starting to think it wasn't such a good idea to keep her away from work after all.

It was Saturday morning, and Caroline was still in bed at ten-thirty. Lyndsey had taken the afternoon off work and took her to see her G.P, and she was prescribed antidepressants.

Raymond was taking some time off away from the office next week. He cancelled all his meetings for the week, and he was going to spend the week with his daughter. He thought it would be nice for them to spend some quality time together. For him to dote on his daughter. He asked Debbie if she wanted to go with them, but she couldn't get time away from college. Besides, she had exams coming up soon.

'Maybe in the summer, dad. You can dote on me all you like then,' she laughed.

Hannah and Tony, and Steve and Lesley were flying home that afternoon, and Raymond thought it would be nice for Caroline to see Hannah again. Danni and Abbie were excited about seeing them all, and couldn't wait till they flew into Heathrow.

It was twelve-thirty in the afternoon and Lyndsey was just dishing up Caroline's favourite. Spaghetti Bolognese. Debbie set the table, and then went upstairs to wake her sister. She pushed the bedroom door open and smiled looking in at her, but then her smiled disappeared quickly. Caroline was hanging half out of bed, her eyes were bloodshot and puffed up, as though she had been crying non-stop for days, and she was just staring blankly at the floor.

'Caroline?' Debbie stepped forward and went to help her back into bed, but her eyes fell to the floor, and she stared in horror at the empty bottle of tablets. She ran to her sister and picked up the bottle.

'Oh God, Cass'. What have you done?' Debbie touched her sisters face, and Caroline looked at her sister.

'I love you, Deb's.' It was barely a whisper as tears ran down her cheeks. Debbie ran from the room as she sobbed.

'Mom. Dad.' She leaned against the wall and slid down.

'Dad . . . Dad . . . Dad . . . Dad . . .,' she screamed hysterically. Lyndsey dropped the two plates of Spaghetti Bolognese she was carrying from the kitchen to the dining room as she jumped, and she and Raymond ran up the stairs. Debbie was sitting at the top of the stairs sobbing hysterically as Raymond got to her, and he looked through the open bedroom door to Caroline, lying slumped on the bed. He saw the empty bottle on the floor, that was supposed to be Caroline's medication.

'Oh God. Caroline.' Lyndsey ran to her daughter and took her in her arms as Raymond dialled 999. Lyndsey could hear him talking to the operator as she tried keeping her daughter focused.

'Come on honey, open your eyes. Keep your eyes open baby.' Caroline kept drifting in and out of consciousness as her mother talked to her.

'Mom . . . Mom . . .' It was barely a whisper as Lyndsey sobbed.

'Come on Caroline, look at me.' She held her face as she gently shook her.

'Caroline, look at me. Come on baby, keep your eyes open.' Lyndsey had been so careful with Caroline's medication. Only giving her the required regular doses and taking the bottle away from Caroline, but she couldn't remember leaving the tablets in her room now. The paramedics pounded on the door as Debbie picked herself up off the floor and let them in.

'Upstairs. Upstairs,' Debbie cried. Danni and Jason and Abbie were all at home, and they all looked out the window and across the street when they heard the sirens, and they went out now to see what was happening. They looked up the street and saw the paramedics go into Lyndsey's.

'Oh, God. What's happened now?' Abbie and Jason ran up the street as Danni ran as fast as she could, whilst holding her tummy. Danni was almost twenty-three weeks pregnant, and wasn't able to run quick enough, but as she got to Raymond's front door the paramedics were bringing Caroline down the stairs on a board.

A couple of streets away a taxi was just pulling into Albion Street, off Bayswater Road bringing Hannah and Tony and Steve and Lesley home from the airport. They turned onto Connaught Street and saw the street lit up from the blue flashing lights, and up ahead they saw the ambulance outside Raymond and Lyndsey's.

Oh, no. What's happened now?' Lesley asked. They saw Danni and Abbie coming out of Raymond's house as Hannah jumped out of the taxi. She tried running as fast as she could as she held her tummy, and she stopped dead in her tracks in the middle of the road as she saw the paramedics putting Caroline in the back of the ambulance. Her hands flew to her mouth, and then she saw Raymond and Lyndsey and Debbie all comforting each other as they cried. Some of the neighbours had come out to see what was going on, and Vera was crying as she saw Caroline. One of the neighbours stood comforting her.

'Danni. Abbie. What's happened?,' Hannah asked running to them.

'Sis'. The girls cried comforting each other as their aunt and Tony came running over. Steve was paying the taxi fare and getting their luggage from the car boot, and he left the luggage on the kerb and ran to see what was happening. Danni composed herself enough to speak, as Hannah held her hands.

'It's Caroline. She's tried to kill herself.'

'Oh my God,' Lesley cried as her hands went to her mouth. They saw Raymond and Debbie now as they stood comforting each other. Lyndsey had gone with Caroline in the ambulance, and Hannah went to Raymond as tears filled her eyes.

The ambulance screamed away up the street with the siren blaring, as Hannah and her sisters stood with their aunt and Steve gathering their thoughts. Tony comforted Hannah as Jason comforted Danni and Abbie, and after a while they got into Steve's car and drove to the hospital.

Lyndsey was just pacing the waiting area when Raymond and Debbie arrived a couple of minutes later, and Raymond went to his wife as they comforted each other. Abbie and Danni sat comforting Debbie as soon as they arrived with everyone else, and it was nearly two hours later when Dr Hanson appeared in the doorway.

'Raymond?' He looked round as the doctor smiled briefly, and the two men shook hands. Dr Hanson appeared sombre for a moment and got them all to sit down.

'Raymond, Caroline is fine. We've managed to get it out of her system, and she's just resting now. But she is very, very weak at the moment, and very lucky to be alive right now. It was a massive dose that she took.' Raymond nodded as he understood, as Lyndsey was crying quietly.

'Dr Hanson, is Caroline going to be alright?,' Hannah asked.

'Yes, she will be fine now. All she needs is complete rest, so I'm recommending that we keep her in hospital for a week. Just for observation.' Lyndsey seemed concerned as she wiped her eyes.

'Keep her in for what? I thought you said she would be fine.'

'Yes she will be. It's just that she tried to commit suicide, and it something not to be taken lightly. I just want to be sure that she is completely better before she goes home.' Lyndsey seemed restless, and Dr Hanson noticed.

'Lyndsey, you know I wouldn't recommend it if it wasn't necessary. You know I only have your daughters best interest in mind. She just needs to recuperate, and the hospital is the best place.' Raymond saw sense in what the doctor was saying, and he tried to convince his wife, but Lyndsey still wasn't sure.

'But we can look after her home Raymond,' she said as she was nearly crying again.

'I know we can, but there's doctors and nurses here to give her the best care.' He kissed her now, and she never said anything else about it. He hugged her as tears welled in her eyes, and the doctor smiled gently.

'You can go through and see her now.' They followed the doctor to the recovery room, and they saw Caroline curled up on the bed. She was facing the wall away from the door, and Lyndsey stood in the doorway as tears spilled down her cheeks.

'Caroline, honey.' Caroline never answered as she cried quietly, and Lyndsey advanced towards her.

'Honey, it's mom.'

'Mom, please go away. I don't want you seeing me like this. I look terrible,' she cried.

'Honey, why won't you talk to us? Let us help you.' It was breaking Lyndsey's heart to see her daughter so upset, and even more so that she seemed as though she was rejecting everyone's help.

'Darling, please let us help you,' Raymond said as tears filled his eyes.

'Daddy please, just leave me alone, please?' Raymond could see his daughter was hurting right now, and it broke his heart to see her like this. All he wanted to do was scoop her up into his arms and protect her forever, but she wasn't letting anyone close. Not even her sister.

'Sweetheart, please . . .'

'Daddy, please just go away and leave me alone,' she sobbed. He advanced towards her, regardless of how much she pleaded with him to leave her alone. She could feel his presence getting closer, and she fought against him to keep him away, but her resistance crumbled with his affection as he picked her up into his arms. Her arms snaked around his neck, and she sobbed uncontrollably in his arms.

'Oh baby, it's alright now. Daddies got you. It's alright.' He could physically feel her shaking in his arms as Lyndsey and Debbie comforted her too. Dr Hanson left them alone for a few minutes, and he went back to the nurses station while he waited.

Chapter Thirty Two

It was Saturday evening, and Caroline was asleep on a private ward in hospital as her parents and sister sat by her bedside. Dr Hanson had put Caroline in a private ward, as he knew her family would want to spend some private time with their daughter.

It wasn't something he did for everyone. It was only because he knew the family, and he had requested it himself, and they were grateful. Debbie was dozing off in the armchair, and Caroline started to stir. She breathed in heavily and turned her head towards her parents, and she opened her eyes slowly as she heard them talking quietly to each other.

'Mom?' Her mouth was dry, and she sounded groggy and drugged up, but her parents smiled now as Lyndsey kissed her daughter.

'Mom, I'm sorry.' A single tear trickled from her eye as her father wiped it away.

'Shh, it's alright, honey. It's alright.' Caroline looked at her father now as he smiled happily.

Hi ya, sweetheart.' He kissed her hand as she asked for some water. Lyndsey poured her some, and she gently lifted her daughters head as she took a sip. She lay back down again as Debbie woke slowly. She smiled gloriously seeing her sister awake.

'Cass'. Debbie pressed her lips against her sisters cheek and kissed her.

'Cass', you have no idea how scared I was.'

'I'm sorry, Deb's.' Caroline looked at her parents now as she thought.

'Daddy, are you angry with me?' Raymond only smiled at her now, and he leaned down and kissed her cheek.

'No darling, I'm not angry with you. But what made you do it?' Caroline started crying now as Lyndsey wiped her daughters eyes.

'I don't know. I just felt so ashamed and so alone and worthless. I thought you didn't love me anymore, and that you didn't want me around.' She cried helplessly now as her parents looked at her in disbelief. Tears filled Lyndsey's eyes as she couldn't believe her daughter was even thinking those thoughts.

'Caroline, what on earth made you think all that,' her father asked gently.

'We love you Caroline. And nothing you do is ever going to change that.' He sat her up and held her face in his hands.

'Caroline, we love you. We always have, and we always will. No matter what.'

'Oh, daddy. I'm sorry.'

That night, Caroline had slept straight through to six-thirty the following morning. She opened her eyes slowly and stared at the ceiling. For a moment she forgot where she was, until she saw a nurse approaching her.

'Good morning, Caroline. How you feeling this morning?' It was a silly question to ask, given the way she looked. The nurse approached and helped Caroline to sit up, and she gave her, her medication. Caroline took a sip of water and swallowed the two tablets, and she just lay there staring blankly at the ceiling.

Lyndsey was going to take some leave from work, and she was going to stay home and care for her daughter. She was going to speak to her manager, Carlos on Monday. She had already taken some time off over the past few weeks, and Carlos's nephew, Benito had stepped in to help out, but Lyndsey was thinking more long term now. She knew she would be dropping Carlos in it, as it was short notice, but all Lyndsey cared about now was her daughters health.

Caroline had spent five days in hospital, and she was back home on the Wednesday afternoon. Raymond was upstairs as Lyndsey came through the front door with Caroline, and he crept down as she went through to the lounge and sat down on the sofa. He stood in the doorway to the lounge with a huge teddy bear, and Caroline smiled embarrassingly as she saw it.

'Oh, dad. You big softie.' He handed her the teddy with a huge cuddle and a kiss.

Caroline was still looking pale and thin, but the doctors had assured her parents that it wouldn't last long. Caroline sat there in her fathers armchair as she crossed her legs. Her face was thin, and she's lost a bit of weight.

That afternoon Hannah and her sisters came round to visit with Tony and Julie, and Lesley and Steve, and Caroline soon started feeling better. She was smiling and laughing as Tony told bad jokes, and Lyndsey smiled watching them as Raymond stood behind her and wrapped his loving arms around her. He leaned in and kissed her neck, and they both laughed watched their daughter.

Hannah looked at Caroline now as a single tear trickled from Caroline's eye, and they both smiled joyfully as Hannah held her arms out to her. Caroline went to her, and they both sat there as Hannah kissed her.

'I love you Caroline. We all love you.' Raymond and Lyndsey disappeared for a while. They went for a walk down the street, and they sat quietly in the memorial garden. They knew their daughter was in good hands.

Over the following few weeks Caroline started showing great improvement. She had stopped having nightmares about the night she was attacked, and she started dressing smartly as she dresses instead of jeans and T-shirts.

It was Caroline's birthday coming up in a couple of days, and her parents laid on a huge spread for her. A surprise party at home, and a barbecue in the garden. Her mother had invited all her old friends from school, and her father had bought her a whole new wardrobe of clothes, and on the morning of her birthday Caroline dragged herself from the warmth of her bed at just after nine o'clock and pulled on her dressing gown. She stumbled to the bathroom and looked horribly at herself in the mirror.

'Oh, man. I look terrible.' She went to the loo, and then dragged herself downstairs. Caroline has never been a morning person, and though her health had improved over the past few weeks she still felt tired during the day. She walked into the kitchen, and she stood there in the doorway. No one was there. The whole house was quiet. It was almost nine-thirty in the morning, and the curtains in the kitchen were still shut.

She frowned as she went to open them, and pulling them back she nearly fell over with fright. Everyone was outside. Family, friends and neighbours as they all sang in unison.

"HAPPY BIRTHDAY!!!"

Her hands flew to her mouth as she screamed, and her family started piling into the kitchen as they all started singing happy birthday. Caroline stood there totally shocked as she tried to compose herself, and tears filled her eyes as her father hugged her. He cuddled her and walked her outside to greet everyone.

'Happy birthday, honey,' her mother said.

'Happy birthday, Cass'. Her sister hugged and kissed her, and she led her to greet everyone. Caroline eyed them all as they slowly greeted her, and Caroline's eyes fell on a familiar face.

'Janet? Janet Becker?'

'It Janet Carver now. I'm married,' she said as they both laughed and hugged each other. Caroline laughed through her tears as everyone of her schoolmates came forward. She saw them all, and just cried.

'Guy's, what you all doing here?,' she laughed. She was pleased to see them all, but she couldn't believe they were all there.

'I think you've got your parents to thank for this one, Cass,' Janet smiled now. Caroline turned to her parents and smiled.

'Happy birthday, sweetheart,' he father said as he went to her.

'Thank you daddy. Thanks mom.' She hugged them both now, and afterwards she engrossed herself in her friends. Many of them long lost friends, that she hadn't seen since she left school.

Caroline sat by the pond in the garden talking to Janet and Gemma Harris and George Underwood, and she was smiling as her parents watched, but Janet looked at her seriously now.

'Cass, what's this we heard about you trying to kill yourself?' Caroline was silent for a moment, as she bowed her head. She pushed her shoulder length blond hair back behind her ears as tears stung her eyes.

'I've been going through some pretty bad shit the past few months. I was attacked and raped a few months ago, and things just went from bad to worse.' Caroline looked up at her friends as tears dripped down her cheeks.

'Oh, Cass. I'm sorry,' Janet said. Caroline was attending counselling now once a week to help her through her troubles, and she had promised to talk to people about anything that was troubling. Even if it wasn't her parents. As long as she spoke to someone.

Caroline had enjoyed herself all afternoon with her friends, and was growing quite fond of George Underwood. George was the same age as Caroline, and had always had a crush on Caroline at school, but he always thought her to be too posh and way out of his league, but they were hitting it off quite well that afternoon.

They sat alone on the bench in the garden for a long time as they talked and caught upon their pasts. When they were at school, George had tried many times to get her attention. To get her away from her friends, and one day he was lucky enough to steal a kiss from her.

They were just fifteen, and he couldn't have been more in love with her if he tried. From that day on he always hoped they would end up together. Her parents had always noticed he had a shine for her, and watching them together now only pleased them.

He reached out to her now as he pushed her hair away from her eyes. She looked so innocent sitting there. Almost like a child. He wanted so much to just kiss her sweet lips. To feel her soft skin beneath his fingers, but he scared to. His feelings for were too much, that he feared he would scare her off.

Caroline and George disappeared after a while, and they took a walk down the street. He kept his hands in his pockets all the time as they talked and told each other old stories. Caroline was wearing one of her long flowing summer dresses her father bought her for her birthday. A little eye shadow and lipstick.

The sun was shining, and Caroline looked so beautiful in the sunlight. It was difficult to believe she had so much troubling her. George reached out and touched her arm, and they turned to each other.

'Caroline. I don't know if this is the right time to say this, but if I don't say it, I think I'll go crazy.' He thought for a moment as Caroline watched him. He took her hand in his and looked into her eyes.

'Caroline, You know how I feel about you, and the way I've felt about you since we were at school. I loved you when we were at school, and I don't think I've ever stopped loving you.'

'George . . .' She went to speak, but he put his fingers to her lips.

'I don't expect you to feel the same for me, and with what you've been through, I thank my lucky stars that I'm even standing next to you, and If we were to never see each other . . .' It was Caroline who put her fingers to his lips now as she smiled.

'George, I think that you are the first man I've let come near me in months. Except of course my father. I did love you at school, I think I was just too shy to approach you. You're the first person I ever did love, and yes I think in some way I am still in love with you, but these past few weeks has put a new perspective on my life.' She touched his face and ran her fingers through his dark brown hair, as he closed his eyes and savoured her touch.

'George, I think I am still in love with you, but I need some time to mend my ways. I nearly died last week, and at the time I couldn't wanted it more, but now, seeing you and Janet, and everyone from school it's made me think how precious life is.' George smiled as a single tear trickled from Caroline's eye, and he wiped it away with his thumb.

She held his hand and leaned into him. Their lips met as she closed her eyes. Tears filled her eyes, and she pulled away from him.

'George. I think I do love you.' They both laughed as she leaned in and kissed him again, and they held hands as they slowly walked back to the house.

Chapter Thirty Three

It was almost six o'clock in the evening when Janet and George left Caroline's party. All her other friends had all gone, and they sat in the living room talking for an hour, and George smiled as he stood up. He held his arms out to Caroline as she went to him as her parent smiled. Caroline had laughed and smiled all afternoon, and it pleased her parents.

'Well Caroline, it's been fantastic to see you again. We've got so much to catch up on, and I hope I have the pleasure of your company again soon.' He leaned in and kissed her cheek as she smiled.

'I'd like that. Thank you for coming.' He winked at her, and then she saw Janet. She held her arms out to her, and Janet kissed her cheek.

'You look after yourself Cass'. Keep your chin up.'

'OK.' She smiled and went to her father as they watched them leave, and Caroline waved as they drove off.

'Well, I think that was a success. What do you think, sweetheart?'

'Thank you daddy.' She wrapped her arms around him and he kissed the top of her head.

'So, it looks like I've got my little girl back.' Debbie laughed and went to him.

'Hey, what about me?' She stood there with her hands on her hips as her parents laughed.

'Yeah, OK. You're my little girl too.' He laughed and kissed his daughters, and they walked slowly back to the house.

Caroline sat in Dr Mann's office at St Mary's Hospital for another session of counselling, and she was smiling happily, and the way she looked now only pleased him.

'Well Caroline, you certainly look a lot healthier since the last time I saw you. How're you feeling now?'

I feel great. I had a surprise birthday party last weekend, and I was reunited with some of old school chums.' Dr Manns smiled as he listened. He was taking notes as Caroline spoke.

'I had a nice long chat with three of my friends, and I'd like to think it's helped get a few things out in the open.'

'What like?'

'Well, I told them how I was attacked and raped, and how things went from bad to worse. I told them how I felt when I tried to kill myself.'

'And how did you feel once you told them?'

'I felt as though a great weight had been lifted off me. To be able to talk to someone about it. I think talking to someone my own age was a big help too.' Caroline's parents were sitting in the room as they listened to their daughter, and they smiled at how much she has progressed.

'And how do you feel now about the attack. Do you still feel angry towards your attacker?'

'No. I just pity him. I feel sorry for him. I just think he needs help if he has to go out and attack helpless people.' Raymond and Lyndsey were so proud of their daughter as they sat listening to her. Though Raymond wouldn't have said the same. If his daughters attacker past him in the street now, he'd still want to kill him.

Carson Davies was sentenced to fifteen years to life for the attack and attempted murder of Caroline, and taking his past crimes into account, the judge had told him he would not be eligible for parole for at least fifteen years. His mother was sentenced too for aiding and abetting, and harbouring a known criminal. She had got ten years in Holloway.

Caroline felt happier once the judge had passed sentence, and Bill had delivered the happy news himself. Caroline had cried in Bill's arms after he told her, though she did pity him. But she knew she would be safe again, and be happy to get on with her life.

Caroline had started seeing more of George Underwood over the following weeks, and her parents were happy for her. Caroline was still taking her medication that Dr Hanson prescribed, but not so often. Sometimes she felt as though she could go days without it. She had started controlling her own medication now, and carried it with at all times, but only used it when she needed to.

It was Thursday afternoon, and Caroline was sitting on the swing in the garden day dreaming. She was smiling as her mother approached, and she didn't seemed to notice her at first. Lyndsey stood watching her for a moment.

'Caroline.' She never answered as she was staring at the ground, and her mother advanced towards her.

'Caroline?' She reached out and touched her arm, and Caroline looked up smiling dreamily.

'You OK hon'?'

'Hmm.' Lyndsey sat on the swing next to her as she thought.

'You really like him, don't you?'

'Like who?'

'George. Who do you think?,' she laughed nudging her.

'I'm not sure. I mean I do feel comfortable with him, and he makes me happy. I told him about everything that's happened to me, and he understands.' Lyndsey smiled listening. She was happy for her daughter, and that she's coping a lot better now. Caroline looked mischievously at her mother now and smiled.

'I kissed him that afternoon of my birthday. We were walking along Hyde Park Street by the memorial garden, and he told me how he still loves me, and we just kissed.' Caroline giggled, and for a moment she sounded like a little girl again as her mother giggled with her.

'I'm so happy for you hon'. George is obviously good for you.'

'Mom, I think I'm still in love with him. I can't stop thinking about him.' Lyndsey touched her daughters face and pushed her hair back behind her ears, and she seemed maternal for a moment as she tried to smile.

'I am happy for you honey, I really am. But I just want you to be careful. Take it slowly, OK?' Caroline smiled and hugged her mother, and Lyndsey kissed her cheek. They pulled away from each other after a few seconds, and they slowly walked back to the house, as Lyndsey seemed all girly.

'So, come on, tell me all about it. What's George like? Has he changed much?' Caroline laughed out loud as they stepped through the patio doors into the kitchen, and Lyndsey almost cried hearing her daughter laugh again. It had been so long since she even saw her smile.

'Mom, he's fantastic. He is so sweet, and so easy to be with, and so understanding.' They both talked for the rest of the afternoon about George, and at five-thirty when Raymond walked in through the front door, Caroline ran to him and hugged him.

'Wow, what a welcome.' He kissed her, and he held her in his arms.

'What have I done to deserve this?' Caroline stood on tiptoes and kissed his cheek.

'I love you daddy.' She skipped away then to her bedroom, and Raymond laughed a little watching her going up the stairs.

'I think she's in love,' Lyndsey said now as she started preparing her husbands tea. Raymond raised his eyebrows hopefully as he sat down at the kitchen table.

'Who with?'

'George Underwood.'

'Well, George is a nice lad. He'll take care of her.' That evening Caroline had spoke to George on the telephone for nearly two hours. They had arranged to meet that weekend, and Caroline couldn't wait.

It was Saturday morning, and Hannah and her sisters decided to visit their parents and Mikey's graves. It was a glorious morning with a gentle breeze, and the girls walked over to the graves and kissed the gravestones and greeted them, as they always did, and afterwards they sat replanting some of the flowers that had been carelessly pulled up by vandals, and plant the new ones they had bought. The girls tried to visit at least once a week, but with everything going on over the past few months, they haven't spent as much time as they would like.

They were thinking of going back to Bude this year, and maybe move back into their house after Hannah and Danni have given birth in September. They had discussed it further with their aunt, but now Hannah was married, she was still thinking of finding a place just for her and Tony.

Hannah and Tony had discussed it together that evening, and they agreed to start looking after the baby was born. Hannah was almost twenty-seven weeks pregnant now, and everything she did it tired her out so easily. That afternoon after they finished at the graveside, Abbie had to drive home with Hannah in the back seat. She was only in the house five minutes before she fell asleep in the armchair.

The girls had given up going to the office entirely now, and they were getting concerned. Hannah had said just the other day, that she didn't feel right leaving it all to Raymond and Desmond, but the two men didn't mind.

Even when Duncan was there, Raymond and Desmond were often left in charge. They were practically Duncan's right arm. Duncan admitted he couldn't run the business without them.

That evening, Caroline sat at her dressing table applying her eyeliner. She was wearing one of her summer dresses, as she and George were going out for the evening. Debbie sat on her sisters bed watching her as she smiled, and Caroline caught a glimpse of her in her mirror.

'What?,' she smiled embarrassingly. Debbie only shook her head.

'We're all happy for you Cass'. The way you've improved over the past few weeks. I was beginning to think I'd lost you at one point.'

'You won't lose me Deb's. I just wasn't thinking straight, and I did a lot of crazy things, and I'd like to think I'm over that now.' Caroline stood up and wrapped her cardigan over her shoulders and turned to her sister and smiled.

'Well, how do I look?' Debbie smiled and shuffled off the bed and held her arms out to her sister.

'You look fantastic Cass'. Caroline laughed a little as she picked up her handbag.

'You'd say that even if I was wearing scraggy jeans and a frumpy jumper.' They both laughed and hugged each other, and they made their way downstairs to the lounge where George was waiting for her. Caroline smiled as she saw him, and George stood up to greet her.

'Hello George.' Caroline was wearing her hair lose this evening with a red ribbon tied up into a bow. She kissed his cheek and they sat down as George finished his coffee.

'We won't be too late back to Mr Layton. I promise to have her home by nine-thirty.' The nights were getting lighter now, so Raymond didn't worry so much about his daughter being out so late. Besides, he knew George would take care of her. Caroline smiled and looked up at him.

At twenty-five years old, George Underwood owned his own computer business in Chelsea. His thick black hair and deep blue eyes was what Caroline liked about him. He was wearing his blue jeans and a white T-shirt this evening, with his denim jacket. They went to leave at seven-thirty, and Caroline kissed her parents.

'Where you taking her, George? It's just so we don't worry,' her mother asked.

'We're just going for a meal at the Cigala Spanish restaurant on Lamb's Conduit Street.' Caroline smiled as she looked to her mother.

'Really? That's where mom works.' George looked at Lyndsey as Caroline seemed excited.

'You'll enjoy it there George. It's got a nice menu,' Lyndsey said. Caroline kissed her parents and sister, and then they left. They walked along Connaught Street holding hands as they talked.

'Does your mom really work at the Cigala?'

'Yeah. She's been the head chef there for nearly twenty-one years. Though she hasn't been working for the past few weeks since I was in hospital.' Now Caroline was a lot better, Lyndsey was thinking of returning to work. She was going to speak to Carlos on Monday, but she didn't like to keep messing him about.

Lyndsey knew she couldn't help it, and Carlos understood. He had got his nephew to step in to help while Lyndsey was away, but Lyndsey was thinking she and Benito could run the kitchen together now. They had worked well together in the past when the restaurant got really busy. Lyndsey was going to suggest it to Carlos on Monday.

Caroline and George walked into the restaurant just before eight o'clock. George had booked a table for two, for a romantic candlelit dinner. Caroline slipped out of her coat and smiled as she saw one of the waitresses.

'Hello Louisa.'

'Caroline. It's wonderful to see you again. Your mama has just called to say you were coming.' Caroline introduced George, and then Louisa shown them to a table.

Louisa gave them some menus, and left them alone for a while, and moments later Carlos and Benito came through from the kitchen. Caroline stood up as she saw them, and she smiled gloriously.

'Benito. It's been a long time. How are you?'

'I am very well, thank you. And it's so wonderful to see you looking so well too. Your mama said what happened. I'm sorry.' Caroline greeted them both, and then they went back to the kitchen as George smiled looking around the restaurant.

'It's so friendly here.'

'I know. Mom has put a lot of years and hard work into this place. Mom and Carlos has practically made this place together.

They both talked about old times, and about when they were at school together as they waited for their food. They both ordered the Paella de marisco, a combination of rice with monkfish, langoustine and mussels.

There was a decorative display of flowers on their table, and Louisa had lit a red candle for them, and as they held hands across the table there were a few looks of admiration from the other diners.

Caroline had looked so beautiful that evening. Her soft skin shining against the flame of the candle, her silky smooth blond hair loose. At twenty-five years old, Caroline had always took care of her appearance. Her ample bosom and her tiny waist was perfection.

They walked along Connaught Street and Hyde Park Street to the memorial garden, and Caroline told him all about Grace and Duncan and Mikey, and how the sisters had had the memorial garden done for them. It was only nine o'clock, and they had half an hour before George walked her home.

They sat in the garden talking, and Caroline flicked her hair, and he saw how her eyes dazzled as she smiled. He was aching so much to just touch her and hold her in his arms, but he was afraid of scaring her off. He just sat there listening to her soft voice in the moonlight.

'George, you know I love you, right?, and you know how I said I wanted some time to get my life in order again, but I can't hide my feelings for you anymore. God knows I've tried, but I just love you so much.' He reached out and touched her cheek as she closed her eyes. He touched her soft hair, and they leaned into each other.

Their lips met, and they kissed as she ran her fingers through his thick curls. Her eyes still closed she felt his hands go to her waist. She wanted to stop him, as she wondered where his hands would end up, but she didn't. She wasn't sure of what she wanted. All she knew was she had butterflies in her tummy. Her heart was melting, and the more her mind said that she didn't want it, the more her heart said that she did.

From that moment on, she knew that George Underwood would be in her life forever. He walked her home, and they kissed on the doorstep, and moments later he waved as he watched her go into the house.

Chapter Thirty Four

It was almost the end of July, and Hannah was thirty two week pregnant. She was sitting in the rocking chair in the nursery listening to some gentle classical music, when Danni walked in.

Hi sis'. How you doing?' Danni sat in her rocking chair, as they both listened to the music.

'It's so quiet around here now. It's driving me nuts,' Danni said.

'Where's Jason?'

'Oh, he's gone shopping for the twins with Tony.' Hannah smiled and looked at her sister now.

'I can't believe you're having twin, sis'. You're so lucky. How you feeling now?'

'Exhausted.' They both laughed, and Hannah took a sharp breath as she felt the baby kicking.

'Sis', You OK?'

'Yeah, Junior's kicking.' Hannah had had a restless night as the baby kept her awake. She had got up several times in the night just to walk about. She had got out of bed carefully, so not to disturb Tony, but he got up too in the night a found her pacing the kitchen.

Just the other night he woke up when she had got cramps, and he sat with her on the bed as she did some breathing exercises.

Tony and Jason had spent the day shopping at Mothercare and looked around Harrods for baby clothes and toys and other essentials, and just after six o'clock they walked in the house with armfuls of bags and accessories.

'Blimey, what you two been doing? Buying out Mothercare?,' Danni joked.

'We've just been buying all the good stuff for my little boy,' Tony said. He kissed Hannah lovingly, and bent down and kissed her tummy.

'How's my little boy today?' Hannah and Tony still didn't know what they were having. They wanted it to be a surprise, but Tony was sure he was having a boy.

'Well your little boy kept me up half the night.' she laughed. He stood behind her and snaked his arms around her waist and kissed her neck.

'Why didn't you wake me up?'

'I was alright, don't panic. Besides you looked so cute I didn't want to disturb you.' He smiled embarrassingly now as Danni laughed.

'I just came downstairs a walked about. I was fine after I had some camomile tea.' She kissed him and the girls started looking through the bags to see what the boys had bought.

Hannah and her sisters were all girly as they looked through some of the baby clothes, and after a few minutes Jason and Tony left them to it as Abbie came upstairs to see what they had bought.

Jason and Tony sat at the kitchen table after they got themselves a can of beer from the fridge. They were all still living at Lesley's, and Julie came over that evening with Hollie and her daughters. Julie and Hollie had disappeared upstairs with Jade and Keeley to see Hannah and her sisters.

All the girls sat in the nursery talking about the babies and the births, and their futures. Julie was so jealous, as she had always wanted children, but she has never found the right man to have them with.

At twenty-six years old, Julie had never had a serious relationship. She was twenty-one when her father was diagnosed with throat cancer. She had devoted all her time to care for him. He survived another seven months, until one afternoon he died in her arms.

Her friends and her fathers business were her life now, and had no room in her life for a relationship and babies, though it never stopped her from brooding and getting all maternal. Though she enjoyed visiting the sisters and talking babies, she was extremely busy at the office.

Hannah and her sisters barely saw much of her now, and were thankful for her company when they saw her at weekends, though recently she hasn't visited at weekends either. There was a big case she was working on, and she put in all her spare time to see it through. It was one promise she had made to her father before he died, that she would always put the business first, but she was slowly driving herself into the ground, and Hannah had said just as much to her.

Julie had cried in Hannah's arms that night after Hannah told her to be careful.

'You're going to drive yourself to an early grave if you're not careful, Jules.' she had said gently. Julie had promised to ease off a bit at work, and spend some leisure time with her friends, but she couldn't help remembering her promise to her father.

Over the following few weeks Hannah and Danni started preparing for the births. There was only four or five weeks to go before they were due, and they didn't want any last minute problems.

Hannah had wanted a home birth, but was told it might be too risky being her first child. The girls had made their checklists, and their aunt had made sure everything was sorted into piles.

It was the second week in August, and Hannah and her sisters were sitting in the lounge with their aunt and Steve when Caroline knocked the front door and walked in. Tony was there, with Jason, and Julie was there too.

'Hello.'

'We're in the lounge,' Lesley called out. Caroline popped her head round the door and walked in. George was with her too, and Caroline introduced him. They sat down in the lounge after Danni sat up and leaned against Jason, and Hannah couldn't help wondering where she had seen George before. She knew he was at Caroline's birthday party, but there was just something very familiar about him.

'Haven't I seen you somewhere before, George? What school did you go to?'

'Marylebone C of E.'

'I knew it.' she laughed

'I'm Hannah Philips.' George almost laughed out loud as he couldn't believe it.

'Well, actually I'm Hannah Craven now. I got married in May.'

'Hannah Philips. Oh My God.' He recognised Danni and Abbie then, and he couldn't believe he was actually sitting in the same room as the Philips sisters.

'You know you and Danni used to bully me all the time,' he said looking to Hannah.

'Well, a girl's gotta defend herself. If I recall, you used to peak at us girls in the changing rooms,' Danni said. Caroline was shocked as she looked at him, and she slapped his arm as they all laughed.

'Well, I was only thirteen or fourteen, and very curious.'

'Ha. Yeah, right,' Abbie laughed. They all laughed and cried as they all exchanged stories, and Lesley was shocked when Hannah told everyone that she had streaked naked across the school playing field.

'Oh, darling. What would your mother say,' Lesley laughed.

That evening Frank and Sally dropped by, and Frank's wife and daughter were there too. Steve had got up and greeted them, as Lesley went to the kitchen and made some more coffee. It was almost six-thirty, and Danni was getting cramps.

'You alright, babe?,' Jason asked worriedly as everyone looked at her.

'Just cramps. They'll go away in a moment.' Just then she sat up quickly and breathed in sharply. She held her tummy as the pain ripped through her. She felt as though someone had just ran a sword straight through her belly. No one had even noticed that her waters had broke.

'*Oh shit.*'

'Danni?'

'I think the babies coming. Oh Jesus.'

'Danni?,' Jason jumped up wondering what to do as Steve and Frank helped Danni up and out to the car.

'Come on sweetheart, hold onto me,' Frank said as everyone dashed about. Danni kept wanting to squat with every step she took, but Steve and Frank just urged her along to the car.

'Oh God, Steve. The baby wants to come now,' Danni was crying in pain as she tried to control her breathing. She tried to remember everything the midwife taught her, and everything she learnt in the antenatal classes.

'Not now darling. Waiting till we get to the hospital.' They lay Danni down on the back seat of Steve's car as Hannah carefully got in with her.

'Jason. Get in quick,' Steve said. He got into the passenger seat and Steve sped off quickly before Jason even shut the car door. Everyone else jumped in their cars and followed. Caroline had followed with George in his car, and when they got to the hospital she called her parents. Even Frank and his wife and daughter followed them.

Steve screeched to a halt outside the hospital and jumped out quickly. Danni was still screaming in agony as Steve ran inside and grabbed a wheelchair, and running straight back into the A&E with Danni, Steve called out for Dr Hanson.

'We called ahead. Dr Hanson is expecting us,' Hannah said. A nurse guided them through, all the time Danni was trying to convince everyone that the baby was coming now.

'Why doesn't anyone believe me? My babies are come now,' she screamed holding her tummy. Dr Hanson approached and ran along side with them to the delivery suite.

'Don't push yet Danni. Wait till we get you into delivery room,' Dr Hanson said. They pushed their way through the huge flap doors into delivery suite and Danni let out an almighty scream as they lifted her from the wheelchair to the delivery bed. A nurse was standing by and ushered Hannah and Jason into the delivery room as she swathed them with gowns and masks, and they went to Danni's side.

'Sis'. Danni, listen to me. I'm right here with you, OK? We're going to do this together.'

'Sis'. Please don't leave me,' she cried.

'I'm not going to leave you Danni. I'm right here with you. OK? Jason's here too, and we'll do this together.' Danni looked to Jason who was smiling at her behind his masked.

'I love you Danni. We're going to do this together.' She nodded as Dr Hanson urged her to push. Everyone from the house had followed, and they stood outside in the corridor waiting and pacing impatiently. Raymond and Lyndsey were there with Debbie, and Desmond. Frank and his wife and daughter and Sally and Julie were there too. Danni dropped back in Hannah's arms now. Exhausted and scared, she cried out.

'Sis', I can't do this. I can't do it.' Hannah wiped her forehead and kissed her.

'Danni, I know you can do this. Jason and I will help you, OK?' Hannah looked to Jason, who was looking a bit peaky now.

'Come on Danni. Just one big push,' Dr Hanson said. Danni took a deep breath and pushed with all her strength. She exhaled and dropped heavily into Hannah's arms again.

'I can see the head, Danni. I can see the head,' Hannah said.

'Come on sis'. One last push. We'll do it together.' The three of them screamed and Danni pushed, and the baby fell crying into the Dr Hanson's hands. Danni fell back into Jason's arms and cried as the doctor passed the baby to the nurse.

'It's a girl,' Jason cried. He kissed Danni now as she tried to look.

'We have a girl. We have a baby girl,' she cried. Danni took a rest for a few minutes as she gathered her strength, and the nurse held Danni's daughter to her, and Danni cried touching her face.

'Hello, my precious baby.' She looked to Jason as tears coursed down her cheeks, and she kissed him. Just then she felt the urge to push again.

'Oh God, sis'. Oh Jesus.'

'OK Danni, here we go again. You've done it once, you can do it again.'

'OK Danni. I want you to do everything you've just done again, OK?,' Dr Hanson said.

Danni started breathing as she counted, and moments later Dr Hanson told her to push. She took a deep breath and pushed with all her might. Hearing her daughter crying only urged to push harder. She was longing to hold her in her arms. Jason wiped her forehead and kissed her.

'Come on baby, push it out. I'll push with you,' he said. Jason was encouraging her, whilst Hannah was encouraging Jason. Jason had started to feel a bit queasy earlier, but instead of seeing what was happening between her legs, he was focusing on Danni now, which he thought was a lot better.

But nearly fifteen minutes later when Danni stopped pushing and flopped back down into his arms he was a bit concerned. The doctor was holding the baby in his hands, but it wasn't making any sound. Hannah watched in horror as the doctor and the nurse tried to help the baby, and tears filled her eyes as Danni was getting impatient.

'What's happening? Where's my baby?' Hannah folded her arms across her chest and looked to Danni as she was nearly crying. The doctor was still trying to revive the baby as Danni started crying, and he looked up at Hannah now as tears coursed her cheeks. She went to her sister, and her silence only confirmed her worst fears.

'Hannah,' where's my baby?' Her bottom lip quivered as she looked to Jason, as he stood crying quietly.

'No, please. I want my baby,' she cried. Hannah and Jason comforted her now as they all cried, and Dr Hanson stood there as he too felt like crying. He slowly took his cap off and pulled his mask down from his face.

'Danni,' I'm so sorry.' Danni sobbed uncontrollably now as the nurse covered her up and took the stillborn away, and Dr Hanson stood there trying to encourage her to take her daughter.

'I want my baby,' she sobbed clinging to Jason. Jason took his daughter from the doctor now, and Hannah went out to the others as they were still waiting impatiently. She walked out slowly holding her tummy, and she stood there as tears ran down her cheeks as they all looked round at her.

'Hannah, what's happening? Is Danni . . .?' Lesley stopped talking as she saw Hannah's tears, and her hands flew to her mouth.

'Darling, what's happened?,' Lesley asked nervously going to her. Hannah just sobbed and clung to her aunt now as they all feared the worst.

'Darling, what's the matter?' Lesley held her niece as they all waited, and moments later she pulled away from Hannah and wiped her eyes for her.

'Danni's had a little girl, but she lost the boy.' Lesley cried now as her hands went to her mouth. Steve comforted her, and after a while Lesley and Steve and Abbie followed Hannah to where Danni was. They stood in the doorway looking at her as she sobbed in Jason's arms. Jason was still holding the baby as Lesley approached her niece.

'Darling.' Danni looked up through blurry eyes.

'Auntie, I want my little boy,' she cried.

'Darling, darling. It's alright.' She went to her and took her in her arms as Jason stood holding his daughter. Abbie cried going to him, and he put an arm around her as she took the baby from him, and she smiled down at her niece as she went to her sister.

'Sis'. Danni looked up through damp eyes and Abbie only comforted her. Abbie pulled away from her, and she placed the baby in Danni's arms.

'Danni, why don't you hold your daughter?' Danni looked down at her baby as tears coursed her cheeks, and she kissed her daughter for the first time.

'Hello my precious girl.' She held her daughter close to her chest and kissed her. The baby gurgled contentedly, and Danni looked up at Jason as he sat on the bed comforting her.

Chapter Thirty Five

Danni sat up in bed at home as her daughter slept in the basket beside her bed. Jason sat on the bed holding Danni's hands as he watched his daughter sleeping. Everyone had piled into Danni's bedroom cooing over the baby, and Abbie picked the baby up and sat on the bed with her sister.

'Have you two thought of a name yet?,' she asked. Danni smiled and kissed her daughter. It has been almost five days since Danni gave birth, and they were still thinking of a name for their daughter.

'Yes,' Jason said.

'We're going to call her Grace Elizabeth Thomas,' Danni smiled.

'Grace Thomas. I like that,' Lesley said going to her niece. She kissed her, and Jason took his daughter from the basket and sat on the bed with Danni, as Danni looked to Frank and Sally. Frank and Sally had visited almost everyday now since Danni gave birth, and Frank smiled watching the mother and daughter.

'There's something else that Jason and I have decided on.' She held her hand out to Frank, and he sat on the bed and held her hand.

We decided some time ago, that we would like you and Sally to be our babies godparents.' Frank looked stunned for a moment as Sally fought back the tears. She went to Danni now and cuddled her.

'Frank, you and Sally mean the world to me. You mean the world to all of us. If it wasn't for you two, God knows how long it would have took us to find Abbie and bring her home after mom and dad died. You helped to bring us together at a difficult time, and I'll never forget that.' Her bottom lip trembled and Frank touched her face and smiled.

'You're welcome sweetheart.' He kissed her cheek and took his new goddaughter in his arms as Sally, and Frank's wife and daughter crowded around.

'Oh dad, she's gorgeous,' Penelope said as Grace yawned. Penelope seemed excited for a moment, and she looked to her mother.

'Does that mean she's my god sister mom?'

'I think it does, my love.'

'Cool.'

Hannah sat on the bed with Danni as they all cooed over Grace, and moments later Hannah held her tummy and breathed sharply.

'Oooh. Aagh.' Everyone looked to Hannah now as Tony tried to soothe her.

'Darling?' Lesley went to her, and Hannah looked up at her aunt.

'Auntie, I think it's my turn now.'

'Oh, no, here we go again.' Hannah leaned on Tony as he helped her off the bed, and Steve stood the other side of her as they helped her downstairs.

Danni and Jason stayed at the house with their daughter as everyone else followed Hannah. Penelope was excited now. Two sisters pregnant, both giving birth in one week. It was almost ten o'clock in the morning, and as they pulled up outside St Mary's, Steve went for the wheelchair as Tony and Lesley help Hannah out of the car.

They went inside and asked for Dr Hanson again, and moments later he appeared looking a bit tired, but he smiled as he saw Hannah.

'OK Hannah. Take it easy. Nice deep breaths.' The delivery suite was all set up ready after Steve called ahead, and they gently lifted Hannah out of the wheelchair. Lesley and Tony both put on gowns and masks, and Tony held Hannah's hand. Hannah was getting worried now since her sister lost one of her babies, and as she lay there waiting to push she was wondering what they had done with the baby.

'Dr Hanson, I'd just like to know what will happen to Danni's baby?' He looked up from between Hannah's legs and smiled gently under his mask.

'Let's just deal with this for now Hannah.'

'Please, I'd like to know what will happen to my nephew.' Hannah was in pain as she breathed heavily, but she was determined to get an answer now.

'He'll stay in the mortuary until he's either given a state funeral or Danni and Jason decide what to do with him.' He didn't want to go into detail, and Hannah seemed happy with the answer she got, so he just carried on with the situation at hand. A single tear trickled from Hannah's eye as she thought of her dead nephew now, and moments later Dr Hanson was encouraging her to push.

Everyone gathered outside the delivery suite waiting to hear news of Hannah. Caroline sat twitching her knees, and Debbie went to her and put her hand on her knee.

'Cass', I sure Hannah will be fine.' Debbie knew that her sister had grown fond of Hannah over the past few months, and she realised what it would do to her sister if Hannah lost the baby.

Hannah screamed and clutched the sheet beneath her as she gave one almighty push.

'That's fine Hannah, you're doing so well. I can see the head,' Dr Hanson said. Hannah fell back into Tony's arms as he wiped her forehead and kissed her.

'This is it babe. One more big push and it'll be over.' Hannah felt the contraction, and she started breathing heavily.

'Oh no, oh no, oh no, here it comes.' She clenched her teeth and scream, and pushed with all the strength she had left.

'Arggggh.' Tony screamed with her, and seconds later the baby fell into Dr Hanson's hands. Hannah heard the baby crying, and she cried with joy.

'Where's my baby? Give me my baby.' Dr Hanson passed the baby to the nurse, and the nurse smiled showing Hannah her baby.

'You have a son,' Hannah.

'I have a boy. She kissed him as she and Tony laughed. The nurse took him away to clean him and Tony kissed Hannah again.

'We have a boy,' he cried. Moments later the nurse passed him back to Hannah, all snug and wrapped in a blanket. Lesley stayed with Hannah, and Tony took his son in his arms and took him out to show everyone while Dr Hanson cleaned Hannah up.

'Oh look at him, mom' Debbie laughed.

'Tony, he's gorgeous,' Caroline said hugging him.

After a while they all went in to see Hannah, and Tony passed the baby Hannah.

'Congratulations darling,' Steve said and kissed her.

It was almost three-thirty in the afternoon when Hannah was finally settled on the ward. Everyone was still there, though they had gone outside earlier to get some fresh air while the nurses got Hannah settled. Frank and his wife, Patricia and daughter, Penelope were still there, and Sally and Desmond were there too.

They all stood around Hannah and Tony and the baby now as they all smiled and cooed over the baby. Danni and Jason had arrived with Grace after Raymond went to pick them up from the house, and George was there too with Caroline, and Julie was there as well.

'Hi sis'. How you feeling now?,' Hannah asked gently.

'I'm OK. Grace keeps me smiling,' she said happily. Danni and Jason will never stop pining for their lost son, but they knew Grace would help them through their grief. They had decided to let the hospital give their son a state funeral, as it would be too tearful for Danni and Jason to deal with. Danni had picked out a light blue rosette to go with the white coffin, and she had found that too tearful.

Hannah was on a private ward, and they all gathered around her and the baby now as Abbie held her new nephew in her arms.

Well, what we calling him sis'?' Hannah smiled holding Tony's hand now.

'We are going to call him Michael Duncan Craven. Mikey Jr.'

'Mikey Jr? I like that,' Abbie said. She kissed him and smiled.

'Hello Mikey. I'm your auntie Abbie.' Abbie passed him around now as they all greeted the new arrival, and as Caroline stood holding the baby in her arms, Hannah smiled and called to her.

Dr Hanson had given them all permission to be on the ward together. Normally it was only a maximum of five visitors to a patient, but as he knew them all, and it was a one off, he allowed it just this once. Caroline sat on the bed holding the baby in her arms. She leaned down and kissed his cheek as Hannah smiled.

'Cass', Tony and I have got something to ask you.' Hannah touched Caroline's cheek and pushed her hair back from her face.

'We were wondering if you would like to be Junior's godmother.' Raymond and Lyndsey smiled now watching their daughter, and Caroline had tears in her eyes as she looked to Hannah and Tony.

'Me?'

'I think that you are a very special person, Cass', and I know you will make a wonderful godmother,' she said gently. Caroline was crying now as she looked to Junior, and she leaned down and kissed him.

'And I think every child should have a godfather too,' Hannah continued.

'George, as you are Caroline's partner now, how would you like to be our son's godfather?' George smiled as he fought back the tears, and he went to Hannah and held her hand.

'Thank you Hannah. I would be honoured.' He leaned down and kissed her cheek and he shook Tony's hand, and then he took his new godson from Caroline and held him in his arms, as Tony looked to Debbie.

'Deb's, Hannah and I were also thinking that how wonderful it would be for Junior to have a second godmother. How would you like to be his godmother as well?' Debbie laughed now as she hugged Tony, and she just smiled and kissed him.

'Thank you, Tony.' She hugged Hannah, and then took Junior from George and held him in her arms.

Hannah and Tony smiled watching Caroline and Debbie and George with Junior now, and as Hannah looked around the room to everyone, she realised that everyone she loved was there. She looked to her sister, Danni as she and Jason cooed over their daughter. She looked to her aunt and Steve as he leaned in to her and kissed her lips, and to her sister, Abbie as she stood in Desmond's arms. And a single tear trickled from her eye as she finally realised that she had got her family back.

The End

Printed in the United Kingdom by
Lightning Source UK Ltd., Milton Keynes
138433UK00001B/10/P

INBAL Travel Information Ltd.
P.O.B. 39090 Tel Aviv
ISRAEL 61390

QUESTIONNAIRE

In our efforts to keep up with the pace and pulse of South America, we kindly ask your cooperation in sharing with us any information which you may have as well as your comments. We would greatly appreciate your completing and returning the following questionnaire. Feel free to add additional pages.

Our many thanks!

_____

To: Inbal Travel Information (1983) Ltd.
18 Hayetzira Street
Ramat Gan 52521
Israel

Name: _____

Address: _____

_____

Occupation: _____

Date of visit: _____

_____

Purpose of trip (vacation, business, etc.): _____

_____

_____

Comments/Information: _____

_____

_____

_____

_____

_____

_____

_____

_____

_____

_____

_____

_____